Orphanage Boys

Orphanage Boys

By

A.N Arthur

Orphanage Boys published by Rangitawa Publishing, Feilding, New Zealand. 2016.
2nd revised edition September 2018.
©A.N.Arthur

Cover image Shutterstock 116881636

www.rangitawa publishing.com
rangitawa@xtra.co.nz

ISBN 978-0-9941382-1-7

Dedication

To my husband who holds the shadows and monsters at bay. And to my mother. For always being there.

Acknowledgements

To SF who has always been my (mediocre!) creative helpmate and punch bag and DW who read it all beginning to end and advised, advisedly. I cherish you both.

Cover design by CA Lines and Team

Also by this author

Between Two Worlds

Part I

1

Nelson
New Zealand
1897

Jimmy woke suddenly. His eyes flicked open and he lay in bed for a moment or two wondering what caused him to wake. Beside him ten year old Samuel sprawled on his back hogging most of the bed, snoring softly. But it wasn't Samuel who woke him nor the snoring.

Not moving from the warm spot he'd made, Jimmy moved his eyes cautiously about the room from the window, where the frost had slipped inexorable fingers through the gaps in the warped wooden frame, over the bare wooden walls and finally to the closed bedroom door. Nothing moved.

Jimmy told himself he was too old at seven to hear ghostly noises in the dark and went to snuggle back down beside Samuel's back when it came again. Strained, low groaning reached his ears. Jimmy scarcely dared to breathe for he was sure it was the ghost of the old Māori chief Samuel said followed them home from the grave they discovered last month. Samuel had sworn the Old One chased them home, feather cloak flapping against brown, bare legs, blood-stained greenstone mere for killing raised threateningly in his hand… '*Ka mate, ka mate, ka ora ka ora. Tenei te tangata pu-huru-huru.....*' Samuel had chanted the haka all the way home. Jimmy hadn't been able to sleep well since, not until his brother came to bed anyway. Even so, every breeze ruffling the cloth at their bedroom window became the Old One's breath, every creak his step.

Jimmy slid nearer to his brother's warmth. If the Old One attacked, at least there would be two of them to fight him off and Samuel at ten was almost grown up. He'd beat the Old One, Jimmy was sure of it.

The groaning noise came once more, deeper, louder and this time Jimmy realised it didn't come from their bedroom but from somewhere else in the house. The Old One had discovered Mam and Father! A rush of panic flooded Jimmy and he sat up. He shook Samuel hard, not pausing to consider the buffeting he would get for disturbing his sleep.

"Sam! Sam! Wake up."

Samuel gave a groan of his own. "Shut your mouth, Jimmy or I'll lam you one." He dragged the blanket back over himself, disappeared under the rough cover until only the top of his dark head showed.

Fear for his parents gave Jimmy courage as the groan sounded again.   He hauled the blanket off, sat astride Samuel who fought back sleepily, no real strength in the cuffs he gave Jimmy but as his sleepiness fell away, he grabbed his younger brother, easily threw him back onto the bed. Now awake and eager for a fight, Samuel picked up his feather pillow, began to pummel Jimmy about the head with it.

In a final plea, Jimmy held onto the pillow, "The Old One's found Mam and Father!"

Samuel grinned, tugged the pillow out of Jimmy's hands, gave him another whack about the head just because. "What are you on about, Tiny Tim?" His mocking name for his younger brother, taken from Mam's favourite story. It never failed to send Jimmy into a rage but to Samuel's surprise, Jimmy heaved him away, began to cry. Samuel's exuberance stopped and he dropped the pillow in concern.

"I can hear him groaning, Sam. And it's getting louder." Jimmy wiped his nose on the bed cover. "He's got Mam and Father." Samuel looked sceptical. Jimmy held his hand and pleaded. "Listen" and sure enough both boys heard it this time, long and deep, the groan sounded through the dark.

It was Jimmy's turn to be surprised for Samuel just grinned. "It's not the Old One, Tiny Tim," and this time the barb found its mark.

Jimmy threw his pillow at Samuel's head.   "Don't call me that. And how d'you know?"

"It's our Mam's time." And he smiled at his younger brother's face, suddenly all round-eyed wonder.

"The baby?"

"Yes, the baby."

Samuel was already out of bed, reaching for his trousers. Jimmy followed, his fingers fumbling with buttons in the cold, his fears of the Old One completely forgotten.

Fraser sat on the edge of the box bed, holding Jeannie's hand as the contraction eased. Once they slept in a carved kauri bed Fraser had made, its matching chest of drawers beside it and on those, the fine silver candlesticks which had been a gift from Jeannie's favourite aunt, the only member of her family to support their marriage. Once, the curtains against their window were long and full, their rich colours glowing in the sun or candlelight and they had gazed around their belongings with pride. Then came the day Fraser suffered an accident at work on the farm and the hard times came and one by one, they'd had to sell all their fine things.

The candle sticks went first, then the chest of drawers.

"We can use the sea chest, Fraser." Jeannie had told him matter-of-factly. "It served us well once, it can do so again."

Jeannie even managed to look brave when they sold the kauri bed with its thick feather mattress. She'd loved the kauri frame more than any other piece they owned for Fraser had made it for her soon after they'd arrived in New Zealand.

When the carters came for the bed, Jeannie stood tall and proud holding Fraser's hand. She could feel him trembling beside her, still weak, still sickly but it was shame that made him shake she knew. She also knew that shame had never left him.

Now, their box bed was big enough for the two of them to be sure but the mattress was straw and neither of them admitted how much they missed the comfort and beauty of the lost bed.

Tonight the room was lit by a single candle on a plain wooden box beside the bed. Both boys stood close to their father as he soothed their Mam. Jeannie's face screwed up in a grimace and as she groaned Jimmy sought reassurance, slipped his hand into Samuel's. "It won't be long." Jeannie told them all. "Samuel, you and Jimmy must carry on working in the field until Father comes for you." She paused as a pain seized her, smiling again when it passed. "There's bread and cheese wrapped in a cloth in the pantry. Take some cold tea as well. And Samuel? Look after your brother. "

Samuel promised, awed and frightened in equal measure at seeing their calm, gentle Mam with her hair coming unbound, her face pale, her hands white-knuckled as they gripped Father's so tightly.

Jeannie loosed Fraser's hand and he rose, ushered the boys out of the room into the kitchen. He took a small bundle off the pantry shelf, signalled Samuel to fill a bottle with cold tea from the kettle.

"Your Mam got quicker with each of you boys." He smiled reassuringly at their concerned faces. "The Doctor didn't arrive in time for Jimmy."

Both boys grinned at the well-loved story.

"You delivered me, didn't you Father?" Jimmy smiled, knowing the answer.

"I did. Mewing and crying before I could lay you in your Mam's arms." Fraser handed the bundle to Jimmy and nodded approvingly to Samuel who carried the cold tea. "Now, I want you to run to Doctor Evans before you go to the field. Tell him Mam's time is come and work until I come for you."

Fraser saw the boys to the back door, opened it onto a pale dawn where frosty sparkling light glistened and danced on the outside world. Samuel whistled softly as he walked towards the road but Jimmy turned back.

"Father, will we have a sister?"

Fraser grinned, shed years as his eyes crinkled. "Aye, with God's blessing, lad."

That was encouragement enough for Jimmy. Giving a whoop, he ran after his brother.

Hours later Samuel wiped the sweat off his face as he stretched and gazed around the paddock to check their progress. Jimmy picked up two more stones and placed them carefully along the paddock's edge and his brother smiled at the look of intense concentration on the little boy's face. He was small for his age but for all that, he worked hard at their chores, never grumbled or complained as Samuel heard other boys as young as his brother grumble and moan at hard work.

Still, he could tell Jimmy was tiring for it had been a bloody long day. They had removed their jackets hours ago, their shirt sleeves rolled up as they slogged. Mr Collingwood paid poorly for stone clearing work on his properties but Samuel was only too aware how their family depended on this small income.

The light leeched out of the winter day leaving the air already tinged with ice. Samuel checked the position of the sun and thought, another hour at most and they would call it a day. He placed two fingers in his mouth and whistled. Obedient as always, Jimmy bounded over.

"Can we go home?"

"Has Father come for us? No, we'll work on a bit longer. He wouldn't expect us to work into dark, though." He grabbed the last bit of bread and cheese, divided them equally and offered half to Jimmy along with the remains of the cold tea.

Jimmy wiped his mouth, handed the bottle back. "Why hasn't Father come for us? Mam said it wouldn't be long." But his brother could only shrug as he settled himself back against a rock. Jimmy looked towards the direction where their home lay. "I hope it's a girl."

"Me, too." Samuel rubbed his arms, feeling the cold now they had stopped working. "One baby brother is enough."

"I'm not a baby, Sam. I'm nearly eight." Jimmy grumbled, dodging the condescending hand that ruffled his hair.

Samuel merely pulled a face then laughed at Jimmy's attempt to out-ugly him. "If the wind changes, you'll stay like that."

By the time they came within sight of their house it was full dark, the only light showing from their parent's bedroom. They jogged closer, nearness to home giving them energy.

It was when they reached the front gate puffing and laughing that a a scream rent the night air. The boys froze, heard a woman sob out in despair and another scream tore through them. Mam! Jimmy couldn't move. His face drained of all colour as he stared mutely at the lighted window.

"Jimmy, come with me into the kitchen." Samuel jogged off, stopped when he realised he was alone. "Jimmy."

Another scream shuddered through Jimmy and Samuel didn't wait. He picked his brother up, carried him round the back, kicked the door open and moved straight to the fireplace, instinct telling him Jimmy needed warmth. There, pacing restlessly around the small kitchen was their father, his face as pale as Jimmy's, his eyes shadowed and fearful.

Jimmy slid out of his brother's arms onto the rag rug and drew his knees up to his thin chest. He wrapped his arms around them, eyes locked on the fireplace, rocking to and fro as the gasping cries from his mother continued, stuffing his hands over his ears in a vain attempt to block the sound out.

"Father, what's happening? I thought the baby would come easy this time."

"We thought so, too, but it won't come." Fraser looked down into Samuel's anxious face. "Doctor Evans is doing everything he can."

Another scream, bitten off in mid cry. Samuel grabbed his father's arm. "It's not enough!"

Fraser threw off his son's arm, sought to put distance between them.

Hours of fruitless, hopeless waiting as Jeannie's pain grew and grew, her composure giving way to the pain then fear as her agony continued throughout the day, Fraser's own strength collapsing a little more at the sound of every cry.

"We must get her to the hospital." Doctor Evans told Fraser only for Jeannie to cry out she didn't want to….. didn't trust….wanted to be here….. the boys….

Both men had soothed her as best they could but when Fraser bent to kiss Jeannie in her eyes he saw the utter despair of an animal caught in a trap.

"Sweetheart, I have to get the boys." He whispered and his heart broke as Jeannie struggled to smile, her fingernails scoring the skin on his hand as she clung to him.

"Tell them…. Tell the boys….. love them…." And another pain wrenched Jeannie away. Dr Evans murmured to her in a low voice as Fraser backed out of the room, unable to bear anymore, even the two boys forgotten.

And now Samuel stood in front of him, demanding effort, demanding something, anything and Fraser had nothing to give, no words of hope, no assurance that all would be well. He realised his fists were clenched and forced himself to breathe out, relax his fingers. Slowly the temptation to lash out at a boy terrified for his mother passed. Instead, Fraser pulled Samuel roughly towards him. He felt the tension in his son's body, neither of them drawing any comfort from the hug.

The door to the kitchen opened and three faces turned to Doctor Evans.

"Fraser. You must come now. "

Samuel stood right in front of Doctor Evans. "What's happening?" but the doctor didn't reply leaving Samuel unsure he'd even been noticed.

Fraser gestured towards Jimmy and the two men disappeared.

The screaming stopped, the house eerily, frighteningly still. The chill of the winter's night crept under the doors and through the windows, easily defeating the warmth from the wood stove.

Samuel stood for a moment confronted by the closed door before he wrenched it open. He pulled Jimmy to his feet and guided him to the hallway where the bedroom door was ajar. Motioning for quiet, Samuel sat on the hall floor, his back against the rough wood wall while Jimmy settled on his lap, his head pushed against Samuel's chest, eyes tightly closed, wanting the comfort, not wanting to see.

Through the gap in the door, Samuel saw his mother lying in the box bed, his father huddled against her, his hands clasped around hers. Jeannie wasn't moving and as Samuel continued to stare, her hands slid out of Fraser's, fell limply. He gave a cry, sobbing his denial as he gathered his wife's body into his arms.

Without knowing he did so, Samuel clasped Jimmy more tightly to him, his young brother so unnaturally still that for a sickening heartbeat, Samuel thought that he and Mam had slipped away together but then Jimmy whimpered and Samuel stroked his hair as their father cried.

Doctor Evans came out of the bedroom and closed the door behind him but not before they had seen the pile of red sheeting on the floor, caught the metallic odour of blood. His glance fell on the two boys as he wiped his bloodied hands on a cloth Jimmy recognised as the one their mother carried tucked into her apron. She'd wiped their dirty faces and hands with it; it had served as a flannel for soothing fevers, a soft cloth for wiping away tears. Now it was covered in her blood.

Jimmy felt sick, thought he was going to throw up all over Samuel and closed his eyes until the dizziness passed.

Doctor Evans spoke gently, "Your mother has gone to God."

"And the baby?" Samuel asked huskily.

"She's in God's care, too, Samuel."

"A sister?" Jimmy whispered.

Doctor Evans gave a ghostly smile. "A sister. Your mother wanted to call her Charlotte."

Jimmy was mesmerised by the sight of the doctor ceaselessly rubbing his hands around the bloody cloth.

"You would be best to give your father time alone. If you need me at all, just come and get me." And he walked back into the bedroom.

Jimmy whispered, "Sam?"

Silence.

When Dr Evans returned he was carrying his bag. He gave the boys a final sympathetic look as they huddled on the floor but there was nothing more he could do. He left, closing the door softly behind him.

Jimmy stared up into his brother's face. "Mam's dead, isn't she?" He knew it was so but needed Samuel to make it real.

"Yes, Jimmy. And our sister, too."

Finally, the tears filled Jimmy's eyes and he screwed his face against the sudden rush of pain and pressed himself back into his brother's arms. Samuel cradled and hushed him softly as he did when Jimmy had been a baby.

The two boys were left alone on the floor in the hallway of the dark house now echoing with the sound of their father's sobs.

***

The day of the funeral was overcast and cold, a hint of rain in the gusts of wind. Fraser, Samuel and Jimmy, dressed in their black clothes, stood beside the gravesite as the minister intoned the final words.

Fraser could only afford one plain coffin so baby Charlotte was laid to rest in her mother's arms. Jimmy tried not to think about that, about them lying together, still and pale under the wooden top. Since Samuel had explained people were buried underground Jimmy's nightmares had changed from The Old One to his mother and sister waking, underground, screaming. Over a few nights his thin face became gaunt, his dark eyes shadowed and Samuel became aware of his own inadequacies for nothing he said or did could ease Jimmy's hurt. Samuel took to going to bed at the same time as Jimmy, lying there unmoving, staring up at the black ceiling for

when a nightmare tore his younger brother from his rest, at least he was there to hold him, soothe him, listen to broken sobs describing Mam clawing at the coffin, screaming to be let out.

On this awful day Doctor and Mrs Evans stood with the family. The minister's wife was there too as she liked and pitied Fraser and his sons. The family hardly knew her, they were only half aware she was even there at all as she stood with her eyes lowered, her hands folded primly around a small bible.

Samuel kept his head up, blinked furiously to keep back the tears.
There'd been enough tears shed. Instead, he tried to blank out the sound of the minister's meaningless words by keeping his eyes out to Tasman Bay. Here in Wakapuaka Cemetery on top of the cliff his mother and sister would look out to sea for ever. Today the sea wore white crowns and murky shades but Samuel pictured it in summer, the clearest of blues, sunlight glinting on the softest waves.

The minister closed his Bible and his wife moved away, pausing at Fraser's side to offer her support should he need it. Fraser barely reacted, her words slipping out of his consciousness as soon as spoken.

Jimmy dragged his eyes from the coffin to catch his father's eye but Fraser was as motionless as a man carved from stone and as unreachable. Doctor and Mrs Beth Evans walked up to the little family, Beth laying a hand on Fraser's arm and he started at the touch as she repeated the sympathy he accepted blankly. While the Doctor drew Fraser to one side, Beth stood next to the two boys staring down into the grave.

"If you need anything, lads, anything at all…." She let the sentence hang for she knew what they needed was beyond her all help, was lying in that coffin. "Just call in. Promise me, Samuel."

He looked into her kindly face and found a small smile. "I will, Mrs Evans."

Silence.

"Samuel?"   He looked into her concerned eyes.   "Is your father….. is he coping?"

He had the oddest feeling that wasn't the question Mrs Evans wanted to ask. He opened his mouth, not sure how to answer without being disloyal when Jimmy spoke up.

"Father's drinking. He never drank as much as he does now. Do you think he should?"

As Samuel met Mrs Evans' eyes he knew that was the question she had wanted to ask. He took a step back from Jimmy as if allowing her permission to draw nearer.

"Sometimes people need a crutch to get them over what hurts them." She explained gently. "I'm sure when he realises how much you need him to be strong, your father will not drink so much anymore."

Jimmy thought this made sense. 'Sam's strong." He confided. "He's strong all the time."

Beth placed herself in Samuel's eye line as she replied, "Well, if Samuel would like to not be strong for a little while he can come to see me. You both can." She added, smiled gently at Jimmy.

"Can I really come?" Jimmy's reddened eyes searched hers urgently. "Can I come anytime?"

"Yes, Jimmy. Anytime at all."

Samuel placed a hand on his brother's shoulder, drew himself up straight. "Thank you, Mrs Evans. If we need you, we'll come over."

But Beth knew as she met Samuel's eye that they wouldn't and it broke her heart to see him shouldering the burdens of a grown man. She glanced in Fraser's direction, struggling with her anger at him. "Just remember I will always be here, Samuel. If you decide you'd like some help." A final warm smile and Beth walked back to her husband.

Alone once more the two brothers stood, side by side as the wind whipped around them and the rain fell

***

The day is hot with a warm breeze. Fraser lies beneath an apple tree. He watches the sun glistening in and out of the green, shimmering leaves, the faultless blue of the sky behind supple, young branches. He closes his eyes, listening to the bellbirds and the tuis, the cheeky chirrup of fantails in the bush beside their cottage.

Soft footsteps pad on the leaf-strewn grass then the swish of long skirts as she lies beside him. Fraser feels her weight and her warmth as she nestles against him, his arm drawing her close. They

***

Fraser jerked awake, heart pounding. Beside him Jimmy slept, his thumb pressed firmly into his mouth, a habit he'd long outgrown. Carefully, so as not to disturb him, Fraser eased out of the bed, drew covers over the sleeping child and saw he wasn't alone for Samuel regarded him bleakly from the doorway.

"He cried himself to sleep again."

Fraser didn't reply. He sat back down on the bed, picking at the cover.

Samuel's voice continued relentlessly.

"Mam's been dead a month. He needs you, Father."

"What about what I need?" was the rough reply.

Samuel shook his head in disgust, left Fraser to his misery.

***

The two boys were back on William Collingwood's land clearing stones, Samuel working like a demon in an effort to burn his anger away. He lifted a large rock with two hands and threw it with all his might, sent it crashing onto the other stones he'd already cleared and as it exploded apart in chunks and chips of stone, Samuel watched the destruction grimly, his chest heaving, sweat stinging his eyes.

He was desperate. The grocer had refused any more credit, asking instead when something was going to be paid off the account.

"I've been patient because of yer Mam and all, but times is tough for everyone." The man avoided Samuel's eye, unable to bear the stunned expression on the boy's face.

Samuel couldn't tell him when. Jimmy's shoes needed re-soling too but he had no idea where the money would come from for that either. Together, they had laid heavy paper inside the shoes over the hole and hoped it wouldn't rain.

The rent for the land their house sat on was overdue, Samuel heard his father beg for more time, Mr Collingwood adamant that they'd had time enough.

"Pay up or bugger off my land." had been the uncompromising reply.

In front of Samuel's accusing eyes Fraser had drunk himself into oblivion and the boy wondered where the hell their father found money to buy drink when they couldn't afford rent.

Last night as Fraser snored heavily, dead to the world Samuel crept into his bedroom. Cautiously he opened the sea chest, looking for something, anything to pawn. It was almost empty. Mam's clothes were gone, father's black suit, gone too. Samuel knew Mam had a few pieces of jewellery, pearl earrings, a green ring among them but they were nowhere to be found. All that remained in the chest were a few pieces of material and some of the boys' baby things. As Samuel picked up a little coat he remembered baby Jimmy wearing hot tears stung his eyes – this was how father could afford to drink! How could he watch Jimmy's face getting thinner, know his sons were going hungry and waste money on booze? Samuel shoved the coat back into the chest. There came the softest thud of sound. On the bottom of the chest sat a small ring of plain gold – Mam's wedding ring. Samuel's face hardened as he stared down at that little gold band. Muttering a swear word his mother would have washed his mouth out with soap for uttering, he scooped the ring up.

It sat in his palm, the last thing of Mam's.

He clenched his hand into a fist, bit his bottom lip. Fraser snorted loudly in his sleep as Samuel dropped the ring safely away in his pocket, gently lowered the lid on the wooden chest and quietly left the room.

Now, with the grocer's words ringing in his head, Samuel lifted his face to the sky and closed his eyes. Slipping a hand into his trouser pocket, he clenched his fingers around the wedding ring. How could he part with this last piece of Mam? The very last? But they were hungry, so hungry and regrets or not there would be food on the table tonight and father and Mr Collingwood could be damned.

Samuel placed two fingers in his mouth and whistled to get Jimmy's attention. "We're finished!" he shouted across the paddock

Jimmy wandered wearily over. "We're finished for the day? It's not on dark."

His brother kicked at a stone. "Don't care." He said. "Feel like sausages for tea?" and for the first time in weeks a smile lit Jimmy's face.

"Sausages? How…..?"

Giving Jimmy a thump on the arm, Samuel told him. "Ask no questions I'll tell you no lies. Come on, Tiny Tim, catch me if you can."

***

Father was out when the boys returned home carrying a brown paper package heavy with half a dozen, fat, pink sausages. Samuel also pulled two onions out of his pocket.

"I never even saw you buy them." Jimmy exclaimed and Samuel just grinned. He hadn't bought them, just picked the moment to slip them into his pocket as they left the grocer's. He'd paid half off their account, bargained a cheap price on the last of the day's bread plus slipped the two stolen onions safely away in his pocket with the coins left over from pawning their Mam's wedding ring. Samuel felt guilty and proud all at the same time.

"You don't see everything, Jimmy. Cut them up, will you? I'll get the sausages cooking."

Jimmy needed no second bidding. He began to peel the skin off the onions, his mouth already watering at the thought of the meal. Samuel hummed away, stoked the dying embers of the woodstove to life, chucked in some kindling and blew into the firebox to make the embers glow. With a prolonged breath they sparked and caught into warm, orange flame.

The onions were sliced and ready. Jimmy grabbed three plates and the cutlery, banged them down onto the scrubbed wooden table in time to the tune Samuel hummed then began to sing. He swung his brother round in a parody of a dance as the two boys sang, turned the sausages, cooked the onions and sliced the day old bread all in time to the song.

At last the food was on the table, Father's share keeping warm in the wood stove. The brothers sat, grinned at each other. As they'd been taught, they ignored their growling, hungry stomachs, bowed their heads.

"Thank you, God for the good food on the table." Jimmy began.

Samuel didn't hear the rest of the prayer thinking with a guilty pang that he'd broken at least two commandments to put that food in front of them. But, he reasoned, God wouldn't want them to starve would He? As Samuel echoed Jimmy's 'Amen' he added forcefully to himself, even if God did their Mam bloody wouldn't!

With no more thoughts or words the two hungry boys tucked in.

For the first night since their Mam and sister died, Jimmy slept peacefully through the night. Samuel lay fully dressed beside him, watching his brother's gentle breathing with deep pleasure for the relaxed face and eyelashes resting tranquilly against his warm cheek were proof that Jimmy's dreams were peaceful ones. There wasn't the hint of a nightmare. It had been worth stealing, Samuel thought to give Jimmy a full stomach and a quiet night.

Restless himself though, Samuel slid softly off the bed and leaned against the window frame to stare out into a drizzly night. The wet found its way in through the window and Samuel absently puddled his fingers in the drips on the sill, the night scene beyond their bedroom window somehow unfamiliar and disturbing.

Father wasn't home and in spite of the drinking and his sadness, he'd always been home at night. Where was he? What kept him? As angry as he felt, Samuel would give anything to have him here. The house felt different without even one of their parents in it, growing ever less like a home.

When Jimmy mumbled something indecipherable and turned over in the bed, Samuel reassured himself that his brother slept quietly on.

Where the hell was their father?

With an impatient sigh, his glance fell back to the window and saw a dark shape moving towards the house. Uneasily he pressed his hands against the cold glass and squinted as the shape seemed to stumble, right itself and then carry on nearer. The boy pulled away with an angry hiss and covered his cold face with both palms, reluctant to take his hands away from his eyes and deal with this.

It looked as if father was making it home after all. Drunk. Again.

Fraser kept his boots on as he stumbled through the back door into the still warm kitchen. Moving unsteadily he placed himself in front of the woodstove to rub some feeling back into his icy, wet hands. Drops fell from his sleeves and spat on the stove top as he pushed more wood into the firebox. Rising back up from his haunches, the stiffness of his legs and the alcohol in his blood caused him to lurch against the stove. By instinct Fraser's hand shot out to steady himself, burning palm and fingers in the process with the sizzle and sudden stench of cooked flesh.

"Shit!" Fraser staggered back, collapsed onto a chair, his burnt hand clutched against his chest. Lost in his own world of pain, he jerked when a steady hand tucked under his elbow and guided him to the sink. Once there Samuel poured cold water into a bowl and shoved Fraser's hand into it.

"Leave it in the cold water for a bit, Father. It will help."

The burn was sobering Fraser up quickly and he felt a hollow sense of shame that his son should find him like this. Not trusting himself to speak, he kept his eyes on Samuel's averted, serious face as he gently pushed cold water around the bowl and up his father's wrist.

"Who taught you to do this?"

"Mam. Jimmy did the same thing when he was little."

"Oh."

"Of course, Jimmy wasn't drunk when he did it."

Fraser was held in the grown up stare his son turned on him until he saw a glimmer of humour in those deceptively old-seeming eyes. With a shame faced grin and a nod, Fraser accepted he'd been fairly caught out.

"I'd hope not."

Silence fell between them filled with the thunder of pouring rain on the tin roof and the gentle sloshing as Samuel dabbled the cold water soothingly over Fraser's burnt hand. After several minutes Fraser pulled his hand away. He cautiously raised his reddened, blistering palm and fingers to his face, winced as the skin pulled and pain seared to his elbow.

"Thank you." He said as his son tipped the water out.

Fraser sat at the table while Samuel grabbed a cloth and took his father's meal out of the woodstove, placed it before him with a knife and fork. Fraser looked at the hot food in surprise.

"Where'd all this come from?" he asked incredulously.

Samuel just shrugged and Fraser decided not to ask any other questions. He knew two things; one, they had no money and two? Well, sometimes certain things had to be done to survive.

After the first bite of sausage though he put his fork down, queasiness bubbling in his stomach. He gave Samuel a small smile. "Not as hungry as I thought."

"Never mind. Jimmy and I'll eat it." Samuel placed the food in the pantry where it sat, already congealing, on the wooden shelf.

Father and son faced each other across the table, a wealth of unspoken thoughts and feelings heaped between them.

"Where were you tonight?" Samuel asked softly.

A pause as Fraser looked down at his work worn hands not seeing callouses and bitten nails while he struggled instead for an answer acceptable for this time of night, for this moment between him and his son.

"Seeing someone" he replied eventually.

Samuel waited for more. No more was offered so he pushed his chair back. "Well, I'm off to bed."

He made it to the door before his father said, "Tomorrow you, me and Jimmy need to have a talk. About the future."

Undefined fear squirmed into Samuel's gut. "We can't talk now?"

Fraser shook his head. "Tomorrow will be soon enough." He replied and after a moment, Samuel shut the kitchen door behind him.

Left alone, Fraser leaned his head back on the chair and stared sightlessly upwards. "What else can I do, Jeannie?" he whispered.

"There's nothing else I can do."

Fraser closed his eyes, held his breath, wished and prayed that Jeannie would speak to him, tell him what to do, offer him some hope.

But all he heard was the sound of rain falling on the roof.

***

They stood once more on top of the cliff of Wakapuaka cemetery where grass was already reclaiming the upturned earth of Jeannie's grave, Nature continuing in the manifest, bountiful way their family had not.

"I wish we had some flowers." Jimmy whispered. "We can plant something in the spring can't we Father?"

Fraser didn't even acknowledge Jimmy's question. In his hand, he held a wooden cross with the names *Jeannie* and *Charlotte* carved onto it. Kneeling at the head of the grave he pushed the pointed end of the cross deep into the ground, secured it upright and strong with his boot.

"One day we'll put up a proper headstone," he said and touched the names with gentle fingers to seal the promise.

For a few moments longer they looked down upon the grave until Fraser gave a deep sigh and moved to the edge of the cliff, gazed out over the sea. He closed his eyes, dreading what he had to tell the boys and when he opened them again, he saw sails out on the horizon as a ship came towards Nelson's port.

There was a time and it seemed so, so long ago when he and Jeannie had arrived on such a ship, leaving the filth and disease-ridden Scottish cities far behind for the dream of new beginnings and a hopeful future. Twelve years, at once just yesterday and a lifetime ago.

He sat on the grass while his sons read the other headstones nearby. Jimmy was about to point out a surname he knew from one of the boys from school when Samuel caught his attention and gestured to their father. Wordlessly they sat either side of him, Jimmy lifting his father's arm to secure it warmly about his shoulders.

"I spoke to the minister last night." Fraser began haltingly. "About what to do with you boys while I find work."

Samuel poked the damp ground with a stick. "What's to talk about? We'll be all right."

But Fraser kept his eyes firmly on the sails drawing closer on the horizon line. "I can't get work here in Nelson. I have to go to the West Coast. There's plenty of work down that way."

Samuel's face lit up at the thought of escaping Nelson. "That'll be great, eh Jimmy?" He grinned at their father, the grin sliding off his face and uncertainty crossing Jimmy's as Fraser shook his head. "I can't take you boys with me." He cleared his throat for even to his own ears his voice sounded much rougher than he wanted. "I'll be working all hours. There'd be no one to take care of you."

Jimmy clutched Fraser's hand. "What about Sam?" His eyes raked his father's face intently. "He's always looked after me." But Fraser continued to shake his head. Jimmy tugged harder on his hand. "Father, please."

Fraser shook off Jimmy's grasp as he stood, moving jerkily away unable to look at the boys as he continued. "No. You both need schooling and proper care. It might take a while to even find work. I'll come and get you when I can."

The two boys exchanged a look and Samuel scrambled to his feet, throwing the stick away. "Come and get us from where?" he demanded.

"They're set up for looking after boys." Fraser continued tonelessly. "And you'll make friends there."

Jimmy also came to his feet but more slowly, his eyes moving from brother to father in anxiety.

Samuel took a step closer to Fraser. "Who are father? What are you talking about?"

Drawing in a deep breath Fraser told them. "The Orphanage at Stoke."

Jimmy gasped while Samuel just as stunned, swallowed hard. "We're not orphans!"

"They don't just take in orphans." Fraser reached out a hand.

Samuel ignored it, his eyes locked onto his father's in horror. "We're not bloody orphans!"

Fraser raised his hand. "Don't you swear at me!"

"How could you even think of this, Father? How can you abandon us?"

"I don't have any choice. It won't be forever."

Samuel's voice trembled, "You're dumping us."

"No." Fraser was adamant. "I have to get work and there's none to be had here. Samuel, you must be reasonable…"

His son cut him off in anger.

"Why don't you want us anymore?"

Fraser's anger rose in his chest.

"There's no money left. I don't have a choice." He repeated, biting the words off as Samuel gave a bitter laugh.

"If you hadn't spent all these weeks drunk we'd have enough money."

With a gasp Fraser lashed out, his hand connecting hard against Samuel's face and sent the boy reeling. Jimmy gave a cry, grabbed Fraser's arm, torn between his brother's tears and his father's rage.

"Father, no!"

Samuel clambered to his feet unsteadily. Jimmy could see him shaking. Lifting his chin, he rubbed a hand over his reddened cheek. "I'll never forgive you for this. Never." He spat out.

Unable to bear anymore, Samuel ran down the cemetery's hill, Fraser shouting after him.

It took a long time for stillness to return to the cliff top. Jimmy felt numb, unable to believe what he'd heard, what he'd seen. The venom from his brother's last words seemed to echo around the gravestones, lingering horribly.

Finally Fraser gave up waiting for Samuel to return. "Come on, Jimmy." He said angrily. "We're going home."

Jimmy didn't move. "What about Sam?"

"Samuel will come home when he's good and ready." Fraser jerked his head. "So come on now."

Jimmy's eyes lighted on the grave where Mam and his baby sister lay quietly, undisturbed by the argument. From further down the hill, he heard his father call for him with increasing impatience and he took off after him as fast as he could. Neither spoke on the walk back and even once they'd reached their home Jimmy remained lost in silence, knowing his father was still furious and unwilling to provoke him further. Worried as he was for Samuel, he was fearful about being sent to the Orphanage, too. Occasionally he'd had seen the Orphanage boys. They were scruffy and if you moved too close to them they smelt damp, mouldy even. Mam had always pitied them but Jimmy never made eye contact with them. You could feel their eyes follow you. It was well known you never picked a fight with a boy from Stoke Orphanage. They fought dirty and they fought to win. Jimmy couldn't imagine living with them, becoming one of them.

There seemed too much to say and when Fraser hauled out their old chest, Jimmy couldn't be inside the house a moment longer. He wandered through the garden restlessly until unable to stop himself, he peeked in through the windows to watch as Father packed their clothes. Why did it feel as if was this was all happening to another family, one he didn't know very well?

It was as he leaned on the gate by the empty chicken coop that it came to Jimmy where Samuel might be. He walked back into the house and found his father, busy sorting through their few belongings.

"Can I go for a walk?

"Where to?"

"Just to, you know, say goodbye to Mrs Evans." Jimmy had never told a lie before, he wasn't even sure why he just didn't tell the truth but for some reason he couldn't mention Samuel's name.

"Of course, lad. Be back before dark." As Jimmy turned to leave Fraser lifted his voice, "Oh, and Jimmy?"

The boy halted in the doorway. "Yes, father?"

But Fraser seemed to change his mind and shook his head. "Just be home before dark."

It took all Jimmy's courage to face it but he ran down the road to where it branched off, took the one that was quickly lost in the thick bush. This was where The Old One's grave lay hidden. Jimmy shivered. What if his hunch was wrong and he ended up at the grave all alone?

Though the afternoon was bright enough, the green canopy above gave evening-like shadows to the ground under it. Jimmy trod cautiously, listened to the birds and the scurrying sounds of small animals.

As he came to the big, lightning-scarred beech tree, he glanced to his right and sighed with relief for there, sitting on a mossy stump was Samuel, his face tear-stained and dirty.

"How'd you find me?"

Jimmy shrugged. "Just knew you'd be here." He plumped himself down on the stump beside Samuel, wiped his nose with his sleeve as his brother asked,

"Aren't you scared?"

"Other things are scarier."

Samuel held a piece of rock in one hand and he scraped the moss off the old stump with it as Jimmy moved to the hump in the ground, the one Samuel told him was The Old One's grave. It looked nothing like their Mam's grave and for the first time Jimmy wondered if maybe Samuel had been teasing him.

"Sam, we should dig it up." Jimmy said slowly.

"Dig what up?"

Jimmy stood on the mound, looking down at it. "The Old One's grave."

Intrigued now, Samuel threw the stone on the ground and joined Jimmy on the grave-shaped hump. He scuffed at it with the toe of his boot. "Why?"

"Just to prove something." Jimmy jumped up and down a few times, then knelt, started to scrabble at the moss and dirt with a stout piece of stick and his hands.

"Prove what?"

"That nothing can frighten us."

Samuel gave a sound between a laugh and a gasp. Dropping to his knees he also grabbed a heavy, thick piece of fallen wood and together they attacked the Old One's grave.

True to his word, Jimmy made sure they were home before dark. The two boys were grubby and tired but there was a sense of elation about them Fraser couldn't understand.

"Did you say your goodbyes?" he asked Jimmy who ignored his brother's questioning glance.

"Yep."

"Don't know how you managed to get so filthy just saying goodbye." Fraser said suspiciously but without a word, he dug out the tin bath, placed it in front of the woodstove. "You need a clean-up" he told them, surprised at the lack of argument.

Instead Jimmy and Samuel sat at the table waiting for the tin tub to be filled, saying nothing, sharing secret looks.

As he tipped enough cold water into the tin tub, Fraser caught the unspoken byplay between the two boys. "What have you two been up to?" looking from face to face as he added, "Or shouldn't I ask?"

At last the water on the woodstove was hot enough. Samuel began to strip. "We've been chasing a ghost."

After adding the hot to the tub and testing the water, Fraser stood back, let both boys clamber in. "Did you catch one?"

Jimmy shook his head.   "No, we didn't need to."

Fraser took the soap and began to wash his youngest son's back. He saw the red of his hand still imprinted on Samuel's clean face and laid a gentle hand against it while Samuel looked up in surprise. "I'm sorry, lad. I shouldn't have lashed out at you." And in the boy's hesitant smile, Fraser found some redemption.

His heart lighter, Fraser pointed to a coating of dirt left on Jimmy's face, laughed as Jimmy wiped at it, still didn't get it clean. Whatever got the boys through, he thought, at least they were happy together for this last night.

Exhausted by the emotion of their day, both boys slept deeply and while they slept Fraser sat on the old trunk at the bottom of their bed and watched them sleeping.

He watched over them all night.

2

The Orphanage was a forbidding, bleak looking building in the eyes of two, scared young boys. Mist shrouded the hills behind it and drifted over the grounds but it wasn't just that damp, chilly, early morning air which made Jimmy shiver. It was the way the hills surrounded them, closed them in as they walked up the valley. The deeper they went, the more oppressive the feeling. He hoped for some small token of comfort from their father, a look, a gesture, something but Fraser's face remained expressionless and taut.

If Jimmy and Samuel had been older they would have noticed their father's clenched fists, the way a tic moved the outer corner of one eye, the way he deliberately avoided looking at either of them and would have known here was a man doing what he felt he should do against all the promptings and desires of his heart.

An elderly man with thin, silver hair stood in the doorway of the Orphanage. The tall windows set in the wooden walls peered out like blank, empty eyes. These were terrifying enough but Jimmy thought he could see white faces peered from behind them and any courage he had slid away. He stopped dead in his tracks, heart racing, unable to move any further.

Samuel pulled at his arm. "Come on, Jimmy."

"I can't." he whispered. "I…. " Tears sparked in the young boy's eyes. "I want Mam!" Jimmy broke down utterly, collapsed onto the stones and sobbed.

Samuel looked accusingly at their father and Fraser already guilty and angry by turns could bear it no longer. He grabbed Jimmy's arm roughly, yanked him to his feet.

"Stop that noise, Jimmy or I'll skelp you!"

With Samuel protesting loudly and Jimmy stunned out of his tears by the painful grip of his father's hand, Fraser strode towards the main doors, stopping in front of Father Aherne, furious, embarrassed.

Breathing heavily, Fraser was aware he still had Jimmy's arm in a vice like grip so his fingers relaxed but just a little, fearful that if he loosed his grip completely Jimmy would take to his heels. Father Aherne smiled at them, seemed not to notice Jimmy's tear stained face or the mutinous glare in Samuel's eyes.

"Good morning, Mr Brodie. Welcome, boys. I am Father Aherne. I have already had the pleasure of meeting your father." He shook hands with them. "This is my Orphanage and you will be under my care." Father Aherne's serene blue eyes regarded them all steadily.

Samuel squared his shoulders and said defiantly. "Me and Jimmy don't want to be here."

Fraser lifted a hand to cuff his ear but Father Aherne shook his head. With no falter in his smile he looked into Samuel's face and spoke gently in warm tones. "I can understand that, Samuel. You've lost your mother and your father has to leave you in our care whilst he looks for work down south. You've lost so much but that's why this Orphanage is here; it's why I'm here. We'll look after you and your brother until you can leave us again."

Samuel's hard fought battle against tears tripped up against this sympathy. He hastily swallowed the lump in his throat, wished the man would look away and was grateful when the priest turned his attention back to Fraser.

"They'll be fine with us, Mr Brodie. Your trunk arrived before you. I'll see the boys have their things." When he realised Fraser couldn't speak Father Aherne added gently, "I'll leave you to your goodbyes." And he moved to stand inside the main doors, watching the family from out of earshot.

Fraser knelt down, hugged Jimmy into his shoulder and held the other hand out to Samuel, half afraid he would be rebuffed but Samuel took his father's hand gladly and was also drawn into a close embrace, none of them wanting to be the first to pull away.

"Now remember what I told you; write to me care of Doctor Evans. He'll send them on so you'll know I'll get them."

When Fraser finally rose, the boys clutched his hands. One final, loving squeeze of their fingers and he turned, strode quickly back down the road, not trusting himself to look back. Samuel and Jimmy watched their father disappear into the mist, not moving until they felt a hand on their shoulders.

"Come on in, boys. I'm sure you must be hungry and you're just in time for breakfast." Father Aherne steered them towards the Orphanage doors.

That first day passed in a haze of frightening images and almost ceaseless noise. The cold, dim rooms, the faces peering at them, down at them, across the table at them, one pale blur after another, some blank, some threatening. Bells, shouts, boots running on wooden floors, the smell of unwashed bodies, so many new impressions crowded in on them and left them dazed.

Then, as the sun dropped out of the valley and the day began to darken towards night, fear wriggled its way into both boys' chests.

At supper they were unable to touch the rough stew and hard bread or face the staring eyes of the other boys who sat around them. Jimmy had no reserves left. He sat slumped over his plate while Samuel somehow knew that to show more fear invited trouble. He forced himself to keep his head up, made eye contact with a tough looking boy whose face bore a livid scar from hairline to nose.

Striving for nonchalance Samuel stuck his spoon into the cold stew and lifted it. As he was about to put it in his mouth, something moved in the sludge. With horror, he noticed a fat, white maggot crawling on top of the stew. There was a sharp clang as his spoon hit the bowl and he gagged, struggled not to spit bile onto the table.

A sharp elbow nudged Samuel's ribs and he turned to face a round faced, red headed boy with sores around his mouth who stared with longing at the full bowl.

"Don't you want it?" was the incredulous question, the incredulousness returned in full as the boy tipped the maggoty mess into his own empty bowl. He ate hungrily, maggot and all. Samuel shuddered, kept his eyes on the stained table top. Father Aherne read the final prayer and all the boys stood, Samuel pulling the unresisting Jimmy to his feet. As the boys lined up in two rows, one row behind Brother Donatus, the other behind Brother Jonas, Samuel put himself and Jimmy in one and they followed the rest out to the wash house where two long metal troughs with taps ran down a cold, unheated room, tall uncovered windows running the length of one wall. All the boys washed hastily shivering as icy droplets fell on bare chests.

Back in their lines, the boys were marched into a dormitory lined with two rows of iron framed beds, heads against the walls of high windows, each bed with a thin mattress and two blankets. Every boy soon discovered these could not compete with the winter's chill. They quickly learned to sleep without moving, the blankets tucked tightly around them, noses barely poking out.

Brother Donatus bade them goodnight from the doorway with his regular admonition for silence. With a final, fierce glare around the rows of boys huddled under their blankets, the two Brothers left.

For several moments quiet reigned until a loud fart echoed round the room accompanied by others less impressive and much giggling. Whispering broke out between a few boys and Samuel listened intently until he heard Jimmy crying softly into his cold pillow trying to be brave, trying not to let any of the others hear him. Samuel lifted his head but no one seemed to be taking any notice of them so he leaned over and whispered, "Jimmy? Are you all right?"

The little boy didn't want anyone to know how upset he was but he couldn't contain his misery and when Samuel said his name softly again, he began to cry in earnest. Unaware how silent the room became, Samuel slipped out of his bed and into Jimmy's to hug him.

The giggling stopped, the whispered conversations too, everything was still until a harsh voice called out, "Crybaby better shut up or I'll come over there and bloody shut him up!"

"Kip Rainey, is that your voice I hear?" The voice was low, sardonic. Brother Donatus had returned.

Samuel felt an unnatural stillness settle on the room, an in-drawn breath of silence. Jimmy's sobbing stopped at the sound of the adult voice though his breathing remained ragged as he tried to hide himself in his brother's arms.

"Kip Rainey?"

The room was so still and quiet Samuel heard the Brother's

footsteps as he strode into the room and stood in front of one of the beds.

"Yes, Brother Donatus. Sorry, sir." All cockiness had gone from the boy's tone, replaced by submissiveness.

"Whom were you threatening, Rainey?"

Samuel and Jimmy scarcely dared breathe.

"The new boy. The crying one. He was keeping us all awake." Rainey's voice was accusatory now.

He was expecting to be told off but Samuel was completely unprepared to be grabbed and yanked viciously out of bed. Donatus's grip on his shoulder was hard and unyielding as he yanked Samuel to within a few centimetres from his face and spat out, "Boys do not share beds with other boys, do you understand that?" Spittle landed on Samuel's face but he didn't dare flinch. Brother Donatus' voice hissed, "It is ungodly."

Samuel tried to pull back for the Brother's breath was foul and meaty but the hand holding his shoulder dug deeper and Samuel gave a cry of pain. Again someone from another bed sniggered.

"Silence!" Donatus's voice slammed into the quiet of the room and every boy stilled in fear. Donatus swung back to the brothers. "There will be no repeat of this foulness, do you hear me boy?" Samuel stared mutely into the red, angry face so close to his own. "Do you?"

"Jimmy was afraid, sir. I was just comforting him." Samuel kept his chin up, his body rigid.

Donatus lifted a hand and slapped Samuel ringingly across his left ear. "I did not ask for you to speak. All boys must become self-sufficient and able to stand on their own two feet. Now get back into your own bed and be thankful that I'm lenient on your first night." Samuel swallowed hard and Donatus shoved him away to look down on the terrified Jimmy shrinking into his blankets.

"And you, James Brodie, will stop snivelling. If you disrupt the night again, you will also come to know my displeasure." Satisfied fear made his point Donatus strode back down the middle row to the door where he turned back into the room. "Kip Rainey, you have duties to attend to, do you not?"

The tough looking boy with the scar across his face slipped out from under his blankets and disappeared down the rows of beds.

Samuel moved as close to his brother's bed as he could and whispered, "Jimmy…?"

But his brother made no sound at all.

Samuel thought he would never sleep yet sometime in the dark and lonely hours before dawn he fell, worn out into a fitful doze.

He woke with a start after what seemed like minutes later, his heart pounding as he wondered where he was. Down the rows of beds the boys were all huddled under their blankets. After reassuring himself that everyone slept, Samuel knelt beside Jimmy's bed. "Jimmy, are you awake?"

Slowly Jimmy uncovered his face, shocking Samuel with the sight of his white face and shadowed eyes. "Did you sleep?" Jimmy shook his head, eyes scared. "It's alright that you didn't." Samuel told him, whispering still. "I didn't either, well, only for a little bit."

One of the other boys turned over, the springs of his bed squeaked and Samuel waited until nothing moved in the quiet. "It will be better now we've had the first night. At least we'll know who to keep away from." Samuel tried to make a joke. "That Brother Donatus…. He's a piece of work." Using a favourite put down of their father's. But instead of smiling, his brother began to shake. "Do you need to go to the dunny, Jimmy? We could slip out now while everyone's asleep." But Jimmy looked even more fearful. "What's wrong?"

Tears welled up in the younger boy's eyes and suddenly Samuel knew. He slipped a hand into Jimmy's covers. "Oh god, Jimmy."

After Brother Donatus' reactions last night they knew a wet bed would be an unforgiveable offence. Samuel came to a rapid decision. Not giving his brother any time to think, he slipped Jimmy out from under his covers, changed trousers with him and pushed him into his own dry bed. With a grimace Samuel slid, flinching slightly into the wet covers, ignoring Jimmy's terrified, muted gestures of protest.

"Hush, Jimmy."

Before Samuel could say anymore, a bell clanged from the doorway and every boy came speedily awake, moving quickly from from deep sleep to wakefulness as Brothers Donatus and Jonas appeared, the latter swinging the bell. Brother Donatus clapped his hands sharply together and every boy threw their covers aside, bare feet pattering onto the wooden floor.

Brother Jonas walked down Rainey's side of the row of beds, Donatus the other, each of them taking in the rumpled bedding and the sleep-flushed faces. As he came to Samuel's bed, Brother Donatus stopped and stared at the discoloured mattress, his lips curling in distaste. Samuel clenched his fists and waited, willing Jimmy to silence.

"A wet bed?" Brother Donatus lifted his voice for all to hear. "Here we have a boy of ten who wets his bed."

Samuel caught the wild glee on Kip Rainey's scarred face.

"What do we do with bed-wetters, Brother Jonas?"

Brother Jonas was older than Donatus. Pink, flaky scalp showed through greying, sparse hair. He had pale eyes of indeterminate colour and his fingernails were bitten to the bleeding quick, the end of each finger wearing a ragged, chewed look as well. Right at this moment he was unmistakeably pleased at someone else's misfortune. His tongue flicked across dry lips as he smirked.

"We make the dirty boy wear his wet sheet through breakfast, Brother." Jonas's voice was harsh with a menacing crack to it. Samuel kept his eyes firmly on the floor. "We also make the filthy boy sleep in his wet bed – no use giving clean, dry sheets to someone with no self-control."

Brother Donatus pulled the wet bottom sheet off the bed and flung it round Samuel's shoulders. "You will wear that through each meal, boy" he said, "and you will wear those trousers all day, too." Samuel felt the moist, foetid breath on his cheek and tried not to flinch. Donatus straightened up and said to the room at large,

"Well? What are you all waiting for? Breakfast."

Brother Jonas left the room, the heavy bell tucked under his arm as the boys hastily donned jerseys and boots. Samuel risked a look at Jimmy who had his mouth open, ready to speak out. Frantically shaking his head, Samuel signalled for Jimmy to dress but not before Brother Donatus noticed this byplay. He frowned at the brothers and the two beds before realisation dawned. The other boys were noisily leaving the dormitory as Donatus stood in front of Jimmy and Samuel.

"You swapped beds."

Samuel looked innocent. "No, sir."

Donatus sneered, fingers twitching at the lie. "You forget I was here last night, boy. You swapped beds."

Samuel shook his head emphatically. "No, sir. You must have been mistaken in the dark, sir." He met the accusing stare unflinchingly.

Brother Donatus swung round to stare down at the terrified Jimmy. "Is big brother protecting the baby?"

Jimmy stood unmoving, unable to speak, his mouth opening and shutting around a tongue suddenly too big for its mouth.

Anxious to spare Jimmy, Samuel faced up to the angry Donatus. "Leave him alone! I told you it was my bed."

Donatus lifted a hand and slapped Samuel across the face, knocking him backwards. "You will not speak to me or any of the Brothers here like that, boy. Now, you will stand at the end of your bed wearing that sheet all day. I will check on you and if you dare to remove it or move from this spot, you shall be whipped, do you hear me?"

Samuel could only nod. The two boys went to pass Brother Donatus who pushed his hand onto Samuel's chest. "And where do you think you are off to now?" he asked softly.

Samuel swallowed. "Breakfast. Sir."

Donatus twisted thin lips in what passed as a smile, light finally reaching his yellow eyes. "Oh, there's no breakfast for piss-a-beds, boy. No lunch. Nor supper." He put his hand on Jimmy's shoulder and pushed him towards the door.

For the first time Jimmy baulked.

"But Sam'll be hungry, sir."

"Better hungry than whipped, James Brodie, don't you think? Or perhaps you would care to join him in the latter and make the comparison?"

"No!" Samuel kept his eyes on his brother's face. "Go to your breakfast, Jimmy. I'm all right."

Brother Donatus blinked slowly. "How very noble."

He smirked and piloted Jimmy out of the room leaving Samuel, standing at the end of his bed, the wet sheet draped over his shoulders, staring at the door.

Jimmy walked into the dining room after everyone else had been seated and Father Aherne was leading the room in prayer. He was painfully conscious of the staring. Brother Donatus shoved him onto a bench then took his own place. Aware of the sidelong glances from the other boys, he chanced a peek and noticed with surprise a sympathetic look on the small, finely boned boy with a cheeky face who sat opposite him. The smaller boy was prodded by a bigger one and the sympathy disappeared. Still, even the glimpse of it heartened Jimmy a little.

Everyone around him muttering, 'Amen' alerted Jimmy to the end of the prayer session. He hastily added his own unthinking invocation, a ragged cross gestured with equal half-heartedness. Breakfast was lumpy porridge with more bowls of hard bread slapped down as well. Jimmy glanced down the table to see if there was cream or sugar to put on the porridge but the other boys tucked into it as it was. He lifted a spoonful, watched the grey stuff plop off the end of the spoon. Feeling eyes upon him, Jimmy looked up to find Brother Donatus staring at him so he ate. After the first mouthful he was surprised when a sudden surge of hunger thankfully took his mind off the tasteless, gluey mass. Reaching for a lump of hard bread intending to eat it with the porridge, Jimmy remembered Samuel. After a careful check to make sure Brother Donatus was no longer staring, he slipped the bread into his trouser pocket.

Breakfast over, the boys were called to stand and again, moved into two lines and marched off. One group including Jimmy left for the schoolroom with Brother Augustus, the other was marched briskly outside to work in the fields with the young Brother Luke.

To his pleasure Jimmy was seated beside the boy who gave him the look of sympathy at breakfast and he was happy to see that the one called Kip wasn't with them. They exchanged hesitant, shy smiles.

"Woss your name?" the boy asked.

"Jimmy. What's yours?"

"Will."

A ruler slammed down on the table in front of them. Brother Augustus growled, "No talking."

Satisfied he had their attention, Brother Augustus moved slowly to the front of the classroom where he mumbled incoherently and wrote sums on the blackboard.

Will spoke to Jimmy out of one side of his mouth. "Let the old bastard tell us what to do, then he'll go to sleep in his chair and we can talk."

It shocked Jimmy to hear swearing like that and about an adult too yet Will didn't seem to realise he'd said anything wrong. He continued to peek at Jimmy in a friendly manner.

Sure enough, after twenty minutes of droning, Brother Augustus gave a self-satisfied grunt as he sat down behind his desk. He glared around the room once before settling back in his chair. Every pair of eyes watched gleefully as sleep quickly overcame him. In minutes Brother Augustus was snoring and the room came to life.

Every boy relaxed and threw down their pens. Will slouched over the table. "The bigger boy you're with? Who's he?"

Jimmy copied Will's negligent gesture, slumped forward onto his elbows. "My brother, Samuel."

"Where's your family?"

"Our Mam's dead and our father had to go and look for work down on the West Coast." Jimmy carefully kept his eyes on the snoring

Brother as he asked, "What about yours?"

Will shrugged. "Dunno. I've been here for years. I can't even remember what they looked like."

Jimmy expected Will to look upset but the younger boy was picking at the rough wood on their table top and seemed unconcerned. "Did you have a brother or sister?"

"Can't remember." Will used the nib of his pen to prise a sizeable piece of wood loose before chucking it on the floor and finding another spot for destruction. He noticed Jimmy's concern. "It's all right, you know. If I can't remember I don't have to remember any bad things, right?" and Will grinned, showing dimples in his cheeky face. "I like Samuel, though. He stood up for you. You're lucky to have a big brother who sticks up for you."

"Sam's always done that." Jimmy sighed. "I wonder how he is?"

Will stopped vandalising the table top. "Would you like to go and see him?"

"How? We're in class."

The other boy gave a contemptuous snort, gestured to the snoring Brother Augustus. "D'you think he gives a shit if we're here or not? He wouldn't notice us leave. We'll be back before he wakes up."

Hope surged through Jimmy. "What about the other boys?"

"No one tells in this lot. A few of the bigger bastards like Rainey and his gang would just to see us get into trouble but they're not here are they?"

Will looked around the room, laid a finger on his lips and gave a complicated hand gesture which must have been a pre-arranged signal among them as every boy nodded. Turning back to the still hesitant Jimmy, Will grinned. "See? Now we're invisible." Jimmy needed no more bidding. Quietly the two boys left the classroom, Will leading the way to the stairs.

"If anyone stops us, leave it to me and I'll tell them you're new and forgot your way to the dunny or something." Will said as they slipped noiselessly up the wooden stairs, ears pricked for the slightest sound but they were alone and in no time at all they stood at the door into their dormitory looking at Samuel, slumped down on the bed, the sheet around his shoulders.

At the sound of footsteps, Samuel leapt to his feet, not realising who had come into the room until Jimmy stood in front of him, smiling, a grinning pixie-faced boy beside him.

"Jimmy! What are you doing here?" Samuel hissed. "If Donatus catches you…"

"He won't. Sam, this is Will. He knows his way around here like a shadow. I wanted to see how you were and bring you this." Jimmy held out the hard bread and Samuel grabbed it, shoved it hungrily into his mouth. "I'll get you some more at lunchtime. I won't have you going hungry because of me."

"I don't care." Samuel wiped the crumbs away and shrugged the sheet back into a more comfortable position. "That Donatus… Will, are all the Brothers like him?"

Will's grin vanished. He glanced fearfully over his shoulder. "Not all of them" he said quietly. "Brother Luke is nice, so is Brother Anthony and Father Aherne is all right when he can be bothered. Brother Donatus and Brother Jonas are the worst of them." Will made eye contact with Samuel. "Don't keep pushing against them, eh. They can do terrible things."

"Isn't this bad enough?" Samuel demanded, shaking the wet sheet but Will shook his head vehemently.

"Trust me. Apologise if you have to but don't you go make it worse."

"What do you mean, worse?"

Will just shook his head as the three boys heard footsteps coming up the stairs. Samuel pushed at the younger boys.

"Quick, don't be seen!" he hissed.

Will grabbed Jimmy's sleeve and dragged him towards the door. He managed to hide them both behind it just as Brother Donatus appeared in the doorway. Seeing Samuel still standing where he was left Donatus gave a nasty smile, moved away again.

Cautiously Will poked his head around into the corridor to peer out. Hearing a door shut further down he gave the all clear to Jimmy.

"We'll be back." Jimmy called softly to Samuel who saluted them. Quickly the two young boys slipped back downstairs. Will paused just outside the classroom, peeking around the door. He got thumbs up from the red headed boy.

Brother Augustus still snored, a silvery sheen of saliva falling from one side of his mouth onto his dusty, faded robes.

"Disgusting old bastard." Will muttered as he and Jimmy slipped back onto their bench.

Behind Will, someone threw a balled up bit of paper. It sailed over their heads to land on Brother Augustus' lap. Will and Jimmy turned round to see another paper bullet being prepared by the boy with red hair. Will leaned on the table behind them.

"Mick, get it in the old bugger's mouth and I'll share supper with you."

The red headed boy pretended to consider this generous offer. "Half?"

Will snorted. "Want me to starve to death? Quarter." And waited confidently for Mick's reply.

"Deal."

Every eye in the room watched in glee as Mick shoved torn paper into his mouth. He chewed on it working plenty of spit into it before hoiking the wet mass into his hand. With intense concentration he rolled it into a hard ball between inky palms, looking at it from this way and that. Satisfied with his missile at last, Mick squinted lightly as he took aim. Every breath was held. Mick lifted his hand, judged the distance and lobbed. The paper wad sailed through the air and landed right in Brother Augustus' wet mouth.

Mick gave the room a quick salute and settled back into his place with speed and innocence while his victim spluttered and choked. Brother Augustus wiped clumsily at his mouth, the paper missile coughed out and lost among the folds of his clothes. Muffled giggles alerted the old Brother that he'd been caught sleeping. He glared around the bent heads, completely unaware of any trick or that the innocent looking Mick, studiously bent over his work was in any way to blame. Brother Augustus checked his watch. It took great effort but he forced himself to stay awake for the remainder of the lesson.

When the bell sounded for lunch, the boys tumbled out of the classroom before the old man had gathered his thoughts enough to dismiss them. Laughing, shoving each other, congratulating Mick they spilled into the dining room, brought up short and to silence by Brother Jonas and Father Aherne who stood waiting. Again, innocence and humility settled on each face and radiated through every posture. Father Aherne led them in prayer then they all sat with the requisite scraping of benches and scuffling of feet.

The fare was a broth with more hard bread but Jimmy didn't hesitate this time. Hunger compelled him to eat the watery soup with its oily layer of fat and few pieces of grey meat. Copying Will, Jimmy dipped the bread into the mess, carefully manoeuvring an extra piece into his pocket for Samuel. Will nudged Jimmy's arm and he looked around in time to see another piece of bread disappear into Will's pocket. They shared a grin as they ate.

Upstairs in the dormitory Samuel was bored. For a while he'd only been cold so he'd slipped on his boots and lifted his weight up and down on the balls of his feet while he moved his arms like windmills to warm up. Feeling better he'd then recited Mam's favourite stories under his breath, the ones she'd read to them in the evenings but thinking about Mam even in an abstract way hurt too much so he stopped. In minutes his mind drifted into the lethargy and blankness of increasing tedium.

After what seemed like a whole day the bell and echoed thunder of feet on wooden floors below signalled lunchtime. Samuel sighed deeply. He'd been standing at the end of his bed covered in the wet sheet since dawn.

Thank god for Jimmy and that boy Will, though. Samuel ached with hunger but at least someone was thinking of him and he knew they would try and get something else to him as soon as they could.

It was surprising how much better he felt knowing that.

As Samuel rocked back and forth on his feet he thought how unexpected it was that Jimmy had made a friend so quickly. It was usually he who made friends while his shyer brother just kind of tagged along, made friends by familiarity.

Yesterday they arrived in this place, only yesterday but it felt like so much longer.   Maybe this punishment had worked to Jimmy's advantage, forcing him to accept friendship on its own terms, there being no one to help him or make the friendships for him?   Samuel didn't know but however it happened or whatever the explanation for it, he was just thankful beyond words that his timid younger brother found someone to help him fit in.

And Brother Donatus….? What could be worse than this? Could he pretend to be sorry to that foul breathed bastard?   Samuel didn't say that last word aloud.   Instead he moved his lips around it, smirking and mouthed it again more strongly this time. Bastard.

Sooo bored.   Samuel let his head drop back and shouted, "So bored!" at the ceiling.

"After a while it is the tedium which overcomes the feelings of hunger and being uncomfortable, is it not?"

Samuel spun round.   There, just a few feet away stood Brother Donatus.   Thankful for what he hadn't said out loud Samuel faced front once more and waited.

"Are you very hungry, Samuel Brodie?"

Unsure if reply or silence would provoke Donatus to anger, Samuel chose silence figuring at least the Brother couldn't use his words against him.

Donatus moved further into the room and to Samuel's surprise, he laid dry linen sheets and trousers onto the bed.

"You have borne your punishment well. I say your punishment but it was James's, we both know that, don't we?" Brother Donatus sat on the side of the bed, patted the mattress beside him with a smile somehow as unsettling as his anger. "Sit, boy."

Taken aback by this unexpected change, Samuel obeyed only to flinch as Donatus reached towards him and removed the wet sheet from his shoulders.

"I admire bravery." Donatus said, still with that same disturbing smile. "Tell me, Samuel Brodie, would you do the same thing again?"

"Yes." A heartfelt, unthinking reply.

Donatus lifted a sceptical eyebrow. "To protect a boy without any courage of his own?"

"He's my brother." As if that explained everything which, for Samuel, it did.

"You deserve better. Someone who would stand up for *you*."

Samuel didn't know what to say. He felt increasingly uncomfortable about Brother Donatus's nearness, that terrible smile. Not wanting to give offence, he shuffled awkwardly, put space between them both as if by accident. He stared at his hands feeling discomforted and uneasy.

After an interminable silence Brother Donatus said, "Well, I think you've learned your lesson. Change out of those wet things and then go and find the others out in the fields. You'll find them to the right behind the main building."

Amazed by this reprieve Samuel needed no further bidding. Swiftly and thankfully changing out of the cold, wet trousers into dry ones, he made his exit an escape. Brother Donatus moved to the tall windows in time to see Samuel explode out of the back door and hare off toward the fields beyond.

Revelling in the feel of fresh air and working cramped limbs, Samuel felt like singing. He quickly reached the main gardens and pausing briefly, spotted people working in the field to his right.
Lifting his feet to run again,he came to a panting stop beside the young Brother who held a shovel.

"Brother Donatus sent me out to work." He explained breathlessly.

"A new boy. And what is your name, my son?" The young Brother's voice was quiet, so quiet Samuel strained to hear him.

"Samuel Brodie, sir."

The young Brother smiled. "Then you must be Jimmy's big brother. I've heard all about you." He wiped sweaty hair from his eyes before brushing off dirt from a filthy hand which he then extended. "I'm Brother Luke, Samuel."

There was something immediately safe and reassuring in the Brother's wide set, hazel eyes, Samuel thought as he accepted the hand shake.

"As you can see, we're harvesting swedes and turnips and will continue to do so until the supper bell so unless you want to find yourself the unfortunate subject of much taunting about how little you have achieved, perhaps you would care to join Jimmy and Will's group?"

"Of course, Brother." Samuel scampered away, Jimmy giving a yell of pleasure at the sight of him.

Immediately Jimmy handed over a chunk of bread which Samuel shoved into his mouth, ruffling his brother's hair. He was surprised but grateful when Will also handed him food. As he ate Samuel related the incredible fact of Brother Donatus's lenience. Will stopped smiling.

"What?" Samuel asked through the thick paste in his mouth. "What's wrong?"

"Donatus let you off?" Will looked troubled.

"Yeah." Samuel threw a turnip onto the pile, stood back up straight. "He brought dry sheets and trousers as well." Jimmy too came to a halt, eyes flicking between Will and his brother in growing concern. "Isn't that good?" Samuel asked in confusion. "I thought I was for the drop and instead I'm let off." Will didn't reply. "What, Will? What's so bad?"

"Samuel, don't….." Will struggled to find the words. "Don't let yourself be alone with Donatus. If you can."

Samuel and Jimmy exchanged puzzled looks. They were so naïve Will thought in frustration. As young as he was he felt years older. Opening his mouth to ask more questions, Samuel twisted unexpectedly and grunted in pain as a swede hit him forcefully in the small of his back. Looking around, he saw a group working behind them with Kip Rainey in it. Rainey wasn't facing their way but Samuel thought he knew who'd thrown the swede.

He forgot about Will and Brother Donatus, he even forgot his own unease as he thought instead about the mean looking Kip Rainey.

***

For the first time since they arrived in this place, Jimmy and Samuel found a few minutes to be alone. Before too long they would be missed yet here they were, unable to move away as they leaned against the long bench in the washroom. Samuel just stared down at the rough wooden floor while Jimmy picked at the dirt caked under his fingernails.

"I want to go home."

"I know, Jimmy but we can't. " Samuel kept his voice low. "And we don't even have a home. We haven't since Mam died. Not really."

They knew they should be washing for the supper meal but still they remained there, reluctant to return.

"Sam, thanks for what you did." Jimmy bowed his head, shoulders slumped. "It should have been me. It was me who….I'm so ashamed, Sam…I'm so sorry."

Samuel gripped Jimmy's arm tightly, forced the younger boy to meet his eyes. "Don't you apologise." he told Jimmy fiercely. "It could have happened to anyone. You've nothing to feel bad about, Jimmy. Nothing." He saw the sheen of tears. "If you were the big brother, you'd've done the same for me. We're brothers, Jimmy. We look out for each other." For the first time Samuel faltered as he added, "And we're all we've got."

Jimmy sniffed hard and said softly, "Till Father comes back for us."

Straightening his shoulders, Jimmy turned to the taps while Samuel found the disloyal thought, "If Father comes for us…." running through his brain as he remembered the drunken, defeated man who sagged, hunched against the kitchen table, his hand burned, his spirit broken.

They made it to the supper table in time for prayers. Brother Donatus proffering Samuel a conspiratorial smile which the boy tried to ignore while not wanting to offend so ended up returning a kind of grimace. Will who missed nothing, certainly didn't miss that.

He leaned over Jimmy to whisper to Samuel. "What was all that with Donatus?"

Samuel shrugged, forced himself not to look back at the Brother in question. "I dunno."

"Remember what I told you, Samuel." Will hissed. "Don't get involved with the bastard."

"I'm not involved!" Samuel's voice was too loud and other boys turned to look at them. He dropped his voice instantly. "I hate the.." All Mam's deeply ingrained teaching struggled against the word but Samuel forced his chin up, continued boldly, "…the bastard. He just smiled at me."

Bowls of stew were dropped in front of each boy and as they bent their heads to pray, Will whispered, "You don't have to smile back." receiving a clip over the back of his head from Brother Jonas.

"Pray for your supper, William Wilson. God knows you need to be thankful." Jonas gave Will one last cuff to make sure he'd made his point as the boys intoned after Father Aherne. Jimmy and Samuel saw the rude gesture Will sent surreptitiously after Brother Jonas. The younger boy gave a shocked giggle as he and Samuel exchanged guilty grins for they knew Mam would never have approved yet neither of them could help liking Will with his wild ways. Though he'd never tell Jimmy, Samuel made a mental note to ask Will exactly what the gesture meant and then use it.

As Father Aherne gave the final blessing, the hungry boys picked up their spoons and began to eat their rapidly cooling meal, Samuel picking cautiously through it, checking for more maggots. None tonight.

Will's mouth was bulging when Mick kicked him under the table.

"Ow, you red headed bastard!   What'd you do that for?" He rubbed

his shin and glared Mick who just passed over his already empty plate and winked.

"Pay your debts, William."

Will had forgotten. Grumbling he spooned exactly a quarter of his stew into Mick's plate and looked mournfully at what was left. "Not enough for a hungry cat," he said in disgust.

Mick spoke, grinned horribly through a mouthful of Will's stew. "If you're complaining, send it my way."

"Piss off, Mick, I'm nearly dead with starvation as it is."

"What and the rest of us are fat as bloody pigs are we?" Mick deliberately took his time to enjoy another spoonful of Will's stew and Will growled, giving Mick even more pleasure.

After listening to all this Samuel carefully divided his stew into two equal measures and scrapped half into Will's bowl.

"What's this for?"

"I owe you."

Looking at Samuel, Will frowned. "I didn't expect half your dinner." He tried to tip it back into Samuel's bowl but the bigger boy gave him a gentle shove.

"It's just a bit of thanks, Will."

He wouldn't be gainsaid so Will gave in. "Well, thanks. You're a kind bugger, you are."

The language unsettled Samuel. A few years ago he'd heard some other boys swear and he then made the big mistake of repeating it in his father's hearing. He had received a thrashing he never forgot, his mouth rinsed with soap and water for good measure. Only once had he heard his father swear. Samuel could still conjure up the feeling of shock. Yet here was Will swearing as if they were just any old words. Determined not to be at a disadvantage again, Samuel strove for a nonchalance he didn't feel and made himself snort with a sudden burst of laughter.

"What's so funny?" Will asked scraping his bowl vigorously in a vain attempt to drag more stew off the all too clean sides.

"Nothing."

Mick flicked a piece of crust at Samuel. "Funny kind of nothing to make you laugh." He belched hugely causing a ripple of giggles up and down the benches and a frown from where the Brothers sat at their own meal.

Samuel tensed, ready to take offence but saw a friendly sparkle in Mick's wide set eyes. He lowered his voice for Will's ears only. "What's the story with that Kip Rainey?"

Will grunted. "He's a bastard. A scarred-face bastard from some shitty little village further south. Why?"

"He hates me."

Will snorted. "You've only just got here. And anyway, don't take it to heart. Kip bloody Rainey hates everyone except Kip bloody Rainey. Just keep out of his way."

Samuel looked over his shoulder to where Kip sat and sure enough, Kip was staring straight back at him. The bigger boy gave an evil grin, ran a finger across his throat and pointed at Samuel who hastily turned away.

'Keep out of Kip Rainey's way?' He thought. 'That's the easy part. But I don't think he wants to keep out of mine....'

That night, only their second night in the Orphanage Jimmy slept, worn out while Samuel lay wakeful, his mind full of every impression, the eye contacts, the gestures, the unsought friends and the equally unsought enemies. He thought about Jimmy wanting to 'go home' and lay there thinking what that meant for them now they had no home, no mother and a father gone.

3

Fraser walked down the muddy road as night came on. He'd been given a lift on the road between Richmond and Wakefield and had then been lucky enough to be given another ride on the back of a farmer's cart to the turnoff to the Howard Valley. There he'd curled up in a wooden hut and slept the sleep of the dead.

Cattle snuffling around the door woke him to pre-dawn light. Quietly amazed at how rested he felt, he stretched out a couple of aches and pains in his back and legs and breathed in the crisp, tangy air. Rummaging around in his canvas bag brought to light the remains of bread and cold meat and he ate ravenously watching the valley hills to the east lighten.

Refreshed, Fraser turned his face towards Murchison. He'd made a plan; at every farm he'd ask for work. Any work.

At the first farm, down a long, potholed farm track, nothing. At the second and third farms, same rough track, same result. With Longford in view Fraser hailed a man bent working in a field. "Excuse me. Any work going here?"

"No. Keep walking." No pretence of interest or politeness.

To the edge of the township flowed the Matakitaki River feeding into the mighty Buller River. Fraser took a breather, leaned on the bridge wall and gazed down into the churning, rain-dirty water. As he stood there an older man wandered across the bridge, saw Fraser and politely doffed his hat. Obviously in no hurry to be anywhere, he joined him in resting elbows on the bridge wall, a cigarette butt hanging wetly between his lips.

"Break in the rain," he said.

"Not for long." Fraser gestured to the clouds. "Be on us before night."

The man coughed, kicked a few pebbles over into the river. "What's the accent?"

"Scottish. I'm from Perthshsire."

"So you're British."

Fraser couldn't tell if the man was joking. He smiled anyway. "Scottish. "

"Didn't think there was a difference." This time there was a smile, slanted sideways as a mischievous grin.

"There is in Scotland." Fraser assured him.

An abrupt yet inquisitive man, strange in a country full of reticence and self-sufficiency, he quickly discovered Fraser's past and his present need for work.

"Well, you could try Lyell but things are tough there, tougher than they have been." The man coughed through his cigarette, finally spat it at the ground. "Men are leaving for the Coast." Something of despair must have shown in Fraser's face for the man dug into his pocket and pulled out a couple of coins, pressed them into Fraser's hand.

"No. I can't take this! I'm not begging." Fraser's face burned with shame and he tried to return the money but the man just quietly shook his head.

"Them that's been there know and understand," he said quietly and Fraser read a hungry past in those knowing, deep set eyes. He gave Fraser a tip of his hat and walked away, whistling to himself.

His face still burning Fraser shoved the coins away, shouldered his canvas bag and walked out of Murchison into the deepening valley gorges.

Despite the warning about the lack of work prospects in Lyell, Fraser stopped there anyway. The greyness of the day and the plain, tatty wooden buildings shared a strange likeness to the worn faces of the people he saw, no one making eye contact with a stranger.

Footsore and thirsty Fraser made his way into the nearest tavern in Cliff Street, handed over one of his precious coins, quietly thanking his charitable friend on the bridge as he sat and ate the thick, meaty stew with dumplings, fresh bread and butter. Fraser had to stop himself from eating like a savage. The woman behind the bar however knew a starving man when she saw one. She casually added another ladle full of hot stew into his bowl, waved away his awkward, stammering thanks.

"Passing through are you?"

"Aye. On my way to the Coast."

"You needing work?" She gave a grimace, replied with a self-mocking, "Stupid question. Who isn't these days, eh?"

"Do you have a bit of food I could take with me?" Fraser, wiped the empty bowl with the last piece of bread, savouring that final mouthful.

She had obviously anticipated this, silently passing him a newspaper wrapped parcel, accepting his money with a warm smile. "Try Greymouth," she said. "Or Blackball. The mines are busy there."

By the time Fraser left, the day was well into afternoon. Mist hung low over the tin roofs and rough wooden buildings, the gloom adding to the knowledge that whatever hope had dwelt here with the gold was long gone.

Fraser buried his chin into his chest, walked around a huge hole in the road and nearly disappeared under the wheels of a cart, laden with a family and what looked like all their belongings in this world. The driver, instead of cursing Fraser for getting in his way, tilted his hat back from his eyes.

"We're to Inangahua if that's any use to you."

"I'll gladly take a ride. Thank you."

With a nod the man waited for Fraser to sit on top of a wooden trunk, three children tucked into places around him. The driver clicked his teeth, set the horses on their way.

"What sends you all away from Lyell?"

The driver looked back over his shoulder once and all conversation from then was carried out to his back. "Mine closure. Only the Alpine left working. Can't survive without work. My brother has a farm at the junction. Offered me work and us a home."

"No gold left?"

A snort.

"There's a couple of old timers still working their old claims but the good times have gone." Again that snort. "Not that there was many except for a lucky few." The driver's voice lowered. "Gold fever's a bitch. Men waste away and die from it." His wife, who hadn't even looked at the stranger in their cart, laid a hand on her husband's arm, a brief glance exchanged between them. Fraser wondered at it. Was it this rough driver who'd felt the sting of gold-fever or someone they both knew? Whatever the answer, there was no more conversation. Fraser settled back as comfortably as he could, eyes drooping, aware of three sets of young eyes on him as he dozed off.

The jolt of the horses coming to a halt just north of Inangahua woke him. He yawned, rubbed sticky eyes, disconcerted to find the children still staring at him. Clambering stiffly out, Fraser thanked them all, lifted a hand as the cart pulled up a long farm road. After a moment the children waved back, shyly at first then more vigorously until the mist swallowed them up. Sitting hunched for so long had seized his back up and it took Fraser a few groaning moments to loosen up enough to walk on. He discovered all too quickly that the little settlement of Inangahua kept its doors closed to a wanderer so he trudged on lonely, sore feet passed the few cottages with warm candlelight beckoning mockingly from tightly shut windows. He smelt supper being cooked for the lucky ones and to top it off, it began to rain, light, misty but soaking rain. Fraser tugged at his coat. He lifted the collar to tuck his chin into its warmth, pulled his hat brim further down over his eyes to tilt it against the worst of the wet and walked on.

Now, as the darkness deepened, Fraser slogged towards the West Coast, aiming for Blackball near Greymouth. He'd once spent time working down a mine in Fife and hoped to never have to do so again. But, needs must.

Just on dark a barn back off the road in a paddock loomed out of the heavy mist. Without a pause, he directed his feet to it and just in time for the heavens opened up as he walked thankfully through the doorway. Ducking under pouring eaves, Fraser threw his canvas pack off his shoulders, himself down onto the nearest stack of hay and groaned as the weight came off his aching feet.

Slowly but surely the tension left his shoulders and back. Too tired to reach for the food in his bag, Fraser just lay there, felt the softness of the hay as its warmth gradually enveloped him snugly. The rain pelted down, thundered onto the roof and a sudden wind pushed it under the wooden doors while it lashed against the small, single window high on the wall opposite. Wearily listening to the thrashing rain Fraser was fervently grateful that the boys hadn't been forced into sharing this hard journey with only uncertainty to end it. At least at the Orphanage they would be warm, fed, have beds to sleep in, lessons given to them and, after a bit of time, friends. Much better that life than this one.

It hurt Fraser too much to think of his sons. To cheer himself up, he dug inside his jacket until his fingers closed over a much creased piece of paper. He didn't need to open it for he knew it off by heart yet he carefully unfolded it for that act alone brought the memories tumbling back. Jeannie had written this to him all those years ago accepting his marriage proposal and reminding him that he may have won her heart but her father would be a trickier prospect. Fraser captured Jeannie's light, playful tone in the words. He pictured her smile, the way it brought out the dimple beside her mouth and set the light in her eyes. He had never managed to win her father's approval but he had won her and together they had left disapproval and dark, grimy cities for a new start in the colonies.

Deliberately focused only on the remembered pleasure Fraser tucked the worn, rubbed letter safely back where it always lay and stretched out an arm to grab his canvas pack. He fumbled with cold, stiff fingers to unlace it and grabbed the newspaper parcel of food finding not only bread and cheese, but a sizeable chunk of meat in there, too.

"God bless the kindness of women," Fraser said out loud.

Careful to save more than half the food for the next day, he settled back into the warm hay again happy in the simple pleasures of food and warmth as the rain teemed down outside.

Tomorrow he would carry on down the Grey Valley, checking for work as he went. If he could find permanent work anywhere he'd be able to bring Samuel and Jimmy to join him and they could be a family once more. But until tomorrow – and knowing his luck, Fraser thought, it will still be bloody raining! – there was the here and now with Jeannie warm in his mind, forever in his heart.

4

It took Samuel over a week to remember they hadn't changed their clothes. Every night the boys slept in their trousers and shirts, every morning they added discarded jackets, unless the night had been bitter and they didn't even remove those. Samuel lifted an arm, sniffed at his sleeve. They still wore what they had turned up in and the sweat and dirt stiffened their shirts and trousers, making them prickly to wear.

"And we stink." Samuel muttered searching under his and Jimmy's beds for their things. After searching under every bed he stood, hands-on-hips. "Where the hell's our trunk?"

Jimmy sat cross-legged not offering to help. "I haven't seen it since we arrived. Ask Father Aherne."

Samuel considered for a moment. "I'll see him after morning prayers."

Will was waiting for the brothers by the door into the dining room. "Where've you been? We'll be late if you don't bloody hurry."

"I want our trunk. We need to change out of these." Samuel tugged at his filthy shirt as they sat down. "I remember Father Aherne telling Father it had arrived before us." Samuel thought hard. "He said we'd get our things."

Will snorted. "You won't see your trunk or anything in it. No one keeps their stuff here."
The brothers began to file in.

"Why not?" Samuel whispered, mouth barely moving.

"Aherne sells anything good, pockets the money as far as we know. We never see any of it anyway."

Samuel glanced up to where Father Aherne stood, his face placid, his white hair framing an innocent face. "He wouldn't do that!"

Will shrugged as Aherne began to intone the morning prayer. "He's an old bastard. D'you think we'd wear these filthy rags if he liked spending money on us?" Will's eyes were fastened on the table top but Samuel saw his bitter sneer.

Mick coughed, alerting them to Donatus's approach and they fell silent.

59

It was the morning for exercises when the boys were all marched outside, placed into rows and handed weights. These hated extras were carried through the whole programme.

As they filed down the corridor which led to Father Aherne's study, Samuel slipped away, stood outside the wooden door, breathing nervously. Hesitantly he knocked and when there was no reply, he knocked again, harder this time. Heart pounding, Samuel heard the scrape of a chair and just when he decided to bolt, the door opened inwards to reveal Father Aherne looking down at him.

"What do you want?" he asked Samuel, his voice harsher, less poetic than when the boys first met him.

"Please, sir, I wondered where our things went. Jimmy and me need to change our clothes and Father put them all into the trunk."

Father Aherne glanced down the corridor. "All your clothes have been added to the rest, Samuel. We hand out your clean clothes on bath night."

"But we're dirty now, Father. Our Mam always made sure our clothes were clean."

"This Orphanage does not have the money to dress every boy like a Prince. We feed, clothe and educate those who have nothing. Are you complaining about the way we do God's work here?" There was no indulgent twinkle in Father Aherne's blue eyes now.
"No, Father. It's just...."
"I think you should return to the others. Better you get some healthy exercise than waste your time complaining about nonsense to me."
"But Father...."
"Go!"
Samuel ran without a backward glance.
Later in the morning, Jimmy came up to Samuel.
"Did you ask?"
"Yes. Leave it, Jimmy."
"But, Sam, what about our stuff?"
"Leave it, Jimmy! We do like everyone else and that's that."

Part II

5

"Why doesn't Father write?" Jimmy demanded of Samuel one Sunday night as the two of them sat in the school room. Inky fingers restlessly tapped the table top as their weary minds sought to frame the necessary words.

"How the hell should I know?" was the terse reply.

Yet as the weeks slid into months and there was no reply to any of their weekly letters, Samuel thought he knew the answer, one he never shared with Jimmy. Out of sight out of mind. And he stopped writing.

Jimmy never did and though they never discussed it, it just seemed to happen that on Sunday evenings Samuel stayed with Will and Mick while Jimmy slipped out and wrote a letter to Fraser, addressed to Doctor Evans. He always signed it from them both.

One evening Samuel walked passed the schoolroom where Jimmy hunched over one of the tables, paper in front of him. Samuel leaned against the door jamb.

"Why do you bother, Jimmy? He's never written to us."

His brother shrugged. "Something must have happened. Maybe he's somewhere letters are hard to get and send. I don't know." He said impatiently to Samuel's sceptical expression. "He'd want to hear from us."

"We want to hear from him." But Jimmy kept doggedly writing. "You're a bloody fool to keep at it!" Samuel said angrily and left, slamming the door behind him.

Jimmy hid how much his brother's words hurt. He yearned for some reply from their father, even a note to show they weren't alone but nothing came. It grew increasingly difficult to pick up a pen week after week and write to an empty void where family used to be but Jimmy kept at it with quiet determination and somehow managed to fill a page with news. But not tonight. Jimmy bit at his thumb, the half-filled piece of paper covered in splodges from his hesitant pen. Something worrying had just occurred to him.

When he tried to picture Father's face, it was blurry and faint, like someone you knew in the distance with the light behind them. With a shock Jimmy realised he was forgetting what their father looked like. He screwed his eyes shut in concentration but all he got was the idea of blue eyes, a thin, weary face. He knew Father had workman's hands, swollen knuckles with rough skin but he couldn't picture them anymore. Mam, too, had faded to nothing more than a recollection of a white face twisted in agony and screams on the edges of a dark, freezing night.

Once, his brother would have expressed sympathy, shared similar fears but not anymore for Jimmy saw that Samuel was hardening. Surrounded by tough boys, hunger and bullying every day, he, too had grown tougher. Never a bully himself Samuel had nevertheless grown impatient with soft emotions. More often than not, Jimmy found himself brushed off or told to "toughen up"' and he did try to. He did, it just…. Jimmy struggled for the right words….. it was just…. He gave up, flung his pen down onto the desk leaving even more ink splatters. Exasperated, he also grabbed the page, screwed it up into a ball and chucked it.

Who was there to talk to? One of the Brothers? Father Aherne, perhaps? Jimmy gave a hollow laugh. Father Aherne had told them to seek him out if they had any problems, any at all and not long after their arrival, they had taken him at his word.

One day he and Samuel had stood in Father Aherne's study, heart pounding, hands clammy as Samuel spoke of their homesickness, their struggle with the constant cruelty of Brother Donatus. Father Aherne had listened, finger tips pressed together, elbows on his desk, rubbing his lips with the tops of those linked fingers as Samuel's voice cracked and broke with emotion until he could no longer carry on.

Finally, Father Aherne had leaned back in his chair.

"Brother Donatus is a man of God. You are newly given into our care and feeling abandoned by those who loved you. Not everyone behaves towards us in ways we understand or are used to."

He gave them a benevolent smile, laced with impatience.

"It's not surprising that you may misread things. What may seem cruel to you is Brother Donatus's way of teaching you independence."

The boys exchanged fearful looks.

"Father Aherne, we're not imagining things." Samuel began. "Brother Donatus.... He's ... he's bad." Samuel faltered, unable to articulate the unspoken apprehension which filled the dormitory when the candle light went out or the regular displays of violence and bullying.

To their horror Father Aherne strode around his desk and towered over them.

"You will not bring disrepute down on an honoured institution sheltering abandoned boys like yourselves. Where would you be without this Orphanage? Who would care for you? Who would feed you?" The boys cowered back expecting to be struck as Father Aherne lifted a hand. They both flinched but all the priest did was flourish the sign of the cross above their heads. "May God protect you and help you to see the error of your ways." He glared down upon them. "Now go and pray for your sins."

They had spun on their toes and ran out of the room, not stopping their headlong flight until they found themselves out in the laundry rooms, shocked and panting for breath.

"If he tells.... "Samuel began, leaning his weight against the copper. "Donatus will have our guts for garters and stew the leftovers."

Jimmy shook his head. "I know he's angry but he won't say anything."

"How can you be so sure?" Samuel asked.

"Because I think he'd rather forget we said anything than have to speak of it."

This insight proved true. Though both boys dreaded the night hours and possible retaliation from Donatus none came and nothing was ever said. After several nights they breathed more easily.

But for Samuel it was the start of his burning hatred against the Order. Never again did he suggest approaching any of the Brothers or Father Aherne for help. If problems cropped up, he told Jimmy forcefully, they would deal with them alone. Which they did.

Jimmy picked up his pen again, dragged another piece of paper in front of him and sighed. What was he going to write? After much thought, he began.
'Dear Father
I hope you are well. Sam as I are still happy here but we miss you every day……'

***

John Rogers blinked slowly as the boys circled him, taunting him like a pack of dogs surrounding a young deer. He was a big boy, easily the biggest in the Orphanage with pale blue eyes placid and dim in a strong looking face on a sturdily built body. Big John could lift sacks of potatoes or swedes with ease, lobbing them onto the back of carts with an effortlessness every boy envied and he could work hour upon hour while even the adults around him faltered. Yet big and strong though he was, there was something lacking. Big John failed to catch any joke, he couldn't read at all though he tried harder than most and maths left him with a reeling mind as Brother Augustus or Brother Jonas brought their cane down on his hands or body time and time again for not knowing the simplest multiplication table. No matter how hard they beat him, Big John just couldn't seem to learn. But though schoolwork left him lost he could make anything out of wood and he adored any animal, especially Fusty, a tiny brown field mouse he kept in his pocket.

Hardworking, slow talking, slow thinking Big John became a target target for Kip Rainey as soon as the latter set foot in the Orphanage. For Kip wasn't an orphan like most of the other boys, like Big John, but one of a dozen or more whose parents couldn't feed him or deal with him so they left him at Stoke Orphanage without a backward glance. A burning rage against orphans, against the world fuelled

Kip's anger and he made his mark from his first hour, punching one of the young boys to the ground for 'bloody looking at me!' and finding himself in solitary confinement during his first night. Nothing had happened throughout his years in this place to soften Kip. He fed on every ill-feeling, stoked the embers of his deep resentment and was the terror of the Orphanage.

Big John was no match for Kip. Like an angry wasp Kip buzzed around him day after day, night after night, reducing the much bigger boy to helpless fury for Big John never threw a punch, never lashed out to land a strike. Provoked to arm flailing impotence, he would roar like a bull, his head in his arms, stumbling around while Kip and his posse poked him with wooden poles, sticks, hoes, anything that came to hand all the while taunting him. Poor Big John, a chained, helpless bear at baiting.

***

Late one night when Samuel was coming back from the dunny he heard laughter and bellowing from inside the dark laundry. Creeping up to the open doorway he peered inside. Moonlight through the windows showed a large silhouette he recognised at once as Big John and when the other boys laughed, Samuel identified Kip and his two friends, Salty and Pike.

Samuel hesitated in the enveloping shadows, not wanting to draw attention to himself yet unable to leave Big John being terrorised like this. The shadowy figure of Kip picked up a heavy wash-stick from beside the copper and moved closer to Big John who gave a yell as the stick was shoved with sudden ferocity into his ribs and now Samuel moved.

"Leave him alone, you bastards!"

The bullies froze. However Kip's thought processes were quick and he instantly realised two things: not one of the Brothers would swear and two, the dark shape in the doorway was boy-sized. Stepping back from Big John, the wooden copper stick swinging in his hand, Kip whispered, "Who's a brave boy, then?" His light, mocking voice sending shivers down Samuel's spine but he stepped boldly out from the shadows into a patch of silver moonlight.

"How brave are you lot?" Samuel scoffed sounding a lot more fearless than he felt. "Three against one?" Kip stiffened at the jeering laugh. "'Who's a brave boy then?" Samuel repeated matching taunt for taunt.

Big John stopped flailing. He stood to one side, scarcely breathing as Kip and his friends lined up in front of Samuel.

"Brodie…. " Kip hissed, turning to his friends he added. "It's our lucky night, lads. Two shitheads for the price of one."

The thugs behind Kip laughed, one of them smacked a fist into his palm, the other spat on his hands. If Samuel knew anything it was that he had to move and move now.

Springing towards a completely unsuspecting Kip, he snatched the heavy wash-stick from his hands, swung it with reckless uncoordination and managed to land Kip and Salty a hefty wallop each. Down they went, moaning. Lost in the rush of adrenalin and tough odds, Samuel swung the stick again, this time aimed at Pike who stood mesmerised by the sudden about face in the confrontation and his comrades groaning on the floor. Samuel caught Pike a blow on the side of his head and Pike, too, hit the ground. Dropping the wash-stick, Samuel leapt at Big John who stared at the writhing shapes on the floor.

Samuel tugged at his arm. "Come on, Big John. We gotta go." But Big John couldn't or wouldn't move and as Samuel pulled vainly at his arm Kip found his way to unsteady feet, the wash-stick lying on the floor between them. Both boys looked at the weapon and each other. They moved as one, arms and legs tangled as they reached it together. Struggling furiously for supremacy, Samuel fought clumsily with a manic desperation as he knew Salty and Pike would be up any moment to join in. Samuel gave the other boy a whack across his face with his open palm and the shock of that stilled Kip long enough for Samuel to grab the wash-stick. Pushing himself up on trembling legs, he faced the three attackers, panting hard, the copper stick gripped threateningly in his sweaty right hand.

"You three better bugger off." Samuel told them. And the swear word fell from his lips naturally, as if he'd always used it. "You attack Big John like that again, you better know he's not alone."
Kip held Samuel's gaze, then spat a bloody froth onto the floor.

"Big words, Brodie." He sneered. "You won't always be within reach of each other or a bloody stick." Kip shoved Pike and Salty through the door, "You sleep more soundly than I do, Brodie…."

Kip melted into the shadows of the night.

Samuel stood tall until he was sure he and Big John were alone and then reaction kicked in. Dropping the wash-stick back onto the bench he leaned against the copper, trembling all over.

"Are you all right?" Samuel asked Big John and was reassured when he nodded. "We better get back to bed. If we're caught out at this time of night….."

"You'll be in quite a lot of trouble." A smooth voice finished from the doorway.

Samuel spun around as Brother Donatus walked into the laundry, a lantern in one hand.

"Kip Rainey told me boys were prowling about in the night. I see he wasn't making things up. Rainey also bears wounds from what he told me was a completely unprovoked attack, Brodie."

"It was not unprovoked! Rainey and his gang bailed up Big John." Samuel's fear disappeared as his indignation swelled. "I was just…."

Brother Donatus lifted a hand. "I'm not in the mood for late night fairy stories, Brodie. He turned to Big John. "Get back to your bed, John Rogers. Now."

Big John needed no further prompting, he disappeared and the sound of his large feet slapping on the floorboards could be heard for a surprisingly long time. Donatus turned back to Samuel. "However, you, Brodie, need to learn we do not settle our differences against helpless boys with our fists."

"Helpless boys? Brother Donatus, Rainey…."

"Nor do we add telling tales to our list of misdemeanours. Follow me."

Samuel held his ground. "Where are we going?"

Donatus grabbed Samuel by the arm. Too scared to say anything now, Samuel focussed on keeping to his feet as Brother Donatus dragged him into a part of the Orphanage he'd never been into before. It looked like a cellar but there were two, tiny rooms with lockable doors on them. Brother Donatus opened one, shoved Samuel inside and the boy heard the door lock. He ran to the door, pounded on it.

"Why am I in here?!" There was no reply. Samuel pummelled the door until his hands hurt. "Why am I in here…?!!"

Nothing.

The boy stared into the blackness. There was no light, no window. He stumbled around, his hands against the walls to gauge some idea of the size of the room. It was he guessed about six foot square. He tripped over a thin mattress and kicked a chamber pot – the only two things in the room apart from the smell of damp and despair. He had no idea how long Brother Donatus was going leave him here but he flung himself down on the mattress, arms behind his head, no choice but to wait it out.

Samuel was damned if the bastard would break him with this shit.

Alone in his bed Big John held Fusty the mouse in his strong hand. Carefully he took some dry bread from his pocket, crusts he'd taken from the supper table and watched the little mouse pick each one up with his tiny paws and nibble quickly at it till it was gone then Fusty would sit up on Big John's hand looking at him expectantly till the next piece of crust came his way.

The boy felt the quivering, warm body in his palm, the tickle of little claws, and smiled in the darkness. Softly, under his breath Big John sang to the little creature.

***

The door to solitary confinement opened, waking Samuel who lay curled up as tightly as a cat for warmth on the filthy mattress.

"Get up, boy." Brother Donatus stood in the doorway as Samuel rubbed itchy eyes. "Go and wash then meet the others in the hall for breakfast."

Eye to eye they stood, these two, each one measuring for the merest hint of softness. There was none to be found in either face.

"Where've you been?" Jimmy whispered to his brother as Samuel arrived to the table halfway through prayers.

Samuel mumbled. "Tell you later."

A pause fell briefly but Jimmy couldn't wait. "Big John said you were in trouble." He whispered urgently.

Samuel eyed the room carefully. "Did Big John say why?"

Jimmy kept his head bowed just moved his eyes in Samuel's direction. "No. He started crying. Kip gave him a whack over his head and told him to shut up. Well, Kip said one other word but I better not say it." Jimmy grinned at Samuel who didn't grin back. "Sam?" He looked round see what had caught his brother's attention.

Kip Rainey and his gang sat whispering. Samuel ignored Jimmy's questions kept his eyes on the gang throughout prayers.

***

6

A river supplied the water vital to the fields and orchards of the Orphanage and keeping it clear was a priority for the boys. Heedless of the farms downstream, Father Aherne decided he needed a more certain water supply for the Orphanage and set his mind to building a dam. To their great joy, he told the boys that a swimming hole would be made among the willows on the river bank.

"Wonder how the Old Bastard'll make money from a swimming hole." Mick whispered to the others after this announcement was made. "There's no other reason for letting us have one."

"Bet it's us'll have to make it." Will grumbled.

"Who cares?" Mick punched Will's arm. "Anything's better than slaving in the fields."

The only boy not happy was Big John who feared water so much he had to be beaten to take a bath.

Jimmy saw Big John's apprehension. "You all right?" he asked they stood for final prayers.

Big John just nodded, unaware of Kip Rainey's unblinking, feral stare.

***

Within a fortnight the work began. First the boys cleared the debris from the riverbanks then they did the same to the mouth of the streams that fed from the river. Old fallen trees were dragged back to the Orphanage, chopped for firewood, stacked away. Even the Brothers seemed to enjoy the work, all except Jonas and Donatus who contrived to sleep the hours away in the shade, leaving the boys to their own devices.

After a few weeks hard work the clearing was finished to Father Aherne's satisfaction and the pool begun. First they used the largest rocks and stones to build a dam across down river and this they did with much splashing and laughter.

Big John kept to the river bank, doggedly avoiding the river itself, focussed completely on dragging away any branches he could find and adding them to the firewood pile at the Orphanage. He was returning from one such foray wiping sweat off his hot face when Kip stepped out from behind the woodshed.

"Dodging the hard work, eh?"

Big John shook his head, walked on.

Slipping his hands into his pockets, Kip fell into step beside him, hissed, "No one likes a shirker, you big, lazy bastard."

Again, Big John tried to ignore Kip. He picked his pace to stride away but Kip grabbed his arm, swung him round and landed a punch in his belly. Big John made no sound, dropped to his hands and knees on the green grass. Kip stepped cruelly on his fingers, ground them with his heel then knelt, grabbed a handful of hair and yanked. Big John whimpered in pain and fright.

"You better get your fat arse down to the river or I'll give you what bloody for. Do you hear me?"

Big John managed a nod and after a pause, Kip slipped into the shadows.

Without thought Big John's right hand slipped into his pocket for the reassurance of a tiny, whiskery face nudging his fingers. Taking Fusty out of his pocket, Big John crooned to him, calming himself. After several minutes, he'd gathered himself together enough to head back towards the river, Fusty safely tucked in his pocket.

From behind a tall willow, Kip grinned nastily.

***

By the end of the month the dam was almost finished. Already the water just above it had filled and deepened into a good sized swimming hole.

Samuel, Jimmy, Will and Mick stood ankle deep in the water, proud and happy. Brother Luke, wet to his knees came up beside them, slapped them each on the shoulder.

"Good work today, lads. How strange none of you are this enthusiastic every day."

He caught sight of Big John still dragging the biggest stones he could and stacking them up ready for use. The boy didn't hear Brother Luke call for him to stop until Luke laid a hand on his arm. Big John leaped at the touch, sweating, his eyes feverish.

"Time to stop, John. You've done well today."

"I'll just get these here big buggers." Big John muttered.

Brother Luke ignored the lewd language. "Right but you must return for dinner straight after that or you'll work yourself to death." Big John made no reply, kept his eyes lowered and returned to the rocks in the bank as Brother Luke whistled to the four boys still fooling round at the edge of the swimming hole. They scampered off just as the dinner bell sounded.

The sweat dripped stingingly into Big John's eyes. He took a breather at the river's edge warily eyeing the swiftly moving water. Remembering the joyful shouts of Samuel and the others as they splashed about making the dam, Big John looked where his toes barely lapped at the river's edge. Slowly, experimentally, he pushed the toe of his boot nearer the water pooled among the stones. After a moment or two he knelt, ran his fingers into the liquid coolness, lifted some in cupped hands to drink then smiled. Feeling bolder, Big John stepped into the river up to his ankles. He laughed out loud at the abrupt, thrilling sensation of cold water on hot, sore feet. He scooped up two cupped hands of water and splashed it over his face, did it again for his neck.

Heart beating more quickly, he took another step. Now the water lapped up around his calves. This was as far as he could go but it was enough. Big John began to laugh and laugh for sheer joy of his discovery.

Two hands shoved him in the small of his back, pushed him so hard Big John stumbled, two steps, three steps and before he could cry out, he'd sunk into sudden deepness. Panic weighted him, his arms flailed as his legs sank beneath him and the water closed over his face again and again.

Brother Luke had seen the three boys into the Orphanage when he realised Big John hadn't followed. Knowing the boy had probably lost himself in his work, he jogged back towards the river and as he drew near he heard splashes, strangled gasps, was in time to see Big John's dark head disappear under the water and not come back up. Brother Luke didn't hesitate, he dived into the river, swam to where Big John had disappeared and pulled the choking boy out onto the riverbank where he promptly vomited water and began to cry.

"John, what happened? Why were you in the river?" Brother Luke alone of all those caring for the boys was sympathetic to John's fear of water. "John…?"

Shaking and crying Big John just shook his head from side to side. He slipped a hand into one of his sodden pockets and gave a howl.

In one gently clenched fist was the tiny, drowned body of Fusty the mouse.

All the boys were seated and eating their supper when Brother Luke and Big John arrived drenched, their sopping wet hair plastered to their heads. Those close enough to see noticed Big John was shaking, his right hand held protectively clenched against his chest, tears mingling with the water. All eyes turned towards them and whispers rustled up and down the tables.

Samuel got to his feet took a step and called out in concern, "Big John!" only to be shoved back down onto his bench by Brother Jonas. "What's happened to Big John?" Samuel demanded and was completely ignored.

Brother Luke spoke low voiced to Father Aherne. No one heard what he said or the reply, they just kept their eyes on the pair as Brother Luke, his arm protectively around the stricken boy's shoulders, led the way out.

While Jimmy, Mick and Will speculated quietly on what had happened, Samuel happened to glance down the table. There sat Kip looking smug and suspiciously happy. He too whispered with his gang and they listened with rapt attention.

Suddenly Samuel knew, he just knew Rainey was involved in this.

And at that moment of realisation, Kip turned, met Samuel's accusatory eyes and grinned, the scar on his face twisted by the action. Samuel felt a hot rush of anger, a swooping sensation in the pit of his stomach. Bastard Kip Rainey, he thought. His eyes burned into Kip's. They stared at each other and Samuel raised a hand, let it cut the air cleanly in a gesture Kip easily interpreted. I'll be waiting was his wordless reply.

"Bloody hell, Samuel, don't get involved in this. Kip and his gang will have your guts, they will. They'll string them up for Christmas." Will was nearly spitting in his effort to get the warning out.

"Do you think I give a shit, Will? I spoke to Big John. He could barely get the words out he was so frightened. He said he heard Kip's laughter as he was shoved in." Samuel began to pace, unable to keep still. "He was holding that little mouse of his in his hand but it was dead. Big John wouldn't let it go." They all exchanged looks at that. "Donatus ripped Fusty out of Big John's hands, threw the body out the bedroom window! Jesus, I can still hear Big John screaming."

They all could for Big John had been dragged into solitary confinement, screaming for Fusty all the way.

"And now Rainey's up to some bloody thing. None of the Brothers will believe us. No good going to them."

Jimmy piped up. "Brother Luke would. He saved Big John, didn't he?"

Samuel swung round to his brother fiercely. "We can't run to anyone for help anymore, Jimmy. Don't you understand that? We have to sort this stuff out for ourselves!"

Jimmy was stunned by the heat of Samuel's temper. He'd never seen him this angry, ever.

With massive effort Samuel hauled his anger in. "It could be any of us next." Samuel reached out to touch his brother, seemed to think better of it and made a fist out of his hand instead. "It could have been you, Jimmy." He looked at the three boys, defiantly. "I'm not asking for you to help me but that bastard Rainey's not getting away with this. I want to teach him such a lesson that he will never do anything like that again." Samuel eyed them grimly. "No more bullying."

Silence.

Will spoke first. "I'll do what I can. I've put up with Rainey's shit for too long. "

Samuel looked at Mick who nodded just once, his fingers cracking as he gripped them into fists.

"Father wouldn't want you to fight Kip, Sam. You know he wouldn't."

Samuel's laugh was bitter. "I don't know what Father would or wouldn't want anymore. Where the hell is he, Jimmy? We haven't heard from him in months." As Jimmy opened his mouth Samuel knew exactly what he brother was going to say and added quickly, "And Mam would want us to do what's right and giving Kip Rainey a lam he won't forget in a hurry is right." Samuel's mouth shut tight, his chin lifted.

***

Big John never considered himself a loner, just someone who was on his own a lot. He knew he had family somewhere. He could remember a man who must have been his father taking to him with the stick he used to beat the dogs.

Sometimes at night, when he couldn't sleep, Big John screwed his eyes up tightly and saw a pale, thin woman who cringed at the far edge of his subconscious. His mother. Big John had no memory of being cuddled or hugged. He had nothing beyond flashes of a heavy stick raised, the jolt of his muscles as a thick-featured, weathered face flashed into his mind, a fleeting image of that pale, tiny woman backing away, the sound of a door closing as the pain splintered into the jagged partial recollections which haunted long, sleepless nights. In hard graft, in sweat, in repetitious labouring Big John found he could think of nothing at all. But then, on the Brodies' first night at the Orphanage all those months ago, he'd heard Samuel stand up for his younger brother and felt a yearning he couldn't place. The always alone boy watched Samuel wear a wet sheet around his neck; he saw Jimmy and Will risk punishment to visit him and one day Big John realised what his yearning was, though he could never have articulated it - to have someone on his side, to not be on his own anymore. To be part of a friendship. To belong to someone. For the first time Big John became aware of his own aloneness and it hurt, became loneliness. He even envied Kip and his gang for in a gang you weren't ever alone.

After his experience in the river, Big John's nightmares came more regularly. He found himself jerked into wakefulness with the dread of undefined menace and threat lingering until dawn and beyond into his days.

Once he'd been let out of solitary confinement he found only work kept those feelings at bay. Yet this gave Big John another worry too for yes, hard slog made him tired and the tiredness made him sleep but when he slept he dreamed. He kept hoping if he worked hard enough he would be too tired even to dream.

Only Brother Luke wondered at the boy's fervour. He did try to talk to Big John but found he couldn't break through his defences. Whatever was going on with him, Brother Luke realised ruefully he wouldn't know what or why it was.

All the young Brother could do, he did. He kept as close an eye on the boy as his time allowed and prayed for him.

***

Samuel hadn't found his opportunity to deal with Kip. To his chagrin, Rainey actually seemed to have repented. Jimmy nudged him one breakfast and Samuel was just in time to see Kip slip some of his porridge into Big John's bowl.

"Maybe Rainey's feeling bad over nearly drowning Big John," was Will's whispered comment and though he didn't want to believe it, Samuel had to grudgingly concede.

7

Big John was cleaning the long sinks in the washroom. Head down, arm moving vigorously he laboured industriously, nothing in his head except the sound of his scrubbing, the smell of soap.

"Should've known you'd be head down arse up somewhere, Big John."

Big John spun round, saw Kip lean nonchalantly against one of the cleaned sections of sink. Reacting with instinctive alarm to that scarred face, Big John recoiled, stunned beyond measure when Kip smiled at him, added, "No one works harder than you."

No one had ever paid Big John a compliment before and he blushed, covered his fluster by scrubbing harder. "I like workin'," he said hesitantly.

Kip picked up a scrubbing brush "I'll give you a hand. You don't mind, d'you?" and received a confused shake of the head in reply.

Together they worked down one whole side. Kip chatted and sang using such bad language that Big John felt heat rise in his face. Yet he smiled shyly, joined in the choruses, softly, in his head.

It took the big, slow boy by surprise when Kip straightened up.

"Job done, Big John."

Big John looked up and down the long sinks and tables in wonder. "That went quickly," he told Kip diffidently.

Kip grinned. "Two pairs of hands halves the work." As he took a step closer, Big John again reacted fearfully, hastily stepped back. The light went out in Kip's eyes and his smile died. "I deserved that," he said quietly, his eyes not leaving the other boy's face. "You know I didn't mean for you to go that far into the river, right?" Kip spoke quickly. "I didn't know you'd go in that deep. I didn't. It was just a joke, Big John."

Big John tried to gather his thoughts but Kip gave him no time. Suddenly he held his hand out. "And I'm really sorry about Fusty. I forgot he lived in your pocket." Kip's eyes implored him. "Brodie and his cronies won't believe it was an accident but it was, Big John. I swear on my mother's grave." To Kip's knowledge his bastard mother was alive and well but the solemnity of the moment needed a big expression.

After an long pause, Big John reached out and shook Kip's hand. Kip grinned and slapped his shoulder.

"New beginnings, Big John. I've got plans for you."

Heedless with the warmth, lost in the idea of friendship all Big John could do was grin back, happy for the first time since….. well, since forever.

Samuel, Jimmy, Will and Mick all watched in disbelief when Big John entered the room surrounded by Kip, Salty and Pike. Samuel and Mick moved swiftly towards the group, thinking that Big John was being kept by pressure. Instead, Kip sneered at them.

"A welcoming committee, eh? Don't need one. " And dropping his voice Kip added, "Piss off why don't you?"

Samuel ignored Kip. "Big John, you coming?" Big John shook his head and Samuel persisted. "Are you sure? You don't have to be near these bastards."

But John spoke up for the first time. "Don't say that. Kip and them are my friends."

"Friends?" Samuel gaped. "Big John, these bastards beat the shit out of you! Kip nearly drowned you. And what about Fusty?"

Again Big John shook his head. "It was a mistake. We're friends." He repeated stubbornly his pride unmistakeable.

Mick and Samuel exchanged bewildered looks while Kip turned Big John away from them. "Friends, Brodie. Did yer hear him?" and with many backward, gloating glances Kip lead Big John to the other table, made a huge fuss over seating the big boy beside him.

"What the hell's all that about?" Mick whispered to Samuel as they sat back down.

Samuel looked grim. "I dunno but I don't bloody like it." He was unable to drag his eyes from the gang.

"Well, if Big John's happy, I suppose that's all good?" Jimmy asked.

Will shrugged. "I've never known Kip Rainey to do anything for nothing. I still think he's up to no good."

Samuel was about to agree when they were called to attention for prayers. "I don't care what Rainey's told Big John, we keep an eye on him," he told them grimly and the other three boys agreed, four pairs of eyes on the retreating backs.

***

Grey, pre-dawn light spilled through the dormitory windows onto the sleeping forms in their metal beds. Someone muttered wordlessly in his sleep, turned over restlessly and settled down, lost to his dream world. Jimmy didn't know what woke him but he was too awake now to drift back off into sleep so he lay there, thinking of nothing.

The door into the dormitory clicked open and Jimmy hastily rolled over, feigning sleep, wondering who it was. He peeked from under the blankets as Samuel returned to his bed. Jimmy shifted onto his elbow.

"Sam?" Samuel spun around to see his brother staring curiously at him. Where've you been?" Jimmy yawned hugely.

Samuel yanked back his covers, slid under them. "Taking a piss."

Jimmy frowned. "Must have been a long piss. I've been awake for ages. Didn't see you go."

"What's it to you, Jimmy?" was the rough reply. "Shut up or you'll have us both in trouble. Go to sleep." And Samuel turned his back to Jimmy, dragged his pillow into his arms.

Jimmy sighed. He couldn't even pretend to try and sleep now. Instead he stared up at the ceiling as the early morning shadows stretched from the windows to cover the floor. Samuel burrowed into his bed as deeply as he could get but still he felt vulnerable. His body ached and he felt the pressure to scream, to cry, build and build in his stomach and chest. He wanted to throw things, punch things and he gripped his pillow so hard his hands cramped and he began to shake.

Donatus waking him from a deep sleep.

"You still have work to do, Samuel Brodie. Follow me."

Samuel getting quietly out of bed not disturbing the rest of the sleeping dormitory. Rubbing his eyes, yawning, wondering what Brother Donatus meant – he has no late work and he finished all his chores didn't he?

Sleepily following Brother Donatus to his cell-like room with a bed not much bigger or better than the boys' but the mattress and pillows are thicker, there are more blankets, too.

"Brother Donatus….? What do I have to do?" Confusion fogging Samuel's tired brain.

Instinct belatedly kicks in when Donatus turns to him. There's a feral look in the man's face, his mouth slack, eyes glazed. Samuel backs away, hands reaching behind him for the door but too late. Far too late. Donatus pulls the boy to him, pushes his wet lips against Samuel's mouth, hands invading his clothes, seeking flesh. Samuel struggles, revolted, terrified. Donatus pushes Samuel, thrashing wildly, onto the thick mattress of his bed. He turns the boy face down and Samuel's world is darkness, the feeling of smothering, heat and sharp pain.

"Relax, Samuel Brodie." The voice soft, coaxing, inflexible. "The more you struggle, the more pain. Relax…. "

Samuel drew in a ragged, hurtful breath, buried his face into his pillow. Damn this hell hole! And damn their father for abandoning them here! His hands clenched. He would kill the bastard if he touched his brother. A sound must have escaped his lips for he heard Jimmy whispering his name as a question. Samuel fought against his hurt, lay as still as he could, muscles in spasm with the effort to lay calm and after a minute or two, Jimmy quieted.

Samuel fed his hatred as oxygen feeds a flame.

***

"What's wrong with you? You look like shit." Will dug his elbow into the unresponsive Samuel as the boys washed at the long sink. "Didn't you sleep last night?"

Samuel cast his eye along the row, saw Jimmy talking to Mick, thankfully animated and distracted. He lowered his voice for Will's ear only. "I had a visit from Donatus last night."

Will drew in his breath sharply. He turned intent eyes to Samuel's bruised looking ones.

"Why didn't you warn me, Will?" Samuel rasped out. "You or Mick could have said something. Bloody anything. Just some warning…." Samuel stopped, the soap slid out of his tense hands, disappeared down the long sink.

Samuel flinched as Will stepped nearer then gave the boy a shamed, apologetic grimace, saw only understanding in Will's eyes.

"I tried but what could either of us say? Maybe you'dve been safe. Maybe he wouldn't have touched you at all. You'dve been wound up for nothing."

Samuel leaned forward on the metal bench, eyes closed and Will hesitated, wanting to show sympathy, knowing how his own body now reacted to touch in any form. After a moment, Will leaned his weight softly against Samuel's shoulder. "It doesn't get any worse, Samuel. Know that."

Samuel gave a jagged laugh. "I forgot to count my blessings this morning. Thanks."

But belatedly he understood exactly what it was Will was trying to tell him – if he could survive this, he could survive anything. And he bloody would.

It seemed unconnected but a thought came to Samuel. "Is it the thirty first today?"

Will screwed up his face in thought. "Yep. First day of spring tomorrow." He gave a snort. "Brother Augustus will be pissing. Father Aherne sends us out into the fields for longer and we get less schooling. " Will spat into the sink. "Not that I give a pig's arse about that." He grinned at Samuel, saw his friend wasn't even listening.

For Samuel was thinking about tomorrow being the first day of spring. There was more to it for him and Jimmy than that.

As the boys trooped unwillingly out into the courtyard for the hated exercises, a stranger waited for them. In front of him was a camera set up on a tripod which they all studied with avid curiosity while Father Aherne beamed at them all.

Each boy was handed weights and took their places in the familiar lines. Most of them had never seen a camera, they couldn't take their eyes off the strange three legged contraption.

"You're having your photographs taken, boys. To show what fine examples you all are." Only Father Aherne looked happy.

The photographer looked bored, the boys apprehensive and Brother Jonas's sunken eyes burned with hatred for all boys, all exercises and photographers, too.

Father Aherne beseeched them all to hold up their weights, look strong and smile. Most of the boys looked terrified while those who did smile had to hold it for so long it turned into a leering grimace. The photograph was taken and the photographer went into the Orphanage with Father Aherne, leaving the boys to their fun.

Samuel spoke to Jimmy between puffs. "It's Mam's birthday tomorrow. I've got an idea."

Jimmy touched his toes, turned eager eyes to his brother. "What?"

"I want to visit her grave. Put flowers on it."

Brother Jonas shouted, "Put some effort into it!" as he tried to touch his own toes and failed at about knee height. The boys in the front row sniggered.

"Yes, Sam, me too." Jimmy felt a swoop of excitement.

"If we slip out when everyone's asleep, we'll be back well before dawn. Mick knows the back roads through the fields and across the hills. He's slipped away himself a dozen times he says."

"Is it too far from here, though?"

"Nah. I told you. Mick knows his way through Stoke and Nelson like no one else."

"And we can see her?" Jimmy eyes lit up, his mouth softened into a smile. "We can tell her about….. things. Do you think she'll hear?"

"Of course she will, Jimmy. When did Mam ever let us down?" Finally Brother Jonas released them and the boys charged back inside. Mick and Will came running up.

"What did he say?" Will looked from brother to brother. "Are we on for tonight?"

"Are you coming, too?" Jimmy rubbed at his itchy, sweaty hair.

Will gave him a punch on the arm. "Of course. You two couldn't find your arse from your elbow without me and Mick."

It was then as he looked at their laughing, teasing faces, that Samuel realised this was the closest to family he and Jimmy had now. Some of the loneliness fell from him and when Mick saw him staring he shoved him down into the dirt laughing.

Samuel forgot Brother Donatus, he forgot his pain as the four of them tumbled their way across the yard.

***

Kip asked Brother Luke for permission to work beside Big John. Surprised but pleased that the ever alone Big John would have company, Brother Luke readily agreed and the two boys worked side by side in the orchard.

"Big John, Pike, Salty and me want you to join our gang."

Big John's mouth fell open. "Me?"

"Yes. We think you're one of us. We watched you fight when Donatus dragged you into the lock up. Definitely one of us." Big John gaped till Kip asked, "Don't you want to?"

"Y..y…Yes!" Big John stammered in his excitement.

"Good." Kip slapped his shoulder. "There has to be an initiation ceremony first, though Big John."

Big John's face fell. "I haven't got no money." And he looked on the verge of tears.

"No, I mean you have to do a dare to prove you are worthy. It's simple." Kip added hurriedly at the fear on Big John's face. "We all had to do a dare."

"You?"

"No, because it's my gang, isn't it." Kip threw a clod of dirt at him. "It's easy, Big John. We'll do it one night soon. And you'll be one of us for real."

"For real."

Big John echoed. His hand slipped into his pocket, expecting to feel Fusty's furry body nudge his fingers. There was pain when he remembered his friend had died but then thought about becoming one of the gang pushed the sadness away. He'd belong for real. Big John decided that when he'd done his dare he'd find another mouse. He'd call it Fusty.

***

The four boys had to wait till they were sure everyone was asleep. With the first snores they pushed their pillows under the blankets to give the illusion of their sleeping forms before slipping softly out of the dormitory, down the stairs to the laundry. Once there it was a simple matter to climb out the broken latched laundry window into the night. One by one they landed quietly on the cool grass. The moon gave plenty of light to see by and enough shadows to disappear into.

Mick was in his element. He loved the hours of darkness and before being picked up by the police for begging he'd spent much of his young life awake during the night, stealing food or pieces of clothing left on washing lines, sometimes just for the fun of it. Effortlessly he led the little group over the hills, through the shortcuts and byways towards Wakapuaka cemetery.

When it couldn't be avoided and they had to pass close by to farm houses, Mick took the opportunity to slip silently into gardens and sheds, returning with a handful of flowers from one and bulging pockets from another.

"Just to keep me hand in, eh," he whispered, handing the flowers to Jimmy. "For your Mam's grave."

From over the fence a dog growled menacingly.

"Can we have a breather?" Jimmy asked. He didn't know why he felt so tired, just needed sit down for a moment or two.

Samuel was instantly alarmed. "Are you all right?"

Will acted as lookout as Jimmy lay on the damp ground. "We get fed shit they wouldn't feed to pigs" he muttered, "and we're hungry all the time. Of course Jimmy needs a break. You two aren't as hard as we are."

Samuel was quick to take offence. "We're not soft!"

"We know that. It's just we've had years to get used to it. And keep your bloody voice down unless you want to be hauled off to the coppers."

After a couple of minutes Jimmy shook himself. "Let's go." But they hadn't taken more than a few steps when he stopped again. "Sam – know where we are?"

Samuel looked around the moonlight, shrugged.

"We're just above the Old One's grave. Can we go see him first?"

"Dunno, have we got time?"

"How many family you two got buried in these parts?" Mick grinned. "Do I have to watch my back?"

"It's just somewhere Sam and I used to go to."

Mick thought quickly, judging distance against their available time. "We could have one stop but if you two want to spend any time with your Mam, it better be quick."

The two brothers looked at each other. A wild look came into Samuel's eyes.

"Do you know what I'd really like to do, Jimmy?"

"What?"

"Go back home. Just to see it."

"There's probably someone else living in it by now."

"I don't care. I just want to look at it. To remember." And though Samuel's voice was a whisper the pain came through to all of them. "What d'you think Jimmy? A final look?"

As one the brothers ran off down the hill, Mick and Will on their heels. Unerringly they found the track through the trees. A quick glance at the Old One's grave as they jogged passed it then out onto the road where they paused just for a moment to reassure each other with a look. Samuel led them the rest of the way.

The small cottage stood dark and defeated. Nobody lived there.

Weeds grew almost to the height of the windows and the one which had been in the boys' bedroom was now completely broken away. Mam's lovingly keep garden had disappeared under the vigorous growth of tall, spindly yarrow, thick clover and vigorous docks. There were no chooks in the chook house and the door to the long drop had fallen drunkenly to one side with no one to repair it.

All at once it became urgent for the brothers to be inside the walls looking back out. Will and Mick followed them, the latter always checking over his shoulder, peering into the shadows. The cottage was quite alone down this road but still…..

Samuel reached the back door first, gripped the handle and tugged. It creaked but remained locked fast. He signalled Mick and they both bent their shoulders, shoved hard. This time the lock splintered easily.

Inside the house their filthy boots scuffed trails in dust lying thickly on the wooden floor. The empty rooms echoed strangely and moonlight made the place eerie. Will easily the most superstitious began to wish he hadn't come.

Samuel reached out and pushed open the door to their old bedroom. There was a frightened scuffle and something flew out of the broken window, startling them all. It terrified Will who muttered, "Wait for you outside." And he bolted.

Mick was unafraid but he saw the Brodies' need to be alone. Quietly, not drawing any attention to himself, he slipped away, too.

Slowly Samuel and Jimmy moved back into the hallway. Jimmy found himself thrown back to the terrible night their Mam died.

Himself in Samuel's arms, there on the floor, the Doctor wiping his bloodied hands on Mam's cloth. …. Mam's screams….. father's sobs.

Samuel breathed in the musty smell of their parents' bedroom. Although he knew there was only emptiness here now, he couldn't help himself, looked down at the floor, half expecting to see blood pooling on the floor, discarded red-stained sheets. He closed his eyes, inhaled deeply and thought he caught the trace of lavender Mam always wore. It scented her handkerchiefs, their linen; she placed little soft bags of it in among their clothes. And with the smell came her voice, urgent, gasping, clear as a bell,

'...*Samuel?... Look after your brother.* '....

Mam screamed and Samuel's eyes flew open, the force of memory so powerful he stumbled, kept on his feet only by Jimmy's quick reflexes.

"Sam…. What…?" Jimmy was close enough to hear Samuel's gulping sob. "Sam…?"

Tears dripped down Samuel's face. He sniffed, wiped streaming eyes and nose on his jacket sleeve. "I'm fine."

"No you're not."

"Where's Mick?"

Without waiting for his brother, Samuel strode out.

Alone now, Jimmy took more time, reluctant to leave the place they'd all been so happy. Eventually he left the bedroom, walked back down the hallway and turned right into the kitchen. The spill of night from outside shone in through the small window, some of the beams falling onto the cold woodstove.

The final bath…..Tension between Father and Samuel…… Warm water…… The clean smell of soap.

It took Jimmy a few moments to snap out of the trap of memories but still he clung to that moment of fragrant warmth, knowing their father was there, sharing, caring.

But it was all gone now. The warmth, the bath, Father too. Jimmy looked about the small room aware he was alone. Where were the others? They weren't in the house and as he walked by the sink beside the back door Mam used for their laundry, he noticed a forgotten piece of rag, laid over the tap. Jimmy reached for it. It crackled between his fingers, stiff with disuse. He recognised the pattern – one of Father's old shirts. Jimmy didn't know why but he tucked the useless thing deep down into a pocket and stepped out into the backyard.

There, near the old chook house the other three boys were arguing. Will threw up his hands, turned away while Mick grinned looking puckish in the silver moonlight. Samuel's face was shadowed and still as Mick held out his hand to him. Something unspoken passed between them till Samuel grabbed whatever it was, rushed passed Jimmy back into the house.

Will faced Mick. "You're a bloody idiot. Why did you give them to him?"

"He's got a right." Mick look undisturbed by Will's anger. "He's gotta do what he needs to. You can't judge him, Will."

Jimmy could hear Will's breathing hard.

"Damn it, Mick…"

"What's Sam doing?" Jimmy asked Mick who just shrugged.

Will's replied harshly. "Something we'll all be bloody arrested for."

"What?" but Will shook his head angrily strode around the house back to the road. Jimmy turned to the other boy, urgently. "Mick, what's going on?"

Before Mick could say, Samuel reappeared. "Let's go," he told them brusquely and he too ran back to the road.

Confused, Jimmy followed mutely. The four of them jogged up the road towards the cemetery. Not a word was spoken. A wind picked up behind them, Jimmy glad of the cool pressure on his back. He felt the wind wanted him to get to Mam's grave as quickly as he could.

They were nearing the bottom of cemetery hill when Jimmy lifted his head, sniffed. "I can smell smoke."

There was no reply from the other boys. Jimmy thought he was imagining things, stopped to look behind him where he thought the smell came from. There, a solid dark shape surrounded by trees was lit by an orange glow, the smoke shot through with moonlight

"That's our house!" He spun round, the others weren't even looking. Jimmy ran up to Samuel, tugged on his arm. "Our house is burning, Sam. We've gotta go back. Do something!"

"Do what?" Samuel pulled free. "And it's not our bloody house anymore. Let the bastard thing burn to the ground!" He didn't lift his eyes to see the smoke, began instead, to climb the hill to where Mam and baby Charlotte lay.

Will and Mick followed Samuel, neither of them looking at the incredulous Jimmy.

"You did it," he told them. "You set it alight!" Jimmy was shouting.

Mick moved snake-quick, grabbed his arm. "Keep your bloody voice down, Jimmy," he hissed. "It's more important now we don't get caught away from the Orphanage, get it?"

Jimmy shook himself free, furious. "Why? Why did you do it?"

Mick stared down at him. "It was your brother that did it. And I didn't ask why. I understand though and you should, too."

"But…." Jimmy couldn't begin to sort out the jumble of emotions and thoughts that whirled inside him.

"Sometimes you have to do a bad thing." Mick said unemotionally. "But you just remember." His finger jabbed into Jimmy's chest. "Your brother has seen bad things and had bad things done to him. He's allowed to do this."

Mick walked up the hill, left the younger boy staring out towards their burning home which wasn't their home any longer. The flames took swift hold of the dry timbers and even as Jimmy watched they seared up the walls. In moments the black night framed them, orange and red.

Standing alone with no near neighbours, the old house burned brightly.

By the time Jimmy reached the top of the hill, Samuel was kneeling at the side of Mam's grave, head bowed. Mick and Will stood right on the cliff edge gazing out to the growing spectacle of the fire. Mick was grinning.

Jimmy placed the ragged flowers at the foot of the cross then knelt beside Samuel and prayed but not to God. He'd given up praying to God. All his prayers were directed to Mam. His shoulder rest against Samuel's and he could feel his brother shuddering until

Samuel slumped down, his head almost resting on his knees. Jimmy could hear the effort he put into not crying.

The ground above the grave was greenly overgrown now, spring urgency covering the small mound. Someone had planted flowers at the foot of the wooden cross Father had made. They were a type of daisy, their petals closed tightly in the moonlight.

Jimmy cleared the weeds poking up around them, satisfied at last that the daisies would hold their own without care till they could come back. With his brother still huddled forward, Jimmy got to his feet, brushed absently at his already dirty legs and lifted his eyes to where their house burned like a beacon now. He thought there were shapes moving on the road near it and was about to say something when a bell rang.

"That's us." Mick said and moved quickly to Samuel. He tried to drag the boy to his feet but Samuel shoved Mick away. Patiently Mick tried again. "Samuel, come on. The bell's been rung for the fire brigade. Now's the best time for us to get back." He glanced up at the position of the moon. "And we'd better not piss about. We've got to be back in our beds before dawn."

Samuel came to his feet, his throat aching and his voice was rough with unshed tears. "Let's go, then."

One last look down on their Mam and sister.

No one spoke on the way back to the Orphanage and dawn was breaking over the horizon when they finally clambered back in through the laundry window.

Jimmy lay back in his bed unable to sleep as flames licked the dark night sky behind his lids every time he shut his eyes. Will was too excited by the whole experience to sleep and Mick couldn't help but think they weren't the only ones awake in the dormitory. His senses told him someone else wasn't sleeping.

Samuel fell asleep as soon as he dragged the blanket up to his ears. Jimmy heard him snoring.

*****

Kip stepped up to Mick as the boys crowded down the stairs.

"So, does your mother know you're out?" he whispered in Mick's ear.

It was the following morning, Mick's nerves still taut from the experiences of the night. He reacted with to Kip's words with a shove but Kip grinned. "Where'd you and your darlings go, then?"

"None of your business, Rainey so keep your big nose out of it."

Kip tutted. "Now, now, Mick. Just trying to be nice. Donatus knows you were out last night. He'll want an explanation." Kip noticed the slight change that came over Mick's watchful face. "You know the explanation he'll be after, don't you." As Mick pushed in front, Kip whispered. "If you won't tell me maybe Jimmy can be persuaded to."

Incensed Mick grabbed Kip's shirt and shoved him hard against the balustrade just as Brother Donatus wandered in. Mick immediately let the grinning Kip loose, strode away feeling his shoulder blades tingling unpleasantly and knew Kip was watching him, Donatus, too.

Brother Donatus stopped at the bottom of the stairs, waiting for the surge of boys to pass. "Where'd he go"
Kip picked at his nails. "Dunno. He won't say."

"Right." Donatus jerked his head, sent Kip on his way.

There were more ways than one to skin an Orphanage cat.

8

A bleak afternoon on a West Coast hillside is no place for the faint hearted. Untamed wilderness, with mile upon mile of thick native forest where hills became peaks, became snow-capped mountains and above it all hawks wheeling against a leaden sky, the late afternoon light fading on a long, hard day.

With forestry tracts opening through the native forests and small towns growing, the demand for new roads was on the increase. Roading gangs had more work than they could handle, foremen moaning perpetually at the lack of hours in a day. There was no stopping for meal breaks when the pressure was on, the men ate as they worked, swigging back cold tea or beer whenever they could snatch a moment. They left for work before dawn, got back to their camp well after dark some falling asleep over their supper, too tired to eat.

Fraser rubbed his back, felt the sweat drip down his skin while beside him Auntie worked away, his arms corded and rough by the long years of labouring. After straining against the jemmy for several minutes Auntie paused to wipe his sweaty face. "You know, we'd get this done quicker with a bit of help from Scotland."

Fraser added his shoulder to the jemmy and both men heaved until the satisfying sound of falling rock signalled job done. Breathing hard they surveyed the edge of the hill from their vantage point. Below them native forest lay dense and still while fantails, all flit and twitter, darted around them, cheeped at them as they caught airborne insects disturbed by the rock fall.

"Dunny's saying one more blow today before the light goes." Auntie said in his soft voice as he gladly let the cold breeze play over his face.

Hugely built, an ex-gold miner from Queenstown, Auntie had followed the gold up the South Island in search of the elusive strike and like most such men, found just enough yellow to keep body and soul together and no more. Finally as the easy gold was taken and the companies moved in, these men gave gold mining away to work for more certain wages. Called Auntie because he fussed around them all like a mother hen, darning socks, caring for those who got sick or hurt on the job, no one knew his real name and Auntie wouldn't say. Such reticence had initially given Fraser concern for why should a man hide who he is? But after experiencing Auntie's care, his unjudgmental acceptance, Fraser relaxed. Auntie's past was his own. All he deserved, all any man deserved was to be accepted for who he was now.

"Fraser?"

Fraser blinked, hearing his name, and came to. "Sorry, Auntie. Lost in a wee dwarm."

 Auntie passed Fraser his bottle of cold tea. "Dwarm?" he queried, one eyebrow raised.

"Dream."

They heard hobnails on stone and turned to see Dunny the foreman, marching towards them. Some said he marched because he couldn't forget his days fighting the Boers. Fraser thought it was because Dunny was an officious, small minded wee bastard.

"Two more." Dunny told them.

"Two? The light's going."

Dunny stared at Fraser. "We're behind schedule, Scotland. If we don't push this road through further today you'll all be docked wages." Dunny ignored the muttered mutiny from the half dozen men around him, their dark looks, the sneers from one or two of the harder ones. "So you'd better shift your arses." He spat and turned on his heels, marched back down towards camp.

"Bastard." Solly said under his breath, the word picked up by Jinn, echoed by them all.

The youngest member of the gang was Rossi. Tall and lanky, nothing seemed to dim the grin that split his face in two but even he looked bitterly after the retreating Dunny.

As always, Auntie acted as the peace maker.

"We'd better get to it," he told the team calmly. "No good bitching like barmaids."

And he picked up his tools, moved towards the road's end.

After much swearing and kicking of stones, the rest followed him.

Solly fixed the dynamite, ran the fuse, called the warning and counted slowly, loudly back from twenty. Not every blaster did that but Solly had seen too many men caught in falling rock and stone to grudge the few seconds of countdown.

Most of the gang would stop to watch an explosion and this one was a beauty. A huge chunk of the hillside collapsed in a thunder of falling rock. Solly was an artist at his work and this one deserved the cheer that followed it.

"How much do we clear?" Fraser asked, surprised to see Solly re-setting straight away.

"No time. You heard that bastard Dunny." Solly looked up briefly and in that look they all realised he wasn't happy about a second blast hard on the heels of the first, not with so much unstable rock around.

Solly set the fuse, counted down. Nothing.

Rossi gave a groan. "Aw, she's not going, Sol!" He moved towards the charge. "I'll grab it."

Solly leapt to his feet, shouting, "No!" moving swiftly towards the grinning Rossi as the dynamite blew a fountain of rocks. Rossi looked around at the other men, a surprised look on his face as Solly made it to him, shoved him hard away and the rocks hit the ground, an earthquake thundering under their feet while they all took cover.

Rossi dived in between Auntie and Fraser, his permanent grin still plastered on his freckled face. "Jesus and Mary, that was close!" but Fraser and Auntie weren't even looking at him. Their attention was back towards the site of the explosion.

Without a word they ran to where Solly lay, legs trapped under a pile of rocks, dust thickening the cold air, blood and smashed flesh exploded over the ground.

Auntie reached the trapped man first, knew instantly he was looking at a dying man. Fraser knelt beside Solly, the man's gasping sobs terrible to hear. With a shaking free hand, Solly reached into his shirt pocket, pulled out a watch and thrust it into Fraser's hand who barely heard the word, "Wife…." before Solly died.

They all gathered around their workmate and friend, stunned as Rossi began to scream.

They made it back to camp well after dark, the unspoken decision among them all that their work mate would not be left trapped there. No one spoke as they worked like demons, shifting rocks and stones, only the harsh sound of Rossi's sobbing disturbed the work.

At last they uncovered the shattered body. Auntie removed his huge coat and Solly was gently gathered in its folds and carried down the hillside. The first person they met was their foreman.

"What the hell took you so bloody long? You better be up in time tomorrow." It was only then that Dunny saw Solly's body carried between Fraser and Jinn. "What the hell happened?" Dunny glared from face to face, demanding an answer. And he got one. Auntie turned to look at Dunny, pulled back one huge arm and threw a punch that knocked the foreman off his feet, out cold.

***

The next morning they woke to mist around their camp and fog in the surrounding valleys. Dunny slunk around with one side of his face black and swollen. He didn't say a word to Auntie, didn't even look his way while issuing his orders between loose teeth.

Fraser was in his tent packing up his kit as Auntie and Jinn pushed under the wet canvas.

"Do you know his wife?" Auntie asked.

Fraser shook his head. "I can ask around. We know Solly's from Blackball." He looked down at the watch in his hand before placing it safely in his jacket pocket.

Jinn held out a small, cloth parcel shaped around some coins. "For the wife and the little uns. Sol mentioned they had five. It won't be easy for her now."

Fraser slipped the money in with the watch.

Outside the tent Dunny was hovering, impatient to have the day's work begun. He saw Fraser carrying his pack.

"Where're you going?"

"To see Solly's wife."

Dunny glowered. "Not if you want to keep your job, you won't. I can't have men disappearing for days on end to run bloody errands."

"It's not a bloody errand! It's for Solly. And I gave my word." Fraser met Dunny's blue eyes with an equally forceful stare.

"Then don't bother coming back." Dunny turned on his heel, stormed away calling for the men to hurry.

Jinn muttered something uncomplimentary under his breath while Auntie kept his eyes on Fraser.

"Are you staying, Scotland?"

"No."

As the two men shook hands, Fraser felt Auntie slip some paper into his palm. It was a five pound note.

"Auntie, I can't take this!" He thrust it back towards the big man.

"You can, Scotland. I've no family and you've got your lads in Nelson to think of. Save it for them."

"But...."

"Take it, Scotland. With my friendship."

Fraser felt a lump in his throat. He said, huskily. "You're a good man, Auntie."

Jinn and Auntie shouldered their tools and Fraser headed away from the camp, leaving Solly buried forever on that mountainside.

9

Big John hoed the weeds between the long rows of baby carrots in one of the large gardens. He hummed a ditty Kip had taught him, still not brave enough to sing the words out loud. Instead whenever Big John came to one of the rude words he compromised by saying it in his head and grinning.

Spread out over the three fields all the boys worked despite their blistered hands, so hungry they pulled out baby carrots or young onions and ate them quickly, one or two sliding into pockets for later.

"…. Show me your lovely breasts. And I will see the rest. God save the Queen….' Kip sang as he walked towards Big John. Brother Jonas shouted out,

"Rainey! What was that I heard you sing?"

"God save the Queen, sir."

Brother Jonas wasn't fooled by the virtue of the reply or the innocence of the face. He strode across the rows, grabbed Kip by the ear and twisted it.

"If I hear that filth from your mouth again by all the Saints it'll be the worst for you." he raged.

Kip felt as if his ear was being twisted off. He knew better than to squirm though, kept as still as possible till Brother Jonas gave a final tug and left. Rubbing his red, aching ear, Kip spat at the retreating Brother's feet, muttered curses under his breath. He carried on towards Big John who had been watching this with wide eyes. Kip affected nonchalance.

"The old bastard," was his greeting.

"Did it hurt?"

It hurt like all hell but there was no way Kip would admit that. Instead he began to hoe the row nearest Big John. "Nah. Jonarse," Kip drew out the last syllable deliberately. "Has to do better than that to hurt me. Or anyone in my gang," he added, slanting a sideways look at Big John who kept his eyes on the plants and weeds. "Big John, it's the time for your initiation."

Terrible hope lit the dull face. "Now?"

"Not now you great numpty. Tonight. When everyone's asleep. Are you still keen?"

Big John felt his heart racing at the thought and fear. "Y…y…yes I'll d…d..do anything."

Kip nodded his satisfaction. "Good, Big John. I'll bear that in mind."

Big John was distracted all evening. He was clumsier than usual at supper, earning himself a clip around the ear from Brother Jonas for spilling a jug of milk over the table, then a whack about the head from Brother Donatus for the plate that fell from his hands and smashed on the floor when they were cleaning up after the meal. But Big John wasn't defeated by the violence as he would have been in the past. In fact, Samuel noticed how Big John smiled when Brother Donatus's back was turned. He hurriedly picked up some dishes to follow Big John into the kitchen. Sure they were alone, Samuel spoke with urgency.

"Big John, is anything going on with you and Kip's gang?"

The other boy continued to rinse the dishes before stacking them ready to be washed. .

"Them's my friends now, Samuel."

Samuel grabbed Big John's arm, forced the bigger boy to look at him.

"They're not good for you, Big John. Remember how they used to treat you?" Samuel saw no emotion on the boy's face. "You have to be careful, Big John. I don't trust Kip. I don't…."

Whatever he was going to say was lost as Big John shoved him back with all his might. Samuel hit the floor and skidded backwards, smacking into the legs of the huge wooden table which ran the centre of the room, his head thudding painfully on the floor.

Big John stood at the sink, pointed at him. "That's all past. I'm going to be part of their gang tonight." His voice echoed the pride glowing on his face.

Samuel clambered unsteadily to his feet. He placed a finger gingerly in his mouth, wincing when it came out bloodied.

"You can't just be part of their gang. You have to do things."
Samuel felt a pang of fear at the wild look of hope on Big John's
face. "What are they going to make you do?"

Big John didn't know and said nothing, carried on rinsing plates as
if it was the most important thing he'd ever had to do.

"Big John, please…."

With a roar Big John spun round, the look of anger on his normally
placid face so frightening that Samuel fled, stopping outside the
kitchen door. He leaned against the wall before carefully peering
back around the doorway, heard Big John singing softly under his
breath.

"….show me your lovely…… And I will see the rest. God save
the Queen.'

"We have to follow them. Wherever they go, we have to be there."
Samuel confided his fears about Big John to Mick. "He said 'I'll be
part of a gang tonight.' Tonight, Mick! What the hell are we going
to do?"

Instead of leaping instantly into some plan of action as he normally
would have, Mick spoke cautiously. "Look, they have initiations –
some stupid bloody things. But we can't stop it happening."

"Mick, it's Big John. They hate him. They hate all of us and I
don't know why Kip's playing the friend when I know he's got
something bad planned."

In exasperation, Mick sighed. "What, Samuel? What has Rainey
got planned, Samuel? Tell me what."

"I don't know!"

Samuel's frustration was all the greater because he had no proof
yet the feeling had continued to squirm relentlessly away inside him
ever since Rainey became Big John's friend.

"Tell me you can't feel it, too," he begged. "Tell me you don't
think Rainey's not up to something."

And as much as he wanted to, Mick couldn't. "What does it
matter what we think or feel?" He grabbed a sizeable stone and
hefted it as hard as he could towards the birds pecking in the fields

they had worked in that day. "We can't do anything."

"We can stay awake tonight and watch. I want to be wherever Big John is."

Samuel looked at Mick's averted face. There was something going on here, too. Why was every bloody thing so difficult now?

"Mick? Are you with me?"

Mick weighted another stone in his hand, looked at his friend then threw it towards a blackbird pulling worms out of the newly hoed earth. A king hit. The blackbird was knocked several inches away, dead.

Finally, Mick faced Samuel. "Rainey knows we were out that night." No need to be more specific. "So does Donatus."

That took the wind out of Samuel's excitement. His face paled. "How?"

"Don't matter how." was Mick's rough reply. "We can't get caught out and about again. You know what Donatus is, what he does. Do you want that to happen to Jimmy?"

Samuel leapt for Mick, grabbed his shirt front as Mick shoved back until Samuel finally stopped Mick with a knee planted firmly on his chest. "Don't you ever mention that. Don't you ever, ever bloody say that!" Samuel spat out.

Mick's leg swung up and round, knocking Samuel off, quickly jumping to his feet, ready but conciliatory. He held out his hands, palms down in a gesture of apology. "Sorry. I'm sorry. But not saying it doesn't mean it can't happen."

Samuel was breathing hard, a glimmer in his eyes.

"We've got a choice. We look after Big John or Jimmy." Mick's eyes searched Samuel's face. "I can't see it any other way."

The slump of his friend's shoulder gave Mick the answer he needed.

"It's not like Big John's going anywhere, is he? Once he's in the gang, he's still part of us. He's not the bastard Rainey, Salty and Pike are. I reckon once Big John knows what they're like, he'll want out. Then we can help him."

There was a lot of sense in this and after a while, Samuel let out the breath he'd been unaware he was holding and nodded.

It was silent in the dormitory. Brother Jonas stood in the doorway as Brother Donatus came to stand beside him.

"All quiet?" he asked softly.

"Who are we after tonight?" Brother Jonas peered through the doors into the shadowed dormitory.

Brother Donatus smiled. "Mick. He knows who was out of their bed that night and why. I think he should tell us, don't you?"

"Is this about the Brodie house burning down?" Brother Jonas didn't possess the sharpest brain in the order but that piece of news had flown through from Nelson to Stoke as only gossip and the suspicion of drama can.

"Let's find out, shall we?"

Brother Donatus walked softly into the room. There was no movement from any bed yet Kip, Salty and Pike were all wide awake, Kip hoping tonight wasn't his night and when the soft footfalls went beyond his bed, he relaxed.

"Mick. You have work to finish." came the soft, oily voice.

Mick awoke so completely he doubted he'd even slept. He stared up into the shadowed face and pushed back his blanket. Avoiding Brother Donatus's hand, he walked out of the room.

As the soft footsteps died away, Kip smiled maliciously into the dark. There was no sound as he moved to Big John's bed and to Kip's exasperation he found him sound asleep. He wanted to punch the sleeping head instead he swallowed his anger, placed a hand over Big John's mouth and flicked his ear until the boy's eyes flew open. He stared wildly, saw it was Kip and relaxed. Kip placed a finger to his lips, beckoned him follow, Salty and Pike trailing behind them.

Mick dreamed of killing Brother Donatus, dreamed of taking the heavy crucifix in the chapel and choking him with it or sharpening the end of it and stabbing it into his chest. Brother Jonas would occasionally take a boy out of his bed at night, too but in Mick's experience, all that pathetic piece of shit wanted was someone to hug. That was disgusting enough though once or twice Jonas had fumbled under their clothes. He would rub against them, rub himself, whimper helplessly until he cried or shoved them away. They knew the sad bastard couldn't even get it up. No boy feared Jonas. They just despised him.

But Brother Donatus.....

Mick walked into the Brother's bare cell and stood weighting his balance on the balls of his feet ready for flight.

"Turn around, boy."

Mick did, hands clenched into fists, eyes widening when not only Donatus but Jonas came into the room, the latter closing the door behind them.

"Where'd you go the night the Brodie house burned down?" Brother Donatus came straight to the point. "You had work to finish that night, Mick. You can imagine my shock when I went to your bed and found it empty."

Mick said nothing, arms folded against his hammering heart.

"Boys aren't allowed out at night, Mick." The soft voice continued. "You know the rules. And you weren't the only one, were you? There was quite a little team of orphanage boys wandering the night." Donatus leaned closer to the boy. "So what were you all doing?"

Still Mick said nothing, his eyes empty. If Donatus knew who had been out with him, he would have mentioned their names. Mick gathered strength from the fact that at least the other three were safe.

The slap around his face stung but Mick snapped his head back round, kept his expression blank.

Donatus absently picked at the boils on his neck. He glanced at Brother Jonas who watched eagerly from the door.

"Seems our young friend is dumb tonight." And Jonas gave a giggle.

Hatred surged through Mick, a charge of emotion so strong he momentarily lost his breath.

"The Brodie's house burned to the ground. Seems quite a coincidence, don't you think? That two Brodie boys were out the night this happened?"

Still Mick remained mute, his eyes never leaving Donatus's predatory ones. The light from the solitary candle burning by the bed gleamed in those hunter's eyes.

"If you tell us where you went last night and what you did, I will make sure you alone are spared punishment, Mick."

The boy knew anything he said, anything at all, would place them near that house. One single hint and they would be handed over to the law. The bastards could assume, they could bloody guess but if all they got was silence, they would never know for sure. Mick coughed, spat hard onto the floor.

"You little bastard." Donatus shoved Mick down on the bed.

It had been bad before but nothing like this for finally, Brother Jonas's body responded to the show of violence and he gleefully joined in. Now he knew what it took and how to get it.

Throughout the ordeal, Mick didn't make one sound.

Big John tripped over something as he lurched through the dark night, his wrists tied in front of his body, eyes covered in a rag. He grinned from ear to ear. Even now, lying face down on the damp ground, hearing the sounds of small nocturnal creatures rustling near where he lay, Big John couldn't stop smiling so sure this was all part of his initiation. He dragged himself back up to his feet, using his bound hands for leverage and pushed on through the undergrowth with only the vaguest of idea where they were headed. He could hear Kip moving somewhere in front of them. On either side of him, Pike and Salty tripped and stumbled too, swearing as they did so. Kip's voice came to them, light, amused. "Keep to your feet you clumsy bastards." He gave a high, excited laugh. Big John laughed, too.

It felt as if they'd been walking for hours when Kip brought them to a halt. Breathing hard, Big John stood obediently still as the three gang members whispered together. Fumbling fingers unbound Big

John's wrists and removed the bandage from around his head but even with it gone, he could see nothing but inky blackness.

"Are you ready for your initiation, Big John?" Kip whispered in his ear. "For it's do or die." Amusement softened the edges of Kip's tone.

Taking a moment to nerve himself, Big John became more aware of his surroundings, the denseness of the bush, the smell of damp, native earth and the sound of running water. Big John's heart lurched. Running water….They were standing near the riverbank.

"Well, Big John? Now or never."

Big John swallowed hard. The river. In a rush he recalled the sickening sensation of feet no longer touching stones, water closing over his face but there was no time for him to gather his thoughts. Kip was growing impatient.

"Now or never, Big John!"

The boy nodded frantically. "Y..y..yes." He stuttered. "N..now or n..n..never."

Pike and Salty stood so close to Big John he felt their warmth in contrast to the cool of the air. His hands were lifted, a rope placed around his waist, tied firmly. Pike sniffed loudly, wetly in Big John's ear.

"We have to face our fears," he said and when Big John turned, Pike lopsided grin showed missing teeth.

"Do or die." Salty repeated, giving the rope a final tug.

Kip, Salty and Pike moved to the edge of a patch of moonlight. Big John saw them as dark shadows with pale, indistinct faces.

"You have to cross the river ,Big John."

Big John gasped.

"Salty and Pike will hold this end of the rope so you'll have no fear of drowning. I'll be right beside you." And their initiate exhaled, sagged in relief. "Can you do this Big John?" Kip's voice caressed the air. "Do you want to be part of our gang?"

"Y..yes."

Without another word, Kip beckoned Big John through the trees to riverbank, where a silvery sheen of moonlight played on the tips of the water. Pike picked up the end of the rope, Salty grabbed a part just in front of that and together they planted their feet firmly on the stones.

"Ready?" Kip whispered in Big John's ear, "The other two don't know this but I picked out a crossing that means you'll never be too deep."

Big John braced himself, stepped into the chilly, black water, blocking out the giddy, sick feeling that swooped through his stomach as he strode deeper in the river. True to his word, Kip kept reassuringly close to his side. Big John kept one hand on the rope snug about his waist, felt the gentle pull of the other end from Pike and Salty. He felt braver, lengthened his strides as the water became deeper. Kip spoke soothingly, softly but Big John only heard the sound of his own harsh, gasping breaths.

The water was suddenly up to Big John's chest and he began to panic, his feet faltering, his arms flailing but then the rope tightened, steadied him and Kip was right at his side, not touching Big John but reassuringly there.

"Come on, Big John. Don't stop now."

Somehow Big John found the strength to take one step, then another and before he knew it he was standing on the other side of the river, water rushing off his sopping clothes, his legs trembling as he stepped right out of the water and turned to look where they'd come from. There lit by bright moonlight he could see Pike and Salty waving their arms and across the dark water came the sound of their cheers. Big John closed his eyes, unable to believe he'd actually done it.

Kip shook his hand. "Nearly there, Big John. You've just gotta get back again."

A little surprised but undaunted now thanks to the ease of his first crossing, Big John faced the gleaming black water again but as his feet stepped into the flow he felt Kip's hands on the knot of rope about his waist. Before Big John could stop him, Kip held the untied rope above his head and threw it into the water. It disappeared instantly from view, swept away on the current.

Big John froze.

"There's only one way back, Big John. The way we came." Kip heard a soft, frightened moan. "It's your initiation, Big John. It's not supposed to be bloody easy."

The darkness hid the wicked grin on Kip's face.

"If you don't finish, you don't get in the gang." Kip's voice was unforgiving. "'Cause me, Salty and Pike…? We don't like cry-babies and sissies."

Kip spun around, jogged towards the water and dived smoothly in. He swam strongly towards the opposite bank, Salty and Pike's enthusiastic voices echoing across the river.
Big John watched in dismay as Kip emerged from the water and the three boys disappeared back into the shadows of the trees on the riverbank.

The deceptive quiet of the night returned. There was stillness and hush yet insects chirruped from the trees, the river danced over the stones and a breeze stirred the edges of the night as Big John stood, wide eyed and shivering on the riverbank.

Kip, Salty and Pike paused at the laundry window with the broken latch known to every boy. Quietly, Salty slid it up, holding his breath as it squeaked. He thought he saw movement inside near the sink and stopped.

"What's the hold up?" Kip hissed in Salty's ear.

"Thought someone was in there." But even as he spoke, Salty relaxed and swung a leg over the sill. Silently the other two boys followed, Kip's feet squelching on the floor.

Carefully, Salty pulled the window back down and they were almost through the room when Pike crashed into Kip's back as the latter came to an abrupt halt, peered into the shadows.

"Who's there?" he whispered, heart pounding, hoping they hadn't stumbled onto Donatus or Jonas unsatisfied and looking for more prey.

No one answered. Only the darkness oddly deepened against the opposite wall warned Kip they weren't alone. Quick as lightening,

Kip pounced, grabbed the shape, thankful it was the same size as himself.

"Who the hell are you? Why are you spying on us?" he demanded of the boy, his voice low and tight.

The boy shook Kip's hands off, answered angrily, instinctively pitching his voice to match Kip's. "Piss off, Rainey. What are you doing out and about?"

Kip recognised the voice. "None of your bloody business, Mick. I asked you first."

"Yeah? Well, it's none of your bastard business either so why don't you and your boyfriends piss off back to bed."

"How was Donatus? Hope you gave him a good time."

Mick didn't answer and Kip had his exit line. Salty and Pike slipped out the room, heading for the dormitory as Kip followed. He'd made it to the door when Mick's voice came out of the darkness.

"Where's Big John?"

Silence.

Kip opened his mouth but no words came. Mick stepped closer. "Where's Big John, Rainey? You had some bloody gang thing tonight, didn't you?"

"Again, none of your bloody business, Mick." Kip closed the distance between them both so Mick felt warm breath on his face as he continued. "There's plenty going on in this place that everyone knows about and no one says a word. There's other things no one knows and no one will. Wanna guess what my business is?" Mick said nothing and Kip gave a jeering, soft laugh.

"Thought not."

Kip made a point of banging hard into Mick's shoulder as he passed him. Mick let his breath out, the ache of his body returning in force now the tension left it. Limping, Mick made his way back to the sink, grabbed the cloth he was using before the window had opened and slowly, gently wiped his sore body down, wiping away the brutality of the night, wishing he had somewhere else to go, knowing there was nowhere for him but this place.

"Where's Big John?"

"How the hell should I know, Brodie."

Was it Samuel's imagination or did Rainey look shifty.

"You had some gang thing last night – and it's no good saying you didn't because Big John told me you did. He was going to be part of your gang, he said."

Kip gave a scoffing laugh. "That fat lump in our gang? Piss off, Brodie. You'll be telling me you want to join us next." With a sneer, Kip shoved himself off the wall he'd been leaning against and sloped away.

Samuel bit down on a thumb nail as Will approached him, shaking his head.

"He's not in the dining room. And I checked the orchard before that. Nothing. "

"Or upstairs." Jimmy added, panting a little as he jogged up just in time to catch Will's words. "What did Kip say?"

"That he doesn't know where Big John is and there was no initiation last night." Samuel scuffed his boot along the wooden floorboards. "He said there was no way Big John would be allowed to join."

"That's shit. What about what Big John told you?"

Will glared at Samuel.

"Don't look at me like that, Will. I'm just telling you what bastard Rainey said. I don't believe him either."

Will looked around them as if expecting Big John to walk into the room or pop up from underneath a bench. "Then where is he?"

Before anyone could say anything else the bell rang summoning them to the dining room.

Jimmy looked uneasily at the other two boys. "Anyone else feel bad?" he asked them. Then, as they jogged off, Jimmy turned to Samuel. "And where's Mick? I haven't seen him all morning either."

Samuel stopped dead in his tracks, thinking. "He told me he was going to see Brother Luke about Big John. But that was ages ago…"

Will pointed to the top table. "Brother Luke's there."

It was Jimmy who asked what they were all thinking. "Then where's Mick? And where the hell's Big John?"

The three of them slipped away from the boys all crowding into the dining room. Samuel ran through the building, headed out to the fields.

"I told you I couldn't see Big John out in the orchard." Will panted.

Samuel didn't drop his pace, said grimly. "I'm not heading to the orchard."

"Then where.....?"

Not looking round, Samuel dug his heels in, ran faster, called, 'The river," over his shoulder.

Will and Jimmy exchanged horrified looks then sprinted after him.

As Samuel ran under the willow trees lining the riverbank he heard the sound of stones being thrown, exclamations of effort. He slipped under the biggest trees, approached the swimming hole. The first thing he saw was Mick, breaking the dam. He called, "Mick!"

Mick didn't even look up. He shoved hard against the weakened dam wall and after a massive heave a section of it gave way, the water flooding downwards.

Samuel cupped his hands. "Mick! What are you doing?!"

After a long minute, Mick pointed and Samuel followed the gesturing finger. Jimmy and Will arrived panting hard and together they bent double to try and catch their breath as Samuel's eyes widened. Without a word he waded into the water, crossed to the other side and knelt at the body huddled on the stones.

"Jesus…. Big John.."

But there was no answer from Big John. His sightless eyes stared up at the clear sky.

Samuel touched the boy's face, pulled away at the coldness of the wet skin. By now Jimmy and Will had reached them. Neither of them came too close.

"Jimmy, run and tell Brother Luke what's happened."

Pale and scared looking Jimmy said, "Shouldn't I tell Father Aherne?"

Samuel glared at his brother. "Brother Luke is the only one who gives a shit. Tell Brother Luke, Jimmy."

Jimmy ran off and Will folded up onto the stones of the river. He didn't make a sound but wouldn't move when Samuel tried to lift him. Leaving him, Samuel waded into the river towards Mick, still destroying the dam.

"Mick?"

Mick couldn't stop. There was desperation in the way he shoved at the dam walls, the way he picked up the smaller stones and heaved them away. Samuel grabbed his friend's arm but Mick threw him off, kept lifting, picking up rocks, throwing, pushing, lifting, shoving, throwing…..

Samuel glanced back – Big John's body cold on the stones. Without another word, he stood beside his friend and together they destroyed the dam.

"Samuel!" Jimmy shouted across the river.

Brother Luke ran as hard as he could to the riverbank. Without pause the young Brother waded into the water, pushing desperately against the flow to get to Big John. Behind him on the riverbank, Father Aherne, Brothers Donatus and Jonas all waited.

Samuel was close enough to hear Brother Luke's quiet cry as he gathered the dead boy into his arms. Samuel looked away, unable to deal with someone else's loss. Mick still worked in a frenzy, ignoring Father Aherne's shout for him to desist. Eventually, Brother Donatus made it to Mick's side, grabbed the boy's arms. Mick gave a yell, shoved Brother Donatus so hard the Brother lost his balance fell into the water. Mick fell on him, throwing punches, sobbing, shouting incoherently. It took Samuel and Brother Jonas to drag Mick off Donatus.

"Bastard! You keep off me!"

Mick fought, he struggled, he swore and cursed until Donatus and Jonas managed to drag the struggling boy towards the Orphanage.

Jimmy knelt next to Will. He didn't touch him, just sat as close as he could while Will wept.

Across the river, Brother Luke gathered Big John's body into his arms and carried him through the water to the riverbank under the willows. From where Samuel stood, waist deep in water he saw Kip, Pike and Salty emerge from under the trees, heads bowed as Brother Luke carried Big John's body away.

And at that show of pity and respect, Samuel snapped. He shoved his way through the water, made it to the other side. He didn't pause for thought, made straight for Rainey and his cohorts.

Kip saw him coming and grinned, safe in the knowledge his gang flanked him.

"Brodie. Come to ask to join our gang, have you?"

It registered too late with Kip, the rage that burned on Samuel's face. With a cry, Samuel punched both Pike and Salty to the ground then he grabbed Kip by the throat, shoved him backwards against the nearest willow.

"You killed him!" Samuel spat out. "You bloody killed him!"

Kip's eyes slewed wildly to where Pike and Salty sat on the ground.

"Of course I didn't." Kip croaked, Samuel's grip on his throat was choking him. "Get off me." He shoved with all his might, but Samuel kept his balance, threw a punch with all his might into Kip's stomach. He let Kip go, watched him fold up onto the ground.

Pike and Salty stared. Samuel swung round to them, pointed. "You two, bugger off out of it!"

To Kip's horror, they did just that. Samuel turned back to his prey.

"Own up."

"Piss off."

"Own up or I'll punch the shit out of you till you do."

Kip pushed his back against the trunk of the tree, used it to get to his feet. He wiped at his bleeding mouth with a hand that trembled.

"Not so brave without your little gang, are you Rainey?" Samuel jeered.

"Yeah? I'm not dead though, am I?"

There was four seconds of shock before Samuel gave a yell and launched into Kip. Punch after punch. Kip hit the ground. Samuel straddled him as a wail of noise like a train whistle screamed inside his head, cutting off all thought, all feeling except his rage. He didn't hear Jimmy and Will's pleas to stop, didn't feel anything until strong arms linked around his chest and hauled him off the bleeding Kip. Samuel was still swinging. He didn't shout, he made no noise at all. He just kept punching.

"Brodie! Cease this minute!"

Kip wasn't moving. Father Aherne didn't dare let Samuel go. He made eye contact with the dazed Jimmy and Will.

"You will run, boys and fetch Brother Anthony and bring him to Kip."

Both boys stared as Samuel struggled in Father Aherne's arms.

"Go!"

They went, Jimmy casting urgent glances back over his shoulder.

"You've the devil in you, Samuel Brodie," Father Aherne hissed in Samuel's ear. "And there's only one good way to cast the devil out of wild boys."

With a desperate heave, Samuel pulled himself free of Father Aherne's arms only to run straight into Pike and Salty. Hearing Father Aherne's shout, they launched themselves at Samuel as he ran for freedom without knowing where freedom was. They dumped him onto the ground and took their retaliation until Father Aherne reached them. Father Aherne pulled Samuel to his feet, marched him towards the Orphanage and his study.

As the door shut behind them, Samuel stood there trembling with reaction, not noticing where he was, feeling nothing but his own despair.

Father Aherne caught sight of his dishevelled, red faced reflection. He hastily patted his hair back down, drew deep breaths to calm himself as he opened his desk drawer.

"God watches us, Samuel. He watches our every move. He knows the best and the worst of us." He circled the defeated boy. "It is given to some of us to guide boys in the ways of rightness. God saw you beat Kip Rainey. He saw the blackness of your heart and the evil in your soul when you laid into him." Father Aherne bent to hiss in Samuel's ear. "An eye for an eye, Samuel Brodie. Do you know what that means?" But to the priest's annoyance, Samuel didn't move. He reached out, grabbed the boy's chin, forced eye contact as he lifted his hand. Samuel's eyes stared blankly at the leather strap. "You've been a problem since the day you and your brother arrived in our Orphanage." Father Aherne smiled nastily. "Lift your shirt and put your hands on my desk."

When Samuel didn't move his filthy, wet shirt was yanked over his head and he was shoved across the desk. Murmuring prayers for the boy's soul, Father Aherne lifted the thick, heavy strap and brought it down heavily on young, fragile skin. Samuel's silence didn't survive the third whack. He strove not to give Father Aherne the pleasure of his pain out but he couldn't stop the cries of pain when the strap was laid again and again across his back. Father Aherne continued striking Samuel's buttocks and the back of his legs until he could barely lift his arm again. Panting from the effort, he finally stepped back, regarded the reddened, bruised body with satisfaction. God, he felt, would be pleased.

The beating wasn't the end of Samuel's punishment. He and Mick were put into the little cells, the doors locked and there they were left.

Each knew the other was just on that side of the wall. Samuel dragged his mattress across so it was next against Mick's wall. If they both lay on their mattresses and tapped, it was contact of a sort.

During the loneliest times that soft rap on the wall became a beacon, a way to keep the darkness at bay. Though neither boy could know, they had set their mattresses up the same way, slept with their heads and sore bodies pressed softly against the wall. Tap, tap. I'm here. Tap tap. I'm scared, too. Tap tap. I'm here. I'm here. I'm here.....

***

Three weeks later Brother Luke released them. He had argued against the locking up. Wasn't it enough they were both beaten? Could their behaviour not be explained by John's death? Father Aherne hadn't even bothered to reply and Brother Luke didn't push the matter. All he could do was make sure that both boys were given food and water regularly – in fact, he often slipped extra into their bowls when backs were turned. And he wanted to be the one to turn the key and free them. His kind, sympathetic face was the first the boys saw but they only had eyes for each other.

As soon as they stepped out into the corridor they saw almost identical puffy eyed, grubby, pale faces and considered themselves brothers. Somehow they managed a fleeting smile, the briefest of recognitions of thanks and reassurance.

10

Fraser trudged along the dirt road. The valley deepened and the hills with their mingled green bush-clad sides rose to be lost in the thick clouds resting on their tops. There was a coach service into Blackball from Greymouth but Fraser wasn't in a hurry to arrive for walking held off the inevitable painful meeting with Solly's widow. He'd been warned about the close knit Blackball community, insular and parochial, suspicious of strangers, anyone who wasn't 'one of us.' But Fraser knew mining communities, knew that clannishness, knew, too the strength of their trust in each other, the hard, dangerous work of the miners mirrored by the hard graft of the wives, the families. To be accepted was to be accepted for life.

Fraser reached the bottom of another hill, decided to have a rest before walking any further.

"Heave away you rolling king. Heave away, haul away.
Heave away and hear me sing. We're bound for South Australia…."

The shanty was being sung with great feeling from the trees near the road. As Fraser removed his canvas bag, he noticed thin smoke rings spiralling up from the dense green under the trees.

"And as we gallop round Cape Horn. Heave away, haul away.
You wish to god you'd never been born. We're bound for South Australia."

Curious, he walked a few steps further and there lying in the grass on his back was a man with a craggy, contented face, eyes closed, one hand resting lightly on an enormous canvas pack, surely as big as the man himself.

Deeply set eyes flicked open. "Anything more than a stare is half a crown, cobber." The odd man's face crinkled into rivulets of wrinkles and his wide smile revealed plenty of missing teeth. "Smoke?" He held out his tobacco. Fraser shook his head and the man patted the thick green grass. "Take the weight of yer feet then, cob."

Fraser threw himself gladly down. "Too many hills on the coast." He removed his hat, wiped at a sweaty face.

"Well, this is your last one before the Blackball plateau." Noticing

Fraser's interest in his pack the man continued amiably. "I'm Jacko. Take things to small places like Blackball, up the rivers to the gold miners, not that there's many of them left up this way. Not like the old days when the place was thick with the bastards, just a few of the old timers and a few Chows digging at the dirt, still hoping for that lucky strike." Jacko took a final suck on his cigarette before nipping the end and tucking it behind his ear. "Poor old sods. Just can't seem to stop, some of them."

"I thought there was plenty of gold still?"

"Depends who you are, cobber. It's the companies who run the big mines now. There are smaller operations around up Moonlight and such - I'm heading to Moonlight next, s'matter of fact but the only real money is made by the big boys." Jacko gave a wheezy laugh. "It's mainly about the coal these days. And the big bastards make the money off the sweat and blood of the workers."

Fraser frowned. "That's communist talk." Undaunted by the frown, Jacko began to ferret about in his huge pack. "Don't make it less true, cob. And if you're heading to be a miner, you'll hear more of it." Jacko glanced at Fraser, quirking an eyebrow. "Times are a-changing. I noticed it in 'Stralia and it's growing here. I heard Tom Mann speak in Auckland last year, great Socialist that man. Ah ha! Got it." Jacko dragged out a pile of pamphlets. He ran his eyes down the first one. "Henry George, Karl Marx…. They all talk sense." Jacko held the pamphlet out but Fraser shook his head.

"If it looks like a galah, sounds like a galah, prob'ly means it's a galah, cobber. Can't deny the truth." Jacko waved the paper under Fraser's nose.

"Not for me, Jacko. That's dangerous stuff you've got there." Jacko shook his head, disappointed. He replaced the pamphlets into his pack and stood. "It's a sad day when it's the truth that's dangerous. You remember that." He deftly swung the huge pack onto his back. "If you're needing a place to stay in Blackball, check out the pub. It's a good 'un."

Jacko gave a companionable grin before turning his face on the road to Moonlight.

"In South Australia I was born, heave away, haul away.
In South Australia around Cape Horn.   We're bound for South
Australia.
Heave away you rolling kings, heave away haul away.
Heave away and hear me sing. We're bound for South Australia."

Fraser could hear him singing until Jacko turned a corner and was lost from sight.

It was mid-afternoon by the time Fraser reached Blackball township. He smelt the thick smell of burning coal before he saw any buildings. The road was bordered by small, rough wooden houses, some with tin lean-tos tacked on the back, all on fair sized sections. Every chimney was puffing coal smoke that hung in the cold air, formed its own, sulphurous atmosphere on this still day.

Slipping his hand into his coat pocket, Fraser's fingers closed around the little bag of money and the pocket watch. Solly Denham. In a small place like Blackball Fraser wasn't expecting any difficulties finding Solly's wife and this proved true. The barman in the pub gave Fraser direction's to May Denham's place but only after Fraser revealed his reasons for needing to find her.

"Solly dead, eh? Poor bugger," was the laconic reply yet Fraser knew, by the end of the day the community would have rallied round. There would be meals cooked and a bit of money gathered for Solly's wife and children.

The Denhams lived on Brodie street, Fraser noting the coincidence. Their cottage was built right off the road ringed by tall macrocarpas. It had a dismal garden out front, growing little more than sooty cabbages and mounds of what could be potatoes. Fraser removed his hat, used two hands to smooth down his unruly hair as he stood at the front door, digging deep for the courage to do what had to be done. He gripped Solly's watch, still safe in his pocket then knocked and waited.

The door was finally opened by a small, plump woman with a sweet face and a smeared and creased apron over her long dark skirt and white blouse.

"Yes?"

"Ma'am, are you Mrs May Denham?"

A wary look settled in her eyes. "Yes."

"My name is Fraser Brodie. I worked with your husband." Too late he realised he'd used the past tense but she didn't seem to have noticed. Fraser twisted his hat nervously in his hands. "May I come in?"

She stood back from the door, wiped her hands on her apron and smiled. "Of course, Mr Brodie. Please do." She had a soft, deep voice and a warm smile now she knew this man wasn't a complete stranger to their family. "Do you mind if we talk in the kitchen? I've something cooking."

"Not at all."

They walked down the hallway into the kitchen where a baby crawled on the floor and a small child sat in front of the rough table, banging pot lids together. Fraser smiled at the homely picture they all presented, the smell of something savoury bubbling on the stove, the spicy scent of something baking in it.

"The boys are about somewhere. They're supposed to be at school but," May gave a soft sigh. "They spend more time up trees and in the hills than in the classroom. Of course, they'll be toeing the line once their father's home." She gave unshadowed smile.

Fraser stood awkwardly feeling evermore uncomfortable. May pulled out a chair, gestured him into it.

"Can I get you a cup of tea, Mr Brodie? Maybe something to eat?"

Fraser found the strength to croak, "Nothing, thank you. Mrs Denham, I need to talk to you."

She turned to him, unsuspecting of any trouble he might be bringing into her home.

"Of course, Mr Brodie."

She sat, her bright eyes on his face.

Fraser fidgeted on the hard wooden chair. He took the watch out of his pocket and laid it down, gently pushed it across the table to May. She stared at it, still smiling but as Fraser watched, her expression changed and when May lifted her eyes he read apprehension in them.

"I'm so sorry." Fraser said and watched helplessly as her fear became reality.

Silence.

"How?"

"A rock fall. He saved a young lad in our work party."

May reached out for the watch. It lay in her work roughened palm and with gentle fingers she caressed its battered cover. Fraser passed over the little cloth bag.

"From Solly's workmates. He was a good worker. A good man."

Unable to bear the woman's frozen stillness, the look of loss on her face, Fraser focussed on the baby crawling about on the floor. The baby's sister kept banging pot lids together, the noise rubbing on Fraser's nerves. May seemed unaware of it. After long minutes she lifted tearless eyes.

"Sol didn't want to go down the mines. He lost his grandfather and father to the black lung, saw them suffer terrible deaths…" May gave a harsh laugh. "He said it was too dangerous. Said he wanted to grow to be an old man." Her tears came at last, rolling suddenly down her face, dripping onto the table. "He didn't want his sons working in the mines either." May gripped the watch tightly in one hand. "Lots of things Sol didn't want." She seemed to become aware of Fraser once more. With massive effort, May wiped her face on her apron and gave him a watery, proud smile.

"But none of that is your concern, Mr Brodie. Thank you for bringing me this news of my husband."

"If there's anything I can do…." But she cut him off by standing abruptly, picking up the crawling baby.

"We'll be all right, Mr Brodie. Please thank Sol's workmates for their generosity."

She gave him no time to say he wouldn't be going back, would never see them again just led the way to the front door and let Fraser out of it as three young boys came hurtling down the path, all red heads like their father. Their faces were lit with the joyful, heedless games of the day as they tumbled inside the house.

Just before May closed the door, she bit down on her bottom lip to keep her voice from trembling. "Sol's buried up on the mountain?"

Fraser nodded bleakly, May surprising him with a brief, smile.

"He'd like that." And meeting his eyes for the last time, May swiftly closed the door, shutting them in with the grief to come.

Well into the dark of night, Fraser lay on the lumpy bed in a tatty Blackball boarding house. The sight of Solly's three boys, their shining, eager faces had brought his own sons to mind.

He lit the stub of a candle on the box at his bedside then leaned over to where his pack lay on the floor, reaching into its depths to pull out a notepad and pencil. He tried to write every week, dutifully sending the letters off trying not to be disappointed when more time passed and still the boys didn't write back. He'd not had one word from them.

.... an overcast Nelson day, the earth damp under their feet..... Jeannie's grave....the little babe.... their names carved onto the wooden cross.... White caps in the bay, white sails on the horizon.... Samuel struggling against the tears. 'You're dumping us!....'
Jimmy's stricken face. Samuel's taut with despair. 'I'll never forgive you for this.' .....white clouds scudding across a grey/blue sky.... Jeannie's agony filled voice, 'Look after the boys....' The muscles corded in her throat, her scream..... the white cross against the green grave.....

Maybe Samuel couldn't forgive him, Jimmy following his big brother unable to forgive him either....

But what could he give his sons? He had no job. No home. No hope of either. The new page on the paper mocked Fraser with its blankness. It wasn't that he had nothing to say, there was so much he wanted to pour out to them. How sorry he was but how glad they were safe when everything was so uncertain for him. How he missed their arguments and rare fights, the way they teased each other. Samuel's serious eyes. Jimmy's youthful grin. Fraser closed his eyes and recalled their last hug, there in front of the Orphanage. He concentrated on the feel of their warm bodies against his own, the clean smell of their hair. The way Jimmy clung to him. The way Samuel struggled not to cry.

He had to get full time work. He had to find somewhere for the three of them to live. And there really was only one recourse. Fraser rolled over on his bed and stared out into the night no darker than the bottom of a mine shaft.

Solly wasn't the only person to lose family to the mines. Fraser too had lost his father in an explosion where thirteen other families were left grieving when the pit siren sounded. Young Fraser and a handful of others had escaped the mine alive but a fear of enclosed, dark places was one of the legacies he carried from that day.

Fraser licked the point of his pencil, smoothed the paper on the notepad and began to write.

'My dear sons. Tomorrow I am to see the mine manager here in Blackball. I am hopeful of work as the mine is busy……'

As his pencil moved over the paper, Fraser remembered the five pound note tucked at the bottom of his bag. He'd put it in the letter for the boys. Tell them to buy what they needed. And he smiled, thinking of the pleasure they would get. Maybe they would write to him at last.

***

Part III

11

The meagre fire in the dining room did nothing to combat the cold. Every boy shivered from the moment they woke till the moment they went to bed, their breath smoky white in front of them.

"Why can't the old bastard use all the wood we gathered at the river in summer?" Mick grumbled, blowing on his hands. "He might as well not have the bloody fire at all for all the good it's doing."

"The fire in his study blazes away all day." This from Will who had lifted his bowl off the table and was scraping so hard at its emptiness, Jimmy half expected to see the spoon break through the bottom of it. "Guess he don't want to waste wood on us."

Mick snorted. "Looks like we're in for hard times, then." He muttered something under his breath none of the others caught but they guessed its blasphemous content easily enough.

Samuel slumped forward over his elbows. "We haven't had hard times yet?"

"You don't know nothing." Will ran his finger around the inside of his bowl now. "A few years ago we near ate the rats out of the barn."

Mick belched impressively. "A bad harvest means a tough winter. The old bastard won't spend money on food just 'cause we don't have enough put by. He'll just keep watering the soup."

Will finished licking his bowl. "Bastard," he echoed, casting his eyes up to the table where Father Aherne and the brothers all sat.

As he scrapped at the table top with his spoon Samuel frowned in thought. "You know, we could feed ourselves."

"How?" Mick asked. "We can't steal from the kitchens if there's nothing there to steal."

"No." Samuel said steadily. "But we can steal from where food is."

He had their attention now. Three pairs of eyes watched Samuel intently.

"What do you mean?"

"I mean there are other farms all around us. The big houses have their dairies and pantries. All we need is an unlocked window." Mick grinned, immediately excited. "Count me in."

Jimmy's face mirrored his unease. "You mean stealing, Sam?"

His brother shook his head. "I mean surviving, Jimmy."

Before Jimmy could say anymore the doors into the dining room burst open and banged heavily against the walls either side. As everyone turned to look, in marched a wiry, dark skinned boy, bouncing on his toes as he walked, Brother Luke on his heels.

"Wait, Conn."

"I'm bloody hungry, man," came the sharp reply as the dark eyes took note of the watery looking stew in the bowls. "I'm so bloody hungry I'd even eat this shit."

Father Aherne stood, unsuccessfully hiding his distaste of this new arrival. "You may be hungry but you are in our home. You will show some respect here, young man."

But the Māori boy was unimpressed. He gazed around the room, grinning at whoever met his eye. He caught sight of the better food being served to Father Aherne and the Brothers. "I'll have some of that, man. That's not shit."

Laughter and giggling came from the boys. Father Aherne stilled it with a look. "Brother Luke, show this young man to my study and I shall come through directly."

As Brother Luke's hand came down onto Conn's shoulder, the boy pushed it away.

"I can walk by myself, man!"

This would have earned Conn a thick ear with any other brother but the gentle Brother Luke who just smiled tolerantly and gestured the way. Conn marched out as proudly as he had marched in, Brother Luke following in his wake.

A storm of whispering broke out around the tables.

"Father Aherne doesn't like Māori boys." Mick told them. "He treats them bad."

Samuel's imagination failed him at that. Māori boys were treated worse than the rest of them….?

Will seemed impressed by what they'd all just witnessed.

"Yeah, but Donatus hates the black fellas too so at least he won't put up with his shit."

"I can't see him being worried about anything." There was awe in Jimmy's voice. "He walked in like he was a King or something."

A wicked light glinted in Mick's eye. "Rainey hates Māori boys. Well, he hates everyone but he really hates blacks. There's gonna be some big sparks in this bloody place now that boy's arrived." Mick let a pause fall before adding gleefully, "And I can't bloody wait."

The first spark was struck in the dormitory that night. Brother Luke brought Conn in as they were settling in for the night. There was one empty bed – next to Kip's. As Conn walked over, Kip leaped out of his bed.

"I don't want no black bastard near my bed."

Conn didn't hesitate. He met Kip nose to nose. "And I don't want to be near no bloody white bastard like you."

He shoved Kip hard in the chest. Kip shoved back and before Brother Luke could do anything at all, the two boys were rolling on the floor punching, the others gathered around cheering and stamping their feet. Brother Luke managed to grab each boy by an arm and haul them to their feet.

"Stop this! You mustn't behave like savages."

Kip wiped blood away from a split lip and sneered. "That's all these black bastards are. Savages."

Conn gave a yell, struggled to get at Kip's throat but by this time Brother Donatus had arrived. He pulled Conn nearly off his feet.

"Behave!" Donatus dragged Conn's face close to his own.

"That white bastard called me a savage!" Conn tried to put some distance between the two of them but Donatus held him close.

"Then you would do well not to prove that's what you are."

Brother Luke let Kip go. "Brother Donatus, you shouldn't speak like that."

Donatus didn't take his eyes off Conn. "If boys behave like animals they will be treated like animals." And without another word, Brother Donatus raised a hand and brought it stingingly down onto the youthful brown face.

Conn gave another bellow and lashed out wildly at the man holding him. With effort, Brother Donatus forced Conn back on the bed, held his face down onto the mattress until the boy stopped struggling. Only then did he relax his hold, the boy choking and gasping. Conn glared up at Brother Donatus, rage shining in his dark eyes but even he didn't dare to resist anymore.

"There will be no more noise from this dormitory tonight." Brother Luke was about to administer to Conn when Brother Donatus took his arm. "We will leave them all now, Brother. I'm sure they will settle down together."

They left the room together, Brother Luke shooting worried, backward glances at Conn. Every boy prepared to clamber into bed, trying not to stare at the new boy who sat on the edge of his mattress.

Kip grinned as he pulled back his blankets and slid under them. "Black bastard." He whispered just loud enough.

Conn lifted his dark eyes and stared at Kip who just grinned more widely and turned his back.

No one dared offer sympathy to Conn. Some felt afraid of the Māori boy and didn't want to be at the receiving end of his rage. The more perceptive among them weren't sure how to offer sympathy to someone so proud without it appearing like pity. While the fearful and the prejudiced whispered, the kindlier ones offered Conn their sympathetic silence. It was all they had to give him.

***

"Dunno where my parents are. Pa worked on the wharf when he could get work but he buggered off to Auckland last I knew. Ma…" For the first time a shadow crossed Conn's face. "She took up with my uncle and he's a bad 'un. Handy with his fists. Drunk all the time. I dunno why she went with him. The first hiding he gave her, I told her to get rid of him. But she wouldn't. She said she loved him…." Conn leaned back against the willow trunk. "Maybe she did. My sisters were taken by whanau in Blenheim. No one wanted me." There was no tone of self-pity in Conn's voice. "Not that I wanted to live with those bastards. So I just hid where I could.

Stole what I needed. Sold what I didn't." Here, he looked round them all, his eyes crinkling as he grinned. "But the bloody coppers chased me down one day and here I am. With a heap of bloody Pakeha." Conn laughed showing strong, white teeth.

They shouldn't have be out here at all but the chance for a temporary escape had come unexpectedly. All the Brothers and Father Aherne had a meeting with some members of the Church. The boys were given time to themselves under strict instructions to stay indoors. Of course they didn't.

The evening light beckoned them irresistibly and before anyone could spot them, Samuel, Mick, Jimmy and Will slipped out down towards the river and up in the willow tree they claimed as 'theirs'. They were all interested in Conn so he had been taken along with them and standing beneath the willow he'd watched as the other boys slipped up into its branches as easily as monkeys. After a pause, he grabbed the lowest branch and began to heave himself up. Mick was the bravest so he sat in highest branch. Will had the branch opposite Conn. Jimmy tucked himself into a big hole in the trunk while Samuel had made himself a nest out of the past spring's growth near Mick.

Will nibbled on the sweet stem of a blade of grass as he thought about Conn's words. "What about Hirangi? He's a Māori."

Conn spat away from the tree. "He's Ngai Tahu. I don't mix with them."

This surprised them all. As far as they were concerned there were Māori. They never thought there were different kinds of Māori.

"Why not?" Samuel asked for them all.

"I'm Ngati Toa." Conn punched his chest proudly. "Te Rauparaha is my ancestor. Ngai Tahu are soft as shit." He looked round their puzzled faces. "You Pakeha don't know nothing."

"All we know, "Mick said slowly, "is that Māori fellas were cannibals." His eyes twinkled wickedly as he added, "Still are I reckon."

They expected Conn to violently disagree. Instead, the Māori boy smiled widely. "We ate the hearts of our enemies. It gave us their strength."

No one said anything at all. Will and Jimmy shared the same sudden vision – Conn tearing Kip's heart out with his bare hands. Jimmy swallowed hard. Ever since Sam had teased him about the Old One, he'd been nervous of brown faces. Conn a cannibal…? Jimmy made a private vow to never make enemies with him.

The ignorance of the white boys around him made Conn garrulous. Feeling it was his duty to enlighten them, he spoke with pride.

"Te Rauparaha was the greatest warrior of them all. He lived in the North Island and won the Battle of Waiorua. He won battles everywhere. He even crossed Cook Strait and captured the Ngai Tahu pa at Kaiapoi after a three month siege! Ngai Tahu couldn't stop him. He was the strongest and the bravest." Conn's eyes glowed. "One day I will be a great warrior just like him."

Samuel alone seemed unmoved. He shifted to get more comfortable. "Will you eat your enemies?"

Conn bared his teeth. "Maybe."

Samuel happened to glance down and saw the look on his brother's face. Half fearful, half admiring, Jimmy stared open mouthed as Conn spoke unaware of his brother's irritated scrutiny.

"Is he still alive? Te Rauparaha?" Will chewed the grass stem to a mushy pulp. He swallowed it, grabbed another from his pocket.

Conn pulled a sizeable piece of bark from his branch, chucked it and laughed as it bounced off Will's head. "Nah, he died years ago, before we could kick you Pakeha out of our country."

Samuel bridled. "It's our country, too."

"You white bastards stole it off us, man."

"You Māoris raided our lands!"

"Our lands. Can't raid what belongs to you."

Conn stayed cool and collected and Mick saw by the mischievous look in his face that he was enjoying Samuel's anger. Before his friend could explode though, Mick asked Conn another question about his warrior ancestor, happy when the Māori boy took the bait and forgot he was taunting Samuel in his passion for Te Rauparaha's bloodthirsty deeds.

After half an hour or so of more raids, other Māori being taken for slaves, killing and slaughter, Samuel grew tired of Conn's tales of Te Rauparaha. He yawned theatrically. "Come on. Let's go see Big John." He grabbed the branch just above his head, swung himself down.

Cut off in mid-sentence, Conn watched as the boys followed Samuel. After a pause, he grabbed the nearest branch and dropped himself through the branches, racing them all, laughing as he leaped the final distance, beating them to land on the damp ground.

"Who's Big John, man? I haven't met him."

Samuel eyed Conn's bright face grimly. "Well, you're about to."

Away from the Orphanage sat this wretched place with its few wooden crosses planted over almost forgotten graves. No fence marked the small borders. Conn looked down at the most recent grave where its wooden cross was still unweathered. It bore the name *John Rogers* carved simply and a little crookedly into the wood. Samuel ran gentle fingers over the words, wishing he'd made as good a job of it as Father had on Mam's. At the foot of the cross was a mound of white stones and Conn watched, bemused, as one by one and silently, the boys each took another pale stone out of their pocket and placed it on top of the others.

"Who was he?" Conn asked, peering hard at the name on the cross as if it could reveal more in itself.

"He was a friend." Mick told Conn, a catch in his voice.

"How did he die?" Conn had none of the other boys' awe when faced with the quiet sombreness of death.

"He drowned." Samuel said, shortly.

Somehow it seemed wrong to have Conn here with his questions and indifference. Abruptly Samuel turned on his heel, left the small, sad graveyard, the others following reluctantly. All except Mick. He stood at the foot of that humble grave, as unmoving as the wooden cross.

Mick closed his eyes. He pictured Big John when he first knew him, smaller than all of them until he suddenly seemed to shoot up above them all. So shy they didn't know he could talk at all for weeks and weeks. Mick had tried to be friendly but the painfully shy boy hadn't made eye contact, wouldn't respond at all and it seemed best just to leave him alone. Now he wished he'd tried harder to get to know Big John, wished he'd stood up to Kip and his gang and their relentless bullying. Wished a hundred things.

Tears pricked Mick's eyes and he lifted his head, blinked them away. Crying was soft. It solved nothing. But standing there in the dying light of day he made Big John a vow. Kip Rainey would get what he deserved. Mick spat onto the ground as if sealing the promise before a prickling down his spine made him aware he wasn't alone.

Turning from the grave Mick saw Conn leaning against a fence post, watching him curiously.

"Was that Big John a friend of yours, man?"

Mick shrugged. "He was here for years like me."

Conn's dark eyes studied the other boy who was conscious of the scrutiny and deliberately averted his face.

"You know, man, I hate that Kip bastard."

This time Mick grinned. "Apart from his gang, everyone hates him."

"Whose his gang, man?"

Mick stopped, bent to retie his boot laces. "Salty and Pike."

"The short arse and the one with missing teeth?"

"Yeah."

Conn nodded. "Thought so, man. They hang around him like a fart."

Mick's laugh exploded from him. "You know, you better watch what you say. It's all right with us but you'll get into trouble talking like that."

The Māori boy seemed supremely unconcerned. "They forced me to be here they can't force me to be quiet, man."

"I mean the Brothers, too, Conn. You watch out for Donatus and

Jonas. They…" Mick struggled with his warning, worried this crazy boy would take any caution as a challenge. "they…. "

But Conn cut him off. "Man, thanks for trying but you better save it." He straightened his broad shoulders. "I can take care of myself." And giving Mick a wink Conn strode confidently away.

"You know something, Mick," the boy told himself. "I reckon he probably can."

Later as the boys all lined up in the washroom, Samuel stood beside his friend, glancing down at Conn, whistling cheerfully only to be cuffed about the ears by Brother Jonas.

"Mick," Samuel said softly, "what do you reckon to Conn?"

"He's all right." Mick grabbed the soap for his usual hasty wash.

"Do you believe his ancestor was that chief?"

"Who cares?" Shaking the water off his arms Mick leaned closer, lowered his voice. "He hates Kip. And I reckon we could do with someone like Conn on our side. I've gotta plan."

Scrubbing hard at the dirt on his arms, Samuel looked excitedly at his friend. "What plan?"

A hand slammed down onto the bench top and Brother Killen called out, "Silence in the washroom!"

"Tell you later." Mick said out of the side of his mouth.

But whatever plans Mick had they were lost that night as the weather turned with a vengeance when a storm broke out over Nelson. It whipped up Ngawhatu Valley, tearing into the orchards and burying row upon row of vegetables under the deluge of water the squall chucked down. Only the heaviest of sleepers remained oblivious to the screaming wind and the driving rain battering against the tall dormitory windows. At the storm's peak, Brother Luke carried a lantern outside only to halt at the gate out to the orchard where water now flowed like a river for the river itself had burst its banks, the sheep once cropping there, gone. Drenched, Brother Luke returned inside and gave warning to Father Aherne before heading back out into the night to check on the cows and calves in the barn.

Conn was wakeful. He had spent the last hour calling to Papatuanuku the Earth Mother to calm the rage of Ranginui the Sky Father. He tried not to think of Whiro, as the Lord of Darkness could be invoked by men's thoughts and Conn didn't want evil here tonight, even though the anger of the Sky Father felt like evil. Prayers unanswered, Conn slid out of bed, his firm feet padding on the wooden floor to the nearest window where he gazed out into the darkness longing for fresh air. He needed to feel the rain, the gale, the power of Ranginui.

Fearlessly Conn stole down the stairs to the back door. There, just inside it were two figures. The boy held his breath, moved soundlessly backwards and made his way to the broken latched window in the laundry. Protected from the direction of the gale, this window gave him a safe exit from the stifling interior. Conn dropped lightly onto the sodden ground, lifted his face gladly to the pouring rain.

Somewhere behind the hills lightning flashed and seconds later thunder smashed into the night sky, echoing around the same peaks. A flickering light to Conn's right caught his eye. Squinting he saw a heavily shrouded figure, clutching a swinging lantern as it moved erratically towards the barn. Eager to know what was happening, Conn followed.

As soon as he made it to the relative calm inside the barn, Brother Luke threw off his oilskin cloak. The air was heavy with the smell of this year's hay, cows and their calves and he inhaled the scent, smelling the mingling rushes of cold, fresh air pushed through the the gaps round the doors by the gusting winds outside. Three cows lay sleepily in their stalls, their calves tucked in beside them while the fourth stood, bellowing.

Brother Luke lifted the lantern, moved slowly along the byre, his feet scuffing among the dropped hay and feed until he reached the last stall. The cow moved restlessly, tugging at the rope about her neck, her calf was missing. A quick look around the barn was enough to show Luke the calf wasn't inside.

The young Brother loved all creatures and with this loss a rush of panic seized him at the same moment the outer barn door blew open and banged repeatedly against the wooden walls. The sudden gush of air knocked the lantern out of Luke's wet hand and he felt a sickening dread of flame and fire until he realised the lantern flame had been knocked out, too. All the cows stumbled to their feet, frightened by the rush of noise and streaming air, their calves sounding their own fear in youthful bellows.

Hastily and now in darkness, Brother Luke wrestled with the door. He was about to latch it when the sound caught his ear, almost swallowed by the storm-lashed night. He pushed the heavy door ajar enough to get through then carefully latched it, all the while listening anxiously. It came again. From the direction of the wind he heard it, faint and plaintive, the lost calf calling for its mother. Without thought for his own safety, Brother Luke went outside. He was bent almost double and shoved against the wind, pausing when the bellowing stopped, waited with a rapidly beating heart until it sounded again. Rain blinded, Brother Luke kept moving forward the cries of the calf growing louder and finally Brother Luke knew where the calf must be. He turned to his left, thrust himself through the water to the small graveyard and there was the small, shivering calf only barely keeping upright on the pile of white stones the boys had left to honour John. Uttering soothing noises, Brother Luke picked the trembling animal up into his arms. It struggled, almost overbalancing them both but something of Brother Luke's urgency must have communicated itself to it for the calf gave a final bellow and stopped wriggling, Brother Luke bearing its full weight. He shifted it more comfortably before turning his face away from the wind and rain to head back to the barn.

He'd reached the deepest part of the flood when from up-river a cracking noise detonated through the storm followed swiftly by the sound of heavy wood smashing into the water. Resisting the urge to look behind, Brother Luke forced his way through the flood as quickly as he could. He was almost waist deep in water when the branch struck him, knocking his legs out from under him. With a gasp he fell heavily but he didn't release the calf and they both disappeared under the weight of the water. Frantically Brother Luke struggled to his feet, only to have another fallen branch smash against him. As it flashed through his mind that this was it, he would be swept away, the calf was dragged out of his arms and the release of that weight gave him the impetus to find his feet once more. Disoriented now he stood panting in the flood, looking desperately about for the calf, unsure which way to go. A voice shouted his name and he turned thankfully to it. The voice called him on, encouraging him and after an age Brother Luke reached dry ground near the barn and collapsed onto his knees, retching shock and flood water. He was dimly aware of someone at his side. His hand flailed out, gripped the other person's arm. "The calf.... Where's the calf?"

"Safe, can you stand?"

Brother Luke shook his head and the person at his side took his weight and guided him to the barn where he was placed gently down onto a pile of hay. As he gathered his wits again he saw the calf was now being nuzzled by its mother.

"Who can I thank for the timely rescue?" he asked, wiping uselessly at his face with a sopping sleeve.

A match struck against timber and suddenly warm lantern light spilled around, darkening the shadows around them, lighting the cheerful, dark face above it.

"It's Conn, man."

Brother Luke stared in amazement at the young face grinning down at him. "Conn! What are you doing out of your dormitory?" He checked himself, hastily adding, "not that I'm not grateful for you flouting the rules tonight., but...." Words failed the young Brother. "Thank you, Conn."

"Better to be fighting the storm than watching it, man." came the nonchalant reply.

Brother Luke smiled at that. He gingerly rubbed his throbbing left thigh and grimaced. His left foot must have twisted when he fell for he could hardly bear weight on it. But it could have been so much worse and Brother Luke offered up a prayer to God's grace and Conn's bravery.

"Where'd you find the calf?" Conn picked up a handful of dry hay and began to rub the shivering animal down competing with the calf's mother as she licked him.

"At John Roger's grave. He'd taken refuge on the pile of remembrance stones." Brother Luke's voice trailed away. "I think John was watching out for that calf, guided him there."

Conn shot Brother Luke a curious look. "I think he was just a lucky bugger, man. And you, too."

Brother Luke looked at the forthright Māori boy with affection. "I was lucky you were breaking the rules, Conn, I'll give you that. But don't tell anyone I said so!"

Conn passed Brother Luke a wad of dry hay and together they rubbed the calf down.

By dawn the worst of the tempest had blown over. Brother Luke and Father Aherne stared at the torn branches in the wrecked orchard, the flooded fields, the destroyed fences. The Orphanage was safe but the cost to the gardens was catastrophic. Brother Luke didn't want to heap more troubles but Father Aherne had to know.

"The flock of sheep beside the stream have all gone. I assume they were washed away when the river burst."

Father Aherne nodded bleakly.

"The cattle?"

"The cows and calves are safe in the barn. I haven't been over to check on the other stock, though, Father. Can't ford the river now."

"No…" Father Aherne's voice faded away, his blue eyes troubled.

Brother Luke faced the Orphanage, thinking of the boys sleeping inside, particularly of the brave Conn.

"At least we're all safe, Father."

But Father Aherne's thoughts were on the lost harvest, the winter ahead and he didn't reply.

The storm heralded an early winter. The autumn harvest died in the fields, withered on the vines or was swept away by the flood. All over the top of the South Island, farmers, shop keepers, families, businessmen, everyone prepared what they could, how they could and expected the worst.

At the Orphanage the boys worked to clear up after the storm, slaving from before dawn dark till after night had fallen. The morning porridge was thinned down almost to gruel and the stew for supper, well, the boys began to joke darkly about wishing there were more maggots in it. "At least they'd be a bit of meat." they grumbled.

With the drop in the quality and amount of their food, illness began to take its hold and as the boys sickened around him, Will found another subject for his perverse, shadow-black humour. "Keep on coughing, lads. Donatus and Jonas don't want to risk their own health cuddling up to us!"

Only Jimmy laughed.

After much soul-searching Samuel had spoken to his brother about Donatus and Jonas, wanting to put his brother on his guard. Jimmy had listened, his eyes never leaving Samuel's face as he tried to understand. Desperate for his brother to grasp the danger, Samuel spoke explicitly and the colour drained out of Jimmy's face so quickly Samuel instinctively reached out, sure he was about to faint. But the younger boy kept to his feet looking sick yet resolute.

Part of Jimmy felt anger at Samuel, for how could he have carried this alone? Yet, he knew why. Of course he did. The reason was right there in his brother's anxiety. Samuel had been trying to protect him and Jimmy understood his brother must have been truly worried to warn him like this.

"I can't always be with you, Jimmy. If he comes for you....." Samuel's voice trailed away.

"I'll do what I have to, Sam. Like you." Jimmy's voice had trembled slightly but there was a change about him from that day. Samuel noticed it almost instantly. Jimmy grew up. And that was why he was the only one to find any reason to laugh at Will's black humour, his laughter as defiant and as bitter as Will's wit.

With their nights safe from predators, Samuel began to plan raids into the surrounding farms and homes. Each night, in groups of three the friends slipped out of the laundry window and disappeared into the night. They expected trouble from Rainey but Kip and his gang left them alone. Samuel wondered if the belligerent, stroppy Conn was most of the reason for that for Conn loved the raiding parties. He called them all 'Rauparaha's Raiders' and insisted he was sent out every night they went. Between Samuel, Jimmy, Mick, Conn and Will, the boys kept starvation at bay.

One memorable raid stood out in everyone's mind. The evening had started off with Conn getting a thrashing for throwing his bowl of watery stew onto the floor and swearing that he, 'wasn't gonna eat that bloody shit!' Dragged away by the collar of his shirt, Father Aherne delivered blows with his supplejack stick while Conn just stood there, hand out, palm up. He didn't flinch a muscle even when the last one landed on his bruised and battered palm and his indifference left Father Aherne at a loss. Abruptly he sent Conn to the dormitory and that was where his friends found him.

Expecting Conn to be in pain and suffering, they were surprised to see him happily leaning out of one of the windows whistling. And spitting. Conn was the best spitter in the Orphanage.

"Show us your hand." Mick demanded.

They all gazed in awe at the bright red palm, the last couple of whacks visible as deep red lines, one across the top of the fingers, one standing out against the rest across the palm where the skin had been viciously broken.

Mick gave an admiring whistle. "Don't it hurt?"

Conn shrugged. "A bit. Don't think the old bastard was trying. My Ma hit me harder than that." Bored with the scrutiny, he flung himself down on his bed. "Look, we've gotta get something good tonight. I'm bloody starving." There was murmured agreement from them all. "So, I reckon we hit the shops in Stoke itself."

That brought the raiders up short. Up till now they had

deliberately avoided the shops, preferring only dark sheds or barns.

"You sure? What about the coppers?" Samuel looked at Mick and Will, read his own disquiet in their faces.

Conn sat back up. "What about them? We're Rauparaha's Raiders and we've never been caught. I reckon we give it a try." He looked intently at them all. "We won't do anything if it looks dangerous." He added impatiently. "Don't you all want something decent for a change?"

Before they could discuss it further, Kip walked into the dormitory, coming to a halt on seeing the others gathered around Conn's bed. Jimmy thought how ill Kip looked, huge shadows hollowed out the shape of his eyes and mouth. Kip coughed, a deep, resonant sound.

"You all right?" Jimmy asked, concerned.

Kip ignored the question, walked to his bed where he kicked off his shoes and slid under the covers as the cough tore through him again.

"He's sick." Jimmy whispered to no one else's interest.

Footsteps on the stairs alerted them to the fact that they should all be in bed. Muted giggling and scuffling took place. Samuel shoved Mick to the floor. Will stole Conn's pillow on his way to his own bed.

With a clearing of his throat, Brother Luke stood in the doorway. "Settle down, boys." He waited for quiet, gave them all goodnight and left.

Conn barely let Brother Luke's footsteps fade away before leaving his bed to sit on the edge of Samuel's. "Well?" he demanded.

Samuel pulled his knees up and wrapped his arms around them. "Well…. " he repeated slowly as the other three boys joined them on the bed.

Conn took that hesitation for the answer he wanted. "I've got an idea who to hit up first. Who's on for tonight?"

"Me." Samuel said quickly, feeling if there was more risk on tonight's raid he'd best be part of it.

"And me." Mick gave Will and Jimmy a very decided look.

Will opened his mouth to argue but Mick shook his head. "No, Will. We're the oldest. It's us tonight."

Will knew better than to argue with that look of Mick's so he shut his mouth while Jimmy hid the relief he felt at being spared this raid. He hated them at the best of times but wanted to do his bit for them all. The thought of the coppers though.... Jimmy suppressed a shudder as Conn made plans.

"We get in and out and quick as possible."

"No. We're gonna piss about!" Mick's sarcasm betrayed his impatience. "Of course we'll be quick, Conn. We're not idiots."

Conn just grinned, elated by the thought of the coming excitement.

While most of the room slept, the three raiders plus Jimmy and Will lay awake until they knew all the Brothers and Father Aherne had turned in. When he judged it time, Conn was out of bed and tapping his feet impatiently as Samuel and Mick put their boots back on, Mick yawning his head off.

At his second, enormous yawn, Will spoke up. "Maybe you should stay and sleep, Mick. You'll wake the dead with that noise."

"I'm fine." Mick replied through another gaping yawn. He raised his hand sleepily. "See you later."

Will watched them leave. "I reckon Conn's too cocky by half." He whispered to Jimmy.

Jimmy too was fearful that the raiders were pushing their luck but before he could tell Will he agreed with him, Kip coughed again so hard that he began to choke.

In a panic, Jimmy moved swiftly to Kip's bed where the boy sat up red faced and gagging. He laid a hand on his shoulder in concern. "Do you think you should see Brother Anthony? Shall I go get him?"

Kip shoved Jimmy away, struggling until he finally managed to control his breathing again.

Will tugged Jimmy's arm. "Leave him alone." He said loud enough for Kip to hear. "Hope the bastard chokes to death."

He went back to his bed while Jimmy stood looking with distress at Kip's huddled figure and listened to the wheezy breathing. After a few moments he returned to his own bed and worried instead about his brother.

"Shhh…"

"You bloody sshh." Samuel growled to Conn. "You're making more noise with your whistling."

Conn beckoned Mick and Samuel. "Do you want the coppers to nab us? 'Cause they will with half a chance. So, shhh." Conn hissed this in an undertone.

Samuel still felt aggrieved and Mick knew it. He grabbed his friend's arm, shook his head warningly. Pitching his voice for Samuel alone, Mick said, "Just remember, it'll be bad enough for us but if a Māori boy gets caught stealing…" He didn't finish the sentence, just raised an eyebrow meaningfully.

It took Samuel a moment till he could swallow his growing resentment for Conn and agree. The two of them looked around, realised they were alone. Where the hell was….? A soft footfall as Conn landed back by the fence, breathing heavily, having taken the short route over the fence rather than through the broken palings further on.

"There's no one around and a broken window on the second story." The bright moonlight glinted in Conn's dark eyes. "I reckon the smallest of us will slip through no problem. Then all we have to do is open the back door."

"We?" Samuel echoed but Conn didn't hear him, or chose not to.

"The mean bastard's selling old bread for new. There'll be some in the back of his shop."

Mick and Samuel looked each other up and down but there was no contest. Mick was smaller than Samuel by a full hand.

"You buggers better give me a leg up, then." Mick sighed.

Using the camouflage of shadows they crept down the fence line to the two broken palings. Easy for thin boys to slip through, though again, Conn preferred to jump it. His foot caught something on the way down and they all held their breath, expecting to hear the whistles and shouts of the coppers as they stood there.

Nothing moved. They all breathed out. Samuel faced Conn angrily. "Stop taking stupid risks! It's bad enough we're in town without you making enough noise to wake all of bloody Stoke."

Again, Conn ignored him making Samuel itch to give him a whack. Quietly they made their way to the back of the shop. Once there he pointed up to the broken bottom window pane. It looked a long way up from where they stood.

Mick shifted uneasily. "Sure you can get me up there?"

"Yeah. Come on, Samuel, the two of us can do it."

As Samuel mirrored Conn and bent his back, Mick stepped up, placed both feet on their joined hands. With a whispered, 'One, two three…' Conn and Samuel hoisted Mick up with surprising ease and the boy reached out, took hold of the sill and dragged himself noiselessly through the window.

Conn wiped his hands on his trousers. "See?" he told Samuel triumphantly, "Easy."

Samuel kept his eyes on the window as a thought struck him. "Conn?"

"What?"

"Does the baker live in?"

Conn pointed to the second story. Samuel was horrified. He got as close as he could to the bigger boy, fighting to keep his anger in check. "Are you saying that we just lifted Mick into the bloody man's house?"

"It'll be fine."

"Will it?" Samuel gave Conn a shove. "How do you even know that's not the bugger's bedroom?"

"Because I've checked this place over before. Relax, man. Look"

Samuel turned to where he was pointing. Mick was opening the back door, signalling that everything was all right.

Conn grinned widely. "See?" And he sauntered off.

It took Samuel several deep breaths to calm down enough to follow him.

The back room of the shop was like Christmas for the boys. Samuel was just about to ask how they were going to carry their gains when Conn pulled an old flour bag out from a pocket. He'd considered everything, Samuel thought sourly.

Quickly, they grabbed loaves and a pile of scones. Conn found a seed cake and grabbed that, too. Like phantoms, with hearts racing, the three boys slipped out of the shop, Conn carefully closing the door behind them. They sneaked back through the fence and ran into the nearest copse of trees where they panted hard, lost in the shadows and unable to believe they'd actually done it.

Conn opened the bag, pulled out three scones.

"Let's try them."

Samuel grabbed them, shoved them back into the bag. "No. We split it evenly."

"But we took all the risks." Conn complained, trying to grab the bag off Samuel who held him off determinedly.

"And on other nights the others take all the risk." Samuel told him firmly. "We share it out. Like always."

"Don't seem fair."

"It wasn't fair when you had us push Mick into the upstairs when you knew the bloody baker lived there!"

Mick's mouth dropped open, aghast. "What?"

Conn sighed heavily. "I told you, I'd already checked that window wasn't his bedroom."

"But he could still've been awake."

This time Conn didn't even bother to hide his impatience. "Look, that's what risk is all about. And it turned out all right, didn't it? Come on, let's head back. My guts feel like my throat's been cut."

He didn't wait to see if the other two followed him, merely jogged off, leaving Mick still staring open mouthed at Samuel. "I could've been caught!"

"I know. And I know we all could've been, but…. But, that Conn….." Words failed Samuel. He muttered under his breath then tightened his grip on the bag. "C'mon."

Mick stood, mouth hanging open. "I could've been bloody

nabbed."

But he spoke to himself for Samuel had already disappeared under the trees. Mick gave the baker's shop a backward glance, staring at the broken window and offered up a hasty prayer of thanks.

Back in the dormitory the three raiders became heroes. Unable to bear the hungry longing on the faces of the other boys now awake in the dormitory, they shared the food out equally among them all. It was a night he would remember forever, Samuel thought, looking around the moonlit room at the starved faces, stuffing bread and scones into their mouths. And even that image paled into insignificance when the seed cake was unwrapped. A reverent hush fell, every pair of eyes transfixed by the sight of a whole cake all for them. Conn, who seemed to have the right thing whatever it was, whenever it was needed, pulled a knife from under his mattress and handed it to Samuel who carefully cut the cake into equal shares.

Jimmy stopped him from handing it round. "You're three pieces short."

"No, I'm not."

Jimmy gestured with his head to where Kip, Pike and Salty sat watching enviously expecting nothing. "They're as hungry as we are, Sam," he whispered.

"They bloody did for John, or had you forgotten?" Samuel asked harshly.

"Of course not, but Sam…."

Not for the first time, Samuel wondered at Jimmy's soft-heartedness, even after more than a year in this place. "Well, I'm not handing it to them." He gave three pieces to his brother, added the last of the bread and turned away from the sight of Kip and his gang sharing their food.

One by one the boys thanked the three who'd risked so much for the food. Conn took the gratitude like the proud warrior he always wanted to be and Mick glowed but all Samuel could think of was the need for them to have to do it at all.

As everyone settled back into their beds, he happened to look towards Kip who was sitting up, staring straight at him. There was a stillness before Kip nodded his thanks. A quick smile flitted across his face and was gone before Samuel could be quite certain of what he saw.

Mam would have been proud of him for sharing with someone he hated. Samuel knew, though, he hadn't done it out of charity or because Kip was sick or any good reason beyond wanting to please Jimmy.

He shoved his pillow under his head, stared out through the big windows. Jimmy would go to Heaven, he thought. At least one of them would.

***

Kip's illness spread like wildfire through the orphanage, Brother Augustus also succumbing and when he took them for classes the room echoed with the sound of the terrible cough, boys hunched over their tables, Brother Augustus leaning against his desk. Eventually Father Aherne sent for a doctor who left medicines and tonics, some of which the boys were given.

Jimmy and Conn were among the few who didn't get sick. It became their job to head out and raid for extra food. Pike offered to join them and though Conn jumped at the suggestion, Jimmy said no, refusing to explain his reasons. Conn was learning that quietly spoken, gentle Jimmy had a deeply stubborn streak. Nothing he said could persuade the younger boy to change his mind. "We could carry more with another pair of hands, man."

"And run bigger risks with someone who doesn't know the places like we do."

"I think you're crazy, Jimmy."

Jimmy folded his arms across his chest. "He's not coming with us, Conn."

So the two boys did the best they could and slowly the cough dissipated from everyone but Samuel, who grew thinner than ever as the cough wore him away. Jimmy looked in fear as Samuel's face hollowed under his cheek bones, shadows darkened under his eyes. He brushed off any concern with, "Don't fuss, Jimmy. Others are sick, too."

But only Kip was as sick as Samuel who struggled to rise from his bed in the morning and would fall into it every night, aching for sleep only to be kept awake by his cough.

In desperation Jimmy longed for their Mam who would have known what to do. Thinking of his brother instead of his lessons, Jimmy remembered something – hot milk and honey. That was what Mam gave them. *'Honey for the cough.'* Her voice spoke softly in his memory. *'And warm milk to build you up, my darling.'*

That was what he would hunt for tonight, Jimmy decided just as a piece of chalk stung his ear and a harsh voice broke through his reverie. "You seem to be elsewhere, James Brodie. Perhaps you need a reminder of where you are? Please return the chalk."

Jimmy couldn't see it until Will pushed it towards him with his foot.

"Hurry up, boy. We don't have all day."

Rubbing his stinging ear, Jimmy walked up to the front of the class, conscious of every pair of eyes upon him. He handed Brother Augustus the chalk and went to return to his table.

"Not so fast, Master Brodie. Twelve times six." Brother Augustus glared down impatiently on Jimmy's head.

Jimmy's mind went blank. Again, Brother Augustus demanded, 'Come on, Brodie. Twelve times six. It's not difficult."

Jimmy cast around in his memory. Twelve times six. Twelve times six…. What the hell was twelve times six?

Mick hissed loudly enough to get his attention. "68."

Jimmy didn't hesitate. He turned confidently to Brother Augustus. "68," he said, smiling.

The smile faltered as a black anger settled on Brother Augustus' features. Jimmy spun round to Mick who was trying so hard not to laugh he'd turned bright red. He mouthed, 'bastard' while Mick folded across his desk and laughed silently, snorts and gasps giving him away.

Brother Augustus roared, "Silence!" before advancing on Jimmy. "72, Brodie. Twelve times six is 72. What is it?"

"72, sir."

"You will spend this evening writing out your twelve times table a hundred times. Now get out of my sight."

Jimmy returned to his table, managing to cuff Mick across the head without being seen while the older boy kept his face hidden in his arms, shoulders shaking with barely suppressed mirth.

Brother Augustus then began his favourite classroom exercise. He pointed to Conn. "Come here, boy."

And when Conn had taken his place reluctantly in front of the blackboard, Brother Augustus folded his arms and demanded, "The seven times table. Now."

Conn barely knew his one and two times tables.

Over and over Brother Augustus made Conn start from the beginning. "Again! Again!" he demanded, whacking Conn on the knuckles every time he faltered.

After a few minutes of this ritual humiliation, Conn the warrior felt himself start to shake and once he did, his mind seized up completely, his tongue lying thick and heavy in his mouth until he gave up and let Brother Augustus' abuse fall on his bent head.

"You will stand on this chair, boy, in front of the class and show them exactly what Māori stupidity looks like."

By the end of the lesson only Mick was smiling. "Your face." He said to Jimmy. "The look on your face."

"Shut up."

But of course, Mick didn't shut up and he unleashed the full spate of his teasing. It was while he was in gleeful flight that Jimmy saw a shape dash by the windows.

Leaving Mick with his mouth full of ready mockery, Jimmy sprinted after Conn, catching sight of him as he disappeared into the barn. Though only seconds behind the other boy, by the time Jimmy quietly opened the barn door, all was still inside. The cows and their calves moved in their stalls but everything was silent and unmoving.

"Conn?" Jimmy whispered.

"Bugger off." The muffled voice came from under a pile of hay, but which one?

"No." Jimmy replied. "And I'll grab a pitchfork to poke around to find you, Conn so where are you?"

The pause went on so long Jimmy feared he'd have to carry out his threat. A rustle sounded at the back of the barn and an arm stuck up, disappearing again as quickly. Jimmy threw himself down onto the pile of hay, causing muffled swearing indicative of him landing on something other than inanimate fodder. Conn sat up, covered in hay.

"You better come back in." Jimmy told him.

"Nah." Conn lay down on top of the hay staring mutinously up at the cobwebby ceiling.

"You'll get into more trouble if you don't." Jimmy watched Conn shrug. "They like punishing us, you know. If you make them do it, they just enjoy it more."

"I bloody hate it here!"

Jimmy lay down on the hay, too. "We all do."

"I'm gonna run away."

"I don't blame you."

Conn rolled over, examined Jimmy's face. "Come with me, man. We can go up North to my whanau."

"Thought they were all bastards?"

"Not all of them. They'll take us in."

Jimmy stuck a piece of hay in his mouth, sighed. "I can't go. Sam's sick."

"So? You're not tied to him, are you?" Conn grabbed more hay to shove behind his head. He finally became aware Jimmy was staring at him. "What, man?"

"Sam's my brother. You look after your brother. He's always, always looked after me."

"All right."

Jimmy sat up. "I'd never leave him behind!"

Conn gave Jimmy an exasperated whack. "I said, all right, didn't

I?" He exhaled deeply. "But I'll tell you man, I'm getting outta here as soon as I get the bloody chance."

There was nothing more Jimmy could do for Conn so he left him in the barn and went in search of Mick, found him with Will and a group of others digging over one of the gardens.

"Can you do my tables tonight?"

Mick leaned on his spade handle. He grinned, thinking it was a joke until he realised the younger boy wasn't kidding. "No." he scoffed.

"But…."

"You got them. You do them."

A flare of anger welled up in Jimmy. "I wouldn't have to do them at all if you hadn't told me the wrong answer!"

Digging his spade into the heavy soil, Mick turned away. "Then you shoulda known the right answer, eh?"

Jimmy stood in front of him, his face red with anger. "I need you to do them."

Mick didn't bother to ask why, he just shoved Jimmy to one side, saying, "I'm not your brother, Jimmy. I don't have to do anything you ask. Now either help or bugger off."

Jimmy walked away fuming. "Damn Mick!"

Will had overheard the conversation. Surprised by Jimmy's rare display of anger he followed him. "What's wrong?"

"I asked Mick to write out my tables tonight and he wouldn't."

"Why can't you do them?"

"I've gotta go out tonight." Jimmy's voice quietened. "Sam's sick and I know what I have to get but if I get stuck writing those tables….." he made an impatient noise. "Bloody Mick!"

Will wiped his running nose on his sleeve. "If you're heading out tonight, I'll come, too."

"Are you sure?"

"And if we do those tables together we'll get them done in no time."

Jimmy beamed. "Thanks!"

"You'd do the same for me."

"I wouldn't for Mick though." Jimmy scowled.

His friend just grinned. "Don't mind Mick. Anything for a joke, him. Come on, let's get this shit done, then."

Thanks to Will, the times tables were done and left on Brother Augustus's desk for the morning.

"Not that the old bastard will read the whole lot anyway." Will grumbled looking down at the scrawled pages. "And our writing's not the same but he's so blind he won't notice."

As they left the classroom Jimmy and Will heard rain against the windows and shivered, neither of them cherished the thought of heading out into it later.

"It's for Sam." Jimmy said determinedly. "And maybe Kip as well, but don't tell Sam 'cause he wouldn't understand."

"*I* don't bloody understand. Rainey bloody deserves what he gets, which should be nothing."

Jimmy shook his head. "No one deserves to be that sick. Mam would do it," he added decidedly.

"Is Conn coming tonight?"

"No." Jimmy's reply was emphatic. "Just you and me."

With the rain coming down harder on the darkness of the night, Jimmy began to regret his decision not to ask Conn to come along even if it was only to share the misery for he and Will were soaked within minutes of leaving the Orphanage and the place Jimmy planned to raid seemed miles away.

"So which house?" Will asked. He seemed oblivious to the weather, jogging alongside Jimmy as easily as if they hadn't a care in the world.

"You know Broadgreen House?"

Will scoffed. "Course I do. The Langbein's place."

"Their dairy is outside the house, opposite the kitchen."

"How'd you know?"

"Father had to go there once, dunno why but I went with him and saw it."

"So?"

"So, Sam needs milk. And honey but milk first."

Will came to a sizeable puddle. Instead of going round it, he ran straight through it as he figured it just got to a point when you were so bloody wet it didn't matter. "We get milk at the Orphanage."

Jimmy wiped uselessly at his dripping face. "No. We get cow's piss with all the water that's in it. Sam needs proper milk. And honey for his cough."

"How d'yer know that?" Will asked.

"Mam told me."

They spoke no more after that, saving their breath for the jog to Broadgreen House. It stood, two stories high, white walls gleaming in the darkness. The two boys, awed and wary, peered at it from behind tall trees.

"They've gotta be so rich." Will breathed, trying to imagine the amount of wealth in front of them.

Jimmy frowned. "Then they won't miss a bit of milk, will they?"

Keeping low and to the shadows, they darted forward. Expecting dogs to be patrolling, they waited, breathing hard in their excitement, nerves jangling. Nothing moved except the falling rain.

Glancing at Will, Jimmy gestured with his head and they moved to the dairy door. Jimmy tried the handle. It turned smoothly in his hand and he grinned at Will as he slowly pushed it open. He hadn't expected it to be this easy. Once they were both safely inside Jimmy quietly closed the door.

It was then the voice said, 'What the bleedin' hell do yer think yer doing in 'ere?"

Instantly panicked, the boys scrabbled at the door, but their wet hands couldn't grip the handle in their fright. The figure in the room with them moved swiftly, pushed both boys away from the door and leaned back on it.

"Thieves!" The voice was younger than Jimmy expected and female.

"P..p..please…," was all he managed to stammer out.

There was the sound of a match being struck and a candle in its holder was lit. The girl swung the light round on the two shivering boys who cowered away from the revealing light. Molly wasn't big but she seemed to tower over them. With their raggedy clothes and drenched hair they were like starving little mice, she thought and her anger faded.

"You two are from the Orphanage." It wasn't a question but they nodded anyway. "Yeah, I can tell." Molly wrinkled her nose. "You don't half stink for one thing. And you're dressed like scarecrows for another." Not wanting her prisoners to bolt back out into the night, she kept her back against the door, placed the candle holder on the bench beside it and folded her arms. "Stealing food, were you? Or trying to, rather."

Will and Jimmy exchanged looks, far too scared to actually answer.

"Well, if the cat's got yer tongues I might as well get the coppers in."

As Molly made to move Jimmy found his voice. "Please, ma'am. Please." He blurted out. "We weren't stealing. Well, we were but not for ourselves, ma'am." He stopped, his eyes flicking from Will to the girl.

Molly leaned back against the door as she examined Jimmy's face for the lie. "Then who was you stealing for, then? Queen bleedin' Victoria?"

"No, ma'am. It's Sam. He's so sick. He needs milk and honey. Milk to build him up and honey for his cough, ma'am." Jimmy's voice rose and fell urgently. "He's so sick, ma'am."

"Firstly, I ain't no ma'am so you can stop that right out. My name's Molly and you can call me that. Now, if I was to move away from the door would you give me your solemn promise not to bolt for it?" Molly waited till both boys agreed. "Right. Well, how about you two sit on that bench. Not that one! That's my bed, that is. Can't you see it's got blankets on it? Or are you blind as well as dumb? I don't want no dripping wet, smelly boys sitting on my bed, do I?"

The boys nodded, then paused, shook their heads, confused by the questions, not knowing which to answer. Molly laughed, the sound bouncing off the close stone walls, shaking the black curls tumbling under her night cap.

"You're a right pair and no mistake. Look, I'll make a deal with you. I'll give you some milk and you give me the whole story. Right?" Molly held out a hand, gravely shaking Jimmy's then Will's.

They sat stiffly on the wooden bench, straight as arrows, hands on their knees watching Molly as she poured out generous measures of creamy milk into two clay cups. She handed them out. Neither boy moved.

"What's up? Don't you want it?"

Though he longed for the drink, Jimmy kept his hands clenched in his lap. "It's not for us. It's for Sam and Kip."

"Oh, two sick boys now is it? If we keep talking will it be twenty?" Molly was only being sarcastic for the effect so she was taken aback when both boys nodded. Needing a moment to think she pushed the cups into their hands. "Look just drink this, all right? You can take more back with you if you're good and answer my questions without telling me no lies." Neither boy moved so she said, impatiently, "It ain't bleedin' poisoned."

Slowly they tipped the milk into their mouths. The thick, creamy stuff tasted so good they downed it all in one, taking the cup from their lips, looking at each other and grinning at the sight of their milk moustaches.

"That's better." Molly told them and to their incredulous delight she topped the cups up. "Right. Names."

"I'm Jimmy, this is Will."

"Can't Will talk for himself?"

"Course I can!" Will said indignantly.

"Good. Just checking. So why are you two out stealing at night for sick boys? Don't you have food at the Orphanage?"

"Yes." Jimmy began slowly, not wanting to get into deeper trouble by telling tales. "But Sam needs fresh milk and our milk has water in it."

Molly considered this. "I thought you said there were two sick boys?"

Will grimaced. "Well, there is Kip Rainey but we hate the bastard. Only Jimmy wants to help him."

"Why's that Jimmy?" Molly asked, curious to know.

"Mam told us to help anyone who needed it."

Molly looked to Will, "And why do you hate this Kip?"

"He's a bastard bully." Will met Molly's eyes defiantly.

She shook a finger at him. "You can't go on talking like that. So I don't want to hear any more bad language, all right?" She held Will's look with a glare until the boy gave a shamefaced nod. "If you've got a Mam, Jimmy, why are you and your Sam in the Orphanage?"

Jimmy hung his head. "Mam's dead and Father had to look for work down south."

Molly sat down on the edge of her bed wondering what to think. She'd heard stories about the Orphanage and there was no doubt that everyone knew the raggedy little scarecrows needed more care. It was just no one did anything more than whisper. And it wasn't as if she could say anything. No one would guess it but she wasn't much older than the two boys. No one listened to girls or servants did they? But there was something she could do and she was determined to do it.

"If I help you, will you swear not to tell? I'd get into such trouble if the master found out I was takin' his food and this is a good job. I don't wanna to lose it. Cross your hearts? Promise?"

Both boys immediately crossed their hearts already captivated by Molly's generosity and warm smile.

"Good. Now just sit 'ere and don't move. I've gotta go into the kitchen for the honey." Slipping her feet into warm slippers, Molly left the room.

Will sat on the bench, stunned. "I thought we were for it."

Jimmy blew his breath out long and slow. "Me, too. Wonder why she didn't dob us in?"

"Who cares? She didn't. That's enough for me." Will leaned back, his stomach full of milk, the panic forgotten.

Jimmy did wonder though. Molly's kindness made him think about Mam. Her face took on Molly's features when he pictured her but Jimmy didn't realise that, feeling happy to be able to picture Mam's face once more. He too, leaned back on the bench, eyes drooping in tiredness.

Within seconds both boys had fallen asleep which was how Molly found them, heads bent together, lost to the world. They looked so thin, so vulnerable her heart went out to them. She put the jar of honey down on the bench and tipped some milk into the bottle she'd brought back from the kitchen along with the honey. She didn't want to wake the boys but knew the trouble they'd all be in if they were caught here.

After a few minutes more she gave Will's shoulder a gentle shake amazed at how quickly the boy woke up, eyes darting around looking for trouble.

She laid a hand on his shoulder. "It's just me." She said softly as Jimmy yawned. "Look, here's a bottle of milk" she handed it to Jimmy. "And here's the honey." This was passed to Will who held it as if he'd been offered the Grail. "One spoonful of honey into a cup of warm milk for each sick boy, got it? And yer better get on yer way."

She checked outside in case anyone lurked, relaxing at the silence. "Right," she whispered. "Get you gone. And when that bottle's empty, you bring it back at night again and I'll fill it up." They stared up at her, unable to speak. "Go." She told them giving Jimmy a push. He turned back, smiled at her, his gratitude shining in his eyes. "Blimmin' go!" Molly hissed, smiling back but waving them on.

***

Though neither boy truly expected it, Molly's kindness continued. On Jimmy and Will's second, hesitant visit she handed Jimmy a small glass bottle wrapped in a piece of cloth.

"It's somethin' to add to the milk. I told Cook I was feeling poorly and she made it for me."

"Thank you." Jimmy tucked the precious bottle deep into his pocket.

"I kept an eye on her as she made it, so if you need more, just say." She reached under her bench, pulled out a clumsily wrapped parcel. "An' this lot was supposed to be chucked out for the hens but I thought you lot would probably like it." Will gathered it into his arms. "It's just scraps from the kitchen but watch yourselves 'cause I popped a bit of meat pie in there for Sam." Molly grinned at Will, added mischievously, "And Kip, too, of course." And when Will scowled, she cuffed him playfully about the head.

The look Jimmy gave her was adoring.

The meat pie, the cordial, the fresh milk, it all helped. Kip and Samuel threw off their coughs, began to get stronger and sleep better. Samuel asked where it was all coming from.

"We're not even stealing it." Jimmy said, piquing his brother's curiosity further. "It's Molly. She's got ever such blue eyes, Sam! She's a kitchen maid at Broadgreen House. She found me and Will trying to take milk and when I told her about you and…." Jimmy hesitated. He was going to say, 'and Kip' but thought better of it. "and she wanted to help."

"Won't she get into trouble if she's caught? Why's she risking it?"

"Dunno but she's nice, Sam. Like a sister."

A shadow passed across Samuel's face. He said gruffly. "We haven't got a sister."

Jimmy's face fell. "I know. She's just like I thought a sister would be, that's all."

Samuel wouldn't say anymore and in the weeks that followed he had to listen as Jimmy spoke of Molly's kindness, generosity, bravery and god knows what else. Used to being the person Jimmy looked up to, Samuel felt resentment peck away at him with every mention of the girl's name. He was grateful, of course, for the risks she had taken on their behalf, on his behalf, but after a few weeks of

Jimmy's incessant, 'She didn't have to help us, Sam, you know? She's so kind.' Or 'No one has been so nice to us, have they? I think I like her more than anybody.' Samuel's gratitude grew increasingly powerless against his jealousy and it became harder for him to hide it. But, if he struggled with his feelings for Molly, Samuel knew just how much he owed his brother. For his sake Samuel gritted his teeth and listened.

12

The yellow glow from Fraser's headlamp shone just a few feet of light around the wet ground underfoot. It could be treacherously slippery at times in the muffled darkness. Around him Fraser heard the sounds of hewers at work, pair by pair, the noise of the trucks rolling behind the pit ponies, the signaling bells, the coughs, occasional shouts of laughter, he could smell the god awful stench of shit and piss and saw the coal dust shimmering in the lamp light. filling nostrils and lungs with every breath.

Each pair of hewers worked their own little rooms off the main tunnels. Just the two of them, throwing pickaxes into the coal face, shoveling it into the metal trucks. Sometimes they had to blast the coal face and at those times Fraser always felt a frisson of fear, remembering Solly trapped under a pile of rocks, the sound of the pit siren and his father lost underground.

Miners learned to trust their instincts down in the deep. That unexpected rattle of falling coal, that unusual creak of the supporting legs and bars holding the tunnels together.... might be an earthquake, might be a fall, probably nothing at all. They listened, ear bent to the sound, gauging, judging, wondering. Nine times out of ten it was nothing. The tenth time it was a fall or something like the Brunner mine disaster eight years ago– sixty five men and boys dead. But miners were like soldiers, they didn't expect to die or no soldier would ever pick up a gun or a miner his shovel.

Miners slaved, back bent, till crib time – fifteen minutes and not a minute more. Not enough time to finish that bit of food and drink, just time for tired muscles to relax enough to ache like billy-o. Then back into it until the end of the shift, day after day.

The bell rang, the call went up for crib followed by the sound of shovels being dropped to the ground, thankful groans, boots scuffing the ground, even the pit ponies sharing the brief rest.

Fraser and Charlie had barely unwrapped their bread and cheese when a cough and glow of light heralded an arrival. The man approaching them gave a huge sniff and spat. "Lads, just spreading

the word. There's a meeting at the pub tonight. The union's called it. We need some sort of mandate about Arbitration."
Charlie groaned theatrically. "Bloody hellfire, Alfie! How many meetings does it take till the union realises what we say don't matter?"

Alfie's laugh was a rumble. "Then we start the union shouting that we do bloody matter. Come on, Charlie, if we don't keep fighting for us, who bloody will?" Alfie turned to leave, his light leading the way back. He called over his shoulder. "And you need to be there, too Fraser. You're a union man now."

Fraser grimaced glad that Alfie couldn't see. Yes, he was a union man now because that's what miners were. But he thought unions were the cause of workers discontent, not the outlet for it. Not that he would ever say that out loud. Not here.

After what seemed like moments, the bells rang up and down the mine. Crib time was over. Up and down the mine men packed away their remaining food, hastily washed down the last of their drink and picked up their shovels. Fifteen minutes break in a twelve hour slog.

***

The pub was thick with cigarette smoke and the smell of warm beer. It was crowded with men sitting at tables, on tables, leaning against the bar and every wall. Voices rose and fell in fervour and it took Alfie Carter a few shouts to get everyone's attention. His wide set, innocent blue eyes looked out onto the world from a weather-beaten face with benevolent good humour but Alfie was nobody's fool.

"Look, you can't get around the bloody facts. Wages have increased by, what, eight per cent since the Arbitration Act but the cost of living has risen by over twenty per cent. If that's not a reason for the unions to walk away from the Arbitration Act, I don't know what is." Alfie sucked deeply on a cigarette, blew smoke out over the heads of his listeners. "And what about the delays at arbitration? The delays only benefit the bosses. They do bugger all for the workers."

There was a bellow against the language and Alfie raised a conciliatory hand. "I apologise for saying bugger," he told the room to laughter.

Michael Conti stood against a far wall, frowning at the language and the anti- government feeling in the room. He lifted his voice. "You unionists can say what you like, but the Arbitration Act and its system are vital to continuing the peace between employers and workers and the stability of wages."

Laughter broke out on all sides at that.

"Stability of wages is one thing, Michael. Keeping them so stable they're bloody stagnant is another." Alfie replied strongly. "And I don't see company profits stagnating, do you?" He received a round of applause which he acknowledged with a graceful nod.

"When did your workers get their last pay rise, Conti?" someone jeered.

"None of your damn business!" Conti snapped and picking up his hat he jammed it down on his head, left the room angrily.

An older, grizzled man sitting near the fire banged his empty glass on the table to quiet the room. He looked round the faces turned his way. "If employers looked after their workers well, there'd be no need for unions. Of course, the buggers don't so we have to fight. And fight hard."

Alfie gave the old man a salute, called out, "Well said Clem."

While another voice called out, "King Dick looks after the workers, Alfie Carter. He always has and he always will."

More laughter, some of it bitter for plenty of working men felt betrayed by their hero. Alfie spoke up again. "Aye. But remember what Labour MP Barclay wrote a few years back, Harvey and I know you remember it because it was you that showed me," Alfie held up a much creased article '*The present government has given up consideration of its old friends the Labour people. The workers are now regarded as a negligible quantity. They must keep their place and not presume.*' " Alfie lifted the piece of paper high. "King

Dick's tired and he's doing deals with the bosses and the companies to keep us workers down."

The roar this time was deafening.

"King Dick's done more for us than anyone else! He's one of us." Harvey shouted.

Alfie pitched his voice louder. "I'm not denying he did good in the past. But it was In The Bloody Past! We need a new leader. We need a party of our own."

Back and forth the arguments continued to rage. Most of it was good hearted but Fraser sitting quietly by the door was able to study the faces of everyone arguing. There was more than simple dislike on both sides, he saw. There was hatred there, too.

Having stayed long enough to say with good conscience that he'd been at the meeting, Fraser slipped out, unnoticed and walked gladly out into the cool night air. Slowly behind him the hubbub from the pub dissolved into the soft sounds and whispers of night time.

A hazy drizzle was falling. Fraser tilted his head back let it cool his hot face. He breathed the crisp, fresh air deep into his lungs, revelling in the cleanness after a day in the mine. He'd only worked at the seam for a short time but already when he blew his nose or coughed, he brought up black coal dust. He knew how bad the working conditions were and not just in the mines in New Zealand – Solly's death was proof of that. But for the life of him, Fraser couldn't see how antagonising the men who paid the wages would help. All he wanted was to work hard and find a home so he and his boys could be a family again.

He was just about to turn in at the gate when a shadow moved towards him from the dense shrubbery. Fraser tensed. "Who's there?"

A small voice said, "It's just Davy, Mr Brodie."

Fraser relaxed again. "What are you doing creeping around scaring honest men at this hour of the night, young Davy? Shouldn't you be a-bed?"

Quietly opening the back door into the kitchen, Fraser beckoned

Davy to follow him inside, placing a finger to his lips to warn of the need for quiet. The woodstove was warm and welcoming and his landlady always kept a night time lantern burning for her boarders.

With a groan of pleasure, Fraser sank into the chair beside the stove, pointed Davy to the other one and the boy perched on its edge, twisting his hands nervously on his lap. The warm light from the lantern caught in the boy's red hair, Solly's hair.

Fraser had kept an eye on May and the children whenever he could. He helped Davy chop the firewood and do the odd chore or two that needed a man's touch. As the oldest of five children Davy considered himself almost grown up and Fraser knew that was the bone of contention between him and May for Davy wanted to work in the mine and May was set against it, wanting her son to finish his schooling and find work anywhere else.

"Do I have to guess why you're visiting me, Davy?" Fraser quirked an eyebrow, smiling to show he wasn't angry.

"You have to speak to her, Mr Brodie. Tell her I have to work now Father's dead." Davy's large, blue eyes held Fraser's. "We need the money. And school's no good." he finished firmly.

Fraser knew exactly who 'her' was but what could he say? It wasn't his place to tell May how to raise her children and May's word was doubly important now there was no Solly to play the hard man when necessary yet nor could he deny Davy's argument. The boy had four younger siblings with two brothers at school with him. Why couldn't they stay and let him go to work?

Davy jiggled his feet, his right knee pumping up and down. Unlike most boys his age he knew when to shut up, kept his eyes on Fraser's face, bit at his thumb nail while waiting for a response.

Leaning back in the comfortable chair, Fraser laced his fingers together and brought them up to his face, thinking hard. "I'll tell you what, lad. I'll speak to your mother after church on Sunday but no guarantee. If she says no, that's it. I'll not ask her again. Deal?" Hope radiated from Davy's face. Unable to keep sitting, he bounced up, held out his hand with a grown up gesture to seal the bargain.

"Deal." He said happily shaking Fraser's hand.

"Aye. Now bugger off back to your bed."

With a happy grin, Davy buggered off leaving Fraser tired enough for his own bed but too tired to stir. He pushed his back into the chair, stretched out his legs and closed his eyes, just for a few minutes he told himself.

A little after dawn when his landlady walked into the kitchen tying her apron that was where she found him, dead to the world and snoring.

13

Conn was missing. He hadn't been seen all day and night was closing in. All the boys in his dormitory had been taken to Father Aherne's office. Do you know where he went? Did he say anything to you about running away? Every boy shook his head.

Only Jimmy had his suspicions where Conn might have run to. He remembered the conversation about family up north somewhere but he held his tongue to give his friend the chance to get away.

They had all turned in for the night when the sound of wheels on gravel woke Will. He lay there for a moment until he heard muffled shouting. Not wanting to miss any excitement, he pushed his face against the window. Down below was the police wagon and between two coppers a boy struggled violently. Someone moved silently beside Will giving him the shock of his life.

Samuel yawned widely. "What's the shouting?"

"The coppers have brought Conn back."

They knew what that would mean for him. Moving quickly and stealthily to the stairwell they saw the front door being opened by Father Aherne.

"We found him sleeping at the Cathedral, Father."

Conn struggled wildly. "Bloody let me go you bastards! I don't want to be here!"

One of the policemen cuffed Conn's ear hard enough to stop him struggling. "Watch your mouth, son."

"Piss off!"

That earned Conn another thick ear. Father Aherne stared down at the boy in distaste. "We know how to deal with this kind of behaviour, officer. If you would follow me?"

"We've already given the little bugger a whipping, Father. It seemed to bounce off him."

"Well, you know his type, officer. They're little more than brutes." Conn roared, yanked so hard he managed to break free of the arms restraining him but only briefly. He was shoved onto the floor by the bigger of the policeman who pressed his knee into Conn's back, snarled into the boy's ear. "You want another whipping, you black bastard?"

"Bring him this way."

Conn was dragged to his feet then hauled along, protesting all the way down the corridors.

"Solitary." Will and Samuel said together and exchanged helpless looks. Conn would be flogged and then he'd be locked away, god knew for how long.

"Poor bastard." Will whispered thinking of that wild spirit beaten and caged.

***

"When are you coming to visit Molly?" Jimmy asked for about the hundredth time.

Samuel kept his eyes on his schoolwork. "Dunno."

"You promised you'd thank her."

"I know."

"I have to keep making up excuses for you and Molly's not stupid, Sam. She thinks you don't want to see her." Jimmy didn't see the shadow cross his brother's face. "Course I told her you did. It's just difficult to get away. Then she asked how I managed to get away and you couldn't." Jimmy laughed, biting the laughter off at the glare Brother Augustus gave him. "She's a card, Sam. You have to meet her."

Samuel shoved Jimmy surreptitiously with his shoulder.

"Shuddup, will you? Do you want us getting whacked?"

Jimmy turned his attention back to his work. For about a minute and a half. "So you'll come tonight?" he persisted.

Samuel gave up. Exasperated he looked at Jimmy's eager face. "Yes, all right. I'll bloody see her tonight. Now, shut. Up." Happy now Jimmy did just that. He couldn't wait for Samuel to meet Molly. On his last visit he'd gone on about his brother so much, Molly laughed at him. "You'd think he was an angel the way you rabbit on."

"Sam's the best, Molly. You'll like him."

"I better, hadn't I? But you know, Jimmy, 1 feel like I'll be meetin' God!"

That night the two boys made their way to Broadgreen House, Jimmy eagerly watching for the little window with the candle burning in it. Molly left it there every night now, in case he needed her.

Samuel stopped walking. He didn't want to meet the girl. He didn't want to owe her anything even his gratefulness. Jimmy's hand tugged at his.

"Come on, Sam," he whispered urgently. "Nearly there. Don't be scared. No one will catch us."

His brother took offence. "I'm not bloody scared!" He forgot to keep his voice low in his indignation. Jimmy shushed him, pulled him forward.

In spite of himself, Samuel was awed by the size and grandeur of the house. He pictured Molly as a posh servant, the ones he and Mam had seen occasionally when they had gone into town, dressed like ladies with their noses stuck up in the air. If he and Mam got to close to one of them, they would pull their skirts in close to their bodies and the look on their faces! Like he and Mam stank. Samuel had hated the look of meekness and deference on Mam's face. He would say something stupid just to see her smile again and they'd hurry through the shop, get home as quickly as they could.

"Sam, come on."

Samuel followed reluctantly as Jimmy moved confidently up to the door on the dairy, knocked softly and in seconds Molly opened the door inward, a smile lighting her vivid face. Samuel's first thought was, Jimmy was right about her eyes.

"Well, hurry up and get in," she scolded them.

Jimmy again took charge of his brother, showed him the bench where they sat, then he looked at Molly with a pleased grin. "Told you he'd come, Molly."

"I thought maybe Jimmy was makin' you up, Sam. Like you was a ghost or something."

Samuel stiffened at her teasing tone, the way she called him, 'Sam'. As she handed them a cup of milk each, he said stiffly. "My name's Samuel. Only Jimmy calls me Sam."

But Molly didn't take offence. "Fair enough," she said agreeably. "I hate to be called, Moll. Makes me sound like a bleeding furry animal."

The two boys had no idea what she meant. There were no moles in New Zealand.

"I want to thank you, Molly. For sending us the things you did." Even to Samuel his voice sounded wooden and unnatural.

Molly quirked an eyebrow at Jimmy before saying, "S'alright, Samuel. I couldn't do nothing, could I?"

"Well, thank you." And that was the extent of his conversation.

The girl seemed oblivious to his unease and happily chatted on, while Samuel sat there, watching the glowing look on his brother's face. He put up with it for so long then gulped the last of the milk and stood. Jimmy's voice died away uncertainly.

"We gotta go, Jimmy." Samuel out the cup down. "Thanks for the milk."

"Are you sure, Sam? We've only just got here."

Hating himself for it but wanting to get out of there, Samuel played the invalid card. "I don't feel too good. Must've walked too far or something."

Samuel couldn't meet Jimmy's anxious eyes. He glanced up at Molly though and the knowing look on her face made him blush a little as he made for the door.

Unwillingly Jimmy stood up. "Thanks, Molly." She hugged the little boy warmly.

"Don't be a stranger now you've met me, Samuel."

All he could do was nod. Molly watched them leave, Jimmy waving so hard, his arm hurt.

"Did you like her, Sam? I told you she was nice. Why didn't you speak to her? You hardly said anything."

"You spoke enough for both of us and she was hardly lost for words, was she? How could I get a look in?"

His brother accepted his words at face value.

Later when they were safely in their beds Samuel tried to get his thoughts into some order. There was nothing about Molly not to like but he hated her. He hated her casual kindness and the way she looked at him as if she knew he was lying but most of all Samuel hated the look on Jimmy's face when she had hugged him.

It was as if he was hugging Mam.

***

The big man sat in front of Father Aherne's well-polished desk. Not a tall man, this fisherman, but thick set, the muscles prominent along sturdy, irregularly tattooed arms and down the bulky neck.

"I'm getting meself another boat, need deckhands and haulers. I niver thought 'bout getting' a youngster till a Skipper I met in Greymouth told me he'd a couple of orphanage boys on board." Captain Riley had removed his cap in deference and he wound it round and round in large hands, their misshapen knuckles, callouses and scars revealing hard days and tough seas. "Good workers, the Skipper told me and used to hard times." Here the big man's head dipped. "Niver had youngsters of my own, thought a boy could learn from me, mebbe take over from me one day when I'm good only for fish bait."

Brother Luke was in the interview and he felt a surge of happiness that one of their boys would get such a promising start. He met Father Aherne's calm face with a hopeful glow on his own. Receiving his superior's silent approval, Brother Luke leaned forward in his chair.

"Boys aren't like puppies or kitten, Captain Riley. What happens if you get sick of them?"

Captain Riley grimaced. "An' I'm not a fool, Brother. I didn't make this decision lightly. I need a boy to learn my ways. He could

end up taking my boats. I niver thought to chuck them overboard."
Captain Riley's eyebrows ran in a riot over his brow and now they
were raised comically in his anger.

Brother Luke raised his hands in apology. "Mea culpa, Captain.
We care for the boys, that's all."

Captain Riley was careful to keep the scepticism he felt out of this
face as he turned his face to Father Aherne. "I don't mean to rush
you, Father but I've a tide to catch. Will you consider my proposal?
I can return in three months."

"I see no need for such delay, Captain Riley. Mick Leary is a
strong boy and a quick study, wouldn't you agree, Brother Luke?"

"Oh, yes, Father. A good, hard-working boy."

Captain Riley lifted one of his massive eyebrows. "Now, you're
not palming me off with one of your troublemakers, are you?
Troublemakers niver last long on board ship."

"Brother Luke, please fetch Mick to us. I believe the boys are at
breakfast." As his subordinate left the room, Father Aherne smiled
at Captain Riley. "If you find in young Mick what you need, maybe
you will offer opportunities like this for more of our boys, Captain.
We wouldn't want to jeopardise that."

"Let's see how it goes, Father," came the cautious, rumbling reply.

A quick knock on the door before it swung open and a fearful Mick
was guided in, his apprehension even more pronounced when he
noticed the other man in the room.

"You wanted to see me, Father?" Mick swallowed hard. The
Captain took in the red headed boy with one sweeping glance. The
slightly grubby look to his pale skin, the scabby sores about his
mouth, the dirt on hands used to hard work. He also noticed the
tremble of those hands, the way the boy wiped them nervously up
and down his trousers. This was a boy expecting a hiding, he
thought. He came to his feet, held out a calloused hand which Mick
shook hesitantly.

"It's me wanting a look at you, Mick, lad and I'm Cap'n Riley. I
need a deckhand. We fish, lad, out in the Tasman or Pacific. And

it's tough work. Hard." He bent down so their eyes were level. "But if you do the work and learn the trade, mebbe you'll get to make Skipper." He saw Mick's eyes widen at that and Captain Riley smiled. "You'll need to be bloody good for that, though, lad. If'n you're keen."

Some of the colour had come back into Mick's face. He was dazed at the suddenness in his change of fortune.

"I'll work hard, sir. I'll work harder than anyone!"

And Captain Riley threw his head back and guffawed, his hand slapped down in Mick's shoulder, the boy buckling a little at the knees.

"You'll do for this old Skipper."

The final deal was done and Captain Riley signed the necessary paperwork. Brother Luke came over and shook Mick's hand, too. "Well done, Mick. You make the most of this opportunity."

"I will, sir! I will." A thought occurred to him. "Can I say goodbye to the others? To Samuel?"

Brother Luke was about to give consent as Father Aherne's negative cut across it. "No." But at the sight of the frowning Captain, Father Aherne adopted a more conciliatory tone. "We've found, and understand, Captain that we've had much experience at this, that the boys are too unsettled by farewells." Father Aherne met the Captain's eye innocently. "Not all boys are as lucky as this one, Captain Riley. For those who are left we need to be careful they don't feel like the last bun on the shelf." He gave a slightly unpleasant smirk. "Though, of course, there will always be those boys."

"But…. But my friends…."

Father Aherne glared at the boy.

"Mick, do not be so ungrateful to Captain Riley. He needs to catch the tide and he doesn't need you playing up. Do you want him to change his mind?"

Terrified he'd said the wrong thing, Mick spun round to the Captain, tugged at his sleeve.

"I'm sorry, sir. Truly sorry. I won't make trouble, I promise!"

Shocked by the fear in Mick's eye, Captain Riley reached out, placed a gentler hand on the boy's trembling shoulder.

"Easy, lad. You've done nothing wrong." He eyed Father Aherne. "Can he not say his goodbyes, Father?"

Father Aherne shook his head sadly.

"I'm afraid not." He stood up behind his desk. "Now I must carry on. Mick has nothing to gather Captain; for the boys invariably arrive with nothing more than they stand up in. We let them take the clothes they're wearing, though." he added as if confirming a tremendous gift.

Captain Riley took in the ill-fitting clothes Mick wore and again held his tongue.   Keeping his hand on Mick's thin shoulder, Captain Riley left the room, smiling and shaking hands with Brother Luke on the way out.

Mick walked out through the doors feeling too overwhelmed for any sense of freedom. A small donkey cart waited for them.

"Come on lad. First things first. How'd you like a slap up feed?"

The Captain considered himself well repaid by the smile which briefly lit Mick's face.

As they turned down the drive, Mick heard someone shouting. He looked back over his shoulder and noticed someone leaning so far out of the dormitory window he looked dangerously close to falling. He was waving furiously. Mick knew it was Samuel and he stood up on the seat of the cart, waved and shouted just as hard until they were too far away and Samuel left his view.

Mick flumped back down on the seat swamped by his loss.

"Friend?" Captain Riley asked.

"Yes. Best friend I ever had." A tear dripped down Mick's face, hastily wiped away.

"You can cry for your lost friend, Mick." Captain Riley told him softly and after a pause he added, "You know we're not out at sea forever. We can come back if you like, next time we're in port."

Mick stared up with round eyes.

"Truly?"

"I niver break promises, lad."

Mick turned and sat so he could watch the Orphanage slowly slip behind them.

Captain Riley cleared his throat and began to sing in a deep, tuneful voice.

"'Oh, the times were tough and the wages low. Leave her, Johnny, leave her.
And the grub was bad and the gales did blow and it's time for us to leave her.
Leave her, Johnny, leave her. Oh, leave her, Johnny, leave her.
For the voyage is done and the winds don't blow and it's time for us to leave her."

Mick turned to stare incredulously at Captain Riley as he sang.

"How did you know what it was like?" he gasped, so sure was he that the song was about the Orphanage.

Captain Riley smiled at the boy. "I've got eyes to see and ears to hear. But this is an old sea shanty, lad. And if'n you're to be a sailor, you'd better learn her."

He lifted his voice and sang again,

"The old man swore and the mate swore, too.
Leave her, Johnny, leave her.
The crew all swear and so will you.
And it's time for us to leave her."

Mick turned back over his shoulder for one more look. He could no longer see even the tip of the tower. Facing front he settled beside the Captain and joined in the chorus.

"Leave her, Johnny, leave her.
Oh, leave her Johnny leave her.
For the voyage is done and the winds don't blow

***

Samuel had stood at the window long after the cart had disappeared from view until forced away by Brother Jonas. For days afterwards he caught himself staring down the road as if expecting Mick to return, a lump in his throat making it difficult to eat or swallow, his feeling of loss like grief.

No matter how Jimmy tried he couldn't break through his brother's sadness.

"There's still most of us here, Sam." Jimmy pleaded with him.

"For how long?" Samuel's eyes were troubled. "I didn't realise that we could just be taken away like that. I thought we were here till our family took us back."

"What about those of us without families?" Will asked. "Did you expect us to grow old here? How many oldies do you see?"

"I dunno. I hadn't thought about it. But it could be any of us next, couldn't it?"

Will dug his shovel into the pile of cow muck they were supposed to be shifting. "Most of us end up leaving when we're old enough to be taken on for full time work somewhere. I've always hoped I'd be chosen for a family. But…" he heaved the stuff, clotted with hay and muck onto the wheelbarrow. "Apparently I'm special. At least, that's what Brother Luke told me once before you two came." Will gave them a shy, not-fooled smile. "And you have to be a favourite, too. Not like with Donatus, but someone Father Aherne thinks worth the chance." With a grunt, Will shovelled on the last load the wheelbarrow could manage. "You can take this lot and dump it, Samuel seeing as you've bloody done nothing else."

But Samuel didn't move. He was watching his brother with an anxious face. "What if I get taken?" he asked Will. "Or what if Jimmy does? We can't be split up. Have you known brothers split up?"

Will shrugged unwilling to meet those searching eyes. His

reluctance answered the question, though. Samuel grabbed the handles of the wheel barrow and shoved it outside the barn to the compost pile.

He hated it here but at least he'd thought being here was temporary – until Father came back for them. Even though they'd never received a letter, there had always been a part of Samuel deep down that thought Father might be too busy to write but he would come back for them.

He snatched the shovel, began to fill the compost pile automatically. Suddenly the certainties he'd felt shifted ominously under him for if Father didn't come for them before someone else did, they'd have to go, wouldn't they? And what if only one of them was chosen…?

Samuel leaned on the shovel staring at the ground. He wouldn't go. He wouldn't. They could choose someone else. Like Conn. Like Will….. like…like… Samuel gave an exasperated sound, kicked uselessly at the compost heap before taking the wheelbarrow back to the barn for the next load. He'd think of something.

***

Conn was finally let out from the cell. He kept his eyes lowered as he walked passed Brother Donatus, fearing if the Brother saw his eyes he would read the hatred there Conn had nursed like a favoured pet ever since they had turned the key in the lock and left him.

The first news he was given was Mick's adoption.

"That lucky bugger. No one will adopt a black bastard like me, man." Conn scratched his head vigorously.

"Yeah, well, they don't want most of us, d'they or else we'd all have homes."

Samuel walked behind Conn, checked the nape of his neck and hair. "You've got nits like bloody weevils."

Conn tore at his scalp.

"Must've picked them up in the cell."

"Go see Brother Luke, he'll shave it all off again."

Conn grumbled. "When I get outta here I'm not cutting my hair no matter how many nits I get."

Samuel, Jimmy and Will followed Conn out. "You and Jimmy'll be out as soon as your dad turns up, won't you?"

"Of course we will." Jimmy's reply was unhesitating and he looked confidently at his brother expecting to be backed up.

Instead Samuel kicked at his boots, shrugged. "I dunno." He muttered eventually. "As long as he comes in time, I guess."

Jimmy frowned. "What do you mean, 'in time?'" Samuel wasn't looking at him. "Sam, what do you mean?"

"Stop bloody going on at me, Jimmy! Jesus, I don't know every bloody thing, do I?"

As Samuel skulked off with Conn Jimmy stared open mouthed at Will. "What's all that about?"

"He's missing Mick."

"He's got me."

"I know." Will gave Jimmy a sympathetic shoulder barge. "But Mick was older. I reckon Samuel liked not being the oldest one for a change."

The two boys sat down on one of the storm-broken branches that hadn't been cleared away for firewood yet.

Jimmy slumped his elbows onto his knees, his chin in his palms. "Do you know what Sam meant by Father having to come in time?"

The pause dragged on so long, Jimmy turned to regard his friend questioningly.

"I guess if someone comes here looking for a worker, what's to stop either of you being taken? Or both of you?"

Jimmy was horrified. "But we're only here till Father comes."

Will rolled off the log to lie with his back on the damp grass. "I know and maybe it'll all be all right but Samuel's not sure of that anymore. So he's worried."

Another pause which stretched companionably until Jimmy slid onto the grass as well, lay beside his friend and together they stared up into the puffy white clouds set against a faultless blue sky.

"Samuel is always worried about something." Jimmy grumbled.

He decided he'd talk it over with Molly. No fear that Sam would ever know because no matter how often he was asked he refused to see Molly again.   Jimmy couldn't understand why and Samuel wouldn't say. He'd even tried to talk his brother out of returning, something Jimmy steadfastly refused to do.

The boy gazed up into the clouds as Will pointed out one that was a particularly rude shape. As Will sniggered, Jimmy felt calmer. He'd talk to Molly. She'd know what to do.

14

To the joy of every boy in the Orphanage, Father Aherne announced they were all going to have a picnic at Tahunanui beach.

"With much thanks to be offered for the pious generosity of two good catholic families. The next fine Sunday morning we will go after prayers."

The boys cheered wildly, taking some time to settle back down. Under the guise of bent heads and thoughtful minds, much whispering took place.

Samuel nudged Conn with his elbow. "Even a treat for you black fellas." He grinned.

Conn turned his dark head and at the look in the boy's black eyes Samuel's grin faded. "I don't care about a bloody picnic, man. I want to get away from here."

"You tried it once. How'd that turn out?"

"I know but I did it on my own." Conn's black eyes searched Samuel's. "Will you help me?"

What could Samuel say but, "Of course." All the while thinking Conn must like whippings for he'd already had more than his fair share of them.

It was Conn, Samuel and Kip's turn to do the dishes that night and as they began to work Conn stepped up as close to Kip as he could. "You better be deaf to what's talked of in here tonight, Rainey."

Kip refused to lower his eyes, holding the eye contact till Conn was satisfied.

"I've gotta get out of here and I reckon I'll be all right so long as I can get my arse onto any ship heading out of port," he told Samuel. "It don't even matter where the bugger's headed. I'll be away from bloody Nelson and that's all that matters to me. It's just….."

"Getting your arse onto that ship?" Samuel guessed.

"Yeah but more than that, man. I need time before the old bastards here miss me. I reckon slipping into the hold of a ship will be easy enough but there has to be enough time for the bloody ship to catch the tide and get away without any bugger setting up hunting parties for my black hide."

Samuel whistled softly. "You've put some thought into this, haven't you?"

Conn slammed a plate down onto the table so hard Samuel and Kip expected it to shatter. "Man, I had all the time the bastards had me under lock and key with nothing else but my bruises." He looked into the middle distance. "But I've got it planned out. I just need that time after I scarper and before the old bastard here raises the alarm." Conn gave a cold smile. "If he even gives a shit."

They worked for a while until Kip reached for a plate, said softly, "I think I know a way."

Samuel looked sceptical. "You do?"

Kip smirked his twisted grin. "You'd have to be prepared to wait a bit Conn and we'd need most of the boys on our side."

"Well, the ones who don't like me are too scared to dob me in." Conn replied. "Tell us your plan."

"I'll need to bring Salty and Pike in on it." Kip flicked his tea towel at Samuel. "And you have to trust me."

Samuel scoffed. "Trust you? Why the hell should I do that after everything you've done."

And to Samuel's surprise Kip's eyes welled up with tears. He wiped at them with the tea towel ashamed and angry at himself but he answered the question honestly.

"Because of everything I've done" he said with emphasis. "Without Jimmy's help and the food and everything... I wouldn't have made it when we was sick." Kip's voice dropped to almost a whisper. "I didn't deserve it."

Samuel's tone was unyielding. "You won't hear me disagree with that."

"Thought you hated black bastards, man?" Conn jeered.

"I thought I did too." Kip gave Conn a sheepish smile. "But you're the same as us. And you helped get the food."

Conn and Samuel didn't know what to say. Samuel fought against all his old prejudices where Rainey was concerned and Conn mistrusted most Pakeha just because.

Kip faced them squarely. "Look, what I have in mind will mean a thrashing for me as well."

"As well?" Samuel queried. "As well as who?"

"Most of us. They'll take to most of us. But it'll give this black bastard the time he needs to get away. I promise that."

Kip waited while Conn and Samuel came to a silent agreement.

"All right. We'll trust you, Rainey. What's your damn plan?"

So Kip told them.

***

It took three weeks for the weather to settle enough so a full day could be relied on to stay bright for the picnic. Breakfast was served, prayers said, no boy listening, lost as they were to the beams of sunlight streaming through the windows. Some of the younger ones were too excited even to eat, their food quickly shared out among the lucky ones who got to it first.

Four big carts pulled up outside the main doors and all the boys scrambled up on board, laughing, shouting. They noticed hampers in each cart and every mouth watered at the thought of picnic food while Brother Luke led the singing. The drivers gave the horses a click of teeth and, 'giddup' and they were off towards Tahunanui Beach.

They were passing the shops when Jimmy gave Samuel a sharp nudge with his elbow, pointed towards one of the doorways, excitedly. "There's Molly, Sam. Look, there she is!"

Samuel peered into a shadowed doorway and saw her standing there with a basket over one arm and another at her feet. She returned Jimmy's enthusiastic waving with more restraint but her smile was wide. Jimmy pointed at himself, just in case she didn't realise who he was, and then at Samuel. Molly nodded her under-standing, laughing at the boy's eagerness nor did she miss the unsmiling, serious expression on Samuel's face.

Cook came out of the shop in time to see Molly waving to the back

179

of Jimmy's head.

"Who was that?" Cook demanded.

"Jus' the boys from the Orphanage, Cook. Must be off on an outing, lucky things."

"You don't need no outings to be lucky, my girl. You've a job and a roof over your head." Cook dropped her parcels into Molly's basket and sailed off down the street, leaving the girl to carry both baskets and trail in her footsteps.

Molly didn't need telling about how lucky she was, especially since Jimmy and Will had told her about their life at the Orphanage. Poor little blighters! Still, she smiled, they were going to have some fun today.

At the beach, under the sun the boys had the time of their lives. A couple of cricket bats and balls were produced and in no time at all, cricket was being played up and down the sand. Smaller boys foraged along the high tide mark for shells or odd pieces of wood and other treasures to fill their pockets, others snuggled down out of sight among the sand dunes and let the sun warm them while they dozed.

Conn hated all games. He made sure he kept so far down the beach he was in no danger of having to play and repeated the plan over and over in his head.

He'd tucked the knife from under his mattress down one sock and could feel it with every step. He also had taken another shirt from the laundry, made sure it was a smaller fit than his usual one so he could wear it unobtrusively. He couldn't wear a coat on a day like today because it would look strange when no other boy wore one. Kip had also handed him a stub of pencil, some tightly folded pieces of paper and some string to put in his pocket.

"You might need them." He said, brushing off Conn's thanks with a careless gesture.

Conn fingered these treasures, reassured by the feel of them. He intended to make sure he ate as much food at the picnic that he could get away with and maybe slip some into his pockets as well.

As he stood on the sands, Conn shaded his eyes and looked out to the port where the ships sat moored at the wharf. His stomach gave a lurch, something akin to excitement and fear. Wherever he ended up, he thought, it would be bloody better than this shit hole.

The sun was heading back down in the sky when the boys were all rounded up from along the beach, among the sand dunes, playing or sleeping so the hampers could be opened at last. Sandwiches, hard boiled eggs, two kinds of cake, apples and cold meat passed from hand to hand and from hand to pocket. Conn kept getting food given to him surreptitiously until his pockets were bulging and he had to refuse anymore.

As the final pieces of food were eaten and the Brothers reluctantly began to rise from the warmth of the sand, Kip looked round, met Conn's eye then Samuel's. Salty coughed, Pike sniffed loudly and Jimmy was given a none too gentle poke in the ribs. Kip was going to start things off and made sure he had their attention. As a cold breeze blew up, Father Aherne issued orders to the Brothers and the boys began to sort themselves into their cart groups.

"Head count, Brothers. We don't want anyone left behind."

All the friends were in the same cart. Brother Luke smiled on each one as he lightly touched their heads, counting them off. When every boy was accounted for, Kip gave a snarl and shoved Samuel so hard, the boy flew backwards onto the ground, gasping. He got to his feet with a yell, launched himself back at Kip, dragging him to the sand, Kip flailing ineffectually.

The fight was on. Salty and Pike made a point of punching a couple of boys they didn't like who came over from the other carts when the shouting started. They too joined in and in no time at all nearly every boy, even the smallest ones were yelling, punching and kicking each other all around the carts. No one saw Conn slip away, no one except Kip who was keeping a weather eye out. He saw him melt into the crowds of people gathering excitedly to watch the Orphanage boys fighting. They stood there, these staid, honest citizens tutting, shaking their heads disapprovingly while watching avidly.

Kip grinned to himself, winked at Samuel to let him know Conn had made this first step safely then punched him in the mouth.

***

"Jesus, Rainey, did you have to punch me quite so bloody hard?" Samuel complained as he ran a finger around the inside of his mouth. He gave a gasp as he found a loose tooth, gasped even more when it came out completely. "Would you look at this?" He shoved it under Kip's eyes, then passed it to Jimmy and Will.

Kip grinned. He was injured too, holding a bloody rag to his nose. "Well, you weren't exactly holding back were you?" He pulled the material away from his nose cautiously. He groaned melodramatically, lay down on his bed, only to have to stand again. The flogging he got for being one the one to start the brawl meant he would have to sleep on his stomach tonight.

They were all aching from being thrashed. Only those who were seen to stand fearfully on the boundary of the melee escaped punishment. Kip looked at Will with his black eye, Jimmy, clutching a painful arm, Samuel still bitching over his lost tooth. Pike and Salty had been locked in the cells. They'd kept throwing punches after the Brothers dragged them apart, Brother Jonas copping a black eye to rival Will's.

Kip gingerly felt his own busted nose then laughed, making them all look up in surprise. "It was worth it," he told them triumphantly. "They've no idea Conn's missing and won't till after prayers tomorrow morning, longer if he's lucky."

Samuel stuck his tongue in the gap where his tooth once sat, grumbled. "I think you're enjoying this too much, Rainey."

***

As he left the shouts and screams of the melee behind him Conn had one thing on his mind; he had to find somewhere to wait for the

182

cover of darkness. Against the cliff along the newly completed Rocks Road was a small boat shed and with a look about him to make sure he remained unobserved, the boy made straight for it. It wasn't locked and after a nonchalant survey to make sure no one saw him, he slipped inside. A wooden boat sat there, a pile of canvas sheeting dumped in it. The perfect place for a tired runaway.

But first, Conn investigated the shed. He found an old coat. It smelt of damp and fish but where he was heading that would be a bonus. He put it on, the arms hanging down far over his hands before he rolled them up. A packet of matches, a small ball of fishing twine, a couple of hooks and three sinkers all found their way into the deep coat pockets. His fingers rubbed along the things Kip had scavenged for him and Conn spared fervent thanks for the friends who risked a whipping to set him free. He had to make it away safely to make their punishment worth it.

Determined now, he climbed into the boat, curled up on the canvas and dragged a chunk of it over himself until he was hidden from view. Relaxed and warm, his pockets bulging with food and treasures, Conn dozed off.

A clatter of wheels on the gravel road woke him. In fright, Conn forgot where he was and panicked, struggling to throw the heavy canvas off. Breathing hard, eyes wide, he stood, banged his head on something hanging from the ceiling and swore under his breath. He rubbed his crown, calming down belatedly as memory kicked in. There was now no light but moonlight. Conn felt a surge of nervous excitement. Suddenly desperate to be away he clambered off the boat and out of the shed. Another cart was approaching from the direction of Stoke.

Keeping to the safety of the shadows, Conn waited and watched. There was one driver, no passengers and the cart was loaded with sacks and boxes. Seizing his chance, Conn crept up to the back of the cart and in one smooth movement, pulled himself onto it. He manoeuvred among the sheltering sacks, grinning. The driver of the cart was obviously in no hurry, the horses plodded calmly as the man whistled contentedly. Conn softly hummed along as he watched the moonlight dancing on the waves breaking along the gravel road. He planned to get off near the entrance to the wharf.

However, the boy's good luck held for the cart turned onto the wharf itself, a busy place even at this hour for ships had to be loaded and got on their way. It didn't matter to him which ship he managed to hide away on; whichever one it was would be leaving and that was all that mattered.

A voice hailed the driver. "What you doing, mate?"

"This here stuff's for Sydney."

"Right. Over there."

The cart jerked, moved off again, came to a halt further along. Knowing he had to be out of the cart before the unloading began, Conn waited until the driver started a conversation with a watersider before dropping silently off the end. He looked wildly around and noticed men and boys carrying things from the wharfside, up a gangway into the hold of the huge wooden ship moored by.

Thinking quickly, Conn grabbed a sack, joined the workers. He took his time placing the sack among the rest in the hold and as soon as he found himself alone, he jumped the stored goods, threw himself as far back as he could and there between sacks and ship hull he crouched. Scared though he was he couldn't help but grin. Let the old bastards find him here!

In a surprisingly short amount of time, the tooing and froing, the shouts and whistles, all came to a stop. Only then did Conn make himself comfortable among the sacks and boxes. He pulled the sleeves of his coat down and did the buttons up glad of its warmth now. Out of his pocket came a couple of sandwiches, worse for wear and crunchy with sand but they were a feast to the happy boy. He gave a sigh of pleasure and lay there listening to the creaking of the wooden ship. He didn't know where the hell Sydney was but it wasn't Nelson, was it?

There was no way of telling the time but it was completely dark and the creaking timbers were the only sound until heavy footsteps sounded on the stairs down into the hold where Conn lay huddled.

A man coughed, hoiked up and spat, muttering to himself. Yellow lantern light spilled over Conn's head and he dared to peek through a gap, saw the outline of a vast shape and shrank back. What was the big bastard looking for? Had someone seen him? The man picked up a sack, threw it and dust exploded over Conn's head. His nose tickled and he felt a sneeze coming on. Eyes watering he held his breath, clamped his lips tightly together but the sneeze when it came still gave him away.

"Who's down here?"

Silence.

The man lifted his lantern, the light deepening the shadows around the walls and wares. "I'm not an idiot. Show yourself!"

Conn didn't move, frozen to the spot, barely breathing. More swearing and the man started shoving things to one side. Conn closed frightened eyes seconds before a huge hand grabbed the collar of his too big coat and hauled him up so high the boy's feet touched the top of the boxes and sacks.

"What the hell have we got here?"

Conn struggled but the hand on his collar held on tightly. "Piss off!"

The man cuffed Conn's ear. "You don't talk like that to me, boy."

Opening his eyes Conn looked into a huge brown face entirely tattoed in moko. He stopped squirming and stared. He pointed at the part of the moko which covered the man's forehead. "Ngati Toa."

It was the man's turn to gape. "And how would a blackbird like you know my iwi?"

"My iwi, too. Te Rauparaha is my ancestor." Pride shone on Conn's face.

The big man sat him down on the sacks, bemused. "E haere mai koe i hea?"

Conn looked blankly at him, shrugged. "I dunno what you're saying, man."

"You don't speak our language?"

"Nah."

The big man shook his head in disbelief. "Boy, what's your name?"

"Conn."

"You don't speak Māori. You don't have a Māori name. It's not enough to wear our skin, boy."

Con thumped his chest. "I will be a great warrior like Te Rauparaha."

A shout from on the upper deck made them both jump. The man swore, regarded the odd figure looking at him so boldly. "Why are you on this ship?"

"I want to get away." Conn crossed his arms over his chest. "And I don't ever want to come back."

Another shout and the ship creaked heavily.

Conn reached out, grabbed the man's arm, pleading. "Don't chuck me off, man! Please."

For several seconds they stared at each other before the man turned, shouting abuse and left the hold.

Conn stayed where he was shivering from fright and pretending it was the cold. After what felt like hours to the nervous boy, the big Māori returned. He gestured for Conn to get off the floor, pointing to a crate where he obediently sat.

Man and boy took each other's measure until the man came to his decision. "My name's Arana, boy. You will stay down here. I will find you a pot to piss in. I will feed you and you will learn our ways and you will learn to speak our tongue."

"I can't."

Arana gave a wide smile that didn't make him look so formidable. "I te tae atu koe ki poihakena e tama ka mau ia koe te matauranga."

Conn looked lost. "What, man?"

"We have from here to Sydney, boy. You'll learn."

As Arana picked up the lantern and turned to leave, Conn said. "And my name's not boy."

The big man turned back. "Then I will call you 'Te manu nohi

nohi manga.'"

"What does that mean?"

Arana smile became mischievous.

"When you've learned what it means, I'll feed you."

"That's not fair!"

But Arana shrugged.

"Life's not meant to be fair, te manu nohi nohi manga. Kia mohio ko wai koe me to whakapapa." Arana leaned in closer to Conn and laid a gentle hand on his shoulder. "You need to understand who you are and where you come from."

The light disappeared with Arana but Conn didn't care. He was safe and he was leaving.

Making his hidden nest more comfortable, he set out his treasures and took out the rest of his food. Then he lay on his back and grinned at his luck.

Above him the sails caught in the wind, the ship ploughed smoothly towards the Cut heading out into the Tasman Sea.

***

Brother Luke stood anxiously in front of Father Aherne's desk, thinking he must have misheard his superior. "But the boy's gone, Father. We have to do something."

"Do we?"

"Of course! Conn is in our care."

Father Aherne leaned forward on his elbows. "He was in our care, Brother. He chose to run once and was returned to that care. He has run again and this time I'm inclined to let him go."

Brother Luke was aghast. "Father….."

"No, Brother. We have many boys here and every week new ones arrive. If we keep having the trouble like that one boy brought, our authority will be called into question. Then where would all these poor, homeless boys be?"

Father Aherne held Brother Luke's troubled gaze.

"One bad apple, Brother and a whole harvest lost."

And before Brother Luke could marshal his thoughts and present any more arguments, he was dismissed.

15

"I want us to run away."

Jimmy stared at Samuel. "Run away?"

"Yes. Conn managed it. We can too. I want out of here, Jimmy. I can't stay here any longer."

Jimmy's mind raced. His brother looked….haunted. He couldn't think of another word. Haunted. Almost as if he were sick again, Samuel's face was pale, his eyes were shadowed.

"Father will come for us."

Samuel exploded. "Why would you think that? Why? We haven't had one letter from him. Not one and we've been here nearly two years! That's two years too long. And not one bloody letter, Jimmy." Samuel paced to and fro, his brother watching him with fearful eyes. "If Conn can make it, so can we." He repeated and stood, hands on his hips, resolute and unrelenting.

Jimmy's mouth went dry. His tongue flicked nervously between his lips and he struggled to find the right words. Or any words. "I….I don't know."

"Why don't you know? Do you like it here, Jimmy? Do you?"

"No! I hate it."

Samuel glared impatiently. "So what's the problem?"

"Father." Jimmy raised troubled eyes to Samuel's hard ones. "He said he'd come for us. He promised."

"He promised he'd write, too" Samuel was unwavering." Where are his bloody letters, Jimmy? And what if we're separated? It could happen, you know." He saw the tears fill Jimmy's eyes.

"No." the boy whispered.

"Yes, it could. What if someone takes me and doesn't want you. What then, Jimmy? Huh?"

"I don't know!"

At the end of his tether, Jimmy shoved himself away from the bench he was leaning on, willing the tears not to fall. He dashed at his eyes in anger, angry at himself for crying, at his brother for everything else. They were only yards apart from each other in the barn yet the distance between them increased with every word.

"I know why you're like this." Samuel said harshly. "It's Molly, isn't it? You don't want to leave her behind."

Until Samuel said it, Jimmy wouldn't have thought so but as soon as the words were spoken he realised the truth of them. He lifted his chin. "She's our friend."

Samuel gave a bitter laugh. "She's your friend."

"She'd be yours too if you let her."

"I know who our mother is." Samuel saw the shock on his brother's face but he couldn't stop himself. "You might have forgotten her but I haven't."

Jimmy stepped forward, his face red. "Take that back."

"No." Samuel held Jimmy's stare.

With a cry, Jimmy launched himself at Samuel who was taken by surprise at the attack and the effort it took to hold his brother off. After some furious wrestling he finally managed to throw Jimmy down on the hay strewn floor, keeping him there by pushing a knee onto his chest.

"For god's sake, Jimmy, what's the wrong with you?"

"It's you, Sam. You're wrong. Let me up." He struggled against his brother's weight. "Let me up!" he demanded again and Samuel stood, freeing Jimmy as they glowered at each other.

The door to the barn swung open and Will's head poked round it. He smiled at seeing them, wandered in. "There you are. I've been looking for one of you." Will grinned. "They reckon trouble comes in….." his voice trailed off into uncertainty. "What's up?"

"Ask Sam." Jimmy spat and ran out, the barn door banging shut behind him.

"Samuel?"
The boy drew in a shaky breath. "Leave it, Will. It's not important."

"I've never seen you two like this before."

"I said, leave it!"

And with that Samuel also stormed out of the barn leaving Will frowning after him.

"What the hell's going on?"

It had been a long day in the kitchen at Broadgreen House but Cook had finally told Molly she could go to bed and here she was, brushing her dark curls, humming away to herself wondering if Jimmy would turn up tonight.

When Aunt Mabel wrote asking for Molly to join her in the new country, the girl had one regret, Ben, the baby brother she missed with all the pieces of her heart. Jimmy was gentler than her brother but there was something about his smile which reminded Molly forcefully of Ben.

The brush snarled in her hair and she tutted, was picking at the tangle when someone knocked on her door. Still with the hairbrush caught up in tangles, she opened the door. "'Bout time you showed up. I thought you'd forgotten me." Molly's eyes widened in surprise as she realised she was looking at an unsmiling face. "Sam! I mean, Samuel. Come in."

He didn't move. "I want to talk to you but not in there. I'll meet you out under the big oak tree."

"Wait a mo." Molly pulled at the brush, grimacing as it yanked out a chunk of her hair when it finally pulled free.

"I'm not talking to you in there."

Molly was astonished. "Why not? What's wrong with it?"

Samuel didn't reply, he slid into the shadows, headed towards the oak tree. Of half a mind to leave him, Molly closed the door. Curiosity got the better of her though and she hastily bundled her hair under her nightcap before grabbing a warm shawl for round her shoulders.

She saw Samuel's dark shape against the big oak tree and casting glances all around to make sure no one was about Molly stood in the shadows with him.

"So what's all this about, then? Where's Jimmy?"

"He's not here."

The words were out of his mouth before Samuel realised the inanity of them. Sure enough Molly picked up on it. She gave a laugh that grated on his ears.

"Yeah, well I can see that for meself, can't I? Why isn't he here?"

she demanded.

With Molly standing in front of him, Samuel began to wish he hadn't been so impulsive. Everything he wanted to say had gone from his brain.

A cool breeze picked up dry oak leaves off the ground and swirled them around their feet. Molly pulled her shawl closer around herself and shivered. "What do yer want, Samuel? I can't be standing about here all night."

"I want to take Jimmy with me and run away," he blurted out, instantly regretting his honesty. After a second's thought though Samuel realised he might not like Molly but she'd done nothing to prove she couldn't be trusted.

On her part Molly wished she could read the boy's face. All she could see of him was his shadowy outline. "Why tell me?"

"He doesn't want to go."

"Why not?"

There was such a long silence Molly thought Samuel wasn't going to answer her. She opened her mouth to repeat her question impatiently when he spoke again, so quietly she had to strain to catch his words.

"He doesn't want to leave you." Samuel heard her intake of breath.

"Well, what can I do about that?"

"You can tell him not to keep visiting you."

To buy herself some time Molly shifted her shawl over her head, held it tightly against her throat. "Can't we talk inside? I'm bleedin' freezin' out here."

But Samuel didn't move. "Will you tell him?" he demanded

"No."

"You have to!"

Molly caught the despair in the boy's voice. "I'm sorry Samuel but I like Jimmy, too. And I think he needs me. He misses his mum."

Silence.

Molly heard only the shifting of the wind on the branches above them. "Samuel?" she said softly.

"You are not our Mam." His voice was shaky.

"I know that. But I could be your sister?" Molly waited. "Samuel?"

He must have moved closer to her for his voice trembled against her ear. "We had a sister. She died."

Molly heard soft footfalls moving quickly away among the leaves. She called again, softly, urgently, "Samuel?"

But he'd gone.

***

The early morning light danced on the river which since the storm had gained so much more land that Will was now able to sit in the willow tree and dangle his feet in the water.

He'd left Samuel and Jimmy to themselves over the past weeks unable to know what to say anymore. He'd tried talking to an angry looking Samuel then an upset Jimmy but neither would speak of the other or tell him what the argument was about.

Will kicked his feet against the trunk disconsolately. No Mick or Conn, new boys arriving almost weekly after the terrible autumn and winter. The only silver lining Will could see was the continuing absence of Brother Donatus and Brother Jonas from their dormitory. Well, it was a silver lining for their dormitory, he thought, not for the new boys.

He leaped lightly down into the water and took his time gathering up a pocketful of nice, flat stones. He squinted across the river and took aim, skimming each stone skillfully across the top of the water. He tried not to think about those frightened new boys. Nothing he could do about it. They'd just have to do what the rest of them did and find their own way through it all.

It wasn't just the Orphanage which had changed, either, Will thought. Samuel was almost unrecognisable from the wary, withdrawn boy he'd first been. As much as Will liked him, he was a bit afraid of Samuel nowadays.

Quick to anger, grown hard and sardonic, no one crossed the oldest Brodie boy if they could help it. If Samuel didn't have such a sense of right, Will thought he would have made the worst bully ever. Thankfully, though, he never picked on the weak or helpless. He was dismissive of weakness but that was as far as he went. Still his forbidding expression and brusque manner could be as intimidating as any show of violence.

Best leave him to whatever was eating him, Will thought, he'd come round eventually.

He pulled back his arm, let another stone fly and watched with satisfaction as it skipped ten times before sinking.

"Not bad. You'll be as good as me, soon."

Speak of the devil Will thought as Samuel sauntered up to him, tossing a thin, round stone from hand to hand as he walked.

"How'd you know I was here?" Will asked.

"Didn't. Just couldn't sleep, thought I'd take a walk." He turned the stone round and round in his fingers. "Nice to see you're getting a bit of practice in. I said you'll be as good as me but……" Samuel shook his head in mock sadness.

"You're all talk, Brodie. Beat ten."

"Easy." Samuel stood beside Will on the riverbank. "Gimmie a challenge why don't you?"

They shared a grin, their stances identical as each boy measured the distance across the water and the weight and shape of their stone. Samuel threw first. He shaded his eyes as they both counted, "…seven, eight, nine, ten..eleven.."

Will grimaced as Samuel crowed. He held up a hand.

"My turn. Watch and learn, Samuel. Watch and learn."

Spitting on his hands for luck, Will rubbed his palms together. He set his feet, turned his arm over a couple of times.

"Maybe you should just admit I've won." Samuel chided. "Save yourself the pain of trying and failing."

Will ignored him, focussed completely on the river and the stone in his hand. His arm went back. Pause. Then Will skimmed. Again, they counted under their breath together.

"….ten, eleven, twelve, thirteen."

Will didn't crow, not straight away. He looked at Samuel, trying to keep his face straight and almost managed it. "Thirteen. Did ya count them? Thir-teen. What did you get?" Will pretended to think hard. "Eleven, wasn't it? That's right. Eleven." Will shook his head sadly. "Maybe with a bit more practice…." He let the sentence hang between them unfinished until Samuel laughed, looking less careworn than he had for ages. Pleased to hear his friend laughing Will continued to mock him until the older boy threw up his hands in surrender.

"All right. You win. Happy?"

"Yep."

Samuel plonked himself down on the stones, letting his face fall back to watch the sun peek over the hills and Will throwing the last of his stones. After another couple of skims – neither as good as the winning one – Will joined Samuel. Together they looked out over the water.

"What's wrong with you and Jimmy?"

Samuel closed his eyes and his mouth turned down, all good humour vanished.

"Nothing."

"Don't give me that shit. I'm not stupid. Jimmy cried himself to sleep last night and he hasn't cried forever." Will faced the other boy determined. "We're friends, aren't we?"

"Yeah."

"Then tell me."

There was a pause as Samuel dragged his legs up and rested his arms over his knees. Keeping his eyes firmly to the front, he mumbled something indistinguishable. All Will could make out were the words, 'Molly' and 'out of here.'

"What? I can't hear you."

"It makes no difference to anything."

"It does when you two aren't speaking to each other."

Turning his head to lay his cheek on his arm Samuel sighed. "I want outta here, Will."

"We all do. Christ, I've been here most of my life! But if no one takes us, we leave to work. That's what I'm holding out for." Will played distractedly with the stones. "Five more years, I'll be gone."

"Five more years?" Samuel was incredulous. "Jesus, five more years and I'll have hung myself if I'm still here!"

Will tried to find their usual turn of black humour to answer him. He wracked his brains uselessly for five years was a bloody long time. Instead, he shoved himself up onto his feet. "Look, talk to Jimmy. He's miserable. You're miserable. We're all bloody miserable."

Samuel lobbed a stone into the water. "You're such a bloody nag."

"And you're pissing everyone off. Even Rainey's better liked than you."

Samuel scowled at that. "That's not fair."

"True, though." Will told him. "I think only the bastards Donatus and Jonas are hated more than you. And even then….."

That got the response Will was after. Suddenly Samuel was on his feet, heat in his face, mouth open to argue the toss. Will grinned, wagged a finger. "Got you."

He laughed and there was an appreciable pause before Samuel laughed too but when he did, it was genuine and Will offered up a silent thank you to whoever was listening to them and watching them. He wondered if it was Big John.

As the two boys made their way back across the fields towards the Orphanage, they noticed a farm cart and two horses being driven towards the main doors.

"He's early. Someone else looking for help?" Samuel suggested to Will's unconcerned shrug.

It appeared that Samuel was right though for as the boys worked out in the fields that day, the man with the battered farm hat seemed to be watching them. When Samuel and Kip fetched the cows in for milking, he was leaning on the fence near the barn and while they milked the cows, he wandered in, asked them some questions and wandered out again.

"Whose he?" Kip asked.

"Dunno." Samuel replied. "But he looks like a gruff old bugger."

When the chores were over for the day and the boys went into for supper, everyone whispering excitedly that one of them could be the lucky, chosen one. Samuel had gone out to the dunny and when he returned he saw the man disappear into Father Aherne's office, Brother Donatus following.

Samuel checked no one was looking at him and slipped quietly along the corridor. The door into Father Aherne's office wasn't shut. Samuel edged quietly along to an alcove beside it, tucked himself behind the curtain and listened avidly, hoping Will's chance had come. How he'd like to take that news to him!

"I'd take an older boy but my wife wants someone younger." The man was saying. "Has to be used to hard work."

Father Aherne's amusement came through his voice. "You can be sure, Mr Benn that our boys learn the benefits of hard work. Of course, boys will always complain but on the whole they're a good lot."

John Benn grunted. "Well, I told you the boy I liked the look of Father. Samuel, was it?"

Samuel froze in his hiding place.

"Yes, Samuel Brodie." There was a weighted pause. "I have to be honest with you, Mr Benn and warn you that Samuel Brodie is a troubled boy."

"Is that so?"

"A troublemaker." That came from Brother Donatus. "From the first day he arrived here. I don't know how often he's had to be disciplined." Donatus' harsh voice was unrelenting. "The younger boys fear him, the older ones dislike him. Maybe there was another boy who you noticed today?"

Samuel heard a chair leg scrape on the wooden floor of the study. He burned with anger at Brother Donatus's lies. After a moment or two, Samuel realised the men were still talking and he was shocked to hear his brother's name.

"… young James Brodie." Brother Donatus was saying. "A good lad, wouldn't you say so, Father?"

"Indeed I would. Different to his brother. Much different."

Samuel's hands began to shake.

"Wouldn't it be cruel to separate brothers?" There was hesitancy in the farmer's voice. "Are they close?"

Brother Donatus made a dismissive noise. "Not at all. In fact, I would go as far to say that James would welcome the opportunity to get away from his brother. It would be the making of him."

The shaking reached Samuel's legs and a strange ringing noise sounded in his ears. He was struggling to breathe as he forced himself to listen on.

"Well, it would be nice to think the boy was getting the benefit from the start.' John Benn said. "I'd like to take him today if that's possible. I don't like being away from the farm for too long."

"No problem at all, Mr Benn. Brother Donatus, if you wouldn't mind bringing Jimmy to us?"

"It would be my pleasure, Father."

Brother Donatus had hardly moved one step when a boy came screaming at him from the corridor.

"You bastard! You bloody bastard!" Samuel launched himself at Brother Donatus and they crashed heavily to the ground. "You can't take Jimmy! You can't!"

Father Aherne leapt to his feet and John Benn watched in horror as the boy, incoherent with rage, attacked Brother Donatus. The Brother was no match for Samuel's out of control fury.

It took John's intervention to drag Samuel off Brother Donatus long enough for the man to get to his feet. Together they restrained the sobbing boy who fought with every bit of strength he possessed, curses falling from his lips, his eyes wild. Brother Donatus wore a cut above one eye and a bleeding lip before he finally managed to take control of Samuel. "I'll take him, shall I Father?"

The boy was dragged out of the room. John could hear him yelling all the way as Father Aherne gestured him back into his seat. "That's who you'll be saving young Jimmy from, Mr Benn. A wild boy, indeed."

The farmer looked back out into the empty corridor which still echoed with Samuel's rage. "What will you do to him?" he asked as the boy's yells were finally cut off.

"Oh, he has to be punished, of course, Mr Benn. Spare the rod and spoil the child. But we never punish unduly. Suffice to say, young Samuel Brodie will be a wiser boy after the event." Father Aherne was comfortably seated behind his desk once more. "Now, shall we have a look at the paperwork?"

Turning his attention back into the room, John shuffled his chair closer to the desk.

In the smallest cell Brother Donatus lifted the whip once more, thrashed it across Samuel's hunched body.

"You'll be in here till you rot, Brodie." Brother Donatus hissed softly. "Think Father Aherne will want to see you after that outburst? You'll be all mine."

Samuel grunted with effort, lifted his face. With all the strength he could muster, he spat into Brother Donatus's smirking face and then cringed back as he was flogged again and again.

Up in their dormitory the boys heard the shouts and the slamming doors.

"What's going on?" Jimmy asked.

Kip leaned over the stairwell, trying to see or hear anything.

"I dunno. Someone's been taken away for a thrashing." He pulled back from the stair rail, hissed at them all. "Someone's coming!" at the same moment Jimmy realised Samuel was missing.

"Where's Sam?" he asked. "Will, have you seen Sam"

Before Will could answer, Brother Donatus appeared in the doorway. Every boy took note of the split lip and eye. Jimmy felt a rush of alarm.

"James Brodie, you're to come with me."

Jimmy didn't move. "Why?"

"Don't ask questions, boy. Father Aherne wants to see you."

Before he followed, Jimmy exchanged a meaningful glance with Will.

"Brother Donatus, have you seen Sam?" Jimmy thought he hadn't been heard. He spoke a little louder. "Brother Donatus? Did you hear me? I asked if…."

"I heard you. And yes, I've seen your brother." He gave Jimmy such a darkly mocking look the boy lost his courage, asked no more questions as he followed meekly behind.

At the door to Father Aherne's office, Brother Donatus stood back shooting Jimmy a look the boy couldn't interpret as he gestured and said, "After you."

Samuel was pacing his cell. It hurt too much to sit or lie down but he couldn't settle anyway. Back and forth he paced, round and round, his mind whirling.

When the knock sounded on the door he thought he had imagined it and paced on. It came again, this time with a voice saying, "Samuel, are you in there?"

Samuel moved as quickly as he could to the door, leaned against it. "Yes. Will, yes! Where's Jimmy?"

"Why are you in there? Did you give Brother Donatus a hiding?"

"Never mind that now. Where's Jimmy?"

"Bastard Donatus has just taken him into Ahearn's office."

Will heard a low moan. He checked the corridor, pressed closer to the door. " Samuel. Are you all right?"

"Will, can you get the key? I need to get out."

"I don't know if…" Will's voice broke off hastily. "I'll be back."

Samuel slammed his shoulder repeatedly into the door, until he slid to the floor where he sat, rocking backwards and forwards.

In spite of all Will's best efforts it wasn't until the Orphanage slept that he managed to get the key to Samuel's cell. As soon as he pushed the cell door in, Samuel grabbed him, Will utterly taken aback by the desperation in the bigger boy's face.

"Where's Jimmy? Will, where's my brother?"

the words stuck in Will's throat. He tried to speak, couldn't and Samuel shoved him aside.

"Samuel, for God's sake…"

To Will's horror Samuel went straight to Father Ahearn's office. Pausing briefly to press his ear against the door, Samuel walked in and immediately strode to the big desk, began to shuffle through all the paperwork on the desk.

"Jimmy's gone, hasn't he? That farmer…?"

"What are you looking for?"

"Something, bloody anything to tell me where he's taken Jimmy."

Samuel stopped his furious search to look at Will. "I'm going after him."

"To do what?"

"I don't Ladino it if you think I'm staying here while my brother is taken away…" Samuel couldn't continue. He clamped his lips together, picked up another pile of papers. He skimmed them, chucking the useless ones onto the floor, heedless of the mass. Will hovered the doorway, reluctant to invade Father Ahearn's privacy but after listening to Samuel's fevered, "Where the hell is it?" He gave in, began to help.

"I can't see a bloody thing." Will hissed.

Samuel lit the candle in the holder. "Better?"

The top of the desk yielded nothing. Together, they knelt behind the desk, began to attack the drawers. All opened but the top right hand one. Samuel yanked at it.

"Damn it!" he lost his temper, tugged and tugged at the resisting drawer until Will pushed him to one side.

"Let me."

"It's locked."

"I know." Will scrabbled around the top of the desk for a letter opener.

"What are you doing, Will?"

Not bothering to reply, Will concentrated, tongue poking out between his teeth. After a few moments something clicked. Will grinned, pulled the drawer open.

Samuel gaped. "How the hell….?"

"Long story."

Heads together they emptied the contents of the drawer onto the floor. Samuel grabbed a bundle of letters. "Hey, these are Jimmy's letters to Father." He frowned in confusion as his eyes fell on another, bulkier pile, the top one addressed to him and Jimmy.

Slowly, Samuel undid them all, opened the first one with shaking fingers.

'My dear sons,

Tomorrow I am to see the mine manager here in Blackball. I am hopeful of work as the mine is busy. I think you would both like it here in Blackball. The hills are on top of us and the forest stretches for miles. Imagine the fun you would have.

I've enclosed money with this letter. As you see, it's a lot of money but it was given to me for you boys and I would rather you have it to buy what you need. Save two pounds for when I can write and say I have a place for us all.

I'll write again soon.
Your loving Father'

Will had been hunting through the other drawers. He gave a soft crow of success, held a form in his hand. "Got it, Samuel! He's gone to Murchison with John and Emily Benn. You'll be able to……" Will became aware of Samuel's frozen stillness. "Samuel….?"

"The old bastard kept his letters."

"What?"

Samuel raised his face. "Aherne. Our Father has written to us all this time. Look." He held the parcel under Will's nose. "But Aherne kept them and didn't send ours… Jimmy's, I mean." Samuel took the letters they wrote, the later ones Jimmy did alone and stroked them. "And Father sent money, Will. We never saw it, did we?"

Will would rather Samuel raved and stormed. Instead his voice was steady, his eyes dry and when he looked at the other boy Will thought how much older Samuel looked. Only his hands betrayed him, trembling as he tucked both lots of letters away in his jacket.

"Where's the form?" Samuel asked.

Will handed it to him and that, too Samuel folded away as he spied a few coins in the letter drawer. He grabbed those thinking they were probably his and Jimmy's anyway.

Samuel stared around the room. "I'm done here." Turning to Will he implored, "Come with me. We'll find Jimmy and go, somewhere. Anywhere. Anywhere that isn't here." Will's eyes widened and Samuel gripped his shoulder urgently. "We'll get work. You don't have to stay here, Will. They never brought Conn back, did they?"

After an internal debate, Will shook his head. "Thank for the offer, Samuel but no. I'll stay." Surprising himself as much as Samuel with these words.

"Why?"

Will shrugged. "Dunno. Maybe, better the devil you know?" He gave Samuel a small smile. "I'm not brave like you. Like Conn. And anyway, I'll stay, tidy up here a bit, lock your cell door and maybe that will give you a bit more time to get away."

They were unable to break their gaze.

"Thank you." Samuel said huskily. "For tonight. For..." he laboured to find the right words to express just how much Will meant to Jimmy and him and failed. He dug into his pocket, passed over a couple of the coins but Will refused to take them.

"You'll need it. Just bugger off. I'll be glad to see the back of you."

And that was the best gift Will could have possibly given, Samuel thought as he disappeared out the window and into the shadows of the night. The black humour they used to survive gave him the grin he needed for courage.

Will waited at the window till Samuel was lost from sight before he let the curtain drop back down and faced the mess. Knowing he couldn't put it back exactly, he did his best. The key to the top drawer was missing, too. Father Aherne probably carried it with him.

Aware just how much time had lapsed, Will gave the room a final once-over before closing the door carefully behind him. As he moved down the corridor he checked his steps, thinking a shadow moved further on but as he stood there, senses tingling, nothing else stirred.

Releasing his held breath, Will walked softly on to the cells where the door to Samuel's lay open. He reached for the latch, pulled the door closed and turned the key in the lock.

"Where's Brodie?"

Will slowly turned and faced Brother Donatus.

"Where's. Brodie?" Brother Donatus's yellow eyes seared into Will.

"Dunno."

The slap across his face made Will gasp but he stood his ground, kept shaking his head.

"Then what were you doing in Father Aherne's study?"

Will aimed for nonchalance and lifted his shoulders in an offhand gesture. Brother Donatus dragged the boy behind him as he returned to the study. Shutting the door Brother Donatus immediately noticed the still burning candle, the candle Father Aherne was careful to snuff out every night. There was a messiness to the top of his desk which was out of character and the corner of a dropped piece of paper poked out from under the desk. He frowned, shoved Will in front of him. "What were you looking for in here?"

"Nothing." That earned Will another slap across his face.

"What. Were you. Looking for?"

Breathe, Will whispered to himself. In… out…. In ….out….

Brother Donatus looked closely over the desk and though he knew – oh, yes he knew! – that Will had been through things, he couldn't work out what the boy had been after.

"You know what I can do to you, boy." He hissed into Will's face The boy flinched. He managed to wrench himself free and backed towards the door, a hand behind him to find the door handle.

"I've had enough!" Will pointed at Brother Donatus, keeping his voice steady. "You won't touch me. You won't touch any of us again. I'm going to Father Aherne and if he won't listen, I'll tell someone. Anyone." Will talked desperately. The only other person outside the Orphanage he knew was Molly. But he'd tell her.

He scrabbled for the handle, found it but though it turned, the door wouldn't open. In a panic now, Will turned his back on Brother Donatus, tugged at the locked door, heard a low laugh behind him.

"I've got the key, Will. You're not going anywhere."

"Didn't you hear me?" Will demanded bravely. "Tomorrow, I'll tell. I'll bloody shout till someone listens!" A stab of pleasure hit Will for Brother Donatus was suddenly motionless. "No one gives a shit about us here" Will persisted. "But they would if they knew what you did." He gave Brother Donatus a smile shot through with triumph. "And Samuel is out there somewhere. You think he won't tell?" Will sneered.

The man's face remained shadowed until with a snake swift movement, Brother Donatus had Will back in his grip. Without another word he unlocked the study door and dragged Will to the cells. Opening the one where Samuel had been he shoved Will in before reaching up onto a high shelf where the Brothers kept the supplejack stick every boy dreaded.

Brother Donatus swung it round in his hand as Will lost all colour, receded further back into his cell until unable to go any further. "Shout all you like." Brother Donatus whispered. "You think anyone will hear you down here?"

Brother Donatus turned the lock on Will, replaced the stick and frowned. Where did Brodie go? Churning the thought over in his mind he returned to Father Aherne's room and circled it, thinking hard. It would only take one boy willing to risk reprisals to bring Brother Donatus's life crashing down around him. All his years in the church would count for nothing against such accusations. As he stared into the candle still burning, inspiration struck. He searched the paperwork on Father Aherne's desk. Where would Samuel be? Wherever his brother was. There was no sign of the form, nothing. The letters from Fraser Brodie to his sons and the boys' to their father were gone, too. Father Aherne had told Brother Donatus about the letters, showed him where they were kept locked away.

"I did think of burning them. "Father Aherne confessed. "But thought they may come in handy one day."

Donatus had agreed with the sentiment. He would have done the same.

But now, Samuel Brodie was out there with the letters and his hatred. Brother Donatus's pacing became increasingly agitated, his mind swirled uselessly, his own hatred of Will, of Samuel, of all the boys combined to bring him close to panic.

Breathing hard, thinking wildly, Brother Donatus stared into the candle flame. With a snarl he swept the desk clean, the candle falling among paperwork, catching it alight. Instinctively Brother Donatus lifted a heavy book to smother the flame but at the same moment another thought kicked in and instead of dowsing the fire, he took a step back, watched the flames leap from page to page on the floor. Dropping more paper into the small fire, he grabbed another candle and lit that. He opened a window to let the air circulate and feed the flames before leaving the room, locking the door behind him.

Moving quickly, Brother Donatus made for the cells. There was no sound from Will. In the next cell he kicked the blankets and bedding into a corner then knelt, set the candle against the lot, blowing on it, encouraging it to burn. As the flames took hold Brother Donatus smiled. Samuel Brodie, a known trouble maker escaped the Orphanage but not before setting it alight. Whenever he was caught, whatever he said could be easily discredited.

Smoke from the blankets filled the cell. Coughing, the Brother left the door open, paused at the locked one to whisper, "Sleep well, Will."

Brother Donatus took up his position in the dining room. He

would time his alarm just so.

And there would another nail hammered securely into the coffin of Samuel Brodie's reputation.

***

Molly had settled into her small bed with a sigh of relief. Cook had been crotchety and bad tempered from the moment she woke to the last minutes of the day, wearing all the kitchen staff out with her demands. Now, Molly was too tired to read or even lie there thinking. She blew the candle out and snuggled under the blankets. She was drifting off when the knock came. "Who is it?" she asked softly and received an indistinct mumble in reply.

Reluctant to leave her bed though she was, Molly slipped out and cautiously lifted the latch of her door and peeped out. Someone was standing there in the moonlight.

"Who are you? What do you want?"

"It's me, Samuel."

Molly pulled the door wide open. "Is something wrong with Jimmy?" Without giving the boy a chance to reply, she dragged him into the dairy, shut the door. "Gimmie me a sec and I'll light the candle."

"No. Don't." Samuel's hand clamped down on Molly's as she reached for the matches.

"What's wrong?"

"Jimmy's been taken away." Molly strained to hear his words. "A farmer from Murchison."

"Oh, Samuel…. When?"

"Today. I'm going after him."

Stunned, Molly sat down on her bed. "Why?"

Samuel shifted uneasily. "I can't leave him, can I? And I can't stay without him." He began to pace. "I only came to tell you because Jimmy liked you. I didn't want you to wonder why he wasn't visiting anymore."

Molly drew her legs up, covered herself more warmly in her shawl.

"How will yer find him?"

"There's one road to Murchison. I've got the address where the people live." Even though Molly couldn't see the gesture, Samuel shrugged. "I'll find him."

"And then?"

"I dunno. But at least I'll have found him." He was eager to be gone now he'd done this duty. "Well, I gotta go."

Molly slid off her bed. "Wait a mo."

She scrabbled about under her bed, pulled out a small box, threw the lid open and pushed things aside till she found it, a little purse with coins in it. She grabbed Samuel's hand and tipped most of them into it.

"No." Samuel shoved them back at Molly who wouldn't take them. "This is yours. I didn't come here to take your money!"

"I know." Molly held Samuel's clenched fist between her two warm hands. "It's for Jimmy, really. He'd want you with him, Samuel."

She could hear his unsteady breathing and when he spoke, tears edged his words.

"I'll pay you back."

"If you want."

"I will!"

The boy reached for the door and pulled it open, checked the moonlit night before looking back over his shoulder to her.

"Thanks."

The horses were labouring on the uphill slope.

"C'mon. C'mon."

John Benn clicked his teeth at the horses, his voice soft, encouraging them on. He turned to the silent boy sitting with him on the cart. Between them sat a handsome sheepdog, Wolf, tongue lolling, ears pricked. Jimmy eyed him warily.

John gestured with his head to the left ahead of them. "Gaukroger's Hotel."

A sturdy two story wooden building with a veranda running along the front sat on the left of them. Numerous outbuildings surrounded the property, the substantial barn to the south set amidst well laid out paddocks, young oak trees growing behind the homestead. Yet, all the miserable little boy saw was an imposing building with the setting sun casting pinky light over its face.

"We'll stop here to rest the horses overnight. And you'll be hungry." John Benn smiled through his beard but the boy didn't respond beyond a nod.

John wasn't a garrulous man at the best of times. Quiet and unassuming, most people meeting him for the first time thought him shy which he wasn't. He just didn't have small talk nor did he consider it a good use of time that could be spent on his farm in the Matakitaki Valley.

He cast a sideways glance at Jimmy, pale and unhappy beside him and thought he'd rather the boy was happy as not. John accepted Jimmy would be feeling lost, he would certainly be missing his brother even if that brother was a bully and made his life difficult so, unable to articulate his thoughts, John wisely decided not to try. There was nothing he could say or do to make this unhappy boy feel any better so he kept things as natural as he could and hoped things would improve given time.

He wasn't often away from his farm and even more rarely away from Murchison. On the times he had to go to Nelson he chose to

stay here at Gaukroger's. He'd always enjoyed the company
of Charles Gaukroger who died, John thought hard, 1892…? Must
have been. It was that hard-working, slow-talking man who built up
the farm, then the first hotel on the site. Charles and John shared the
hard slog of men building a farm from the bush clad country.

The older man had sold John a fine ram for his new sheep stock
and Wolf was descended from the first sheepdog puppy Charles gave
to the eager man with the drive to hammer out farmland in the
unrelenting hills of Murchison.

When ill health finely got the better of Charles his son, also named
John, took over the running of the hotel and farm with the help of his
sister Libby and then his wife, Anne. John Benn remembered talk of
Libby.   Small, darkly beautiful and intense, she'd married the
famous George Moonlight – prospector, gold digger, hotel keeper,
Mayor of Murchison when it was named Hampden, a fine man,
much missed in Murchison.

Lost in his ghosts, John didn't realise the horses had come to a stop
outside the hotel. He blinked, saw Jimmy watching him quizzically
and gave a shamefaced smile. "Lost in my thoughts, Jimmy."
A stable boy came out and led them to the barn. John unhitched the
cart and stabled the horses, Wolf sniffing around at their feet and
scaring the tabby farm cats which lived in the barn keeping the
population of rats and mice down.
When it came to grooming John said, "We look after our own." He
tipped his hat at the stable lad who gladly scarpered away to his
supper as John picked up a curry comb. This he handed to Jimmy
who took it silently and began to brush the horses down while the
farmer saw they had food and water. Wolf kept so close to Jimmy
the boy kept tripping over him and John wondered if the big dog
picked up on the boy's unhappiness or was just keeping an eye on a
strange, new creature. Wolf's wagging tail swept the barn floor
clear of fallen hay and feed and when the boy reached out a tentative
hand the big dog licked his fingers. For the first time, Jimmy smiled.
Feeling brave, he began to brush the horse's neck gently with one

hand, patted it just as softly with the other.

John picked up a second brush. "Like this, Jimmy." And he began to brush the other horse vigorously, pleased to see the boy copy him instantly.

"Do they have names?" Jimmy asked, uttering his first words since leaving Father Aherne's office.

"The black-maned boy here is Hardy. The chestnut? She's called Flip." John finished the feeding. He stood in front of Hardy, stroking the horse's velvety nose. "They've put in the miles, both of them. Seen us through a lot of hard times." Now he dug into his pocket, pulled out two sugar cubes, gave one to each horse. "That's why this boy's called Hardy. He was born in the middle of our hardest winter. We didn't think he'd survive. But you did, didn't you, boy?"

Jimmy laughed out loud when the horse gave a soft whinny as if in reply. John smiled, too. "I don't know about you, Jimmy but I could eat a dead dog backwards, as my old dad used to say."

Jimmy put the curry comb down. "Does that mean you're hungry?"

"Very." He pointed to the dog. "Wolf. Stay. Come on, Jimmy. We'll eat then put our heads down. Mrs Gaukroger keeps comfortable beds." John walked off, stopping when he realised Jimmy hadn't moved. "Don't you want supper?"

Hesitating Jimmy bit his lip, then his words came out in a rush. "Mr Benn, could I stay out here? With Wolf? And the horses? I…. I'd like be with them."

John studied the anxious young face. "Well, I don't see why not. I'll send the stable boy back out with your supper." He frowned slightly. "Do you mean to sleep out here, too?" He was surprised when the boy accepted eagerly. John thought for a moment or two. "Then I'll see you in the morning."

Jimmy found his tongue. "Thank you."

John tipped his hat as he walked towards the hotel. Jimmy copied the gesture, thinking it looked very smart.

He worked at grooming the horses until the stable boy arrived with his plate of supper. As hungry as he was Jimmy shared his meal with Wolf, sitting together in the hay under Hardy's head, listening to the soft whickering of the horses, breathing in their warm, comforting smell.

With a huge sigh, Jimmy pushed his empty plate away, lay on his back and tried to get his mind around everything that had happened today. Wolf whined and to Jimmy's surprise and pleasure, the big dog lay beside him, pushing his nose under his hand. He patted Wolf, enjoying the feel of the dog's warm body breathing against his. Turning over onto his side, Jimmy put his head on one arm, played idly with Wolf's ears with the other.

"What about Sam, Wolf?" he whispered. "Sam must have heard I was chosen….. he must be so worried….. I'm glad, glad to be gone from the Orphanage but I couldn't say goodbye to anyone. To Will…. I miss Will already. And Sam. I miss him most of all." Warm tears slid down Jimmy's cheeks. He buried his face in Wolf's ruff. Mr Benn seemed nice. He didn't want to seem ungrateful. "But….. what about Father? He won't know I've gone, Wolf! And I… I can't visit Mam's grave anymore."

At that Jimmy gave into his unhappiness, Wolf whining and licking his face until the exhausted boy had cried himself to sleep.

John checked on Jimmy before turning in for the night. He held the lantern carefully, lifting it to see where the boy was and found him, curled in the hay in Hardy's stall, Wolf beside him. The big dog wagged his tail at his master's approach but didn't move.

John knelt down, patted Wolf and noticed the dried trail of tears on Jimmy's dirty face. Even in sleep the boy looked unhappy. Sitting back on his haunches, the man thought deeply. He needed help on the farm. He and Emily had no children and a farmer farmed for his sons. Emily begged John to adopt a boy and he had resisted until he felt the stiffening of the joints in his hands and fingers, his back and knees – all evidence of hard work in all weathers. So, to Emily's joy John said, yes. All right. He'd go to

Nelson, find a suitable boy. In the abstract it seemed such a simple solution and that was exactly what he had done. But…. He gazed down on the young, sleeping face. A flesh and blood boy was quite a different proposition. He was a personality in his right and he wasn't just help, he was a responsibility, John's responsibility as much as any child of his own blood would have been. He hadn't expected that somehow. To feel so strongly for a child he'd just met, hadn't expected that at all.

Rising carefully, John grabbed a blanket off the back of the cart, tucked it round Jimmy.

"Look after him, Wolf," he told the big dog softly.

***

John Gaukroger hadn't wanted to be on the road so late but the meeting in Wakefield had dragged on interminably and now it was the small hours as he rode towards Foxhill and home.

Everything was quiet. Occasionally a dog would bark on hearing horse's hooves on the dirt road so late at night but otherwise it was John, his horse and the soft sounds of night under a full moon. Mind you, full moon or not, John Gaukroger prided himself on finding his way on the darkest night.

He lifted his eyes to check the way ahead and caught movement on the roadside. It wasn't unusual for stock to end up on the road but as John peered through the moonlight he realised it wasn't a four legged animal but a two legged one. Again, men walking for work or farm to farm was a common enough sight yet as he drew nearer there was something about this shape that puzzled him. It carried no swag bag and it didn't seem adult sized.

Definitely curious now, John held the reins more determinedly, used his legs to force the horse into a trot. The figure kept moving as he came alongside it, glancing down at a boy faltering with tiredness.

John brought his horse back to walking pace. "You all right, son?"

"Yes, sir."

"Where you headed at this time of night?" No reply. "I don't mean to pry but it's late to be out walking."

Samuel stopped, breathing hard. "My father's on the Coast working. I'm on my way to him." He began walking again.

"That's a long journey for a boy." John mused and received only a shrug in reply.

"I got a ride with a man from Richmond to Wakefield. I'm fine, sir." The words were no sooner out of Samuel's mouth than he stumbled over a large stone.

John dismounted, took the horse's bridle in one hand and walked beside Samuel companionably. "Look, son. I own a hotel a few miles up the road. How about I give you a ride that far at least? You can sleep in my barn, rest yourself up."

Samuel stopped walking, looked the stranger up and down, seeing an average height, solidly built man with honest eyes. He looked at John as intently as John regarded him.

After an appreciable pause, Samuel said, "That's kind of you, sir. Thank you."

"Well, it's not like it puts me out any." Samuel caught the humour in the voice. "Do you need a foot-up?"

The horse seemed enormous to the exhausted Samuel so he was grateful for the man's cupped hands under his foot as he pulled himself onto the saddle. Staring down at the ground suddenly a long way away, he made room as the man mounted lightly up behind him and picked up the reins. While Samuel gripped the pommel tightly in both hands and tried not to look down, the horse walked on once more.

"I'm Mr Gaukroger."

"Thank you for this ride, sir. I didn't realise how tired I was till I stopped walking."

"Usually it's just me and the horse heading home so a bit of new company is always welcome."

Samuel listened as the man chatted on. It seemed no time at all when John pointed to a handsome wooden building. "Home." He said and Samuel felt a pang as he heard the affection in the man's voice. Home meant that to him once.

Less than half an hour later Samuel sat at a big, well-scrubbed kitchen table eating hot, thick soup. As hungry as he was, he found it hard to keep his eyes open. A brief spurt of laughter and Samuel's eyes snapped open to find John Gaukroger looking down at him.

"You nearly ended up face first in your dish."

Samuel looked down at the empty bowl. He couldn't remember finishing the soup. Yawning, he gave John a sheepish smile. "Just tired."

"You surprise me."

John put a lantern in Samuel's hand, warning him to blow it out before sleeping and directed him towards the barn. "Sleep where you like, lad. There are a couple of bunk beds out in the back room if you'd like one."

The short walk in the cool night air was reviving so Samuel reached the barn wide awake again. He walked by a heavily laden farm cart that looked ready to be hitched up and taken and had a nosy poke around it until he discovered it had been expertly tied down.

As he quietly pushed open the barn doors, he heard a low growl and froze, not daring to move. Mr Gaukroger hadn't mentioned a dog! Samuel cautiously lifted the lantern, peered into the gloomy shadows of the barn. Two horses chomped hay in their stalls and it was from that direction the growl sounded. Not seeing a dog, Samuel stepped warily forward, saying softly, "I'm allowed to be here."

The low rumble sounded from the dark shadows once more and again, Samuel froze. "Mr Gaukroger said it was all right."

There was a sudden rustling of hay, a gasping of breath and a face peered round the wooden partition of the stalls to the boy holding the lantern.

"Sam?" The voice was incredulous. As incredulous as Samuel.

"Jimmy?!"

Before either boy could do anything else, Wolf erupted from Jimmy's side and stood, hackles raised, lips curled back in a snarl, growling at Samuel who swallowed hard and closed his eyes fearfully, waiting for the bite that never came as his brother said,

"Wolf, no!"

In three steps, Jimmy covered the space between them and Samuel pulled him into his arms. Jimmy clung, unable to believe that his brother was actually here with him.

"Where's the man who took you?"

"In the hotel."

"Why didn't he let you sleep there?" Samuel asked indignantly.

"I wanted to sleep out here." Jimmy smiled. "With Wolf and Hardy and Flip."

"Who?"

"The dog and Mr Benn's horses. I just like them."

Intuition flashed between them and Jimmy knew what Samuel's next question was going to be. "He's really nice, Sam. Mr Benn. He doesn't say much but he's kind."

They settled themselves back in the nest Jimmy had made for himself, Wolf sitting between them, happy now to acknowledge Samuel as friend.

"I didn't want to go." Jimmy caught the look on his brother's face, added, "I don't want to go but if I have to…." He held Samuel's look. "Then at least Mr Benn's nice." Jimmy smiled. "And I like his animals."

"Well, I guess that's good but Jimmy, Father won't know what's happened to you. To us."

"So? You were right, Sam. All along." Jimmy cuddled Wolf. "He dumped us and then forgot us."

Samuel fell over his words in his hurry to get them out. "No. I know I thought that but he didn't. Look here." Samuel yanked the letters out of his jacket, dumped them onto Jimmy's lap.

"What are these?"

"Father's letters." Jimmy picked one up, began to read as Samuel continued, "All of them, Jimmy. And these." Samuel held out the second bundle. "These are ours to him plus the ones you wrote on your own."

"Where….?"

"In Aherne's desk." Samuel said grimly. "Locked in a drawer. Me and Will found them looking for the papers to say where'd you'd been taken."

Dazed, Jimmy opened each letter, read the first couple of sentences. "I don't understand why Father Aherne would do this."

Samuel's laugh was bitter. Wolf raised his head enquiringly.

"There was money in some of the letters to us, Jimmy. Didn't get that either, did we?"

Although the question wasn't meant to be answered, Jimmy shook his head, his mind numb as he struggled with this knowledge.

Samuel gripped his brother's arm, excitedly, his eyes glowing in the light of the lantern. "But now we know where Father is. We can get to him, tell him everything. I bet he's been worried about not hearing from us."

"Maybe he thinks we've forgotten him?" Jimmy's eyes were anxious but Samuel could only agree.

"All the more reason why we have to get to him, then."

Jimmy held out the pile of Fraser's letters. "Can you read them to me, Sam? Please?"

They snuggled down together, Jimmy's head on the complaisant Wolf, his legs over his brother's as one by one, the sound of Fraser's words made them a family once more.

The lantern had been blown out, only moonlight shone through the cracks in the big doors and dirty windows. The boys heard scuffles which meant the farm cats were earning their keep. Wolf snored between them as they lay on their sides facing each other sleepily across him.

"Do you have a plan, Sam?"

"I do now."

"What?"

"Well, Father Aherne will look for me like he did for Conn and he'll know that I would have followed after you."

Sudden fear widened Jimmy's eyes. "Then he'll catch you."

"No. He won't. Listen, Jimmy. I'll be gone by the morning." Samuel was grinning into the dark, staring up at the endless ceiling, seeing only a brighter future for the first time in nearly two years. "I can hide away on your farmer's cart to Murchison. Once we're there, you'll be fine and I'll find work somewhere, anywhere for a few months, just long enough to earn a bit of money so we can get to Blackball where Father is. Easy."

Triumphantly Samuel turned looked at Jimmy. Both his brother and Wolf were sound asleep.

***

John was out at the barn just before dawn yet even in spite of the early hour he was surprised to see Jimmy was awake and grooming the horses, Wolf chasing one of the cats.

"Wolf, no!"

As the cat disappeared through the doors, Wolf, his tongue lolling sat at Jimmy's feet. John hid a smile.

"Morning, Jimmy. Ready for an early start, I see?"

"Yes, sir."

The change in the boy was startling. His eyes had lost their scared look and he smiled easily.

"Good. Now, Mrs Gaukroger has some breakfast for you. I've had mine. Why don't you run over and have it while I hitch up the horses?"

There was no hesitation from Jimmy this time. He shot off gladly while Wolf stood at the barn door whining after the boy.

John turned to his dog. "Thought I was your master?"

Wolf returned to John, licked his hand, but before long he had his nose poked back out through the door, waiting for Jimmy.

By the time Jimmy returned, his pockets full of breakfast for Samuel, John and Wolf were sitting on the cart, waiting for him.

Jimmy made a show of pushing something back under cover on the cart, managed to slip his brother food before clambering up beside John and Wolf.

"Is it far to Murchison, sir?"

"One more night on the road. I have a couple of things to deliver on the way." John clicked, the cart jerked as the horses pulled forward. "So," John turned to Jimmy. "You've all the time in the world to ask me anything you want to know."

"About the animals?"

"Yes, about the animals. And anything else you may want to know about Mrs Benn and myself or the farm."

"How old's Wolf?"

John Benn burst out laughing.

***

16

Emily glanced at the clock for the umpteenth time, chiding herself that time would not move more quickly just because she wanted it to. John and the boy would be here as soon as they could be. Until then… Well, until then Emily wandered aimlessly around their home.

Upstairs to the little room under the eaves she had prepared for the boy. She pulled the covers a little straighter. Would he like the quilt? She had made it herself but maybe he'd prefer blankets? A toy soldier sat on the pillow but perhaps it was too babyish, after all, she had no idea of the boy's age and John was keen on an older boy for the work. After painful indecision, she scooped the toy up and took it into the only other room at the top of the stairs.

She rarely came into this room. John never did. Inside it a rocking chair sat near an old wooden chest. As Emily lifted its lid, the dusky scent of rosemary wafted out and enveloped her. Carefully she tucked the toy soldier into a corner near a recently tied posy. She knew where it would be if it was wanted.

For a few moments Emily remained on her knees, head bent, lips moving through the prayer she had offered up every night since John left for Nelson. "Please, God let him love us. Let him be kind and hard-working and we will love him as if he was our own." She lifted her face, whispered, "Amen."

Unsteady hands brushed already immaculate hair back from her worried face. Would the boy think she was too old? She gave an impatient sound. It didn't matter what he thought, she scolded herself and marched out of the room, down the tiny set of stairs to the kitchen.

Here her glance fell once more on the clock and she hurriedly looked away, choosing instead to poke the woodstove's firebox. She lifted the lid on the fragrant meal keeping warm on the stovetop and also ran her hands lightly over the plates on the table. Perhaps they wouldn't want anything when they arrived. John had to stop at Tophouse on the way and would have undoubtedly been offered their usual kind hospitality but better safe than sorry.

Outside, the dogs barked and Emily stiffened. She moved swiftly through to the sitting room and peered through snowy curtains out into the dark night, straining every nerve and, yes there was the sound of the horses and the rumble of cart wheels.

She stood on the veranda as the cart pulled up, her hands clenching and unclenching as John climbed stiffly down from the seat. She could tell how tired he was by the stoop of his broad shoulders. He came straight to her, kissed her. "We made it home, mother."
Tears sparked in her eyes at the word. "You found a boy?"
"James Brodie. Jimmy. He's nine."
Emily's hands went to her trembling mouth. John took them, rubbed warmth back into them. "He's a nice boy who helps wherever he can and has a good heart."
Her eyes raked the cart for some sign of him. John drew her forward to where Jimmy lay curled up under the driver's seat, rolled up in a blanket and fast asleep.
Carefully John scooped the boy up into his arms and with Emily so close she was treading on his heels, he carried Jimmy up to the lovingly prepared room. Emily drew the covers back and as they tucked him in he gave a wordless mutter, pulled his hands up to his face and slept on. They heard claws on the stairs and Emily spun round to see Wolf walking in. "What's Wolf doing in the house?" She pointed back at the door. "Wolf, out!" she hissed but felt John's hand on her arm.
"Em. Wolf's taken to the boy and Jimmy to him. The lad's going to wake in a strange bed in a strange house. Maybe Wolf could stay so Jimmy will know he's with friends."
There was good sense in that so Emily bent to the big dog's ear and whispered, "You can stay but you are not to get up on the bed, Wolf. You hear me?" and she had to smile for Wolf cocked his head to one side as if he understood her every word.
Just as well Emily didn't look back for as soon as she and John were out of the room, Wolf leapt lightly up onto the bed to lie beside Jimmy.

Down in the warm kitchen, Emily fussed over the meal. "Wolf better not think he's allowed inside every day," she warned. "Do you want supper or did you eat at Tophouse?"

John yawned, shook his head. "I knew you'd be waiting. We watered the horses and came straight away. I'd like supper but I'll see to the horses first." He paused looked deeply into his wife's face, her glowing eyes. "Promise me you'll not lose your heart too quickly, Em. We don't know the boy."

"John Benn! I'm not some silly slip of a girl to lose my heart over a boy for nothing, which you should know better than any." She chivvied him out of the kitchen. "Go see to the horses. I'll have supper on the table when you're done."

And John left, thinking that in all ways that mattered, Emily was a girl about to lose her heart too quickly.

Hardy and Flip were stamping impatiently and John rubbed Hardy's ears as he took hold of the harness, led them towards the barn, his undiscovered stowaway still tucked away out of sight.

Hidden under the heavy canvas cover Samuel hadn't dared move. When the cart first came to a stop he listened to the conversation die away as Mr and Mrs Benn went into the house with Jimmy. Even then he didn't move.

After a while Mr Benn returned and Samuel remained quiet while the cart was unhitched in the barn and the horses groomed and stabled for the night. Finally the barn door was shut, the latch dropped down.

Samuel counted slowly up to a hundred five times. Only then did he move his cramped limbs, groaning as he clambered off the cart. He wasn't hungry as Jimmy had assiduously kept him fed but Samuel did have a raging thirst. He found a bucket of water kept near the horses and drank greedily, the water slopping from his hands onto his chest.

Tomorrow he would wait for Jimmy to bring him some food as they planned, then head for Murchison itself. He had to find a job. But for now, he settled once more into a nest rather than a bed, tired from the bone shaking two day journey.

***

Wolf woke Jimmy in the morning. The dog had heard John leave the house before dawn, heading out for the first day's farm work in nearly a week. Wolf wanted to be out there too but the boy slept on so the dog did, too.

A couple of hours later though, he heard his companions barking joyfully out in the paddocks and Wolf whined, dropped one mighty paw on the boy's chest bringing Jimmy bolt upright, gasping, wondering where he was as the dog leapt off the bed, disappeared down the steep stairs.

With a huge yawn Jimmy opened the little dormer widow above the head of his bed and leaned out in time to hear a woman scolding Wolf out of the house. Jimmy watched until the dog disappeared the farm track beside the barn. The barn….. where Samuel would be waiting for him.

The door to the bedroom opened and the woman walked in. She had grey streaked dark hair framing a friendly, anxious face. "Jimmy? I'm Emily Benn. Did you sleep well?"

"Yes, ma'am."

"Call me Mrs Benn, Jimmy. There's a bowl of warm water on the table." For the first time Jimmy noticed the small table against the wall opposite his bed. "I thought maybe you'd like a wash this morning and a bath tonight?" When he nodded, Emily relaxed a little. "I put out some other clothes for you, too." He looked to a neat pile on the end of his bed. "Right, well, I've your breakfast waiting for you when you come down."

She gave him a nervous, bright smile and left the room giving Jimmy time to really take in his surroundings. He hadn't slept in such a comfortable bed ever. Even the bed he and Samuel shared when Mam had been alive hadn't been as deep and warm.

Jimmy washed his face and hands, drying them on the towel left beside the bowl. He noticed a bit of embroidery on one edge and peered closely at it, making out a capital N. When his stomach gave a long, demanding growl Jimmy realised how hungry he was.

Quickly he put the new clothes on, marvelling at the feel of them, noticing a pair of boots, too. He slipped these on and though they were a bit too big he was amazed at how comfortable they were. Staring rapturously at his feet Jimmy bounced up and down a few times until a wonderful aroma found its way up the stairs. Sniffing hungrily he found his way down the steep stairs to the hallway as he followed the smell of breakfast to the kitchen.

There, Mrs Benn was frying something. She smiled at the sight of him and tipped the contents of the frying pan onto the plate ready set on the table, gesturing with her head for the boy to sit. She poured a glass of milk to go with his meal. "If there's anything you don't eat, you must tell me, Jimmy."

He shook his head, mouth crammed already full to bursting with sausage meat.

"Well, if there's something you like especially, tell me." Emily tried not to stare at the boy, busied herself at the sink while she spoke to him. "I'd like to cook you a welcome supper."

Chewing thoughtfully, Jimmy considered her offer. "I like treacle tart." He said and watched a delighted smile light Emily's face.

"Treacle tart happens to me one of my favourites, too. I'll make it for tonight. Would you like that?"

"Oh, yes, Mrs Benn. I haven't had treacle tart since Mam died." He added conversationally, surprised when Emily's eyes filled with tears. He stopped chewing in alarm. "Did I say something wrong?" he asked uncertainly.

"No, Jimmy. I… I was just thinking." Emily quickly turned away once more. "But, I hope you'll be happy here."

Jimmy managed to slip a sausage into one pocket and a chunk of new bread into the other while wondering how he could get some milk to Samuel. He looked around the kitchen, the woodstove, the wooden table wistfully. It all reminded him of what home had been.

In a short space of time he wiped his plate clean with the last crust from his bread.

"Can I go outside?"

"Of course. Mr Benn told me you're to get used to the place for a day or two so feel free to poke your nose in wherever you like." Emily smiled. "We expect boys to be nosy creatures."

Jimmy wiped his face on his sleeve, manners forgotten years ago as he pushed himself away from the table and slipped out the door. Emily picked up his breakfast things and washed them up at the sink. Under her breath she began to sing softly.

"About bloody time." Samuel grumbled as his brother found him, sitting on some bales of hay, kicking his heels.

"I couldn't rush, could I? Mrs Benn would be suspicious. Anyway, here." Jimmy passed Samuel breakfast. "I'll try and get some milk for you when….."

"Never mind that." Samuel cut in impatiently. "I've got to find my way into the town and find a job. And I've changed my name to Luke."

"Luke?"

"Just in case anyone asks questions about a missing boy named Samuel."

Jimmy gave Samuel an admiring look. "That's a good idea."

"No need to look so surprised." Samuel muttered in a disgruntled tone. "I'll try to get somewhere I can stay as well as work." He paused. "Are you sure you'll be all right here with these people?"

"Yes Sam. Look! New clothes!" Jimmy proudly strutted in front of his brother who begrudgingly admired them. "It's you I'm worried about. If someone from the Orphanage shows up they'll know what you look like. It won't matter what your name is."

Samuel stretched as he stood. "Don't go borrowing trouble."

"When will I see you again?"

"I dunno. If I can't get a job, sooner than you might think." He walked to the barn door. "Now, stick your head out and see if anyone's around."

"How will you know which direction from here?"

Samuel cuffed Jimmy playfully across the head. "I heard Mr

Benn talking to you from Foxhill to here, stupid. He told you all about the place, didn't he? Now, have a looksee."

Jimmy did as he was bid, peered cautiously around the door. "All safe."

"Right. See you sometime." Samuel paused, handed Jimmy half the bundle of Father's letters. "For you to read."

As soon as he saw Jimmy tuck them into his pocket, Samuel slipped round the barn door and jogged away leaving his brother to his new life and to discover his own.

18

Sergeant Burrell sighed as he shifted his weight back and forth across the balls of his wide, flat feet. It wasn't that he didn't like religious men or institutions but…. Actually, he amended honestly, it was. He disliked their smug self-righteousness, their indifference to any world beyond the bounded walls designated by the church.

He also disliked this man specifically. Father Aherne could speak seemingly without breathing, his soft voice reiterating over and over again the blamelessness of the Orphanage, how they knew the Brodie boy was trouble from his first day, that the rebuild would cripple them but they would do it, of course, as homeless, parentless boys needed care and the care they gave was exemplary.

After so long of this recitation, Sergeant Burrell lifted a meaty hand.

"If I could stop you there, Father." Father Aherne closed his mouth in surprise. "This isn't the first boy who's run from your Orphanage."

"Well, no. Some boys are unwilling to better themselves through the virtues of hard work and church going, Sergeant." The smugly superior look on the man's face annoyed the policeman.

"There are also boys who'd rather be whipped in our cells than taken back to your Orphanage, Father. I have often asked myself why the poor wee buggers would rather suffer that?"

Father Aherne met Burrell's sneer with one of his own.

"There will always be gossip, Sergeant. Surely it's your job to see through that to get to the truth?"

Burrell hadn't always been a policeman and in his time he had taken smooth, plump sanctimonious faces like the one sitting opposite him now and punched them in the mouth.

"It's what I'm trying to do, Father. You have implicated a young boy in the serious charge of arson and have also implied he murdered the young boy locked in the cells – William Wilson?" Burrell checked his notes. "Yes. William Wilson. An accident, surely, Father? Not murder."

Father Aherne crossed one leg over the other.

"Samuel Brodie maliciously started a fire that led to William's death. Not murder, Sergeant? Then what would you call it?"

"An accident Father. A terrible accident."

Burrell leafed through the pages of notes on his desk, wanting to get this bastard out of his sight. He'd returned boys to Father Aherne's care on more than one occasion. What he had seen led him to sympathise with young Brodie because if he'd been under this man's care, he'd have wanted to burn the bloody place to the ground, too. "If Samuel has run away, I'm not sure what you expect me to do."

"I expect you, Sergeant Burrell to do your job. Brother Donatus has given you information relating to Samuel Brodie's possible – almost certain – whereabouts. I ask you to follow that information, Sergeant and find the boy who burned down our Orphanage." There was a telling pause before the priest thought to add, "And killed poor young William."

Pale blue eyes filled with insincere pity met sceptical brown ones

"I'll follow up Brother Donatus's information myself, Father." Sergeant Burrell knew Brother Donatus, too. It would be no lie to say Sergeant Burrell longed for a few quiet minutes alone with him. "Will that satisfy you?"

Father Aherne rose from his seat.   "Justice will satisfy me, Sergeant."

The pomposity of that reply rendered the policeman speechless and it was probably just as well for both men that Father Aherne didn't look back as he left the room to catch the gesture Sergeant Burrell made.

19

Harry Wells whistled as he went about his work at Murchison's Commercial Hotel. A jack-of-all-trades, he could turn his hand to anything. Ostler, miner, labourer, Harry had dug roads, worked on the railways, he'd broken in horses, milked cows, picked fruit and was a crack shot with a rifle.

Middling height but broad in the shoulders with strong arms and a skin weathered by the New Zealand elements he was the kind of man men overlooked and women never did. Now, as he shovelled coal into the bins for storage, Mrs Milly Dray sauntered passed, giving him a smile from under the shady brim of her hat, the smile warm and secret. Harry grinned back, offered Milly a bow that was just short of parody. It made her laugh for the gesture was one her husband used to deliberately exhibit what he considered were excellent manners.

Peter Dray bored Milly senseless. Thinking of her husband, Milly stopped beside Harry, her gloved hands folded demurely in front. "Are you having a pleasant day, Mr Wells?"

Harry leaned on his shovel, wiped his sweaty face. "As pleasant a day as a man can have shovelling coal, Mrs Dray. How is Mr Dray?"

Milly tilted her hat brim just enough to see the devilment dancing in Harry's hazel eyes. "My husband is away, Mr Wells. He has to attend to work in Wellington."

"I see."

"He expects to be gone for over a month." Milly's innocent eyes met Harry's as another woman hailed her. She turned reluctantly at the voice to greet Ann Stewart with forced civility.

"Mrs Dray, how fortunate."

"Mrs Stewart." All vivacity flattened out of Milly's voice and only Harry saw the grimace on her lips as she faced this woman she detested.

One ear on the conversation, Harry began to shovel coal once more.

"You must attend my recital on Saturday night, Mrs Dray.

8 o'clock. I have three new pieces to play." Ann primped the curls under her hat.

Milly's face was a perfect study of misfortune. "Oh, Mrs Stewart I am sorry. I have a prior engagement at seven that same evening which just cannot be altered. Such a shame to miss your recital. Perhaps next time?" Without giving Ann a moment to discover what that prior engagement might be, Milly walked swiftly away.

Harry's laugh developed into a hasty cough. Ann fixed big blue eyes on him, her mouth turned down in massive disapproval. Harry gave his ironic bow which Ann had not the wit to perceive as satire. To his amusement she gave him the barest of acknowledgment before walking away.

Harry lifted his hat brim to wipe at his sweaty forehead. He'd look forward to seven on Saturday night but now he wanted a beer and a break.

It was then he caught sight of the raggedy boy who'd been hovering around the town for a couple of days now. Once he'd been given a cuff round the ears and Harry had thought it was for begging but interested as he was in anything out of the ordinary, he'd kept the boy in his sights as he went about his own work and discovered the lad was merely asking for work in a town where work was scarce, especially for outsiders.

Now Harry knew something of hunger, all kinds of hunger. He also recognised something in this shabby, half fed little scarecrow that he saw every time he caught his own reflection. The lad was running, he'd bet his grog on it.

Taking his meal out into the warmth of the day, Harry was careful to pick up an extra shovel as well. This he leaned against the wall next to him as he sat with his back against the stable wall. Feeling the sun on his face Harry removed his old hat and relaxed, his eyes closing to slits through which he watched the boy draw nearer, sidling closer, nervous but determined.

"I could do with an extra pair of hands on that shovel." Harry motioned toward the one leaning against the wall.

Samuel licked his lips, sudden hope almost painful in its intensity lighting his gaunt face. "For what?" he demanded. "I won't work for nothing."

Harry understood now why this lad had found trouble finding work. He hid his amusement as he opened his eyes, met the proud desperation in those searching his.

"Food." Harry rubbed at his rough chin. "Mebbe if you do good work, a bit of money."

Samuel didn't have to think twice. Keeping his eyes off the man's substantial packet of food, he ignored his aching stomach and picked up the shovel. As the sun beat down, he shovelled hard.

Harry watched the boy as he ate a leisurely lunch. He noted the swift glances at his food and drink, the dogged persistence of someone resolutely proving himself. After a while he picked up a piece of coal and lobbed it at the boy's feet to get his attention.

"I've about had enough to eat. Would you like to finish this off for me?" he asked casually as if it was of no interest to him one way or the other.

Samuel responded in kind, gave a small shrug of his shoulders before placing the shovel back against the wall and sitting just shy of the man.

"I'm Harry. What do I call you?"

Samuel already had a mouthful of bread and meat. He chewed hurriedly, managed to say, "Luke." through the doughy mass in his mouth.

"Right, Luke, I've seen you about for the last coupla days. You want work, I 'spect?"

Samuel nodded, devouring the rest of the sandwich.

"And you want paying, too?"

"Yes."

Harry looked quizzically at him.

"I can't pay much."

Samuel swallowed the last mouthful, licked each finger in turn.

"I only want what's fair," he said. "I'm not a bloody slave."

Harry saw the confusion in the boy's face.

"No one'll pay me more than three pence a week."

"I'll pay you what I think you're worth. Work hard and I'll pay you well."

Samuel stared at Harry from under mutinous brows. "How do I know I can trust you?"

Harry belched.

"You can't, lad. Anymore'n I know I can trust you. But we'll shake hands like gentlemen. Mind you, I know so-called gentlemen, so how's about we shake as men of the world? Deal?"

There was something about this man Samuel instinctively liked. Amusement danced in Harry's hazel eyes yet Samuel understood he wasn't being laughed at personally, this man laughed at the whole world. And besides, what choice did he have?

Samuel held out a grubby hand which was enveloped by Harry's even grubbier one.

***

John stood at the back door ready to head back out onto the farm. "How's the boy?"

Emily was mixing something on the woodstove. "He'll be fine when the fever's broken." She lifted her face back from the heat of the stove top. "I think he's been through terrible times. The things he's shouted out during the fever…."

Her face was so troubled John walked back into the kitchen, heedless of his boots on the clean floor. "Jimmy's got you to care for him now. He'll be fine." John held her close and she clung to him, burying her face in his shoulder so he didn't catch her reply. He bent his head to hers. "What did you say, Em?"

"I can't lose another." Her words hollow, defeated.

John lifted her face to his. "Em….."

But she had swallowed her tears having drawn strength from his warm embrace. She laid her hands over his, stood on tip toes and kissed his lips then pulled away from him, pushing him back towards the door. "Now you've got work to do and so have I."

At the doorway John grabbed her, kissed her again and she struggled out of his arms, scolding. "John Benn! What sort of man kisses his wife like that at this time of the day?"

John smiled, straightened his hat as Wolf appeared at his side, whining. "A lucky one." He reached for the lunch Emily had packed for him. "We'll be late tonight, Em. I'll be helping over at Longford's. Don't wait up. You've worn yourself out nursing Jimmy."

"Don't tell me what to do, John Benn. I'll see you when you come home." Emily had turned back to the stove.

John ruffled Wolf's ears then whistled and they both left for the day's work, Wolf barking happily, dashing around John's legs.

Every quarter of an hour or so, Emily made her way up the steep set of stairs to the room where Jimmy lay in a fevered sleep. He'd had a terrible week or more, his sleep disturbed by wrenching nightmares and then the fever had hit him.

Hour after hour, Emily had sat vigil beside his bed, murmuring softly to him and bathing his hot face. Whenever he seemed awake enough, she spooned broth or soup into him, anxious when he vomited it all back up, grateful when he could keep it down.

To her pleasure, when she opened his door this morning, his pale face greeted her with a dazed smile.

"Drink this, Jimmy. I'll leave it beside your bed but be sure to finish it all."

Emily propped the boy up on an extra pillow, smoothed the covers over him.

"I'm sorry, Mrs Benn," he whispered.

She stopped tidying the bed to sit on it.

"Sorry? Whatever for, Jimmy?"

"For being sick."

His thin face tore at Emily's heart. She gave him a quick kiss, startling Jimmy but pleasing him, too.

"You can't help being sick, Jimmy." She stood up again. "Now lie there, sleep, rest and drink up all your medicine. Can I get you anything?"

He shook his head weakly on the snowy pillow.

"Then I'll leave you to rest."

As Emily bustled away Jimmy laid his fingers on his face where she kissed him. He lay there, kept the feeling of her embrace as sleep claimed him once more.

Waking later in the day, he felt better. He wasn't achy and hot anymore just a little muzzy headed.

Mrs Benn must have opened his window for fresh, warm air moved the curtains gently and when he breathed in, Jimmy could smell the earthy tang from the farmyard below. Now he was feeling better it he became restless and not long after that, bored. He could hear Mrs Benn moving around downstairs and decided to get up.

As he left his bedroom, he glanced to his right where beside his room was another. He'd noticed the door, of course, but he hadn't been curious enough to explore. Until now.

Cautiously he pressed his thumb on the latch and pushed the door into the room. It mirrored his with its small dormer window and sloping ceilings. It didn't have a bed though, just a rocking chair and a trunk under the window. Jimmy sat in the rocking chair and stared at the wooden trunk, so like the one Father had packed his and Samuel's things into.

He knew he shouldn't pry but he was bored, missing Samuel and the trunk sat there, teasing him with its secrets. In moments Jimmy was kneeling before it, lifting the heavy lid. It creaked and the weight of it surprised him so when he rested it back against the wall, it dropped more quickly than he anticipated, thumping loudly, the metal latch making a dent in the wall. Jimmy guiltily ignored the mark, peered instead into the deep well of the trunk. It contained books, boy's clothes, pressed and folded away, sprigs of flowers tucked among them and on top of all sat a small toy soldier.

Jimmy picked the soldier up, tucked it carefully on his lap as he reached for a book, trying to remember the last time he had even held a book, let alone read one. Opening the cover he read, *'To Ned with much love.'* written in a clear hand. Under the books were some pieces of paper, covered in black and white drawings of dogs and horses. Jimmy recognised Hardy from the queer white star on his forehead. He couldn't drag his eyes away from the clever sketches. Sitting back on his heels he pored over them. This picture here looked like Wolf as a puppy and here was Mr Benn carrying a calf on his arms as the rain poured down. Jimmy turned the page over and there...

"I didn't even know he was drawing me."

The pages spilled from Jimmy's hands as he spun guiltily round, hastily getting to his feet, the toy soldier bouncing to the floor. Emily stood in the doorway. Expecting to be told off or to receive a thump around the ears Jimmy saw only her sweet smile.

"I...I'm sorry, Mrs Benn. Truly. I..."

"It's quite all right, Jimmy."

Emily gathered her heavy skirts as she sat on the floor where he'd been sitting moments earlier. She picked up the soldier and patted the space beside her. Slowly Jimmy knelt down and when Emily handed him the soldier he gave shamefaced grin, took charge of it once more while she gathered the pages up, turning them the right way round, smiling at the images on them. She held the last one Jimmy saw, passed it back to him.

"I remember the morning so clearly. Three springs ago. It was warm, damp – perfect for the garden." Her smile widened. "Ned knew I didn't like having my picture done. I always caught him trying and would shoo him off but this morning I thought he was still abed – he was such a sluggard when it came to getting up. Mr Benn was still sleeping. He'd been up most of the night with lambing."

Emily turned to Jimmy but he didn't think she was seeing him. Her wide set grey eyes were lost in that morning of years ago.

"I finished planting out the seeds and I'd been given these little rosemary plants. I love rosemary and wanted to border the whole vegetable patch with it."

Emily stared at the picture of herself, kneeling among the newly dug garden, her hands busy in the well-turned earth. Wisps of dark hair lay against her cheek where a smear of dirt marred its cleanness. She was concentrating on the fragile plants, lips pouting slightly, eyes lowered, intent on the work.

"Ned had heard me leaving the house, slipped out behind me. He was sitting on the back door step – I didn't notice him until I stood back up and there he was, engrossed in drawing this picture."

Jimmy kept his eyes on the drawing. "Did you tell him off?"

She shook her head.

"How could I? He wouldn't let me even see it until it was finished." Emily pointed to the signature at the bottom. "All he wanted to do was draw and paint. He signed everything he drew, just like the real artists."

Now Emily reached back into the trunk and pulled out some larger pictures. She held one up, a boy aged around twelve or thirteen with a serious face and his mother's grey eyes. He was looking right at you, Jimmy thought as if he could read your mind.

"This is Ned. A self-portrait."

"It's wonderful."

Jimmy saw another one of Mr Benn, riding a horse, dogs capering around the horse's legs, sheep on the hill behind him, the Matakitaki river running full between its banks.

"Ned was so clever."

"Yes, he was. Yet it broke his heart."

"What do you mean?"

"There's no call for a farmer's son to draw pictures, Jimmy. Ned couldn't bear to hurt his father to follow his dream and he was our only child."

With those few words Emily hid the years of longing, the miscarriages, the lost hopes, the fear she could give John no children at all, the children she knew he longed for. Then the pregnancy that held, the one that lasted nine months and gave them Ned.

"Without him…." Emily couldn't talk for a moment or two. When she spoke again her eyes were bright with tears. "…without him Mr Benn would have no one to work for." She smiled down on Jimmy. "So Ned began to draw less and less. This one he did of me was the last one he ever did."

A single tear slid down Emily's face, splashed onto the paper near Ned's signature. Jimmy snuggled against Emily, wanting to offer comfort but unsure how to. "I think it's the best one," he whispered.

Emily drew the boy to her, held him closely and Jimmy gave into the feel of warm arms holding him, the rise and fall of Emily's ragged breathing. Something occurred to him and he pulled back, frowning in concern. "I can't draw at all Mrs Benn. Not anything."

Some of Emily's loss melted away. "Neither can I, Jimmy." She whispered into his hair. "Not one blessed thing."

Later that night when the cottage was quiet and everyone but him slept, Jimmy crept back into Ned's room and opened the trunk again. He placed the candle holder carefully beside him and took out the pictures to look at them again, finally holding the one of Ned himself.

There were other things in the trunk and Jimmy rummaged carefully around pulling out a small, material covered box. Sitting back down with Ned's picture propped up on the side of the trunk, he opened it. There were cards in it, wishing Ned a happy birthday or Merry Christmas. Something was wrapped in tissue paper and Jimmy uncovered a thick auburn curl with a little card, *'Our darling Edward. 18 months.'* There was a little collar that looked as if it had belonged to a puppy, some stones with things stuck in them like leaves. Jimmy, all unknowing, ran fascinated fingers over fossils, millions of years old.

Right at the bottom of the little box was a piece of newspaper. It was beginning to yellow and looked as if it had been folded away somewhere before being laid out under these things. Jimmy drew it towards the candle flame.

'The Colonist, Nelson.

Murchison suffered its worst flooding since 1878. Much livestock and property has been lost to the distress of farmers and townsfolk alike.

There was one death when Edward John Benn was swept away by the Matakitaki River three days ago and though a thorough search has been undertaken by the whole community, Edward's body has yet to be found. Edward was fourteen years old and the only son and child of John and Emily Benn. Our deepest sympathies are with the family at this time.'

Slowly, Jimmy returned the article and the treasures to the safety of the little box before repacking the drawings around it. He gazed down at Ned's serious face one last time and placed it on top of the rest.

20

"Harry?"

"Mmm?"

"Why don't you tip your hat to the boss like the other men do?"

They were rubbing oil onto the saddles and leather gear. Outside the barn, steady rain was falling, people dashing between the verandas or taking cover to wait for the heaviest of the rain to pass.

"The man pays my wages, lad but he's not God almighty." Harry rolled a cigarette, placed it between his lips and lit it.

"Silas says you have no respect for your betters."

"Does he?" Harry puffed on his cigarette then tipped more oil onto his cloth. "Well that's the difference between me and Silas. I don't think any man's better'n me."

Samuel thought about this. "What about gentlemen?"

Harry's warm laugh echoed round them. "They're just men with more money, Luke. Don't make them better, 'course, it don't stop the buggers thinking they're better! And," Harry paused, blew some smoke into Samuel's face before adding, "There's a fair few gentlemen that don't have any money either, so what was your question again?"

Samuel had spent enough time with Harry to know that was a didn't-have-to-be-answered question. They usually hid a joke or at least Samuel assumed they did because Harry always laughed after saying them.

"Father always tipped his hat or saluted his boss."

"I'm not saying a man's wrong to do it, lad, just that it's not my way. Finished yet?"

Samuel held the gleaming bridle up for inspection. Harry gave it a once-over and hung it back up on its hook.

Harry had never asked him any questions, Samuel realised. Even at the mention of Father, Harry never asked why Samuel wasn't with him or where was his mother or any other question most people would ask. Yet he never felt that Harry wasn't interested in him, just not interested about him.

"I've never seen anything in the world to make me think the man with all the money should be the man making all the rules, lad."

Harry was full of statements like that. Samuel thought of Father, remembering his cringing subservience in front of Mr Collingwood, his eyes lowered to the ground as Mr Collingwood demanded higher rent or dawn to dark hours of work and he knew Harry would never have done that. Harry would have called the man a bastard to his face and walked off. Harry would never have cringed.

The rain began to pour down in torrents. Small rivulets ran along the stables and the horses shifted irritably in their stalls. Harry was alone in liking the cats that prowled among the hay and feed and as a large ginger tom sauntered up, he bribed it onto his lap with a bit of meat. It settled itself comfortably, purring. Relaxing himself just as comfortably, Harry leaned back, stroked the cat absentmindedly and stared out into the weather. "If it goes on like this it'll flood again. The Buller's a bitch when she gets flooded and this town's already seen its fair share of it."

Samuel sat cross legged in front of Harry, tickled the cat behind its ears.

"We had a big flood last year in Nelson."

"I heard. Not a patch on the ones we get here, though lad." Harry gestured, "The Matakitaki and the Mangles – two mighty rivers pouring into the Buller." He shook his head, repeated, "And the Buller's a bitch."

"Our river flooded, too. Brother Luke was rescued by Conn, a Maori boy when he got knocked into the water by a broken branch. Wish it had been Brother Donatus, the bastard."

Harry kept his tone deliberately casual. "You were an orphanage boy, then Luke?"

Samuel shot Harry a wary look.

"No. Just heard about it, that's all." He watched the man intently, reassured when Harry yawned, made no comment and tipped the protesting cat onto the floor as he stood, stretching.

"I'm away tonight so the place is yours. As is this." Harry fumbled in his pockets brought out ten shillings. "Your pay.

You've done good work, Luke."

Samuel beamed up at him. "Thanks, Harry!"

But Harry brushed his thanks off with a careless gesture, left the stables whistling.

***

John Gaukroger refilled Sergeant Burrell's mug with hot, sweet tea.

"John Benn? Yes, I know John. He and my father knew each other well and John always stops here on his way to and from Nelson."

Burrell drank deeply, trying to slake a raging thirst. What he wanted was a beer but when John Gaukroger offered him a drink, the man didn't mean alcohol. Strange in a publican, Burrell thought, dutifully drinking the tea.

"Well, sir, Mr Benn has adopted a boy from Stoke Orphanage."

"Yes. He had a boy with him. Jimmy..? I think was the lad's name."

"James Brodie." The policeman leaned back in his chair which creaked ominously under Burrell's not inconsiderable weight. "We're looking for this boy's brother, Samuel who we believe has run off after Jimmy."

John busied himself so his face was averted from Burrell's. He remembered a boy trudging exhausted, thin and faltering.

"Is there trouble with this Samuel?"

"I'm afraid there is, sir. It appears Samuel Brodie may have been involved in the fire that burned the Stoke Orphanage to the ground." Burrell didn't mention the death of the boy in the punishment cell. "We just need to talk to him."

John thought back to that night, the boy not much more than a child with desperate eyes. He'd never asked his name and the boy hadn't offered one.

"I did see a boy on the road, Sergeant. He seemed to be heading south. I offered him a bed in our barn for the night."

"That was generous of you, sir. Very trusting, if I might say so."

"He was a scarecrow of a boy, Sergeant, starving and filthy. What I did was nothing more than Christian duty."

Burrell pulled out his notepad, licked the tip of a very short pencil. "Can you remember which night this was?" he asked, pencil poised.

Again, John turned away from the policeman. "Around the same time as John Benn stayed. I can't be more certain than that."

But Burrell gave a contented grunt as he wrote this down. "Thank you for your assistance, sir." He pushed himself to his feet. "If you do think of anything more…?"

"I shall be in touch, Sergeant Burrell."

John walked the policeman out to the front where a young constable waited beside the horses.

With surprising ease for such a big man, Sergeant Burrell mounted into his saddle. He took up the reins and looked down into John's eyes. "Any messages, send them to Nelson Police, sir. I shall be in Murchison for a few days at least."

With a brief salute, the two policemen headed down the South road and John Gaukroger thought of the raggedy boy as he went back inside.

21

Jimmy had his head bowed over his hands as Emily finished saying grace.

"And thank you, Lord for keeping our family safe. We ask that you continue to watch over us, especially our Jimmy. Amen."

As he whispered his amen, Jimmy felt a warm glow inside him that owed nothing to the prayer but everything to Emily calling him one of the family. 'Our Jimmy', she had said. 'Our Jimmy'. He watched as they ate, John, silently and heartily, Emily with the good manners she brought to everything she did. Today John had told him how grateful he was for Jimmy's help. He'd ruffled his hair, told him they would get him his own pony around Christmas. The boy couldn't believe it, gaped after John long after the farmer had walked away whistling at the hard working dogs.

Emily spooned another potato onto Jimmy's plate. He grinned at her, cheeks already bulging.

John leaned over, dug his fork into Jimmy's potato. "We won't need a turkey for Christmas the way you're fattening that lad up."

Jimmy's spurt of laughter sent half the contents of his mouth spraying across the table. Red faced he stood to grab a cloth only to have Emily push him back down and do the job herself, scolding John for the mess, not Jimmy.

"It wasn't me spat my dinner over the table." John protested, winking at Jimmy.

"It was your nonsense that caused it, John Benn." Emily had the table clean in a couple of wipes. "Now, Jimmy, would you like some more?" He shook his head. "Then time for bed, young man. You still look a little pale to me."

"You mollycoddle the boy." John said as Jimmy scampered up the stairs. He caught the scent of rosemary as Emily bent her head to kiss him.

"Be thankful I mollycoddle all the men in my family." She said as Jimmy's footsteps thundered back down the stairs. His faced poked round the kitchen door. "I forgot to say goodnight to Hardy and Wolf."

"Two minutes, Jimmy."   By the time his promise reached their ears he was already halfway to the barn.

Jimmy had barely reached his bedroom when he heard stones rattling on his window. He'd known instantly who it had to be. Now he leaned his weight on the barn door. It gave its usual moaning creak as he shoved against it, walked inside, squinting into the darkness of the barn.

"Sam?"

A figure stepped out of the shadows, Wolf at his heels, a grin spread from ear to ear. Jimmy hugged his brother tightly.

"Bloody hell, Jimmy, anyone would think I'd been gone for a year." But Samuel held him close.

"It feels like it. I can't stay out here long. I told Mrs Benn I was saying goodnight to Wolf." Jimmy didn't mention Hardy's name. He didn't think Sam would understand a horse needing a goodnight. "I'll slip back out later as soon as I can."

"I've been working in the stables at the Commercial Hotel." Samuel told his brother proudly, unable to wait any longer to share this news. "I've already saved nearly one pound!"

"That's great, Sam."

From the veranda of the cottage, Emily called Jimmy inside.

"I've gotta go in. But I'll be back."

Jimmy was as good as his word. He waited until Emily and John had gone to bed then dressed quickly, putting his trousers and coat on over his pyjamas before heading back out to the barn.

The two boys sat on top of a pile of hay, Wolf beside them.

"How'd you know which room was mine?" Jimmy asked, curious to know.

"I've been outside since just before dark. I knew the Mr and Mrs Benn were still in the kitchen so I just chucked the stones when you lit your candle." Samuel looked insufferably pleased with himself.

Jimmy was so pleased to be with his brother again he didn't want to upset him by telling him how sick he'd been. Instead, he satisfied his own worry and curiosity about where Samuel had been and what he'd been doing. "Tell me about your job."

"Well, I'm not working there officially. Harry's taken me on as a help to him but the boss doesn't know I'm there, really. Harry doesn't think I know but he pays me out of his own wages."

"That's really kind of him."

Samuel agreed happily. "Harry's great, Jimmy. He doesn't bow to any man." And the words, straight from Harry's mouth sat a little oddly in Samuel's, not that Jimmy noticed. "He found me some other clothes, too." Samuel held out a sleeve for Jimmy to admire his new coat. "And these." A lifted leg to show off the new trousers. "And I eat three times a day, good meals, too."

Both boys thought about the vast changes in their lives.

"It hasn't been long," Samuel struggled for the right words, "but the Orphanage seems like a dream."

"Nightmare more like."

Wolf proceeded to spread himself over their legs. Jimmy thumped his shoulder, murmured, "Pushy dog."

"Jimmy?"

"Yeah?"

"Are they kind to you here?"

Jimmy saw the concern in his brother's face. "Yes." His eyes brightened. "Mr Benn said he'd get me a pony at Christmas." He waited for Samuel's equally excited reply, saw him frown.

"We'll be gone by Christmas, Jimmy. Don't get too settled."

Jimmy didn't know what to say to that. He rested his head back against the hay.

"Did you hear me, Jimmy?" No reply. Samuel shoved Wolf off his legs, sat up to face his brother. "We've got a plan, remember? I save enough money so we can find Father."

"I know." Jimmy's voice deadened, all the excitement he'd felt gone.

Silence.

"You do want to find Father, don't you?"

"Yes." But Jimmy wasn't sure and Samuel could tell.

More silence as the boys stared at each other. Samuel opened his mouth, unsure of what he was going to say when Wolf leapt away from them to growl at the barn door. Both boys stiffened, ears straining for the sound of footsteps. Instead, they heard horses riding nearer.

Together they pressed against the barn door as the farm dogs began to bark. Through the gaps, they saw candle light in the downstairs bedroom.

"Mr Benn will come out." Jimmy hissed.

"Well, he doesn't know you're here so just keep quiet." Samuel replied, a restraining hand on his brother's arm.

Two horses came to a stop at the veranda of the cottage as John appeared holding a lantern.

"John Benn?" asked the largest of the two men.

"Who wants to know?"

"Sergeant Burrell, sir. Nelson Police."

Emily had flung a shawl over her shoulders. She stood at John's side. "Nelson Police?"

John heard the tension in her voice.

"Yes, Ma'am. We're looking for a James Brodie. We believe you adopted him from Stoke Orphanage."

Inside the barn the two boys were scarcely breathing. Samuel was sure Jimmy would hear the wild thumping of his heart.

John raised his lantern to light the face of the two policemen. "You'd better come inside."

Jimmy grabbed Samuel's arm. "I've got to go in. Will you stay or go back to the hotel?"

"We don't know what they want yet. I'll stay." As Jimmy turned to leave, Samuel gripped his shoulders. "Tell me as soon as you know what they want."

Cautiously Jimmy left the barn. The police were already inside. He moved round to the back door just in time to hear Emily saying in a tight voice, "He's not in his room."

Setting his face to hide his own panic, Jimmy walked in through the back door, yawning, rubbing his eyes as Emily held a candle up to his face.

"I've been to the outhouse." Jimmy stared at the policeman, remembering to act as if he'd just seen them. "Is something wrong?" He didn't have to fake his anxiety.

John placed gentle hands on Jimmy's shoulders, guided him to the kitchen table. While he, Jimmy and Emily sat, the two policemen stood stiffly by the woodstove.

"Jimmy, I'm Sergeant Burrell from Nelson. Have you seen Samuel?" He watched Jimmy's face intently.

"No." Jimmy sat on his hands, crossing his fingers against the lie.

"Well, not since I left the Orphanage." Tightly crossed!

"We believe Samuel may be trying to find you."

"I miss Sam." Jimmy bowed his head, missing the looks exchanged by all the adults.

Sergeant Burrell glanced at John with a questioning look. After a pause, John gave his permission and the Sergeant pulled up a chair to sit opposite Jimmy. He regarded the boy calmly. "Jimmy, we think Samuel did a very bad thing. And we have to talk to him about it."

Jimmy lifted his head, met the sergeant's calm gaze with a puzzled one of his own.

"What bad thing? Sam's never done a bad thing." But in Jimmy's guilty mind was the memory of them stealing food, Samuel fighting and the image of red and orange flames lighting up a dark sky.

"Jimmy, someone set a fire in the Orphanage, burned it to the ground."

Sergeant Burrell was expecting some reaction, but the boy lost colour in a heartbeat. Jimmy shoved the chair back, stood. John reacted instinctively and just in time to keep the boy on his feet as Jimmy stumbled.

"No."

"I'm afraid so, Jimmy. And a boy died in the fire."

If they thought Jimmy was pale before it was nothing to the

whiteness in his face at those words. Not realising what he did Jimmy leaned his weight against John.

"What boy?" Jimmy hardly got the words out through his fear.

"William Wilson."

"No!" Jimmy buried his face in John's arms.

Emily stood horrified, desperate to hold Jimmy, to comfort him. Her hand caressed his hair and she whispered to him, words he couldn't hear while Sergeant Burrell pushed his advantage.

"Jimmy, you understand why it's important that we speak to Samuel?"

"He didn't do it!" but even as he spoke of his brother's innocence, Jimmy felt his own terrible suspicion.

John knelt. He wiped the boy's streaming face with his sleeve. "If he's innocent, Jimmy," John began as Jimmy burst out,

"He is!"

"Then he's in no danger." John continued, warning Sergeant Burrell back with a look as the policeman stepped forward. "But he must speak to the police, Jimmy. They have to ask him questions."

Jimmy looked at John's worried face then at Emily, her grey eyes enormous. He backed away step by step and after a few he spun around disappeared out the door, slamming it behind him. Sergeant Burrell and the constable moved only to have John block their exit.

"He's got nowhere to go, officers. He's frightened and shocked. If I know Jimmy, he'll have gone to the animals in the barn." John gave them a wan smile. "Surely there's nothing else you can ask of him? He's not seen Samuel and we haven't seen a boy hanging around either."

"If you do…." Sergeant Burrell let the sentence hang. "Well sir, we won't disturb you anymore tonight. We'll head into Murchison, ask a few questions and return to Nelson tomorrow."

They walked to the veranda, found their horses cropping the grass on the verge near the cottage.

"You'll know where to find us if Jimmy has any contact with Samuel at all."

As the policemen rode away, Emily stared at the barn. She stepped off the veranda towards it but John caught her arm.

"No, Em. He needs some time alone."

"What if....?"

John gathered her in his arms. "Then he knows where to find us."

Out in the barn, Samuel could make no sense of what Jimmy was sobbing to him. Every time he tried to hold his brother in one place he was shoved back as Jimmy paced round and around, his words incoherent, tears falling unheeded down his face.

"Jimmy, I don't understand. What did the police want? What's happened?"

"Will's dead."

These were the first words Samuel could understand and he couldn't grasp the meaning of them. "What?"

Jimmy faced Samuel, his face twisted. "Will's dead, Sam. He died in the fire."

"What fire?" Samuel could bear it no longer. He pulled Jimmy to face him, held him there. "Jimmy? What bloody fire are you talking about?"

"The Orphanage.... It burned to the ground. They think you burned it to the ground.... And Will, Jesus, Sam! Will died. He died in the fire."

As Samuel's nerveless hands slipped from his arms, Jimmy moved away again. Wolf was whining, his tail down, desperate to give reassurance but ignored by both boys. Samuel wrapped his arms about his body.

"Oh, shit...." His thoughts spinning around a frantic mind.

...The night he left.... Will... Letting him out.... Will helping him.... Papers all over the floor.... A candle burning...... Will refusing to leave..... Will watching him go......

Without warning, Samuel's legs gave way under him and he sank to the barn floor.

For moments beyond thought both boys were lost in their private misery. If Jimmy closed his eyes he remembered how Samuel had changed, he could see his brother's out of control rage when he attacked Kip, the feral look on his face while they watched their house burn.

"Did you do it?"

The question was hesitantly asked and almost lost in the dark shadows surrounding them. Samuel couldn't look at Jimmy.

"No." But more words were dragged out of him. "How can you even ask that?" The final word a ghost on the air as Samuel's tears fell at last, head in his hands, his body shaking.

In halting sentences, Samuel told Jimmy everything from the time he was taken from the Orphanage. How he overheard Donatus's damning of his character, the way he raged and was dragged out to the cells and beaten.

"Will let me out….. he helped me find where you were….. he said he'd clean up Aherne's office to get me more time….. he was going to lock my cell door to make it seem as if I hadn't left…. They wouldn't have known till Donatus went to give me another flogging….." Samuel wiped his nose on his coat sleeve. "I saw Molly, told her you were gone." He lifted his eyes to his brother's. "She gave me some money. She said it was for you 'cause you'd want me with you. Then I ran. And ran." He tried to read Jimmy's face and that surprised Samuel as much as anything for Jimmy had always been an open book. "You know the rest."

Silence.

"Sam, you have to leave."

"I know."

"I mean Murchison, Sam. You can't stay here when they're looking for you."

Samuel faced his brother. "I know." He repeated, getting to his feet. He offered his hand to Jimmy who ignored it. "I have to go back to the hotel. All our money's there."

"I'm coming with you."

"No, you're not."

That brought Jimmy up short.

"Sam, I'm not staying here without you. You can't leave me."

His eyes bored into Samuel's but his brother shook his head.

"It's only me that's being blamed for this. And you have a chance here, Jimmy. I saw you at the table with them, I saw their faces. They want you here." Samuel lifted his hands in appeal. "Don't you see Jimmy? You can be part of a family again."

Silence.

"Damn you, Sam." Jimmy spoke so softly Samuel wasn't sure he'd heard correctly. "We're family. You and me. And you want to leave me? Like father did?" As his brother tried to reach out Jimmy punched his hand away, stepped backwards shaking his head. "Bloody go, then."

Samuel was appalled by the anger on his brother's face. Jimmy pointed at the barn door.

"Go!" he shouted, and as if in reply the farm dogs all began to bark.

"Jimmy….." Samuel stammered.

"I don't wanna hear it." Without another word or glance Jimmy stalked out of the barn, leaving Samuel stunned behind him.

When he reached his bedroom, Jimmy threw himself face down on his bed and hid his face in the pillow, purposefully blanking out his brother's face.

Samuel jogged most of the way back down the valley into Murchison, keeping wary eyes on the road for any sign of the policemen but he made it back to the safety of stables. Once there he gathered up his few possessions, throwing them into a sack he snatched from a bin. Scrabbling at a broken board in the wall, he uncovered the gap he'd made to hide his money. This he tucked into his pocket. He wished he'd had time to get some food. He was going to ask Jimmy to get him some but…..

Samuel drew in a shaky breath as the stab of pain shot through him. He wanted to cry but somehow he knew he'd cried for the last time. With a quick look about him to make sure he had everything Samuel turned to leave. And saw Harry leaning in the doorway watching him, a cigarette burning between his lips.

"I hear the coppers are looking for a boy on the run from Nelson. A Samuel Brodie. This boy burned the Orphanage at Stoke to the ground, they said." Harry sucked the last of his cigarette, dropped it into a bucket of water.

The sack fell from Samuel's hands. His face taut, his fists clenched he lifted his head and faced Harry.

"They bloody lie."

Harry crossed his arms.

"They also said this lad caused another boy's death."

Samuel shook his head.

"No. He was my friend."

"Lad, you're up to your neck in shit."

Why was that so funny? Samuel didn't know, it just made him laugh and once he started he found he couldn't stop. He laughed at the words. Laughed at the look on Harry's face. Laughed at every bloody thing.

In two strides Harry reached the boy. He took him by the shoulders and shook him.

"Stop. For god's sake, Samuel, it's not funny."

Samuel was breathless with laughter. "But it is, Harry. It bloody is." Then Samuel gasped as Harry's slap shocked him.

"Now listen, lad. I don't know what happened in Nelson but if I tell you I was sent to an orphanage as a boy you'll know that I understand what you ran from. Yes?"

Samuel nodded and Harry calmed a little, shooting nervous glances out into the yard in case they'd been heard.

"I told them coppers that I ain't seen no boy named Samuel, which isn't a lie though it wouldn't bother me if it was one. I don't think the sergeant believes you had anything to do with the other boy's death 'cause apparently he'd been locked in a punishment cell and the sergeant had a few things to say about Catholics and punishments which don't concern you none 'cept to let you know he don't think you did it. But the fire? That's something else, lad and he wants to talk to you which we both know means he wants someone to pin it on and you're the obvious choice."

"I didn't do it." Samuel whispered. "I didn't. When I left Will was alive. He saw me leave, helped me go, said he'd try and get me some extra time before anyone found out I'd gone. I swear it, Harry."

"You don't have to try so hard, lad. I'm on your side."

Samuel sagged with relief as Harry, grabbed the boy's sack and tipped it into an old canvas pack of his own.

"This'll be easier to carry. I put a bit of grub in there and you can take Hodge. Come on."

Incredulously Samuel followed as Harry saddled up his own horse. He tied sacking around Hodge's hooves.

"Just to get you down the road unheard. Take them off when you're safely out of the town."

"Harry, what are you doing? I can't afford your bloody horse!"

"Who asked for any money?" Harry gave Samuel a foot up, passed him the pack which Samuel slipped onto his back. "Where were you thinking of going?"

"Father's in Blackball."

"Anyone else know where he is?"

Samuel shrugged.

"I dunno."

Harry bit his lip, thinking hard.

"My advice, lad? Head to Christchurch. Plenty of work at the port or you can get work on board a ship and get right away. Or disappear somewhere in the West Coast where you can lose yourself, mebbe start again."

"Thank you, Harry."

"Never mind that. Just get gone. The coppers are here for the night and were talking about heading further south tomorrow so you've hours to put the miles between them and you."

Still Samuel didn't move, he struggled to say how much this meant. Maybe Harry knew for he smiled, gave Hodge a push on his rump, set the horse and the boy on the way.

"Good luck, lad."

Harry waited long enough to know Samuel had got away unheard and unseen before heading back into the bar to buy Sergeant Burrell a few more drinks. Give him enough, Harry thought grimly and the bastard won't want to go far in the morning. He would guarantee it.

22

Samuel was footsore and weary. Days had drifted into weeks as he left Murchison far behind him. He'd kept Harry's horse until reaching Christchurch then sold it to pay for the coach to Greymouth.

From there he walked to Blackball, conscious that his money had to last him for as long as he could stretch it out.

He couldn't say how long he'd been on the road but the Orphanage and even Jimmy felt so far behind him Samuel couldn't even see their shadows.

The fog smothering Blackball was thick and yellow too with the coal smoke belching out from every chimney in this small town at the end of the valley.

A single question asked casually of one person and Samuel knew where his father was to be found. At that house. Down that path between the gardens. Behind those windows. Behind that door. But once there Samuel stopped, his feet cold on the gravel road, his coat wrapped tightly about him. He ached to knock and announce himself. Why couldn't he move?

Because there was a part of him that feared that he'd not be wanted. Even though finding the letters proved Father hadn't forgotten them, having spent all those months believing he didn't had scarred him, Samuel acknowledged that. And he wasn't the boy his father left behind two years ago.

It took all his courage but when Samuel took one step, the others came quickly enough. Ignoring the front door, he moved round the back; everyone lived in their kitchens. He heard Father's laughter and something swelled in his chest, brought a lump to his throat. It was as Samuel reached out to bang his fist against the back door that he heard boys' voices and his hand froze. Father laughed again, there was giggling, a thud of feet.

Cautiously, Samuel moved passed the door to peer through the uncurtained window. There in the cosy kitchen Father sat at a wooden table reading aloud to three boys. One of them sat on his

lap while the others were looking into his face. As if they loved him
As if they belonged there.

It wasn't the chilly air that made Samuel shiver. He watched his
father's face desperately for any sign, a distant look, a sad
expression, anything he could put down to Jimmy and him being
missed. But Fraser read on, laughing when one or other of the boys
interrupted him and Samuel saw no shadows on his face at all.

Slowly, Samuel pulled his share of the letters he still carried in his
pocket, all creased and grubby from constant handling. He felt the
weight of them in his hand and on his heart.

For a long, long moment he stared down at them.

From inside the kitchen a woman's voice called the boys to bed.
Samuel bowed his head. Carefully he laid Jimmy's adoption papers
on top of the pile then placed them all on the back door step where
they would be seen in the morning.

A shadow himself now, Samuel turned his back on the scene and
melted away into the night

Part IV

23

Wellington
New Zealand
1911

The ship sailed out of the choppy Cook Strait into the calmer waters around Wellington harbour. Two young men leaned against the rails on the deck watching as the coves and bays passed smoothly by. Slowly the hills of Wellington wrapped the ship round and now on one side of them, they gazed at fine wooden buildings dotted amongst the green of Miramar Penninsula, on the other, the bare hills of Pencarrow Heads and all the while a steady wind flapped at their trouser legs and made it necessary to jam their caps hard down over their ears.

Cass sheltered back from the wind, lit a cigarette. "Want one?"

Samuel shook his head, his attention fixed on the newspaper he held.

FREEDOM
A Journal of Anarchist Communism
ALL GOVERNMENTS
ARE ROBBERS
WHY DO YOU
ELECT THEM?

Monthly 1 penny

Frowning in concentration, Samuel began to read the accompanying article. After a few moments he smelt smoke and edged away from Cass's cigarette, realising all too late that it was his paper burning. The flames reached his fingers and he yelped, hastily dropping the flaring pages to the deck where he stomped on them.

"Shit! Bloody hell, Cass. I was reading, that."

Cass just grinned at his friend. "Anarchy," he said by way of explanation.

This time when he passed Samuel a cigarette it was accepted.

Together they moved back out into the wind to watch Wellington wharf draw closer.

"You sure we'll find work here?"

Cass eyed his friend calmly. "Tim's given us a reference and it's his cousin we're seeing so why not? Bit late for your concerns, though innit?"

"Isn't it bad manners to answer a question with a question?"

"I dunno, is it?"

Ahead of them tall, stately brick buildings showed the shape and size of the city and Samuel felt overawed as he stared for the first time at their capital. "You and me, Cass. In Wellington." A sudden rush of excitement flooded him and he thumped Cass on the shoulder in exhilaration.

Now the ship came alongside and the shouts of the watersiders were answered by the crew. Surreptitiously, Samuel lifted the glowing tip of his cigarette to the back of Cass's cap. The wind fed the heat more quickly than he anticipated and as the cap began smoking he shoved himself back from the rail, picked the bag up from his feet and threw it over one shoulder. "C'mon then."

Cass followed, gradually becoming self-conscious of stares and fingers pointing his way. "What're they on about?" he asked Samuel.

"Hey, mate," a watersider shouted up. "Better put that fire out before coming ashore!"

"What bloody fire? What're you on about?"

To Cass's confusion the man just pointed to his own head. He turned to Samuel and the penny dropped as he encountered the huge grin. Cass grabbed his cap as the first flames caught. Cursing he dropped it over into the harbour, watched it smoke as it rocked on the water. "That was my favourite," he grumbled. Unable to bear his friend's grin anymore, Cass leapt at him, grabbed Samuel's own cap and pulled it triumphantly down over his curls. "You're a bastard," he told Samuel conversationally as the two of them stood on the wharf trying not to be too wide eyed at all the bustle.

"Must be why we're mates, then."

Samuel pulled a piece of paper from his pocket. On it was a roughly drawn map of Wellington city with certain buildings circled. He looked about them, spotted a sign on the building opposite them. "This way."

With his head high and striding confidently, Samuel walked out of Queen's Wharf and headed towards the city centre.

Lambton Quay was a real eye opener to the two young men. The Wairapapa Farmers' Co-Operative building rose five stories high with brick walls and lovely arched windows but it wasn't the only one of its kind for almost every building on this long street was more grand than anything they had seen in the South Island. Trams ran down the centre of the wide streets and halfway along Cass stood on the footpath and whistled at the number of hansom cabs parked outside Kirkcaldie and Stains. He whistled again louder when he caught sight of the window displays and the number of well-dressed people being bowed in and out of the glass doors by a doorman.

"How long would we have to work to buy anything in there?" he muttered.

The doorman took note of the two scruffy young men who had stopped on the footpath and proffered a disdainful look down his long nose, a look which did not go unnoticed.

"You're a worker, same as us, not God Almighty in a pretend uniform." Samuel said but the doorman just glared. "Bet if I had a pocketful of money you wouldn't be looking at us like that, mate." To Samuel's chagrin the doorman refused to even acknowledge him. Instead he stepped neatly to one side, opening the ornate glass doors as he bowed to a woman wearing furs and the highest heels Samuel and Cass had ever seen. She wasn't aware of anyone else around her as she left the shop, a servant behind her carrying an armload of parcels.

Cass ogled the woman's long legs as she stepped neatly into a hansom cab, her servant clambering in beside her. Oblivious to the glare from the doorman Cass whistled once more, long and low which improved Samuel's temper no end. He gave the scornful doorman a mocking bow, placed a hand over his heart with exaggerated aplomb as he did so. "See you round, Your Highness."

"Not in this shop I won't. Mate. "

The wind chased their steps up Lambton Quay. They gazed in wonder at the cable car running to the top of the Botannical Gardens. Horses and carts moved through the streets with the occasional motor car. Samuel and Cass gaped longingly at these metal, noisy curiosities knowing there wasn't a chance in hell of them ever owning one.

So distracted were they by the sights and sounds that the afternoon slipped away. As the day darkened, the wind picked up and they huddled their bags to their bodies in an effort to keep warm.

"Where the hell's the boarding house?" Cass grumbled.

"Um….." Samuel peered at his map. "Tory Street."

He moved on and was only belatedly aware he was walking on alone. Turning back, he saw Cass transfixed by the door of King's Theatre. Built the year before, grandly lit, its sign offered, 'Hayward's Pictures Every Evening.'

Cass gave a moan of longing. He dug frantically around in his pockets, pulled out a few coins. "You got any money?"

Samuel grabbed his arm. "Not for the pictures I don't. Aren't you hungry?" Cass kept his eyes glued to King's Theatre until Samuel punched his arm. "Anyway, thought you were all for finding the boarding house?"

"But Sam…. movies."

"We're here to stay, Cass. We can go any time. Come on, can't you? I'm bloody starving."

Reluctantly Cass left the theatre behind him and they picked up their pace, suddenly aware that they hadn't eaten since leaving Christchurch.

The grandeur of Lambton Quay soon gave way to poorer Wellington streets where the buildings grew shabbier and more huddled together, brick gave way to unpainted, weathered wood and the roads became pitted and dirtier.

Finally seeing the sign for Tory Street Samuel stopped again to get his bearings. All around them the tenements crowded together. Children ran amid the filth, women hung around doorways and out of windows, cat-calling, shouting. Cass's looks were noticed, loudly commented on and he perked up.

"I think I'm gunna like it here."

"Huh?" Samuel looked up from his map and the first thing that met his eyes was a well-endowed young woman with her blouse open too low for modesty. She placed her hands on her hips and stood provocatively against the dirty doorway.

"Come on in, love," she called. "If you're new at this, I'll show you a thing or two."

Cass's tongue was almost hanging out. He stammered a couple of words but Samuel yanked him up the street.

"We can't afford a movie, you think we can afford her?"

But indifferent to such things Cass's eyes remained on the girl's obvious charms.

"Halfers?" he pleaded.

Moments later they found themselves standing outside Mrs Huntly's Boarding House. An old dog sat on the doorstep, fleas crawling around its chewed-looking ears and pale eyes.

A small child tottered out of the building, collapsing to the ground in the sudden way of toddlers and laughing as it hugged the dog. They stepped over both into a dark hallway. Upstairs an argument was raging and from down the hallway came the sound of a crying child, a sharp slap immediately followed by a greater pitch of was raging and from down the hallway came the sound of a crying sobbing.

Awkwardly the two young men stood there, their bags over their shoulders as the child toddled back inside. It reached Cass's legs and gripped onto them, smiling and dribbling up at him. Cass was unused to children and he gave his leg a bit of a shake, hoping to dislodge the dirty little hands but the child clung and gabbled at him. "Get it off me," he told Samuel in a panic.

Dropping his bag, Samuel crouched down, held out his arms and the child wobbled towards him. He scooped it up, realising it was a little girl. "Where's your mother, little darling?" he asked her.

The toddler laughed at the sound of his voice. She grabbed Samuel's tie in one hand then lay against him, tucking her head underneath his chin with a grubby thumb shoved in her mouth.

"Well, there's yer character reference."

They turned to the harsh voice and saw a fat, blowsy woman wearing her untidy blonde hair very dark at the roots. She wore a faded black skirt with a white blouse and the flesh bulging around her corset gave her an odd shape only slightly obscured by the enveloping apron she wore. She reached out for the little one who gave a wail and clung onto Samuel so he shifted her weight more comfortably in his arms.

"She's all right." he said.

The woman shrugged. "Peg don't take to people as a rule. She's gotta brother somewhere, called Moss. He don't talk so don't pester him about it." She gave the two men a probing look. "Samuel Brodie and Cass Williams?"

"Yep."

"I'll show youse yer room." As she walked up the creaking stairs she called back over her shoulder. "I'm Mrs Huntly by the way. Don't bother asking for Mr Huntly, 'cause the bad old bugger's six feet under and has been these seven years. And yer can call me Maudie. Everyone does."

Samuel glanced down at the child in his arms and did the obvious bit of arithmetic. Not for him to judge, he decided.

Maudie turned a corner, reached one floor and began to trudge up another. "Yer asked for a cheap room?" She didn't wait for their reply, just kept walking up a third flight of stairs. "'Cause that's what yer've got. Yer lucky, akcherly. It's the last cheap one I got. Suddenly every bugger wants to live in Wellington."

On the top floor were several pokey attic rooms. It was one of these that Maudie opened the door onto.

"This here's it. Breakfast's from five till seven and if yer pay extra, I'll cook a bit of supper. I expect a week in advance and there's no grace for no rent. Yer don't pay I chuck yer out. Got it?"

Samuel and Cass moved with some difficulty past her into the small room. Cass peered out of the window straight out into tenement next door where a woman was standing in her corset.

"We've got it." he said.

Samuel passed the now sleeping Peg into Maudie's arm and took out two weeks rent. He handed it to Maudie who peered at the coins suspiciously before nodding and tucking them in the pocket of her grubby apron. "Welcome." She leered at them and left them to it.

There were two old mattresses on the floor, each with blankets, a chamber pot and nothing else. Samuel dropped his bag on one mattress as Cass did the same to the other. The argument they heard on arriving still raged somewhere in the house. Doors slammed and there was a strange, unidentifiable smell on this floor. Samuel noted the same view from the window that Cass had and then turned to his friend who seemed to be with-holding judgement.

Samuel gave him a wide smile. "It's Wellington." he said. "And we're home."

Cass grinned as the corseted woman in the tenement opposite noticed him staring. She sent a rude gesture his way before grabbing her curtains and tugging them across the window.

"Awww…," he grumbled.

***

Five thirty the following morning saw them both standing on the wharf in front of their new boss.

"So, Tim writes you're both hard workers. You'll need to be. You think Lyttleton's busy, it's more so here. No slacking. Are you both members of the union?" The big man's gruff manner fell away somewhat as they nodded vigorously. "Well, that's something. Youse young fellers don't often seem to have your heads screwed on straight and that's a fact. Right, come and meet some of your workmates and we'll get on with it."

Both Samuel and Cass were used to hard work but by the end of the week their muscles ached from loading and unloading an unending procession of boats and ships. Come knock off on pay day and all Cass wanted to do was grab some supper and have a beer.

"I want to have a gander at Haining Street." he smirked. "Remember what Tim told us?"

They stood aside as a tram rattled along on Courtenay Place.

Cass rubbed his hands together gleefully. "Opium and gambling. I could do with some extra pounds in my pocket."

Samuel eyed his friend. "You could lose them just as easily, Cass. You're shit at poker."

"So you're not going to come along then?"

"Might for a bit. I wanna bath first."

They turned into Tory Street, Samuel marvelling how quickly it had felt like they'd lived here for years.

As they wandered along in no particular hurry Cass made eye contact with a dark haired, dark eyed working girl he'd taken a shine to. "Where's the bath house?"

"Manners Street."

"Right."

Cass dragged his eyes away from the girl and his usual lope became a swagger knowing she watched him. Samuel smiled at this byplay then heard a little voice calling out and his smile widened for Peg was toddling towards him as fast her stubby legs could manage. She stumbled at a pothole and fell just as Samuel reached her. He swept her up into his arms and tickled her tears into watery giggles.

Cass grimaced. "She's got as many fleas as the bloody dog."

"She doesn't stink as much as you do," was the blunt reply.

Two hours later they walked out of Hall's Turkish Baths, the working week's grime gone. They stood together on the pavement, Cass turning his back to the wind to light a cigarette.

"So you're off to Haining Street?"

Cass squinted through cigarette smoke. "Thought I'd see a movie first, then maybe. Saul recommended it."

Samuel watched people walking by, bent into the wind. "Saul?"

"I dunno his last name. Tim's mate."

Sam searched his memory for a face, found it with all its unpleasant associations. "Cass, he's a bloody head case."

"But he won plenty off the Chows."

Samuel scoffed. "So he said."

Cass patted his friend's shoulder in mock sympathy. "That's your problem, mate. You don't trust any bugger."

"Cass….."

"Sam, you're not my father. You do what you want and I'll see you later." He flicked his still glowing cigarette butt at Samuel's feet as he walked away towards Dixon Street, his steps buoyant, hands dug deeply into his pockets and Samuel just knew Cass would be whistling as he went.

He remained standing where he was, not wanting to head back to their room or follow Cass. For the life of him he couldn't see what was so marvellous about the pictures. From what Samuel had seen of them if you'd seen one, you'd seen them all. But then, what to do with himself for the rest of the night?

There was always the option of a pub and a few beers but he didn't feel like sitting alone in a bar either. Uncertain but restless Samuel happened to glance across the street. There an ordinary looking building carried the sign 'Socialist Hall'. As he watched a large number of people walked purposefully into it, talking animatedly.

Curiosity piqued, he crossed the road and read a poster on the door.

No God
No
Master

Two young women walked by and Samuel stood aside for them. One of them looked him up and down with a pair of bright, grey eyes and a sardonic lift to pink lips. As they walked up the set of stairs, Samuel straightened his new cap and came to a decision which he knew wasn't really a decision at all.

He followed the girls.

Upstairs the room was warm with chatter. A table under a set of curtained windows faced rows of empty chairs.

Samuel, cap in hand, wearing his only footwear, his working boots, felt very out of place until he realised most of the people around him were working class like him. Nearby a small table was loaded with pamphlets and magazines. For want of something to do, he picked one up with, 'Freedom' written on its cover. He had just opened it when a smiling woman approached him.

"A new face," she said happily. "Always a pleasure. Mr….?"

"Brodie. Samuel Brodie, Ma'am."

"And I'm Jane Donaldson. No Ma'ams here, Mr Brodie." She led him towards a group which included the girl with the grey eyes. "Now, do you know anyone?"

"Not a soul, Mrs Donaldson. I'm new to Wellington."

"Ah. Well, let me introduce you to some new souls, then."

Again Samuel was aware of grey eyes boldly assessing him. Jane gestured. "Mr Samuel Brodie, this is Miss Alexandra Redburn, Mrs Myra Cole and Mr David West."

They all exchanged smiles and handshakes as Jane was hailed from the other side of the room.

"I'll leave you all to get to know each other."

Only Alexandra's attention stayed on Samuel, the other two

seemed intent upon continuing a heated conversation. Giving the arguing couple a rueful glance, she moved a few steps away, Samuel happy to follow her lead.

"So what do you make of Wellington so far, Mr Brodie?"

"It's very alive, Miss Redburn. Not unlike Christchurch I suppose but Wellington has something Christchurch lacks.

"And what would that be?"

"A Socialist Hall." Samuel let his eyes wander about the room. "I worked on Lyttleton Wharf and there was plenty of talk about unions. Bob Semple and Pat Hickey came from Greymouth to talk to us during the Blackball crib time dispute but we usually stood around in pubs or Cathedral Square." Samuel gave the assembled people an approving nod. "This is…. better." He finished a little lamely.

Maybe Alexandra thought so too for an eyebrow lifted. "It was Phillip Joseph who brought the Socialist cause to light in Wellington. This place is where his ideas come to life. Somewhere people can meet, hear new ideas, socialism, communism or anarchism. We have lecturers from Britain, the United States. Bob Semple spoke here once." Alexandra gave Samuel a wide smile. "A very exciting speaker and a rather attractive man, I thought." And before Samuel could reply to this surprising comment, she lifted her head. "Ah. It's beginning. Would you care to sit beside me, Mr Brodie."

"Thank you, Miss Redburn."

Samuel had taken to politics and socialism with passion, so much so that one of his reasons for choosing to work in Wellington was a need to be in the capital city for the General Election at the end of the year. He'd read whatever he could lay his hands on, so complacently expected to enjoy tonight's proceedings without feeling challenged by them. Samuel thought back proudly to those times when his workmates had listened to his bar-thumping rhetoric in Christchurch. Maybe he would get such an opportunity to do so here? And, he had to admit it, he wouldn't mind showing off a little to the woman sitting with such cool self-possession at his side.

Too his discomfiture however, what Samuel heard overwhelmed him, left him gaping at the depth of discussions offered and he realised within minutes that he wouldn't be offering any of his personal insights any time soon.

Georges Sorel's words were fired at them from the man standing behind the table.

"'Class struggle can only be overcome by creative violence by the working class. Parliamentarianism and evolutionary democracy are dangerous illusions and need to be replaced by realistic strategy or direct industrial action.' Discuss."

A tall, thin man with a querulous moustache rose to refute.

"If we're going to quote anyone, what about Edward Tregear? He has written, 'Strikes have had their day.' We have an Independent Labour Party now ready to take the cause of the working class into Parliament. We must stand behind those who would seek change in the offices of power and through the Arbitration Court."

Some cheered. Some booed.

Alexandra stood, eyes flashing. "No. We should stand behind the New Zealand Federation of Labour – no arbitration. We fight because those in power are not listening to our needs while increasing profits are shovelled into their hands by keeping the working classes to the ground with negligent, dangerous working conditions and subsistence wages. The General Election draws nearer. We need a voice that will be heard. One strong union able to force industrial action – the only kind of action the Liberals or the Reformers will take heed of. And let's not forget that the Arbitration Court is happy to freeze or cut workers' wages but have repeatedly told us that the high profits earned by employers does not justify increasing the wages of those who made those profits possible!"

Samuel joined in the clapping as Alexandra sat back down. She leaned towards him. "Stir them up," she whispered mischievously,

The evening was a revelation to Samuel. He heard from radicals, moderates, from men and women and each person had a point of view and pamphlets to back up their arguments. By the end of the night his head was reeling and he knew he'd found his kind of place and his kind of people.

As she pulled on her gloves to leave, Alexandra turned to him. "Will we see you here again, Mr Brodie?"

What else could he say but, yes.

With his pockets bulging with reading material, his head full of new ideas and passionate silver grey eyes, Samuel paused on the footpath outside the Hall and breathed in the freshness of the gusting Wellington wind.

Haining Street, Alma Street and others of their kind only came alive at night. Haining Street was a one-way hovel, crowded with decrepit wooden cottages some with crudely made add-ons of tin and old wood, the last refuges of the very poor. Rubbish piled up where there happened to be a gap between the buildings but for all its slum-like appearance it was in a part of the city where everyone was welcome, provided they had money enough.

A door to one of the oldest cottages thumped open and Cass staggered out, mumbling his goodnights to no one, unaware of the cold wind and the menacing shapes observing from the gloom. Stumbling, he crashed against one wall where a pair of helpful hands guided him back on the path and with great dexterity lifted the few coins Cass had left in his pockets.

Whatever hell the time was when he eventually made it back to Maudie's, Samuel was stretched out on his mattress snoring. Cass collapsed onto his and lay there contemplating his revelries of the past few weeks.

He knew he lost too much money gambling. The chinks were playing something called fan-tan and he couldn't get his head around it no matter how hard he tried. He'd stuck to poker, feeling that if he was going to beggar himself he might as well do it with rules he understood.

Then came the occasion when someone passed him an opium pipe. For the first few nights he'd handed it on with a shake of the head. Then tonight the chink pressed it on him again, smiling that blank Asiatic smile and Cass gave in. The rest of the night he was lost to a smoky, dreamy haze. He could still smell the sweet smell on his clothes.

Cass fell asleep smiling.

'Dear Jimmy,

It was lovelie to get your letter. No I aint seen Samuel since last time you wrote me. I aint herd nothing of him since when you 2 left tho he sent me that money what I told you abart. 3 pounds! I culdnt believe it then or now!

I got Cook's job for she is too old now. She still works here and gives me a hand wen we are very bisy but still thinks shes the boss!

Did I tell you Im getting married to Joe Green? hes a driver for Newmans. I hope you like yore present. Hope the socks keep you warm. I only just lernt to knit last winter cose Joe says its perishin on the rode.

Love from Molly'

***

Dawn up the Matakitaki Valley in Murchison slid softly over the hill ranges and settled her light across the valley floor. At this time of the year there was plenty to do, cutting hay a priority and it needed every pair of hands which was why John's face wore a discontented look as Emily served breakfast.

He glanced to Jimmy's empty seat. "Twenty one years old and he still can't drag himself out of his bed." John grumbled.

Emily tipped breakfast onto two plates, passed one to her husband, covered the other before placing it in the stove. "You know what this time of the year means to him, John Benn. Jimmy's not still in his bed and if you put your mind to it you'll know exactly where he is."

It was stifling hot even at this early hour of day. Heat hung in the air while the scents of grass and native bush all added their sweet heaviness to the early morning.

John sucked on his pipe as he strode towards the river. After four years he still missed Wolf's vast presence at his side. Cob was a big dog but he didn't have Wolf's sheer mass or intelligence. Cob did exactly what he was told and skilled though he was he never anticipated commands the way Wolf used to. Now, he gave an excited bark, and launched himself towards his brother.

Colt was more like Wolf. He had his father's size and cleverness but he'd been the runt of the litter, an undersized, scrappy, little thing John had been going to drown when fourteen year old Jimmy stayed his hand with pleading eyes.

"I'll raise him, John. I will."

"He'll be a sickly thing, son. Not worth the effort."

But Jimmy had the poor pup in his hands and as it squirmed against his fingers the boy felt an intense surge of love for it. Unable to explain the feeling, Jimmy couldn't speak, just stared mutely up at John, imploring until he relented.

"If it sickens, Jimmy, if it's poorly….."

Jimmy gently stroked the tiny creature. "I will. I promise." He stayed his hand with pleading eyes.

"I won't have any animals suffering."

The boy gave him a confident smile. "He won't suffer."

To John's amazement the boy proved right and Colt grew to be a strong, handsome white and black hound with a thick coat and a mane-like ruff whose superior intelligence was obvious when the two canine brothers worked on the farm side by side. Jimmy didn't gloat when Colt out-classed Cob. Not much, anyway.

This morning Colt sat at the bottom of the willow tree and didn't move when Cob threw himself onto him, expecting to wrestle and tumble. Instead the big dog whined up into the branches of the tree.

"Away, dogs." John pointed behind him and on cue both dogs moved. Colt though only moved a few feet away to sit and watch the willow tree leaving Cob to chase the insects and splash in the river. The long day's work stretched ahead of the farmer as it always did but he never begrudged Jimmy this day of the year. Grunting a little as he sat, John leaned against the tree trunk and stared out over the river. "Mother remembered."

"She always does." Jimmy's muffled voice came down through the pale green foliage.

During the silence John watched Cob chasing waves as they fell over rocks until there was a scuffle above his head and Jimmy dropped lightly down out of the branches, sat beside him.

From a skinny, under nourished starveling Jimmy had sprouted and though he was still lightly built, he was deceptively strong. His hair fell untidily across his forehead while the early light of the day brought sharp cheek bones into prominence in his lean face.

"They were the worst days of my life." Jimmy spoke softly. "But I can't leave them behind me." He sighed deeply, clicked his fingers and Colt was instantly at his side. "We used to sit beside the river at the Orphanage. Big John died in it. Why do I sit here every year beside a river when rivers have nothing but terrible memories? Why?"

It had been in the nights after Samuel left Murchison that Jimmy's nightmares reached frightening proportions. Night after night Emily sat at his bedside, soothing the distraught boy as he spoke haltingly of ghosts, screams in the night, pain and fear. On the worst nights he'd wet the bed, suffering torments of embarrassment and shame.

For two long years Emily and John worked through those terrible events in Jimmy's life, painfully aware of times when the tendrils from the past still had power to reach out and engulf him. Even now he was a young man and no longer a fearful boy, echoes and shadows clung to him on certain days.

Days like today.

"And…. it's Sam's birthday and I don't know where he is. He could be dead for all I know."

"Maybe you should write to Molly again."

Wordlessly Jimmy handed John Molly's letter.

"Father's not heard anything either. Harry said he's only ever had that short note with the money Samuel sent him to repay him for the horse, remember?" Jimmy threw an arm round Colt's neck. "Too much money, Harry said. The horse was only an old nag. But he's sent not even a word to me!" Jimmy's anguished face turned to John's. "I know I told him to go…I know… But I'm his brother and he's never got in touch."

A familiar sense of uselessness swamped John where Samuel was concerned. He knew Jimmy had been devoted to his brother and he understood, too just how Jimmy strove to forget him but neither he or Emily could find the right words to help Jimmy heal this particular wound.

No one knew where Samuel went to after Murchison. During Jimmy's worst months Fraser had turned up at the farm with Jimmy's adoption papers in one hand. Their reunion had been full of tears and happiness and when Samuel's behaviour was discussed and the policemen's visit picked over, Jimmy's tearful side of the story came out as well. He told them about Samuel hiding in John's cart to Murchison; what Samuel said about the fire, the way he, Jimmy, had sent his brother away. And here Jimmy fell mute, shaking and crying in Emily's arms.

Together John and Fraser had travelled back to Nelson. They met Father Aherne and Brother Donatus at the same time other questions were being raised about the way the Orphanage had been run.

Fraser raged at Aherne. He punched Donatus and was nearly arrested. Only John's intervention and well-chosen words to Aherne saw that crisis averted. Both men came away knowing Samuel was innocent of what he was accused of but without proof either way? It was no wonder the boy had run.

Jimmy, ill in bed could barely take any of it in beyond the baldest of facts – Samuel had done nothing wrong. And during his slow recovery, Jimmy was faced with another hard decision. Fraser wanted this one son to live with him on the coast. As he listened to his father's pleading, tears slid down Jimmy's wasted face but he knew the only thing he wanted was to be with Emily and John. The boy would never forget the look on his father's face when he told him he would be going back to the Coast alone. Twice Jimmy had rejected the people who loved him. So Fraser returned alone to Blackball grateful at least for the contact with Jimmy and the need

May's family had for him. He and Jimmy had never lost touch again.

Yet still there was a raw and gaping wound in Jimmy's life, a gap where his brother used to be.

John placed his hand warmly on Jimmy's shoulder. "I don't know why Samuel feels it has to be this way, Jimmy. I don't. Probably never will. Maybe with more time….?" He left the sentence hanging knowing as well as Jimmy that twelve years was already a long time. "Look, lad, I have to turn out for the day. Mother has your breakfast waiting for you – and woe betide you if you don't return and eat it before it spoils."

That earned him a watery smile. John whistled for Cob who galloped up, tongue hanging out, ready to run. "See you on the farm."

It wasn't meant as a question but John felt a sweeping relief when Jimmy turned his face to him and nodded. Snapping his fingers to his dog, John strode away, his mind on the day ahead.

Jimmy ruffled Colt's thick coat. "Twelve years, Colt. Twelve bloody years."

The big dog whined, licked Jimmy's face.

"I'm not going to feel like this every year. Waiting for someone who doesn't want me in his life." He glared at the big dog who thought the expression was for him and his ears and tail drooped. Jimmy shoved himself onto his feet. He had so much to live for here, so much to be grateful for. Memories of Samuel wouldn't poison it anymore, they wouldn't.

He jogged away through the fields towards the house with Colt at his heels all the way, determination feeding off his anger and resentment.

***

In a room set aside for meetings in the Commercial Hotel, a group of Murchison farmers had gathered at the request of Peter Dray whose anger pulsed around them all. He waved the papers at the other men while Jimmy listened avidly.

"Have you read some of the filth that's being printed? Listen to this – *'There must be an abolition of capitalism which must include abolition of the wages system, private ownership and control of industry, natural resources and minerals. There must be an end to a system of control by landowners who earn thirty thousand pounds or more annually while paying their labourers as little fifteen shillings a week. It could begin with a tax on unearned income to control the speculators and farmers.'"*

Dray's disgust was such he could barely prevent himself spitting on the words.

"Massey's the only one who can put those bastards in their place. With the Reform Party in Parliament these militants can be dealt with." Peter Dray threw the newspaper on the table. "This is treason they're spouting. Treason. They should be locked up before they bring good men down with them."

"Is it treason for men to want what's fair?"

John hadn't been going to enter into an argument with Peter who never heeded any opinion but his own but some devil on his shoulder urged him to speak.

Peter gave a disbelieving snort. "Fair? The employers take all the business risks. What does the working man have to worry about apart from which pub to spend his next lot of wages in?"

John lit his pipe, leaned back on his chair. He supported Massey, too but he was damned if he was going to let Peter Dray know that. Instead he played Devil's Advocate. "You do know most working men have families. Have you not seen how some of them live?"

"It's their choice to live in poverty, John. A sensible man, a hard-working man will easily pay his way." Peter thumped his hand back on the newspaper. "It's these bastards who want something for nothing. Foreign agitators Massey calls them and with good reason. If the bastards aren't happy here, they should go back to their own damn country and let God-fearing New Zealanders get on with living their lives according to the rules of Church and Government. Farmers and employers are the backbone of this country's welfare and if these…. Red Feds… don't like that then they should be arrested and bloody shot."

John had had enough. Without apology he got to his feet and picked up his hat. "Well, whatever the outcome of the election, I've still got a farm to run. Thanks for the drink, Peter. Coming, Jimmy?" Giving the young man no choice but to obey.

Peter Dray's angry voice, still loudly denouncing, 'those communist bastards,' followed them outside.

Cob and Colt were lying by the horses when the two men walked into the stables behind the hotel. Harry, busy clearing out, lifted his head as they approached, gave them a nod by way of a greeting.

"Harry. Not having a drink on Peter Dray tonight?"

"I'll buy my own drinks, John. I wouldn't ask the time of Peter Dray."

Whether it was deliberate or chance, Harry spat onto the floor. He happened to catch Jimmy's disapproving expression and wondered for the umpteenth time why it was he just couldn't like him. There was something lacking in the lad. To Harry's mind he didn't have half the character of his brother and he certainly didn't have Samuel's sense of humour. It amused Harry to sense that the dislike seemed to be mutual for whenever Jimmy spoke to him, it was with noticeable reluctance, bordering on disdain.

"You've still no word about your brother's whereabouts?" He received a shake of the head. "Shame."

Jimmy grabbed the reins of his horse and mounted up with one smooth movement. "He can rot in hell for all I care." Jimmy's stare burned the air between them and without another word he left the stables at a trot.

Harry raised an eyebrow in John's direction. "Plenty of anger there."

"Not without reason, Harry."

The two men walked out of the stables, Harry's hand resting on the neck of John's horse. Instead of mounting, John paused, weighing his words. "You seem to hear a lot of what goes on and not just here in Murchison. Do you think much'll come from these Red Feds?"

Surprise showed in Harry's face. He searched the other man's expression as cautiously as John examined Harry's words.

"Peter Dray?"

John nodded briefly as Harry gave a snort of derision. "There is change coming, John. And where there's change, there's resistance." Harry leaned against the accommodating horse. "The way I see it, if you keep a man face down in the dirt with your boot on his head he'll either die in the dirt or he'll finally push back."

John frowned. "Things are that bad? This is New Zealand, not Britain. Not Europe."

"You're a good man, John, a good employer but many aren't. I've worked in factories and I've been a slave on a sheep farm. I even spent time in Brunner Mine a few years before the disaster and it's a hard life being a working man."

"I'm a damn working man, Harry!"

"You're a farmer. A land owner. But what's coming isn't about you. It's not even about Peter bloody Dray." Harry kept his eyes on John's. "There are people out there who want a revolution. I reckon they'll get one."

John looked around the quiet streets of Murchison. Children played, running and shouting, one had an old hoop she rolled with a stick. Women with baskets tucked over one arm walked in and out few shops, pausing to pass the time of day.

"It won't come here."

Harry pushed himself upright, looked at the same streets and saw only the smug content of people who could afford to shop and children from families who could let them play.

"Maybe it bloody should."

For the first time in all the years they'd known each other something moved out of the shadows of their different lives and subtly changed them. They would never be so comfortable together again.

John mounted his patient horse and looked down on Harry who

held his gaze. The farmer tipped his hat politely before riding away.

26

Unmoving, stagnant air felt out of place in Wellington. In a city used to winds from gentle breezes to gales this soft calm was unnatural.

Samuel stifled in the warm, dead atmosphere, longing for the usual freshness of crisp, new air. He ran a finger around his stiff collar, felt the sweat gathering under the inflexible neckband while Alex walked easily beside him, matching his long strides. Her white frock and wide shady hat seemed impervious to the heat and unlike most Wellington women, Alex refused to be corseted, revelling in the ease of movement this freedom gave her. The other benefit of not being encased in hot, punishing whale bone was reflected in her cool face which made a mockery of the flushed, red cheeks of the women who passed them on their walk through the Botanic Gardens. These women targeted Alex with behind-the-hand whispers and judgemental stares, for as she explained to Samuel, wearing no corsets was considered an admission of immorality. Alex pointedly met this haughty disapproval with the aloofness she had long perfected as a weapon.

On this lovely afternoon, she and Samuel stopped on a crest overlooking the Teaching Gardens.

"They have to keep these gardens fenced and gated. People steal the plants." Alex sat on a wooden bench. She pulled out a hat pin to remove her hat, fanned herself with it.

"I don't mind trees but can't see the point in flowers." Samuel grumbled, dropping down onto the seat with an ungainly thump.

"You have no eye for beauty?"

Samuel met Alex's silver eyes with a mischievous glint in his own. "Not for flowers," was his pointed reply.

Alex shook her head at him. "Flattery doesn't impress me, Samuel."

"It's not flattery when it's truthful."

"Again!" Alex whacked him with her hat, much to the scandalous disapproval of a staid couple walking by. She met their glare with a sunny look. "He deserved it," she told them.

The couple turned their faces from hers and walked quickly on as if fearful of contamination.

"Now look what you've done." Alex complained as she watched them, condemnation radiating off their broad backs. "They think me wanton."

Samuel took himself off the bench and threw himself under the shade of an obliging pine tree. With a groan of pleasure he removed his cap, lay back on the grass, let coolness tickle the back of his hot neck. "You should treat men with more respect, then."

Through half closed eyes Samuel saw Alex sit on the grass beside him.

"When I find a man deserving of respect, I shall offer it to him." She laid her hat on the grass and drew her knees up, wrapping her arms around them.

Samuel rolled over, propped his head up on one hand. "I thought Bob Semple was such a man." He watched her lips curl up at the ends as she smiled.

"Charismatic, certainly. Attractive, yes. But he's dangerous, too."

"Dangerous? How?"

"He argues from his emotions, not logic. He can stir people up, make them forget themselves in the fight but when the fight is over I wonder how many are left questioning how far they went for that cause and just what it cost them."

All mockery had left Alex's face and she gazed out over the gardens with an intent, serious look. Samuel admired that about her. The way she leapt from mockery to teasing to seriousness and back again with nothing but a breath between the moods. It made Alex an interesting companion but an uncomfortable one, too for he wasn't always sure when she was teasing. Those silver eyes could be as unrevealing as a mist across a chasm.

"If we're to win a class war, we need men like Semple and Hickey."

"We need moderates, too."

"Moderates don't win wars on a battlefield."

"No. But they can win them in Parliaments." Alex looked at the open, honest face watching her. "Radicals may force a path to power but only moderates can hold that power." She read Samuel's scepticism. "Listen to the debate tonight. I know working people need to strike but to use it as a weapon to bludgeon employers?" Alex sighed. "I don't know."

"But I've heard you speak out in defence of strikes."

"Yes as part of a fight against unfairness, not the whole fight itself."

Samuel frowned. "What other choice does a working man have?"

"I don't know…." Her voice trailed off sadly.

They sat in comfortable silence for a while, watching this hot Sunday afternoon pass them gently by. A nanny in the company of four small children came into view, the nanny's harassment, the children's exuberance a fine show.

"Do you have family, Samuel?"

The question sucked all joy out of his morning. No longer relaxed and somnolent, he lay stiffly on his back, an arm over his eyes as if to shade it from the sun sparking through the branches overhead. "No."

Alex was taken aback by the abruptness of his reply. "Oh." She continued to fan her face. "You mean, never?"

"I've told you, Alex, I was an orphan in Nelson. No family." He sat up now, all pretence of relaxation gone. His eyes were dark and bitter lines cut into his usually good-looking face.

The change in him was so pronounced, Alex pulled back no longer sure of him. "I didn't mean to upset you." she began but he reached out, laid a hand on hers.

"It's not for you to apologise." The pressure of his hand on hers was warm and this time when he looked at her, all hostility was gone and he was the Samuel she'd grown to like once more.

Another couple appeared on the path in front of them, the woman wearing a large picture hat atop her white frock and being chaperoned by a man in an immaculate dark suit. Alex removed her hand from under Samuel's, aware the women had seen the action.

With one smooth movement, she rose to her feet and repinned her hat. "Cup of tea?"

"I'd rather have a beer." He grinned at the look on Alex's face. "But if you're buying, a cup of tea will do."

He offered her his arm which after a pause, Alex accepted. Arm in arm they walked back towards the cable car, talking politics all the way.

***

Samuel whistled as he prepared for the meeting that night in the Socialist Hall.

Cass lay on his mattress, bags under his eyes, fingers picking restlessly at nothing. "You sound happy."

"Why don't you come with me, Cass?"

"And hear a lot of old buggers rambling on? No thanks." He eyed his friend impishly. "Also, I've no bloody wish to play gooseberry."

Samuel reacted too quickly. "What are you on about?"

"I wonder how keen you'd be on your bloody socialism if you hadn't met Alexandra Redburn." To Cass's delight, Samuel's face coloured from the neck up.

"That's rubbish." Samuel looked away from his friend's knowing smirk.

Cass put his hands behind his head, still wearing his smirk. "If you say so."

"She's middle class, Cass. She won't have any interest in someone like me."

"Thought a lot about it though, haven't you?"

Samuel threw a handy book at Cass's head. "Piss off. What will you get up to tonight?"

"Dunno."

"Are you seeing Vi still?"

A shrug.

"Cass, you won't head back to Haining Street, will you?"

It was Cass's turn to look guilty. He shrugged, avoided all eye contact.

"It's not doing you any good, mate."

"I can cope with it."

"You get the sweats, you don't eat, you don't sleep…."

Cass leapt to his feet, rounded on Samuel. "Bugger off, Sam. I know what I'm doing."

"No, you don't."

"I'm warning you, stop bloody nagging!"

In concern Samuel noted beads of sweat forming on Cass's face, the nervous twitching of his restless fingers. He reached out only to have Cass pull away and leave the room, slamming the door behind him.

Samuel followed quickly as Cass turned right out of the front door and headed up Tory Street. What were the chances he'd head straight for the dens?

A little away from Samuel, Peg's older brother, Moss squatted on the road, playing with a couple of marbles.

"Moss, d'you want to earn thruppence?"

The boy rubbed his wet nose across a filthy sleeve, stared at Samuel before nodding.

Maudie was right. Her boy never talked but no one seemed to know if it was because he couldn't or he just didn't. He seemed bright enough, though. Now he held up six fingers, the dirt from the street sticking to them.

"Sixpence?" Samuel looked up the road. There was no sign of Cass anywhere. Samuel hunkered down and picked up a marble, eyeing the one ahead of him before thumbing it off. It missed by yards causing Moss to grin, showing missing top teeth. "Tell you what, Moss. If you do a good job for me, I'll give you a shilling, all right?"

The boy beamed at the prospect of such wealth. In all his eight years he'd never had so much money for just himself. He nodded furiously, stood up, wiping his hands on his trousers, which made little difference to the state of his hands or trousers and held one out to Samuel who sealed the deal solemnly.

"Now, young Moss, just how good are you at following people…..?

As usual it was Bob Semple's voice which rose above the rest in argument as the crowded Socialist Hall turned out again.

"The NZFL has 14,000 members alone. We're becoming a force to be reckoned with by anyone's standard. But if every union walked under the same banner, one union, one major battle against the employers. They'll listen then." Bob Semple's dark eyes flashed around the audience. "Craft unions and the Arbitration Court are things of the past."

James Young gave an exasperated sound, rose to meet Semple's argument. "You are up against a capitalist government and if you have a universal strike you are going to be crushed in the same way as Wade has crushed the miners in Australia. Surely industrial development must go hand-in-hand with political action? It should not exist independently."

Semple sneered. "The Labour Party's middle classes are grovelling to get into parliament on the back of the workers!"

James Young ignored the sneer, kept his cool. "That sort of rhetoric gains you nothing, Bob. No advance can be made in this country until you capture the political machine."

"Back room deals and Machiavellian machinations!"

But James just gave Semple a sorrowful look. "We haven't even made Parliament and you would condemn us for behaviour we haven't committed? What kind of argument is that?"

For once, Semple's ready tongue failed him and in the pause, an odd looking figure stood and coughed politely to get attention. Walter Mills stood under five foot tall and he seemed dwarfed by the two men either side of him but there was something about this American that drew every pair of eyes.

"This country is being run by powerful men with powerful reasons to hold the working man firmly in his place; to make him incapable through poor education, poor health and poverty itself to never challenge those in control of his life. These powerful men do not want to change the status quo, nor do they wish to share their power and wealth among the many. What the New Zealand worker needs is a radical coalition opposed to those economic monopolies which keep commodity prices at high levels and conservative government only interested in maintaining and increasing the power and profits of the ruling class with social inequality."

Samuel leaned towards Alex and whispered, "Who's this?"

"Walter Mills. The Trades and Labour Council invited him to New Zealand to lecture."

While Mills spoke on in his monotonous drawl Samuel watched the men at the table with him. "Look at Semple. He doesn't like Mills."

Alex studied each man's face. "But Mills is arguing for one union which is what the Red Feds want. Why wouldn't Semple agree?"

Samuel shrugged. "I dunno but I bet he won't win Semple over."

Near the end of the meeting, Samuel checked his watch, unaware he'd been doing so for most of the night.

Alex whispered, "Are we keeping you from something?"

"No, no. It's…. I've promised to meet a friend, that's all. He's… well, he's in need of company."

"I see. I hope he's all right."

Applause broke out around the room which they both hastily joined in and it had barely died away when Samuel stood up.

 "Sorry. Alex. I… I've got to go."

Thoughtful silver grey eyes followed him out the door. Seeing Alex's distraction Jane Donaldson touched her arm to gain her attention.

 "Miss Redburn. I'd like to introduce you to Mr Walter Mills."

The little man took Alex's hand in his and bowed over it in a way that made her want to laugh. In an effort to control this unsuitable response she quickly averted her eyes and as she did she saw Bob Semple on the other side of the room watching the little American in a way that reminded Alex of a cat watching unexpected and unfamiliar prey. She mentally saluted Samuel's insight.

Outside on the pavement the scruffy little boy waited patiently, keeping a wary eye out for inquisitive coppers and the kind of men who kept their own look out for young children.

Samuel thundered down the stairs, fumbling to do up his jacket. "Moss. Did you find him?"

A nod.

"Can you show me?"

Fear showed in the boy's eyes and he shook his head. As Samuel frowned, Moss shoved a grubby piece of paper into his hand. Uncrumpling it, Samuel read a street name written in barely decipherable letters.

"Which house?" he asked urgently but Moss shrugged. He didn't go down that street.

"How long has he been there?"

Moss considered this then held up four fingers.

"Four hours?"

Nod.

"Alone?"

Nod.

Samuel passed Moss the promised shilling. The boy stared down at the coin before gripping it tightly in one palm and doing a funny little dance, to show how happy was he.

"You've done good work, Moss. I'll remember that. Now bugger off back home or I'll have your Ma after me."

Skipping joyfully Moss left Samuel lost in his thoughts and it took him long moments to come to a conclusion but decision made, he strode off to find Cass.

Before getting too far up Tory Street, Samuel picked up a short but weighty piece of wood he found in an alleyway and tucked it inside his jacket. He hadn't experienced much trouble on the streets at night but as the working men grew angrier and the election nearer, so the arguments escalated. Scuffles and fights spilled out of pubs onto the streets and it was a brave man who ventured into the darker areas totally unprepared for trouble.

As if to highlight Samuel's expectations, two men stepped out of an alleyway only to back off hands raised in a conciliatory gesture on seeing the homemade baton swung threateningly. Samuel watched until they had disappeared back into the gloom before moving on, shoulders twitching, the hairs on the nape of his neck prickling.

"Are you lonely, Mister?" The voice was young, far too young for the knowing eyes.

"I'm not lonely at all, sweetheart." Samuel gave the girl a few coins.

She added them up quickly, took a step towards him and reached out. Gently, he held her hands, feeling the delicate bones under her skin. "I don't want anything," he told her.

With an incredulous look at the money she held, the girl gave Samuel a bewildered, gratified smile and left him before he could change his mind. As he walked off he heard her calling out to someone else.

Haining Street appeared on his left. Now, which den would Cass be in? Moss had scrawled the name of the street only, obviously too scared to venture down it any further after Cass.

Samuel began to comb stinking dens made even worse by heat and the crush of bodies. In room upon room he saw men lying on crude pallets or just on the filthy floor, their faces blank, eyes dead, lost to the opium.

After the umpteenth room, Samuel found Cass, almost indistinguishable from the other bodies lying near him. He crouched over him, fearfully aware how thin and sickly his friend had become. Cass looked so ill their boss had begun to notice.

"What's wrong with Cass?" he had demanded of Samuel.

"He's just tired."

But shrewd, undeceived eyes met Samuel's carefully nonchalant ones. "Well, he better keep off the Chink's bloody opium, then." Abashed, Samuel promised he would see to it and a weighty hand slapped down on his shoulder. "Get him straight, mate. You're good workers both of you but Cass's not pulling his weight anymore and there's always good men looking for work."

All this went through Samuel's head as he looked down at his friend, an opium pipe hanging listlessly from his fingers.

Through a roughly hung curtain, Samuel heard muted voices, then a shout. Before he had time to move, a man was shoved backwards through the curtain, spitting in rage as he crashed onto two of the drugged, heedless bodies. The man shoved himself back through the curtain.

"You cheating Chinese bastard! Gimmie back my money!"

Again he was shoved out, this time followed by laughter. Enraged the man pulled something out of his pocket. Samuel caught the glint of candlelight on a metal blade and with no time to think the man bellowed, thrust the knife before him and charged back into the room. This time there was a scream of pain and a sudden, enveloping silence.

Four Chinese men appeared, dragging the unconscious body between them and Samuel had a sickening view of a bloodied face with a gaping hole where an eye used to be. In moments the Chinese men were back, wiping their hands fastidiously as they disappeared into the room. A rush of Chinese was followed by exuberant laughter.

Desperate to be out of this terrible place, Samuel lugged Cass to his feet and dragged him outside. There, under the summer moon the unconscious, bleeding body of the gambler lay among the rubbish, a rat already investigating the smell of blood and flesh. Samuel shuddered, stumbling in his haste to be gone. "Jesus, Cass." he muttered. "Do you really want to live like this?"

Not expecting an answer he was surprised when Cass slurred, "It…. makes me…. happy." T

The over-sweet, sickly smell hung around Cass who smiled blankly. Samuel bit back a retort, aware of the pointlessness in arguing with someone lost to a drugged haze. Instead, he shouldered him more comfortably and said grimly, "We have very different ideas about happiness, my friend."

Half way back down Tory Street, Samuel faltered with Cass's dead weight. As he paused to catch his breath a woman stepped up beside him.

"Can I help?"

Samuel turned incredulously to find Alex watching him, concern on her features.

"What the hell are you doing up here?" he blurted out, shocked into impoliteness.

"I thought your behaviour tonight was odd. I wanted to know why."

"So you followed me?"

She gave him that sardonic smile. "So it would appear." The smile disappeared as Cass vomited over Samuel's boots. "Is he drunk?"

Samuel cursed under his breath, held Cass steady until the spasm passed. "No. The silly bastard's not drunk."

As Alex moved quickly to wipe Cass's hair back from his sweaty, pale face, she smelt a distinctive odour on his clothes, in his hair. "Opium." She said, adding softly under her breath, "The bloody fool." She took out a handkerchief and gently cleaned Cass's mouth and chin. "Come on. I'll help you get him home."

Without waiting, Alex grabbed one of Cass's arms, pulled it over her shoulder as Samuel did the same on the other side.

"You shouldn't been seen in this part of town on your own, Alex."

"I'm not on my own. I'm with you and Cass."

The ludicrousness of this reply struck Samuel as funny until he noticed the looks they were attracting from passers-by.

"You know, I think that only makes things worse."

"Have you not yet noticed that I'm not one for caring over much what others think of me?" Alex replied, a little breathlessly as Cass's weight dragged her down.

They made it to Maudie's. Samuel heaved Cass off their shoulders and held him against the outside wall of the front door. "We're in the attic room."

Alex scowled. "You would be!" She sighed theatrically, made to pick Cass up once more when Samuel stopped her.

"This isn't your problem, Alex. I'll deal with him."

"Do you know how to deal with someone with an opium addiction?"

Samuel folded his arms, leaving Cass to slump unceremoniously to the ground. "No."

"Well, I do. You have to clean it out of his system. And it's horrible. But if you don't and he can't beat it, it will kill him."

Samuel forgot they were standing on a dirty street, with drunks weaving past. He didn't hear the rumble of hansom cabs or hear the cat calls. He saw nothing except the pain and understanding in Alex's eyes. "What do I do?"

"I'll show you."

With the help of Maudie who could have carried Cass up the stairs singlehandedly if Samuel had let her, they set him on his mattress and Alex tucked the blanket around him.

"Thanks, Maudie." Samuel said.

"Thanks yerself," she replied in her dismissive fashion but not before Samuel had seen the flush of embarrassment on her face at his courtesy.

Cass whimpered, his hair matted wetly against his scalp. Alex knelt beside him, soothing him as a mother would a distressed child. She looked up and saw Samuel hovering anxiously. "You'll have to stay with him. He can't be allowed out unescorted and it would be better if you could just keep him here. He'll need food he won't want to eat and you'll have to give him boiled water but most of all you cannot let him touch the stuff. It has to wear its way out of his body and it'll hurt him. He'll cry, he'll curse and he'll hate you but you mustn't give in." All the while she spoke she kept her attention on Cass's wasted face.

Samuel knelt beside her "How do you know so much about it?" The pause went on so long Samuel thought she wasn't going to answer unaware that Alex was weighing up the emotional cost of revealing something so personal.

"My brother," she said eventually. "And we couldn't save him." Before Samuel could show any sympathy Alex stood up, straightening her long skirt. "I'll help you. When you need to work, I'll be here with him and I'll see Maudie. I'm sure she'll lend a hand, too."

"What if he's violent?"

"Then I'll shout for Maudie." He opened his mouth to object. "Trust me on this, Samuel. You can't do it alone."

With a final look at Cass, Alex left.

27

The house was the same as every other on the tidy street. Two stories, two rooms wide, the staircase on the right in the front door, three bedrooms upstairs, drawing room, dining room, bathroom and kitchen on the ground floor.

The rooms of this particular house smelt of polish and no dust was allowed to gather on any surface. The grandfather clock in the hall could be heard ticking from the drawing room, the dining room and from the upstairs landing. Alex could even hear it counting the finite length of her hours from behind her closed bedroom door even when she huddled under the bedcovers with fingers stuffed in her ears.

It ticked off the quarter hours, the half hours, the full hours of her existence. Clunk, clunk, clunk, clunk. Alex swore she could even feel the rhythmic dripping away of her life Clunk, clunk, clunk, clunk. The striking of midnight, the clamour of noon. Clunk, clunk, clunk, clunk. Farewell to that quarter hour, that half hour. Farewell to that never to be lived again hour.

Clunk, clunk. Clunk, clunk. Clunk.

That monotonous heartbeat of the grandfather clock reinforced everything Alex hated in her life. She didn't want to be surrounded by well-mannered people speaking carefully placed words whose content depended on whoever was listening. She struggled against the pointless stroll through middle class morality which everyone lauded while it remained determinedly unexamined against its prejudices.

There were days when all she wanted to do was stand with her toes on the edge of a crumbling cliff. To face the storm. To feel the beat of the wind's gusts and fight against them as they threatened to push her over the edge and to fight equally hard when they shoved her back towards safety.

It was this vein of wildness she recognised in Samuel and she found herself increasingly drawn to the understanding that he was holding back, tightly confining things he wanted within the expectations of his reality. Sometimes she surprised a look on his face, especially when he was nursing Cass and she would catch her breath, avert her eyes for she felt she had discovered something so private it was as if she'd walked into the room and found him naked in front of her, exposed and vulnerable, attractive and forbidden. She had experienced nothing like this with anyone in her life ever.

When she had assisted her mother and aunt in Bobby's care there had been no intimate feeling of shared experience, no drawing closer on the edge of approaching darkness. The older women had viewed Bobby's wasted body with obvious distaste, leaving to Alex all the more personal moments a nurse should be hired to undertake but for Father's refusal to have their family shame seen by any other living creature.

Alex alone understood what drove Bobby to seek life in the underground places of the city, where no one cared who his parents were, what they did and what their expectations for his future might be. In those dark rooms, he had whispered eagerly to her, nothing mattered but the feeling as the drug swirled in behind your eyes and into your brain. She'd watched as the drug took even that excitement from him as it took everything else from his money, his self-respect and finally his life.

Until only three were left in a house that reeked of scrubbing and a clock that ticked. Clunk. Clunk. Clunk.

With a glance at her bedside clock, Alex cursed under her breath. She would be late but mother had insisted she stayed home for dinner. Grabbing her gloves Alex reached for her bedroom door when it swung inwards and her mother walked in.

"Alexandra, we need to talk."

This, Alex knew only too well, didn't mean a talk by means of conversation. What would follow would be a catalogue of her failings. "Can it not wait until later, Mother? I really have to go."

To forestall flight, Edwina shut the door and stayed in front of it. She ignored the look on Alex's face and didn't notice or chose not to notice, the tightening of Alex's hands on her gloves or the tapping of her boot. "Your Father and I have hardly seen you for weeks."

"I've been busy."

A pause, weighted and terrible.

"Alexandra, you have been seen in disreputable parts of town."

"By whom?"

"Does it matter?"

"Yes, Mother. Most of your friends consider any street that is not Lambton Quay or Willis Street to be disreputable parts of town. I need to know against whose prejudices I am to defend myself this time."

Silence. Icy and clammy.

Cold blue eyes bored into Alex's. "My friends are not the cause of this discussion."

"It's not a discussion, Mother. It's a railing."

Edwina forced herself to remain calm. Why was her daughter so difficult? "It is unacceptable for a young woman to walk around unescorted."

"Then would you like to accompany me to Tory Street, Mother?"

In spite of her intentions not to show emotion, Edwina gave a gasp of horror. "Tory Street?"

"Yes. I'm helping a friend."

"Which friend?"

"No one you would know."

"That is not as reassuring as you somehow seem to believe, Alexandra!" Edwina dropped her voice hurriedly, anxious not to disturb Edward for her husband preferred to leave all but the most serious confrontations to her. "So Celia was right. You are not only being seen in notorious parts of Wellington, you are there with unacceptable men. This has to stop, Alexandra."

Alex's face stilled. "Men?" she queried, eyebrow raised.

Edwina had the grace to look discomforted. "Well, man."

"How do you know he's unacceptable?"

"Because Celia saw you with someone whom she said was not of our class or background."

"Celia Moore is a self-righteous, busy body who condemns everyone while calling them friend to their face. How dare she make judgments on someone she has never even exchanged words with? And this isn't the first time." Alex made a pleading appeal to her mother. "Can you not see, Mother how appalling her behaviour is?"

But Edwina's face hardened. "Celia's behaviour is not on trial here."

"Oh, and mine is?"

"That's not what I'm saying, Alexandra."

"Actually Mother that's exactly what you're saying." Alex resented having made an entreaty. She drew herself up, retreated into what her parents called her glibness, an accusation she also begrudged, seeing her confrontation of their social dishonesty as anything but facile. "You believe everything Celia tells you and you refuse to see the venom behind her socially acceptable mask." Alex stepped towards the door. "And I'm really too busy to listen to anymore. Believe what you will of me, I truly don't care." Which was a brave lie and one Alex would never confess to.

Eye to eye they stood, Alex unsure of what she would do if her Mother refused to move and equally determined not to show that uncertainty.

After several heartbeats, Edwina stepped silently aside to let Alex stride angrily out of her bedroom, down the stairs and out the front door. She knew she would be watched from behind her bedroom curtains as her father too would peer through his study window.

Alex strode away blinking away angry tears. Why was it that every confrontation with Mother brought back the aftermath of Bobby's death? The way Edwina had broken down into heaving, sobbing distress, throwing herself into Alex's arms, begging for comfort, for denial that this terrible thing had happened while Alex struggling against her own awful, welling emotion held her mother briefly as a switch clicked inside her and she felt nothing, nothing at all beyond disgust at Edwina's despairing need and clutching hands and her own heart as dead as her brother. On the edge of memory Alex recalled the sound of a door closing as Father shut his study door on his wife's sorrow and if he grieved, none but he knew it. So they lived, the three of them in a strange half-life of swallowed emotion and gaping silences with Bobby's smiling picture hanging on the wall above a vase of dried flowers; Bobby, ever the favourite who could do no wrong especially now he was the subject of eulogies.

As the distance from home increased, clean air whipped round Alex's ankles and tugged playfully at her hat. She drew in a long, deep breath, pulling the crispness into her lungs and soul in an effort to purge the pollution of ill feeling. Damn them all!

She knew she had been initially drawn to socialism only because her parents feared the new thinking. It was belatedly that the good sense and humanity of it became apparent to her. The meetings gave her a reason to leave the house and if Alex enjoyed her parents' solid, unspoken disapproval which marked every leave taking, she tried not to let it show or colour her reasons for attending them. There was a passion about the people she had met at the Socialist Hall, a clear goodwill to do good for the best reasons. She encountered no smugness among them and if there was something dangerous about the radicals she had met, all Alex felt was excitement at their zeal.

And now, of course, there was Samuel. A working class labourer, the kind of person her parents and their ilk instantly despised for not being 'one of them'. They would offer him condescension at best, active dislike at worst no matter how sincere he might be towards her.

But here Alex checked herself. A few walks and shared political interest didn't signify that Samuel considered her in any way special. And liking him wasn't easy. He was so different from the men she had grown up with that Alex struggled with the preconceptions her upbringing had given her, finding herself surprised at his perceptiveness or understanding and becoming angry at herself for thinking that someone with no education could be less insightful than herself.

So distracted by these emotions had she become that Alex used her sharp sense of humour to cover her confusion and growing attraction to Samuel. Languid glances from perfectly groomed young men over cups of tea or limp, sweaty hands taking hers in a dance had not prepared her in any shape, way or form for the pure rush of attraction she was now experiencing. In the face of everything she had known Samuel had swept in, different, damaged and good.

Alex had to admit as much as she enjoyed her independence at Socialist Hall it had been Samuel's need for help which gave some meaning to her empty life. The word popped unbidden into Alex's head and it surprised her so much she stopped walking and considered it again. She hadn't thought of her life in terms of meaning before, aware only of a lack, of gaps where something should have been and right here and now that word summed it all up.

Meaning. Noun or verb.

She had little understanding of men in any romantic sense so perhaps she had misread the looks Samuel had given her, the feeling she thought was developing between them. Those differences about him added to this attractiveness and were things she herself had no experience of beyond a natural instinct for compassion.

With effort Alex pushed aside any romantic considerations and focussed her mind on Cass. On getting him well once more.

On finding meaning.

28

When Edwina opened the front door in response to a tentative knocking, the last thing she expected was to be confronted by a filthy urchin holding out an equally grubby piece of paper. Edwina used the door like a shield.

"What do you want?"

The boy thrust the paper closer. Edwina shrank back further, her nose twitching from the sour smell coming off the child.

"Go away."

But the boy just stood there, sniffing, his arm outstretched, the paper flapping.

"Are you deaf? I told you to go away! Now do so or I shall call for the police!"

At the last word Moss took a wary step back. Samuel had been insistent that this note was given to Alex and now Moss was unsure whether to obey Samuel who he liked to or this horrible woman with her face screwed up threatening him with the coppers. Thankfully for Moss, Alex heard her mother shouting and came down the stairs to see what the fuss was all about.

'Mother, who are you…..?" Alex caught a glimpse through the half shut door. She flung it open, ignoring her mother's squawk. "Moss! What are you doing here?"

Edwina clutched at her daughter's sleeve. "Alexandra, you know this…. child?"

"Yes, Mother. This is Moss." Alex was down the steps. "Why are you here, Moss? Do you have a message from Samuel?"

"Samuel?"

Alex didn't hear the question for Moss had handed her the piece of paper and hared off without a backward glance. Alex quickly scanned the note as she moved back inside, Edwina on her heels.

"Alexandra I demand you explain this carry on. Who was that boy? How do you know him? And who is Samuel? Do we know a Samuel?"

Alex brushed off these questions as she would sandflies. Quickly slipping on her coat she grabbed her gloves and hat. "I have to go out, Mother."

"Out? Again? Alexandra!" Edwina stood on the doorstep as Alex ran out of the gate. "Alexandra!" But Alex was already out of sight.

A face peered through the curtains from next door and Edwina gave a ghastly twitch of nonchalance, lifted her hand as if merely waving to her daughter before escaping back inside.

That was the night that Cass turned a corner and they knew he would make it. Samuel and Alex shared the vigil, talking softly. It just after midnight that Cass opened heavy eyes and for the first time in too long Samuel saw recognition and lucidness in them.

"What the hell have you been doing to me, Sam?" Cass croaked, his gummy tongue licking dry, cracked lips.

"Not only me, Cass." Samuel gestured and Cass slowly turned his head, saw Alex sitting on a wooden stool Maudie had supplied. "But saving your life." He held a mug of water to Cass's lips, exchanging a happy look with Alex as his friend drank.

Wiping his mouth on the back of his hand, Cass told them, "You'll give me some time for gratitude?"

"No." This from Alex. "We expect it in full force from this moment."

Cass groaned, ran a hand through hair stiff with dried sweat. "I feel like shit."

"Better that than feeling nothing at all, don't you think?"

Cass met Alex's calm gaze before reaching out to Samuel whose hand he gripped with all the fierceness of his regrets and gratitude.

Samuel said softly, "I couldn't lose you as well, Cass."

And Cass, who understood, pretended not to see the sheen of tears in his friend's eyes while Samuel tried not to notice Jimmy's phantom watching him from the other side of the bed.

Maudie spent most of her hours in the kitchen next to the stove. No matter what time of the night, that was where she could be found so Samuel confidently stopped at the door to let her know Cass was through the worst.

"I'm walking Alex home."

"I'll pop up an' keep an eye on Cass." Maudie heaved herself upright. "So yer don't have to hurry." And she smirked meaningfully at them.

As they left the house, a small shadow materialised beside them.

"Jesus, Moss!" Samuel reached out and gave the boy a smack on his head. "How many times have I told you not to creep up on me like that? And shouldn't you be in bed?"

Moss lifted his shoulders, grinned at Alex who grinned back.

"We're off." Samuel pointed a threatening finger in Moss's face." And no following, got it?"

The boy bent down to fiddle with the laces on his boots, didn't reply. Samuel gave him a searching look before adding, "And bloody go to bed."

There was something to be said for walking with a woman's arm tucked warmly into your own, Samuel thought. It was quiet on the streets and from Tory Street to Courtenay Place they added to that unexpected peace by walking in weary silence.

"Thank you for everything you've done, Alex." Samuel guided her around a large hole in the road. "You were right, you know. I couldn't have got Cass through without help."

"I can't say it was a pleasure, exactly but… well…. Anyone would have helped."

"Not anyone."

A cart rumbled by, the driver seeming asleep as the reins lay lax in his hands, chin on his chest as his horse plodded faithfully on.

Samuel glanced at Alex's profile. "I'm sorry you lost a brother."

"My only brother, only sibling come to that."

"Then I'm even more sorry."

Only when she was sure she had herself under control once more did Alex look into Samuel's grave face. "It was…. terrible." She confided. "And although the rest of us survived our family didn't." She noted the puzzlement on his face. "We were never very close but Bobby was my parent's pride. He was their future." Alex dropped her eyes. "And I just don't measure up. I never have.

Without him, there's nothing left for them, really."

Samuel sought his mind for something reassuring to say. "I'dve thought you'd be even more precious to them. In fact," his lips curved into a smile. "I'm surprised you haven't been kept away from disreputable people like Cass and me."

Alex laughed. "Those are almost the exact words Mother used. Apparently, I've 'been seen in disreputable streets with disreputable company'."

"Ah. That would be me."

"Yes, Mr Disreputable. I'm afraid so."

"And yet, you still came to help?"

Alex lifted her chin. "Of course."

Samuel looked down at Alex's face, its sardonic line of brow and turn of lips softened into sincerity. "You do realise, Alex that there's no 'of course' for most people."

He looked so gently, so lovingly at her that Alex felt pleasure and fear in equal measure and spoke quickly to cover her confusion. "Samuel, can I ask you something?"

"Anything you like."

"What did you mean when you told Cass you couldn't lose him as well?"

The question startled him and Alex felt palpable tension. It was all too apparent that his 'anything you like' did not include this.

"I lost someone," he said shortly.

"Lost who?

Samuel turned his face from scrutiny, taking his time checking the road before crossing.

"My brother. Jimmy." Again, the bare amount of information reluctantly offered.

"I thought you said you had no family?"

Samuel shrugged, unwilling to discuss his previous, painfully built defences.

"I'm sorry, Samuel. When did he die?"

"Jimmy's not dead." The words as flat as Samuel's tone.

"Then what did you mean?"

He gave her a look of impatience.

"I don't want to talk of it, Alex!"

Taken aback by the sudden flare of anger, Alex relented.

"Of course."

After a couple of minutes and as if by chance, her arm slid from under his.

As they walked on, Samuel mentally berated himself. All Alex had ever shown him was kindness and friendship and what did he do but throw it back in her face. He hated himself but couldn't undam the hurt from his past and offer it to her as an excuse for his behaviour. He felt trapped by his inability to open up to her, repressed by his awkwardness and afraid of what releasing it all to her would mean to him.

Samuel looked up from his abstraction to find they were at her front door. Against his will he was intimidated by the smugness which seemed to go hand-in-hand with streets like these. He unconsciously tugged his coat straighter, tried to look more respectable knowing no pig's ear had ever made a silk purse, but hoping nevertheless.

He desperately wanted to say something to Alex, anything to make up for the display of temper she did not deserve but the sharp edges of the words stuck in his mouth which opened and closed around them unable to frame a coherent sentence.

In the end Alex uttered a calm, "Goodnight, Sam." And left him.

Before he even accepted she was gone, Samuel stood alone on Tinakori Road, damning himself for his cowardice.

Alex stood inside the hallway, watching Samuel from behind the curtains, watched him stare at the front door. Watched him leave.

Too restless to head back to Cass, Samuel wandered aimlessly up and down streets, letting his feet guide him unthinkingly until he had left the city centre and headed up Aro Valley. A poor place with a bad reputation where men hid avoiding arrest or the responsibility of wives and families to spend their time drinking and gambling safe in the knowledge that lookouts guaranteed ample warning of any approaching trouble.

Not having good clothes to wear or anything worth stealing, Samuel didn't worry over much, just kept his head down and tried to look as if he belonged. Occasionally he felt eyes watching him from the darkness between buildings or alleyways but no one came near him.

Past the shops, closed and shuttered for the night, the valley deepened and the road to the left and plus the one in front disappeared into thick bush. Samuel was just thinking he wouldn't mind living up this way when he smelt smoke so strongly he looked quickly about for the fire. There just ahead of him was the recently burned out shell of a cottage. Even the trees growing close to the walls had been burned away and the whole house slumped drunkenly. A morepork hooted from the quiet of the surrounding trees while Samuel just stood in front of the blackened wreckage unable to pull his gaze away.

It was a small, wooden, worker's cottage simple, homely and all too familiar. After long minutes he walked closer, heading to the back of the house where the whole kitchen had burned completely away and the roof rest crookedly on the floor. Samuel edged through the broken ribs of the walls to stand in the shattered hallway.

Father's wracking sobs..... Jimmy's shaking body in his arms..... the sound of the front door shutting as Doctor Evans left...... the sharp odour of blood......

'Sam?'

'I'm fine....'

'No you're not!"

'Where's Mick....?'

The smell of flame on dry wood..... the sound of cracking timber.....a homemade cross with Mam's name on it...... their first sight of the Orphanage.....

Donatus.....the hunger.....Jimmy..... looking after Jimmy..... caring for Jimmy.....

Jimmy caring for him......Jimmy shouting at him..... Father with

another family in a warm kitchen..... a boy on his knee......
Jimmy frightened of the dark......
Jimmy and him cooking sausages and stolen onions......
Jimmy sending him out of his life...

Samuel closed his eyes and tears welled through his lashes. He whispered, "You're here, aren't you, Jimmy?"

His eyes snapped open and he peered into the moonlight filtering through the creaking, fractured timbers. Nothing moved.

"You told me to piss off, Jimmy. You told me to and I did."

Somewhere on the very edge of his vision the ghostly shape of a thin, young boy with a scared face hovered, just there, leaning against the wall of the burned out hallway, watching him with sorrowful eyes. Samuel gestured to him, hopelessly.

"I pissed off, Jimmy. Like you said."

The shadow faded and Samuel stared at the spot. "Why won't you?"

29

'Dear Sam,   *April 1912*

I've been here at Waihi for nearly four months and you know I've never liked small towns but I'm warming to the people here. It's a bloody hard life gold mining and they're a tough breed, the men and women. I'm staying with Mrs Annie White who could be sister to Maudie. Tough as old boots and her laugh could pickle your insides but her husband William is the quietest soul. They have a brood of children but I've only spent time with the youngest, a set of twins David and Don who I can't tell apart. The rest have married and most of them live in Waihi and the boys either followed William into the mines or work on the farms hereabouts. Good people all.

Thanks for the copy of 'God and the State'. It's been passed around hand to hand since I finished it. What you say is happening on the wharves is happening up here, too – lots of anger and fear now the Reformers are a power to be reckoned with. No one has a good word to say about Massey but everyone agrees he will do what he can for landowners and businessmen and nothing for workers. These men haven't had a lift in their wages for years. Two pound eight shillings a week don't go far when you've got a family to feed and clothe. There have been several accidents in the time I've been here and never a drop of compensation from the company which Silo says has been making profit hand over fist, increasing every year and not even giving the drippings off their nose to the workers. Bastards.

There's talk of strike action as the only action the company will take heed of. Just my luck to get caught up in it so soon after starting but I'll go out if the others do.

How's Alex? You didn't mention her in your last letter and you don't usually shut up about her. Sick of the sight of you, is she?!

And that reminds me, there's another note in with this letter. It's for Vi from Alma Lane who works at the Royal Tiger. She can't read so you'll have to read it to her. If you don't understand some of it, she'll only be too happy to explain.

307

Anyway, old friend, I better get this in the post. Please send me any pamphlets you can. William Parry here's a strong union man and I need to get my head around some of the stuff he goes on about. He's as bad as you.

Your friend, Cass.'

'Dear Cass   *May 1912*

I hope the pamphlets arrived safely. Mr Joseph also sent you a selection of 'Freedom' magazine. Bob Semple and Paddy Webb are subscribers - it's a goodun. Mr Joseph's has just got himself out of bankruptcy so it's kind of him to give these to you. He's an Anarchist and he's spoken several times at the Socialist Hall being great friends with the best minds who are all preparing for revolution in New Zealand. We have so many lectures and meetings now. If Semple and Joe Savage have anything to do with it, revolution won't be far off. Semple says it will start with the miners. He says all good things start with miners. Of course, he's a miner himself!

If there's trouble in Waihi you can be sure other unions will support in some way or other. We've got to look out for ourselves as no one looks out for the workers except us, eh?

I gave your letter to Vi. She's says you still owe her for one night and, 'don't tell her no shit about being on the opium 'cause you managed to do it well enough so pay up.' I wrote it down exactly as Vi told me. And you're right. She was happy to explain your letter and offered to do so in great detail. I managed to get away with my dignity – but only just.

Also, Maudie sends her best and tells you to come home for a visit, not that I care if I see your ugly mug again but Maudie does. No accounting for taste.

Take care.

Sam.'

'Dear Sam   May 1912*

Well, we're up to our scuppers right enough. The company have formed a breakaway union of the engine drivers. Parry says this is a deliberate attack on our union. I won't write you here of the things some are saying of the drivers for not standing strong but I'm sure you'll guess. Yesterday, Parry called a meeting for all the wives and womenfolk involved with us miners and told them straight how things would go in a strike. He said he didn't want the men out unless they had the support of the women. They gave it, too - standing on their feet and clapping. Everyone's spirits are high and we expect the company to see the error of their ways sooner rather than later. Strikes are hard on those with families most of all but it does your heart grand to see the way the women and even the children rally about with the men.

The Miner's Union Hall has been alive every night with some activity or other. We have concerts and dances, too. Parry says it's all about keeping peoples' spirits up. He says the early days are easiest but when the last pay has been spent, the savings are gone and people get hungry, that's when folk need to rely on their friendships. Annie's best friend is wife to one of the shopkeepers and her husband supports the engine drivers. Annie refuses to shop there now and she and the other strikers' wives have boycotted that shop and any others that think the same. Those shopkeepers in their turn have refused credit to the strikers' wives. Waihi is already a different place with all the sides being taken and the tensions. I hope the strike doesn't have to last long.

We had a meeting with Parry, Semple, Webb and Peter Fraser. They told us their plans to gather support for the strikers' families. Fraser spoke, too about his intention to travel round New Zealand to gather support for our strike. We all left the Hall that night with lighter hearts.

Tell Vi fair exchange is no robbery. She'll know what I mean. Also, tell Maudie I won't be coming home any time soon but give her my best. Does Moss speak, yet?

I also noticed you never mentioned Alex so I won't again either.

She was always too good for you anyway.
   Your friend, Cass'

'Dear Cass

July 1912

I'm sure William Parry will know already but Massey is Prime Minister on the back of two sessions to get a no confidence vote in Parliament. We had a meeting last night at Socialist Hall and all parties are in agreement – Massey will put the power of the government behind the companies and employers. He's already made a statement of his intent to 'crush the enemies of order.' This won't be good for you Waihi strikers, old friend..... And it won't be good for any worker in this country. I think Semple is right to argue for a single union strong enough to push back against the capitalists. If there is to be a revolution of workers, let it start here in New Zealand.

Little Peg had a terrible accident in the street a few weeks ago. A hansom cab knocked her down and the wheels ran right over her legs. The driver got out and yelled at her for playing in the street, screaming and covered in blood as she was! Moss was with Peg and he started bellowing, too, called the driver a bastard and more besides. We couldn't believe it when he spoke so at least we know he can. Maudie gave the driver a punch that knocked him off his feet, spitting blood and teeth. Peg is back home now but Maudie doesn't think she'll walk again. Poor Peg cries whenever she's stood on her feet even for a moment. I made her a little cart and Moss pulls her about in it. He hasn't spoken again since Peg's accident, funny wee lad.

Young innocent as I am, I am not taking your latest message to Vi. She and Maudie are great friends and if it comes to doing what you ask and me getting starved by Maudie for upsetting her Vi, you will have to miss out. I like you, Cass but I like Maudie's stew more. Our shifts are being changed at work so I might be able to see you soon for a day or two. Hope so anyway. Sam.'

'Dear Sam

September 1912

Your visit was a godsend. There are a couple of the lads still hung-over from your generosity and the bottle of whiskey you bought me is sitting under my bed to open at the right time. Silo sends his best and tells you he'd almost forgotten what beer tasted like till you showed and now he doesn't want to ever taste it again and you're a bastard because of it!

We have arbitrationist workers in Waihi now and the company parades these bastard scabs up and down the streets, in front of the Union Hall when they know we're meeting there. There's been no violence yet but the arrogance of the scabs will provoke it. Annie thinks that's why they're behaving the way they are. If we fight back, we'll be the bastards. Won't stop me throwing a punch if I have to.

Yesterday the mine was reopened and the women whose men were arrested took their place in the protest line, waving placards, shouting out. One of their banners was red and had 'Workers of the world unite' written on it. We call these lasses the Scarlet Runners and they are as militant as us men. Our Mrs Matthews and Mrs Hinchey stood up and spoke out for strikers.

Things are getting tougher. We had strike pay in June as you know but it only goes so far. People are hungry now and the Charitable Aid Board refuses to help the families of any striker. Police Commissionaire Cullen has sent in reinforcements to the police. They are as arrogant as the scabs and if they see a striker, they will shove against him if they think no one's looking. Sad to say but more men are returning to Martha Mine now – they've taken strike pay and still turn traitor. Some of them justify what they do by saying they're hungry – well, everyone's hungry!

Semple and Webb turned up yesterday so I expect things will pick up again. Semple's already given a rousing speech at the Hall but it will take more than rousing speeches now.

Annie knitted Peg a doll and I'll send it with this letter. Give her a hug from me and take Moss to the movies. I'll pay you back soon as I

---

can.

Can you ask someone at one of your meetings why a General Strike hasn't been called to support us here at Waihi? Silo mentioned it the other night, how the Red Feds are all for one and we got talking about it and wondering. Semple won't answer but if we need to take collective action as workers, maybe this could be the start of it?

Annie and her friends in the Scarlet Runners are talking about smashing windows so I better go and make sure they don't. Or maybe I'll join them.

Your old friend, Cass'

Nov 1912,

'Jesus, Sam! Jesus Christ. They killed Fred Evans, good as murdered him! The coppers demanded we remove our pickets, then the company closed the mine for the day and the coppers and the scabs marched to the Hall. I don't know what they wanted but all hell broke loose! We had batons smashing down on us, the scabs attacked with whatever they had so we grabbed what we could – I grabbed a bloody paling – and... I don't know what to say..... the coppers just watched us get beaten, they helped, they..... Coppers had pistols, shots were fired... Fred was bashed with batons, bashed almost to a pulp – I couldn't reach him, couldn't do anything but watch... the bastards dragged him away, dumped in a cell and he died, Sam. Arthur Doyle and I fought our way through, Christ he was bleeding as much as me, the scabs and a copper threatening us with a lynching... Arthur took off one way, I went another. I've just found out he hid in someone's house, one of our supporters but the coppers must have had everyone watched, for the scabs found Arthur, they cornered him like dogs cornering a rat... They charged the poor bastard, arrested him and charged him with assault.... Anyone who refused to leave Waihi – anyone with homes and family were all hunted down. No one escaped a thrashing and then we were dumped at the railway station....

Oh god, Sam... not one scab was charged with assault or trespass... and the coppers.... Annie said they was just obeying orders but to do what they did...?! I'll never trust a bloody copper again in my life. Tell them at your meetings, Sam. Tell them what happened.

I'm gonna make my way back to you in Well. Not sure how, no money. I borrowed off Annie to post this before she and the rest grabbed what they could and took off. How can I repay her? I won't know where she went.... But I'm coming home.

Cass'

***

"…….. they would have lost anyway, the poor sods! Why attack them? What was the sense behind attacking them? The mine was open again, the strikers had lost."

"Cullen would be behind it, bloody guarantee it. Massey would have given him orders as Police Commissioner but he didn't have to throw such a vicious attack on unarmed men and women."

"Industrial activity cannot win against the state. If Waihi shows us anything, it's that we have to gain political power so the police and the legal system can't be turned against the workers."

"Keep your damn politics out of this! Those people were hunted down like animals. If the NZFL had called a General Strike…."

"Strikes are useless! Look at what Massey did – he had the power of the state and he used it as a vanguard for the employers."

"But if all unions had supported the miners? If all workers had thrown their support in behind the miners? How could Massey defeat that? How many bloody coppers do we have for god's sake that they could attack thousands of strikers?"

"You're not listening. The government will always find the money to defeat a strike, no matter how big."

"And you're refusing to acknowledge the power of the working man. If you would just….."

Alex put her thumb and forefinger between her lips and whistled.

Alex put her thumb and forefinger between her lips and whistled. All arguments ceased as everyone stared at her in astonishment.

"My brother taught me." She disarmed the room with a brief smile. "Nothing can be settled by anger, gentlemen. We're all on the same side in this room. Waihi was unforgiveable and Massey has shown just how far he's prepared to go to keep the workers in their place." She held up a sheaf of papers. "But every action has its reaction."

One by one they found their seats again as Alex continued.

"'Mother Earth' wrote, 'the strike arbitration laws of New Zealand, so enthusiastically hailed by America reformers as an effective solution of Labour troubles is beginning to show results that fill its champions with anxiety and fear…. For a whole week the myrmidons of capital and government carried on an orgy of violence and during that time, 1,800 men and women were forcibly driven from that place…..'" Alex grabbed another paper. "And, Walter Mills, 'Justice is perverted when innocent miners were imprisoned and no action was taken against those breaking the law in the interest of the mine owners.'" She faced them all proudly. "New Zealand is not alone in her troubles and her workers are not alone in their struggle. Change can be effected. It must be effected and by god, if we can harness the responses to the cruelty and greed of Massey and his ilk, change will be effected."

Alex sat down to rousing applause. She turned a jubilant face to Samuel and he stopped clapping, took her hand in his and raised it to his lips. An unspoken accord moved, softly, completely between them and when the discussions began again, Samuel kept Alex's hand warmly in his.

They were among the last to leave the hall and had walked down Manners Street and onto Courtenay Place before Samuel realised where they were. He came to a halt. "We're heading the wrong way, Alex." He did an about face, surprised when Alex didn't move. He smiled at her. "Did you hear me? We're not heading to your place."

"I know. I noticed."

"Well, then….?" He gestured back the way they came.

Instead, she increased the pressure of her hand on his arm. "I don't want to go home tonight, Sam."

He thought for a moment in confusion. "Well, what do you want to do?"

"I thought, perhaps we could go back to your room." Alex spoke carefully, unsure how Samuel would respond but she felt a sudden need to be held by him, to be loved by him, to experience a life beyond her parents' imagining.

Samuel held her gaze as understanding dawned. "Are you sure?"

In answer Alex drew closer to him and lifted her face. Samuel had no conscious thought of taking her into his arms. He kissed her as he'd wanted to kiss her for weeks.

"Maudie will know," he warned but Alex just shrugged.

"You still haven't remembered have you, Sam?"

"Remembered what?"

She kissed him again, felt the heat of his response and her own desire. "That I don't much care what people think."

Hours later Samuel held Alex in his arms as they lay on his mattress, moonlight shining through the window onto her face. She was sleeping peacefully, a smile softening her lips and he felt a rush of protectiveness. He wished he could have offered Alex a room that wasn't a pokey attic room with no proper furniture or a carpet on the floor.

She moved, murmured something in her dreams and nestled closer to the warmth of his body. He softly tucked the hair back from her face, never so far from sleep as he watched her lying in his arms. It was the strangest thing but Alex didn't seem to notice the poverty of the place. He couldn't understand how someone from her background would not be all too aware of it and even want to be here with him yet he shrank from the thought of discussing it with her fearing such a discussion would bring to light the cheapness of the room, the poverty of his life and Alex would return to her comfortable home in its tidy, quiet street her heart full of regret for what she had done. Instead he acknowledged his own cowardice in comparison to her bravery and determined to love every moment Alex wanted to give him and not begrudge the time he felt sure would come when she had to or wanted to return to her real life.

Slowly the sleepiness came. Samuel settled comfortably down feeling the completeness of sharing a bed with a woman he loved. His eyes grew heavy and as he drifted towards sleep footsteps sounded on the stairs and stopped in the hallway. Sure it was someone for the other attic rooms, Samuel ignored it, until a key turned in the lock and the door opened softly.

Instinctively covering Alex with the blanket, Samuel was on his feet, his hand reaching uselessly for anything to use for a weapon as someone moved into the room and closed the door.

Samuel moved quickly, had the intruder in a choke hold startling Alex awake. "Who the bloody hell are you?" he hissed, hearing only indistinct gurgles in reply.

Alex had lit a candle and the light flared, fell on the two men. "Cass!"

Samuel released his hold and Cass stumbled onto his mattress, clutching his neck and gasping. "Jesus, Sam! What the hell…..?" The words died in Cass's mouth as he saw a naked Samuel and Alex sitting up wrapped in the blankets, wide eyed but vastly amused. He swallowed. "Ah."

Samuel hurriedly reached for his trousers but Cass stood back up, flapping a hand at him. "I'm in the way. I'll talk to you in the kitchen when you're…. ready." Cass reached for the door, turned back. "Nice to see you again, Alex."

"You too, Cass."

With a huge grin, Cass left the room. They heard him relock the door and burst into laughter as he went down the stairs.

Alex eyed Samuel who just shook his head before settling back onto the mattress, pulling her into his arms again.

"I've always hated him." he said. Giving Alex an unhurried kiss, Samuel plumped up her pillow.

"Will you be able to go back to sleep, love?"

But Alex gave him a far from sleepy smile.

"Well, seeing we're both awake...."

And she laughed at the expression on Samuel's face just before he pounced.

Part V

Moss watched Samuel and Cass leave the house and march off purposefully down Tory Street towards Courtenay Place. Rain fell steadily and the gutters above his head, unable to cope with the downpour, dumped water straight onto the already muddy road. Wherever Samuel and Cass were headed, Moss was sure it had something to do with the word he'd never heard before in his life but had heard every day in the past few months – strike.

A scuffling noise at his feet alerted him to the fact Peg had dragged herself out from the kitchen on her worn blanket.

"Moth…..Moth…..up…." Peg lisped as she held her arms out beseechingly. She crowed delightedly when her brother swung her onto his hip, her useless legs dangling, and together they stared out into the wet weather.

Peg pushed a hand out into the rain pouring off the roof and giggled, using both hands the next time wetting them both. Moss made a soft growl in his throat, stepped back into the hallway to put Peg back down on her blanket. He knelt, held her sticky hands between his own and kissed her cheek, ignoring her cries as he dashed out into the downpour.

Following the noise from her youngest Maudie stumped out looking for her. "There yer are, little bugger."

Peg hauled herself to the doorway, heedless of the rain now being blown into the house. She pointed outside, gazed back up at Maudie.

"No, Peg love. You ain't goin' out in that."

Maudie bent with difficulty, picked up the edge of Peg's blanket and began to tow her back into the kitchen.

Peg screamed, "Moth! Moth!"

"He ain't here, Peg. I dunno where he is."

Still calling for her brother, Peg struggled to get back to the doorway. In exasperation, Maudie picked the little girl up and slammed the front door shut.

"If he's out in that with the rest of them bloody fools, then more fool them." And ignoring Peg's wails, Maudie strode back into the warmth of the kitchen. "Them and their bloody strikes."

Moss made his way to Queen's Wharf for that was where Samuel, Cass and hundreds of working men spent hours, waving signs, shouting and shoving. Speeches were regularly made, even on a miserable day like today.

"The company locked us out and now they are using scab labour to do the work of honest men. We cannot back down in the face of this intimidation and threat to our livelihoods. If they are prepared to do this, we must be strong and ready ourselves for the fight!"

The words and answering cheers drifted over Moss's head as he shoved himself through the bodies of men, the smell of wet wool from suits and mud from the road following him through the crowd.

Here and there were well-heeled boots or shoes and smartly cut trousers and the scent of cologne. Beside these Moss paused long enough to slip a hand into a pocket and retrieve coins or silver lighters; he got a good price for silver lighters from Old Vander in Martin Square.

Having pushed his way through almost to the gates themselves, Moss found Samuel and Cass standing tall, heedless of the pouring rain, shouting through the gates, cheering the speechmakers.

Samuel felt a warm pressure against his leg, looked down into Moss's face. "Thought we told you to stay away. This isn't the place for you."

Moss stuck out his bottom lip mutinously but Samuel was adamant. He grabbed the boy by the shoulder of his coat and pulled him away from the thick of the crowd. "Get yourself home, Moss or I'll wallop you."

Still Moss stood his ground. He shook his head, shoved his hands deep into his trouser pockets, scowling.

Unwillingly impressed by this show of defiance and knowing it sprang from the boy's loyalty to himself, Samuel dug into his pocket, pulled out a couple of pennies and pressed them into Moss's hand but Moss shook his head, tried to give them back.

Samuel wouldn't take them. "If you don't want them, keep them for Peg or Maudie and get your backside out of here or Cass won't take you to the movies again."

This threat worked as Samuel knew it would and he felt a twinge of guilt not knowing when either he or Cass would be able to afford the movies again. Cass was supporting them both working wherever he could while scabs worked the jobs the watersiders had done.

Moss eyed the pennies before pocketing them. He made a sign with the fingers of both hands and Samuel shook his head.

"She won't take my letters, Moss, you know that." A deadened feeling invaded his chest.

Moss made another gesture and Samuel snorted with impatience. "There's no point if she won't read the bloody things! Look," he pointed back towards the gates. "I've gotta go. Keep out of the way, Moss. And keep away from Alex."

Moss stared non-committedly at the finger pointing straight at him. Samuel thrust the finger closer to Moss's face just to be sure the boy got the message before turning to elbow his way back through the crush of bodies.

It was still raining when Samuel and Cass returned back to Maudie's, soaked to the skin and shivering.

"I suppose yer off back down to that bloody wharf again tonight?"

"Have to, Maudie." Samuel had taken off his sodden coat, was rubbing his hair with it.

Maudie grabbed the coat and began to take Cass out of his. "Youse two ain't going nowhere till yer've dried off and had a bit of supper."

"Maudie we can't take your food…." Cass began, instantly shut up by having his sopping coat slapped about his head.

"Don't yer like my food?"

"Of course we do." Samuel replied indignantly. "We just can't aff…." He also copped a whack and shut up.

"I'll do what I like with me own bloody stew!" Maudie huffed. "Now, get that wet clobber off so's I can dry it round the stove and get yer arses back down here for some supper or yer'll feel the toe of me boot somewhere yer won't bloody like."

Twenty minutes later Samuel and Cass sat in front of the woodstove in Maudie's kitchen, watching the steam rise off their wet clothes while eating stew and bread. Peg sat on Samuel's lap, picking out bits of meat from his plate or chewing the crusts off his bread.

"So what's the word from the wharf?" Maudie asked, ladling more stew into their bowls, her eyes daring them to mention it.

"The company's using scabs and building barricades." Cass spoke with his mouth full, wiping his lips with the back of his hand. "Bastards."

"So, is it war?" Maudie replaced the stew pot on the stove. "'cause the way I see it, Massey fired the first shots over the union's head at Waihi."

His appetite suddenly gone, Samuel pushed his plate away only to have Peg pull it back again.

"You know, Maudie," he and Cass exchanged a grim look. "I think it might be."

***

59 Ghuznee Street was home to Otto England's Albemarle Hotel. Otto had a nose for those unsympathetic to the socialist cause and many a man had slunk out the Albemarle, cap pulled low over his face having had his request for a drink and his money flung back in his face. Three stories high with a distinctive dome to top it off, it was an imposing building with light always on inside and a fire kept burning in the hearth, a welcoming sight in troubled times for the strikers and their supporters.

It was the early hours of the morning and the front door had been locked hours ago but Cass made unerringly for the back door and knocked softly. Samuel thought Otto must have been standing right behind the door; he opened it so quickly, but they saw why soon enough – the place was packed with men and dense with cigarette smoke.

Otto put a finger to his lips and pointed them through. It was one of the nights when the Albemarle was literally standing room only and men who needed accommodation slept on the floor wherever they could find a space. Samuel recognised Bob Semple, Peter Fraser, Joe Savage and Tom Barker, these men the focus for all eyes. To no one's surprise, Bob Semple was holding forth.

"The men are tough, Fraser. Massey's oppression at Waihi has given us a stronger militancy than we could have hoped for in this fight." Bob's eyes glowed in the firelight.

"You sound almost happy that Fred Evans died, Bob," came a quiet voice.

"That's not what I'm saying, Tom! Of course it's not. But now is our time. Massey and Cullen can do what they will. We have to stand up. We have to take the fight to them. We must…"

"We must all work together on this. Social Democrats, Labour, NZFL – if we have any hope at all in winning this, we can only do it together." Peter Fraser's gentle Scottish voice was urgent. "If we call a General Strike…."

"If?" Semple exploded. "There's no 'if', Fraser."

"There's always an 'if', Bob."

All eyes turned to Joe Savage. Dark haired with striking light coloured eyes, Joe's integrity and dedicated service to the causes of the working class commanded the respect of every man in the room. Since 1908 Joe Savage had kept to a pattern; he would slog for six months then devote himself to fulltime political activity for six months until his money ran out. For some, Semple was too vehement, Fraser too soft, Joe seemed to strike the right balance of passion and purpose.

He kept his gaze on Semple. "You're right in your instincts, Bob but a General Strike calls for a commitment beyond the ordinary. Badly paid though our workers are, a General Strike will mean no wages at all. Do we have the right to ask more of the workers than they and their families can afford?"

"Yes!" Unable to be still, Semple stood, found there was no room for pacing and sat back down again, legs jigging up and down like pistons. "If we don't fight now, Massey will grind the workers down so far they'll never see daylight. This is war, Savage!"

"Then we attack them before they get the upper hand." Cass swallowed hard as every face turned to him. He couldn't believe he'd spoken out in front of their strike leaders but it was too late to shut up now. "If this is a war then we need to be soldiers." Cass fidgeted under the intense scrutiny.

"What's your name, son?" Joe asked.

"Cass Williams."

"Soldiers go to war prepared to die, Cass. We don't want anyone dying in this fight."

Cass glanced nervously at the men around Joe but he couldn't back down now. "Someone already has. I was in Waihi when Fred Evans died. He didn't expect to die and he damn sure didn't want to die and this war isn't of our making but I don't want to come to the end of it and wish I'd done more." Cass held Joe's thoughtful gaze. "I'll do whatever I can, whatever I bloody have to. For Fred Evans."

Samuel couldn't believe this was Cass. In all their years together he'd never known him so articulate, so passionate and he listened to his friend in awe but it came to him then that he had noticed a difference in Cass after Waihi.

For several heartbeats no one spoke, then a roar went up and the whole room was on its feet, shaking Cass's hand, repeating his words. Joe Savage remained in his chair, watching every man's face, listening to their words, worrying, hoping.

The rain had eased by the time they finally wandered home.

Samuel shot a sideways glance at his friend. "What made you come out with all that?"

"I meant every word, Sam. We have to fight."

"We're striking, aren't we? The employers need workers to make their profits."

What little light there was seemed to be held in Cass's eyes. "They've got workers! Bloody scabs. We need to strike in other ways."

"What other ways do you have in mind?"

Cass lit a cigarette and the flare from the match illuminated his grim smile. "Ways they can't possibly ignore."

***

31

The well-dressed family left their house, locking the door carefully behind them. The Mr and Mrs walked a little ahead of their daughter and though Moss was tucked out of their view, he could see how drawn Alex's face was. He fingered the letters Samuel had written.

A few weeks ago Moss had made the mistake of passing the first letter over to the Mrs at the door who had taken one look at the letter and told Moss if he dared show his face at their door again, she would have him locked up. Then she had grabbed the letter, screwed it up and thrown it into a puddle at Moss's feet before slamming the front door in his face. No Alex came to his rescue this time. It had taken Moss ages to dry the letter carefully before smoothing it back into shape.

Trying to find a way to pass the letters to Alex proved difficult. She no longer attended meetings at the Socialist Hall and no matter how many times during the week Moss watched their house or for how long he waited, Alex never seemed to leave it.

He was on the verge of giving up when he remembered Sundays. Lots of people went to church on Sundays. Now, as Mr and Mrs walked ahead, Moss felt proud of his cleverness. All he had to do was….. warily Moss followed the three of them until the Mr and Mrs turned a corner leaving Alex walking alone. In seconds Moss slipped beside her and pushed the letters into her hand. Startled, Alex almost cried out, glad beyond all measure that she didn't when she recognised the small, grubby figure disappearing into someone's garden as Edward came back to see where his daughter was.

"Everything all right, Alexandra?"

Alex slipped letters into her pocket unseen. "Yes, Father."

He held out an arm, obliging Alex to take it. Moss peeked out from behind a large shrub, smirking at his success.

All through the church service, Alex was intensely aware of the letters hidden deep in her pocket. She longed to read them, knew that was impossible until she was alone. Knowing Father kept glancing sideways at her, Alex kept tranquil hands in her lap and a a calm face as the Minister's voice droned on and on.

Face-to-face mother and daughter stood in Alex's bedroom.

"I won't be kept as a prisoner any longer, Mother."

"Don't be so ridiculously dramatic, Alexandra. You're no one's prisoner." Edwina felt the heat rise in her face and she quickly turned away from her daughter's knowing eyes to tweak the items on Alex's dressing table. "Your Father has merely tried to ensure….."

"Father wants to marry me off to that…that…. oaf from the Wairarapa with more chins than acres! I will not marry him. I will not marry any man not of my own choosing."

Edwina looked out of the window and saw Edward returning home. She'd hoped for more time with him out of the house, not wanting him to overhear this discussion. She replaced the curtain with obsessive neatness to buy herself some time to think and when she faced her daughter again, she kept her voice low.

"You leave me no choice, Alexandra. I have to say this to you." But still she hesitated.

The fine thread of Alex's patience snapped. "For god's sake, Mother, say what?"

Certain she had herself under control Edwina faced her daughter, surprised at how calm her voice sounded to her ears. "Alexandra, your behaviour has given rise to some very ugly rumours."

Alex rolled her eyes. "Ugly rumours from an ugly mind." She couldn't help the sarcasm, "Whoever can you possibly mean?"

Edwina ploughed on. "If you do not tread with the upmost care, no man of decent family will have you."

"You are, of course, assuming that a man of decent family holds any interest for me."

"That is exactly the kind of talk that is overheard and judged. Your 'work' with the anarchists..."

"Why did you put 'work' in parenthesis? And I'm a socialist, not an anarchist. There's quite a difference, you know, mother, although you apparently don't know."

Edwina wrung her hands. "And again you drag a conversation away from its salient point. Alexandra, listen to me, please."

Alex drew in a sharp breath at the desperation in her mother's eyes. She wanted to make a smart comment but couldn't, caught as she was in Edwina's imploring gaze.

"You mentioned a young man. A Samuel. He's not one of us. He's a working class labourer who has taken keen interest in a young woman from a well set up family. He has designs upon your honour, Alexandra, your place in society. You cannot risk everything for….."

But Alex finally had enough. She'd held her peace over the past months, shrinking from saying the words out loud. But no longer. "I went to bed with him, Mother. With Samuel. And it was my idea, not his. And I love him." She had been aching to say these words, the sentences burning on her tongue every time Father mentioned marriage with the fat, smug farmer from the Wairarapa. Now they were out, she expected to feel victorious but all she felt was guilt at the sight of her mother's ruined face with its lost expression.

"You…. You…." Edwina couldn't frame the question, kept her eyes on Alex's face while her daughter met her horrified gaze defiantly. A hand flew to her mouth and Edwina gripped the back of the nearest chair to steady herself, afraid she would faint. "Oh, my god…You mustn't….. you can't have….If your Father…. If he…. ever finds out….."

"I want my life back, Mother. I need to do what I believe in and if you keep me here, well…." Alex forced herself to continue. "I will tell Father. I will tell him myself and to hell with the consequences!"

Whenever she looked back on this scene with her mother, Alex couldn't remember, not for the life of her what happened next. She didn't know if Edwina said anything else. She must have left the room but Alex had no memory of her doing so.

She would close her eyes and try to picture herself after all the emotion and saw nothing, felt nothing until coming to herself in the evening air in the garden out the back of the house, sitting on the old wooden swing seat Bobby had put up for her all those years ago, staring over the roofs of the houses behind them.

In her lap sat Samuel's letters. She'd read them over and over, reading his growing despair when he couldn't reach out to her, his feelings of abandonment, the words sprawling drunkenly across the pages as he lost hope he would ever see her again.

Alex drew the letters to her lips and gently kissed them. Whatever her parents thought, she would find Samuel again.

***

32

The streets were bathed in fog and midnight gloom as the men moved swiftly through the shadows to the barricades at the wharf, spurred on by anger and the hunger already biting at the heels of their families. Samuel and Cass led the way, hearts beating fast, knowing the police would show no sympathy if they were caught and Massey and Cullen would use their arrest as an example to others. They reached the Harbour Board buildings and huddled together, eyes constantly searching the streets and buildings around them.

"Remember," Cass said, low-voiced, "Once we're at the barricades you make as much noise as possible. Sam and I need the distraction so we can get onto the wharves themselves."

A thickset man with heavy features slapped a crowbar from hand to hand. "What do we do with the stuff from the barricade when we've pulled it down?"

"Chuck it into the harbour." Samuel said decisively and to a man they grinned darkly.

The bastards would rebuild the barricades, they knew that. But they would keep tearing them down.

"Once you start, don't worry about me and Sam. We'll make our way back to the Albemarle as soon as we can."

A tall, thin man shuffled his muddy boots. "Once we do this tonight, there's no going back." He spoke in urgent tones. "Massey'll be forced to hit back harder."

Cass spun round, heat in his eyes. 'Bugger it, Charlie! He has the force of the police and state behind him as it is and we're only a bunch of ragged arsed strikers." Cass read the fear in the other man's eyes and slapped one hand on his shoulder. "There was no going back whatever we decided to do, Charlie my friend. Massey wants us under the boot of the employer and I don't know about you but I'm no rich man's lackey to be paid wages that don't keep a dog."

There was muffled agreement from the other men but Cass held

Charlie's gaze until the other man pulled his shoulders back and straightened his cap. Without another word the group moved down the streets and reached the barricades near King's Wharf.

Cass and Samuel moved in first, tearing at the wood, while behind them the other men followed suit. For a few minutes the patrols on the wharf remained unaware of what was happening, but only briefly. Before long the handful of men who made up the patrol were uselessly struggling to hold back the strikers as the barricade came down piece by piece to be flung into the midnight waters of the harbour.

In the melee Cass and Samuel slipped unseen passed the uproar to where cargo lay stacked up everywhere, the most obvious sign that non-union, unskilled scab workers were struggling to keep up with the flow of goods in and out of Wellington. Silently, the two men foraged through the crates and boxes, gleefully tipping those labelled for the posh shops into the water, watching with great satisfaction as they sank without a trace.

Behind them the shouts and scuffles continued unabated.

Samuel turned worried eyes towards the noise. "The coppers'll be here soon."

"Won't matter. We got here quick and in enough numbers so the barricade will be down and the lads gone when the first whistle blows." Cass's voice was rich with satisfaction. "Sam, here. What do you reckon this all is?" They crouched down beside some barrels among a big stack of crates and goods. "Murratic acid." Cass murmured, reading the label. "Have you heard of it?"

Samuel frowned, thinking hard. "Dunno. Maybe in the workshop in Christchurch. Rings a bell anyway." He saw the wicked grin on his friend's face. "What are you thinking or shouldn't I ask?"

"I'm thinking, 'bugger them', Sam. That's what I'm thinking."

Swiftly, Cass pulled out a knife from his back pocket and began to prise the lids off the barrels. Samuel grinned, reached for his own knife and in moments they had them open. They kicked the barrels over and the stuff flooded through the crates and goods, Samuel leaping to safety as it came towards his boots.

From out in the streets, they heard police whistles, knew their companions would have heard them, too.

"Grab this." Samuel took hold of a box, shoved it into Cass's arms then reached for several sacks himself.

"What is it?"

Samuel began to run, Cass on his heels. "Supplies." He called over his shoulder and they began to run in earnest.

"Bloody give me the heaviest one." Cass grumbled.

The Albemarle was full of exhilarated men by the time Samuel and Cass arrived there, breathing hard, arms aching. Several times they'd had to hide in alleys as coppers ran past.

With thankful groans they dropped the goods onto the floor in the main bar.

"Thought we'd take the opportunity while we could." Cass told the room. "Tins of meat and some vegetables."

Joe Savage gave a satisfied grunt. "Good work. Jane Donaldson is already talking about organising a Distress Committee – this'll be the first help for those families already suffering."

"The barricade's down. We showed the bastards." Charlie's face was alight with enthusiasm, his earlier fears forgotten as the other men cheered and stamped.

At the bar, Otto reached for a bottle, began to pour out good measures for all.

Joe raised a hand. "You did light a candle today but remember, it has to be a long burning one. Massey'll retaliate and we have to be ready."

"To do what?" someone asked.

"Whatever we have to." was the stark reply.

Bob Semple lifted his voice over the talk that broke out among them all. "Cullen's recruiting more coppers, Special Constables, he's calling them."

"How'd you know?"

Semple tapped the side of his nose slyly.

"Can't say."

Pat Hickey dragged fingers over an unshaven chin, no time to shave and he felt tired, Christ, they were all tired!

"Where will he bring these 'specials' in from?"

"Farm boys." Semple spat onto the floor, Otto cursing him from behind the bar. "He's sending quiet messages out to the country – work the wharves."

Tom cursed roundly. "And they will, too, damn them! But what about the shearers? They've a union of their own. Surely they'll stand behind the watersiders?"

Semple leaned forward over the table, grabbed the beer in front of him. "Don't hold your breath, Barker. Farmers only think about themselves and they've too much too lose to help a bunch of poor bloody working class skivvies."

Pat picked up his own beer, gazed into its depths. "If Massey and Cullen bring in forces against us all we can do is fight back harder."

"And the press will damn us traitors and radicals only fit for hanging." This from Joe Savage.

Pat Hickey lifted horrified eyes. "What if this turns into another Waihi?" He scanned the expressions around him but only Semple had the courage to say what some of them were thinking.

"Then we're buggered."

Pat pushed his beer away and shoved himself to his feet.

"Where you going?" Semple asked.

"We need to make some plans. I've gotta find the others."

Semple watched Pat leave the pub in a panic. He looked at his empty glass then reached over for Pat's full one, lifted it to his lips. "And then what, Pat?" Semple asked his beer. "We'll hold some more meetings?" He gave a harsh bark of laughter before tipping the liquid effortlessly down his throat.

***

In spite of Semple's cynicism, they had little choice. Word of their planned actions had to be got out and mass meetings were the best way to do that. Since October the 6th when sixteen Huntly miners were sacked, Tom Barker and the Wobblies had launched 'The Industrial Unionist' news-sheet. This was produced three times a week and sold on street corners and in the shops of sympathisers. Moss had been co-opted onto this job, selling so many Joe Savage slipped him a few shillings from his own pocket.

But, there were plenty of workers out there who couldn't read or who didn't take in information well in this way. With urgent messages needing to reach as many working people as possible the strike leaders used their best weapon – mass meetings. Wellington had seen nothing like it in her previously well-ordered life.

Thousands of men and women turned up at the Basin Reserve, breaking down the gates to get in when the strike committee was refused a permit. A sea of suits and hats standing, listening, cheering and supporting as men like Treager, Semple, Hickey and Savage spoke, argued, gave them all hope. The police stood back and watched as the crowds poured in.

Cullen screamed blue murder from his office, calling the strikers foreign agitators; an echo of the Prime Minister but without the irony of Massey's Irish accent. Traitors, they called the strikers and their sympathisers and had the Dominion print material stating how the trade unions were causing trouble again and foolish watersiders were being swayed by greedy men into breaking the good faith of their employer. It wrote of the 'lawlessness of mob outbreaks', 'terrorism at the wharf' and constantly emphasised the inability of the regular police to keep any peace as, Cullen claimed, the agitators tore the country apart.

In retaliation, the unions called on their membership around the country to support the Wellington watersiders while in the country centres, farmers and their sons were recruited into an army to fight against the working man.

Massey spoke of starving the strikers and their families into submission to which Peter Fraser replied," If the employers try to starve the strikers into submission, then the workers of Wellington and New Zealand are to get food, and if a few doors have to be burst, like the Basin Reserve, all the worse for the doors."

New Zealand's first class war was underway.

***

33

Maudie was in her kitchen when a familiar face peered round the door.

"Are they in?" Alex pointed a finger to the ceiling.

"They are. Should you be?" was the shrewd answer.

Alex had too much respect for Maudie and too much personal bravery to misunderstand the question or not answer it. "My parents aren't happy about it but it's my life I'm living."

Clear, grey eyes met knowing bloodshot blue as Maudie gestured with her head for the younger woman to sit with her. "He was sick as a dog when he didn't hear from yer." Maudie sucked on her old pipe, kept her gaze at the pot of soup simmering on the stove top. "Thought he'd give it all away and leave."

"I wanted to be here, Maudie, with him but…my parents…" She struggled to find the right words. "They've already lost so much. They see Sam…well…He's not who they hoped for me." Alex was aware of floundering. "To them he's a threat to what they have left." She could tell Maudie wasn't impressed by this argument.

"Thousands would be more than happy to have their leftovers."

"I know."

"You went so far with him then buggered off. Any idea what that did to him?"

"Maudie, I know! And I know you understand that things in this world are never simple. I'm sorry, so sorry for what Sam went through but it wasn't easy for me either. I know what I'll lose with my choice to be in this world, Sam's world." Alex bit her bottom lip. But I hope he can forgive me, Maudie for if he doesn't then I don't know what the hell I'm going to do with all this love."

The wood in the firebox cracked and dropped into the ashes. Maudie took her time re-stoking it to give Alex some privacy to wipe her eyes unwatched. When she spoke again, her voice was softer. "The bastards are up there preparing for trouble."

Alex's head snapped up in concern. "Trouble? Who's after them?" Maudie just lifted an eyebrow and Alex realised her mistake. "Oh. You mean they're preparing to cause trouble. Yes, that does seem much more likely."

She left the kitchen with Maudie's snorting laughter in her ears.

Alex stood in the hallway outside Samuel and Cass's room, uncharacteristically hesitant. As anxious as she was to see Samuel there was always – always – the possibility he'd not want anything to do with her and while she paused out here, she was safe from such inevitability, could fool herself that everything would be fine.

She leaned her back against the wall beside their door, listening to the voices inside raised in argument.

"We ignore all buildings except the sawmill and the factory with it." Samuel's voice was adamant.

"No. We should get rid of it all. The whole bloody lot. If they want to do deals with the devil, they should expect some retaliation."

"They employ workers, plenty of them. And without the means of production, there's no need for workers."

There was no noise except for the sound of hobnailed boots irritably pacing the wooden floors.

"All I'm saying, Sam is there's a mill up north that refused to make the batons because it was a police baton that killed poor Fred Evans. And these Wellington bastards are happy to take the money for producing weaponry." Cass swore under his breath heatedly.

"Then we burn the sawmill and factory. That'll stop the bastards."

The two men heard the creaking of wood outside their door. Samuel shot Cass a quick look, full of meaning. While the latter picked up a metal bar and swung it around one hand, Samuel moved to the door and yanked it open as Cass appeared at Samuel's side, arm raised, face fierce. They froze.

"Alex!"

Innocent eyes moved from Samuel to Cass. "Is this not a good time to call?" She stepped through the doorway.

Cass coughed awkwardly, edged to the door. "Well…. I'll leave you two to…. chat." But he came to an abrupt halt as Samuel's hand slammed down on his arm.

"No need for you to go, Cass. We've nothing to talk about." Samuel lifted his chin, returned Alex's cool stare.

As Cass whimpered in the thick, unpleasant atmosphere, Alex controlled her own panic at the cold look Samuel sent her way. It took effort but she behaved as if nothing was amiss between them.

"So, we're torching Stewart Timber and Hardware tonight, are we?" Alex rubbed her gloved hands together.

Stunned they'd been overheard and even more dumfounded over Alex's apparent expectation that she was to be part of it, Samuel and Cass gaped open-mouthed. They looked so flabbergasted that Alex smiled and Samuel finally found his voice.

"We? No. Cass and I, yes."

Cass's voice was urgent. "You won't tell anyone will you?"

But Samuel ignored that question as irrelevant, focused his attention on the increasing look of determination in the woman's eyes. "This isn't a job for you, Alex."

She ignored his frown, spoke composedly. "And according to my parents, you're not the man for me, yet here I am."

All Samuel's sense of loss disappeared as the meaning of her few words sunk in. He became unaware of anything other than the glow of those silver eyes, looking at him with confidence and love as he reached for her hands, held them against his chest.

Cass sighed heavily, thinking this atmosphere just as trying as the earlier one. Putting on a posh accent he said, "And we've got some arson to undertake so shall we get on?"

They were glad of the foggy night and quiet streets, quieter than they had ever been since trouble erupted around the city. The only noise came from the direction of the wharves where the strikers tore down yet another barricade, overwhelming the police and patrols.

"This might be the last of any easy targets." Samuel whispered, ignoring Cass's snort and, "Easy? Bugger off!"

"Why?" Alex kept close to Samuel.

"Massey's bringing in what he calls 'special constables'. Farm boys with weapons to face us down."

"Turning citizens on citizens! He can't."

"He will, Alex. From what Joe and Semple have discovered, they'll be here any day now."

Never before had Alex been aware of such a sweeping feeling of rage against the men who ruled over them so heedlessly, so arrogantly sure of their own rights that they would destroy any who wanted to challenge those rights or even demand their own.

"And they'll be armed?" she knew it was a forlorn question, needed to hear the reply even if only to confirm her worst fears.

"You bet your life they'll be armed."

Samuel threw out a hand, kept Alex back in the shadows while he listened not breathing as a shout rang out a street or so away from them. No further sound encouraged them to move on into the thickening fog.

"Then I'm glad we're doing this." Alex said angrily. "Anything less to beat the strikers about the heads with the better."

Cass leaned into her ear, whispered, "We'll make a unionist of you yet, Alexandra."

She was about to make a smart retort when Samuel stopped in front of the walls surrounding Stewart Timber and Hardware Company. "Cass, you sure you know which building we're after?"

"Of course. I've done some work here, haven't I? Follow me."

Cass slipped through the loosely bound chains on one of the side gates and they all sneaked towards the two story sawmill and factory. "She'll go up in a heartbeat."

"Set more than one spot alight to get maximum coverage for the flames. We don't want them to rebuild too easily." Samuel held out some matches to Alex. "You sure you want to do this? You don't have to."

"I know. And I do."

Alex was surprised how steady her hands were while she was almost gasping with nerves but finding a likely spot she set her own fire going, turned back to see Cass and Samuel already stoking small blazes of their own.

Moving quickly they started three other small fires then at a signal from Cass, disappeared out the way they came and just in time as a whoosh of moving air joined two of the small fires into one big one. From the safety outside the perimeter fence, they watched the quickly growing conflagration.

"They won't be making their damn batons here." Cass said grimly, adding softly. "This is for you Fred."

***

34

The word flew round the Wellington streets – the cavalry had arrived in port and armed ratings off the British ship, HMS Psyche were on the march. On the wharves here and in Auckland, Massey ordered machine guns to be set up, faced towards the strikers. War had arrived on those ships and Massey wanted all strikers and their supporters to understand the forces now in place against them. Back down or starve became heavily emphasised when machine guns underlined the words.

At first, most people refused to believe their Prime Minister capable of such conduct and it was with a wish for the whispers to be proved wrong that brought thousands onto the streets around Wellington's Post Office Square near the wharf. When they discovered the rumours to be true, disbelief changed to fear and anger, a sudden sense of having nothing left to lose.

"You want fair wages to feed and clothe your families? You want to be a worker, proud and respected? They would have you nothing more than a cog in their wheel of profiteering. They want you uneducated, unfed, poorly waged and unprotected because therein lies their greatest profits." Semple's eyes blazed over the heads of the crowds, echoed around stone buildings. "You are working men and women and you deserve to be acknowledged as the sweat that makes this country great!" Semple paused as the cheering swallowed up his words and Joe Savage, eyes down as he knelt beside him smiled at the man's ability to stir up a crowd.

All at once, Semple raised his arms and the crowd fell silent. "Massey brings his Cossacks against us. Armed with guns and batons they are here to subdue us. Over there are machine guns, pointed straight at our hearts – that's how much they fear us. We ask that you stand with us, shoulder to shoulder for we will march beside you, IWW, SDP, NZLP, radical, socialist, worker. Together we need to be stronger than the strongest weapon Massey and Cullen will direct our way. If we have to fight then by god, let us fight as one!"

This time the cheering went on so long, Joe Savage took the opportunity to speak to Semple. "Bob, you're asking these people to face machine gun fire and who knows what violence to come."

Semple lifted a hand to acknowledge the cheers as Pat Hickey took his place to speak. "No, Savage. I'm asking them to show that some things are worth fighting for."

Joe's piercing eyes ranged over the thousands of heads. "I never thought Massey would call out the military against us."

"He's frightened we will win this and he can't let us."

"Do you know what you're saying?" Joe asked Semple softly and received a grim nod in reply.

"And so do you. You and I both know. This isn't a fight we can ever win."

"Then why are we risking their lives?" For the first time desperation sounded in Joe's voice and the eyes he turned to Semple's mirrored that fear.

Semple fell silent. He focussed on Hickey's words, the responses from the crowd. He saw policemen, patrols, the hope in the faces watching them, knew hunger gnawed at their bellies, knew their pockets were empty. And only then did he look Joe Savage in the face.

"Because, " Semple softened his tone. "There's a world of difference, Joe in being beaten down unheard and unrecognised or going down fighting with your head held high."

Joe drew a shaky breath as a cry went up from the back of the crowds nearest the wharf.

"Here they come!"

Every head spun round at the sound of hooves thundering towards them. Men shoved women hastily towards the safety of the nearest building and instinctively turned to their strike leaders.

"Keep yourselves safe!"

"Bugger that! They're coming straight at us!"

"We fight back they get to say we're the danger!"

Women screamed, scooped up children and ran as the mounted

specials smashed into the crowd, men disappearing under the horses' hooves. Mounted, armed men rode through the weaponless crowd who nevertheless began to fight back. Over a thousand men against the contingent of specials and the specials began to give way under the onslaught.

"You dirty scabs! You're a bastard lot of scabs, not men!" strikers screamed at the approaching horsemen. Men ran through the street towards Lambton Quay, horses on their heels. They grabbed whatever they could as they scarpered, stones, anything useful off carts or on display outside the shops. The riot reached its peak at Whitcomb and Tombs bookshop as missiles flew and batons smashed down on unprotected flesh and bone, where men and women taken by surprise were trampled.

As this part of the city exploded, hasty provisions were being made for the wounded. At the Socialist Hall women of the Distress Committee tended to the badly wounded first while Alex was sent running for a doctor to set smashed limbs and find any nurses who were willing to assist.

It wasn't until the specials fought their way through to the safety of the Buckle Street barracks that the streets slowly quieted and a stunned reaction set in as the protesters wondered at the brutality of the attack and just what the hell would happen next now Massey's Cossack's had shown their power.

That evening the specials charged another peaceful demonstration at Post Office Square, provoking Sir Joseph Ward to question Massey about the provocative behaviour of the specials. Massey did nothing.

***

Whilst the Present
INDUSTRIAL TROUBLE is in
progress,
CITIZENS are urgently
requested
To refrain from congregating in
POST OFFICE SQUARE
JOHN P LUKE
Mayor

October 30 1913

Under the cover of the next evening's riot Samuel and Cass took the opportunity to slip back onto the wharf. They had Charlie with them again and two others they knew well and trusted.

"Your cousin told you it would be safe?" Samuel asked Charlie for the third time.

"Yes, I've told you. He has to work as a patrol on the wharf because he's on the bones of his arse and has six little 'uns but he doesn't like what's happening anymore'n we do. He told me where to get through and he'll make sure there's no bugger patrolling there."

"If this works, I'll buy the bastard a beer." Cass told Charlie who just grinned.

"Better give it to me instead. Arthur, he don't drink."

"He doesn't?"

"Nope."

"Does he smoke?"

"Never."

Cass shook his head in wonderment.

"Still, if he's got six kids we know what he does do."

It was the easiest job to date. Thanks to the invisible Arthur not a patrol was to be seen as they grabbed eight sacks of spuds from a pile on the wharf. They melted back into the night, arriving at the Socialist Hall where wounded men lay around the walls and Jane Donaldson, Hilda Mills and Alex worked with a doctor and two nurses.

The men dropped the heavy sacks into a room turned dry goods store and were offered hot soup which they gladly took, Jane shaking their hands, profuse in her thanks.

"We're getting donations from businesses and families – oatmeal, flour, vegetables, milk. There are shop keepers selling goods under cost for strikers' families and a lovely Italian fisherman who won't give us his name but catches fish every morning and drops it into us." She paused for a moment before adding, "Good people doing good things.”

Cass finished his soup with a slurp. “Here’s hoping the good will outweigh the bad.”

***

In his office, William Massey stared out into the night. With him, around the well-polished tables sat high ranking employers and farmers all discussing the effect the strike was having on them.

“You said Waihi would calm the unionists down, Prime Minister. It appears your response has had the opposite effect. Damn it! How can I run a business if my workers strike?”

“You are hardly alone.” A ruddy faced man, uncomfortable in a tight fitting suit folded his heavy hands on the table. “I’ve hundreds of pounds worth of produce from my farms rotting on the damn wharves.”

Massey turned back to them all, his eyes in shadow. “Once we have enough special constables on the streets, we can take decisive action against the strikers and their supporters.”

“You’re bringing in more specials?”

“I’ll bring in as many as I can. Give them a baton and a pistol, we’ll have order soon enough.”

“If the public find out we’ve armed the specials….”

Massey turned fathomless eyes to the speaker. “The papers will print only what we tell them to print. Anything else we can claim as pro-unionist hearsay or propaganda.”

The farmer hadn’t taken his eyes off the Prime Minister’s face. He considered himself a hard man who earned forty thousand pounds a year and paid his farm labourers ten shillings a week. He had no sympathy for the strikers and little for his own workers but there was one question he wanted to put to Massey and it surprised him how afraid he was to ask it. William Massey the farmer he thought he knew and understood. William Massey the Prime Minister? He wasn’t so sure of him.

"Prime Minister, the machine guns on the wharves." He paused .

"Will you use them?"

Massey's reply was chilling. "I've never been a man for empty threats, gentlemen."

And he turned away from their stares, looked back out into the dark night.

***

Jimmy was hanging over the rail of the ship, retching bile into the waves and wishing he'd never agreed to come with Peter Dray to Wellington.

It had sounded exciting while they talked about it in Murchison – reclaim the wharves from the bastards who threatened all their livelihoods through greed. Jimmy had supported Dray wholeheartedly as the farmer spoke passionately about radicals holding the country to ransom while hard-working farmers saw their goods spoil and waste.

John never attended these meetings and when Jimmy asked him why he would only say, "There's two sides to every story, lad. I might vote Massey but that don't mean I agree with everything the man says and does."

And then Jimmy declared over supper one night that he'd offered himself and his horse to travel with Peter Dray to Wellington as a Special Constable. All John had done was light his pipe and wander outside to the barn, unwilling to forbid Jimmy but unable, too to support his decision.

So here he was, Jimmy thought morosely, spewing his guts up after and all the way through a terrible crossing. What seemed an adventure in the remote hills of Murchison now appeared a ludicrous over-reaction with Wellington coming into view.

Peter poked his head out onto deck and wandered over. He leaned his back against the rail and lit a cigarette. The first smoke he blew out hit Jimmy in the face and the younger man groaned as his stomach heaved viciously and he twisted back over the metal rail, spitting stringy mucus and wiping his mouth with a shaky hand.

"Sorry." Dray grinned and ostentatiously held his cigarette away from Jimmy's face. "What do you think of the capital?"

Jimmy lifted his eyes as they sailed past Soames Island, saw the expanse of buildings before him. Ill as he felt the cityscape overwhelmed him with its presence.

"It's…." words failed him. "Huge." Was the best he could come up with.

Dray sneered. "London's huge, boy. This is a colonial backwater and nothing else."

"It's huge to me." Jimmy responded, watching round eyed as they drew nearer. "I can't believe we're here." Despite his still churning stomach, for the first time he felt a frisson of excitement. "And the people will welcome us?"

"Welcome us? They'll think we're bloody saints come to save them. Shipping's at a standstill in all our main ports because of these communist thugs. I hear Wellington's running short of essentials, too." Dray finished his cigarette and continued smugly. "I don't doubt they'll be cheering in the streets when we arrive."

But Dray's foresight proved woefully inaccurate. From the moment they unloaded at the wharf Jimmy thought he'd ridden into a nightmare. As they rode out onto the streets they were surrounded by the frightening clamour of angry crowds. Not wanting to hurt anyone, Jimmy struggled with his anxious, nervous mount which tossed its head and rolled its eyes in fright at the noise and tension.

It wasn't long before Jimmy's head began to spin. Stunned in all his senses, he looked around at Peter to see if he was suffering, too but Dray sat unconcerned on his tall horse. To Jimmy's shock, Dray kicked out at those nearest to him, brought his whip brutally down on heads, shoulders or faces as the newest specials shoved their way through the sea of people towards Buckle Street barracks.

Where were the cheers and the banners welcoming the rescuers to
a city in torment from a senseless rabble?

Keeping a firm grip on his horse's reins, Jimmy blindly followed
those in front of him, wishing with all his heart he was back home in
Murchison.

Buckle Street crossed the top of Tory and Taranaki Streets where
some of the poorest of Wellington's inhabitants lived in cramped,
damp housing, where they struggled on pittance wages and often
went hungry.

That night at the barracks in Buckle Street, Dray thrived in the
atmosphere of heroes and saviours which permeated any space the
specials occupied. Tonight they ate heartily of meat, fresh bread and
vegetables supplied by the government and farmers who knew the
specials were an investment to be nourished.

Jimmy couldn't eat. He pushed food about his plate while the men
around him traded jokes about the heads they'd cracked on the way
but all Jimmy could think about was the desperation in the crowds,
the pinched, hungry faces they'd laid into. After Dray loudly
declared they would have the strikers on their knees in a couple of
days, Jimmy shoved himself to his feet, dumped his full plate on the
ground for the dogs and walked out.

In one of the courtyards he found sacks of feed for the horses
stacked high against a wall and he clambered up them, threw himself
back against the sacks to stare up at the night sky.

Wellington's usual wind shifted the loose hay and spun it around,
lifted tufts of it up into the air but Jimmy was heedless of anything
but the fear and anger on the faces he'd seen in the crowds today.

A loud belch signalled he was no longer alone. "Thought I saw
you slip out, Jimmy."

"I needed fresh air."

"You didn't eat much. Are you still sick from the crossing?"

Jimmy just shrugged, uncaring if Dray saw his response or not, wishing the other man would just leave him alone.

"New Zealand needs us here, Jimmy. Massey's Cossacks, they're calling us, mocking us." Dray's voice hardened. "But we need to keep the wharves working."

"You said the people would welcome us! I saw no welcome, just anger and desperation."

"What do you expect from uneducated labourers who don't know what's good for them? They're being stirred up by the communist agitators. You think they want this fight?" Dray didn't wait for a reply. "Course they bloody don't! All they want is more money to piss up in a pub on payday."

But Jimmy had had enough of Dray's rants. He slid down the sacks nimbly. "I'm not sure we're doing the right thing," He began, only to gasp as Dray grabbed his arm, digging relentless fingers deep into muscle .

"You keep that talk to yourself, Jimmy!" he hissed. "You think John would be proud to hear you sympathise with the anarchists? Remember where you come from, boy and do your damn duty like the rest of us."

Jimmy wrenched his arm free, strode away his face burning with anger and shame.

***

35

At night from his doorstep Moss could hear the sinister sound of horses patrolling through the streets and he shivered at the jingle of bridle and bit, the slap of whips on rumps, the thudding of hooves on the ground. Though the specials patrolled during the daylight hours, too, there was something more intimidating about them at night, where the shadows were part of the menace hiding eyes, faces and intentions.

Moss knew Samuel and Cass spent most of their nights involved in work for the strikers but he didn't know what it was, just saw them come home exhausted before dawn and snatch a little sleep before rising to do it all again the next night.

Sometimes, he ran messages or acted as lookout but most of his time was spent still selling copies of 'The Industrial Unionist' around the streets. When he took Peg in her little cart, he sold dozens more copies but then Samuel found out and put his foot down about the little girl being dragged about the streets in these dangerous times.

"I don't care how many damn copies you sell with Peg, Moss, you leave her at home!"

Moss obeyed, taking Peg only when he stood on the corner of Tory Street and Courtenay Place.

But tonight, he felt restless. Unable to sleep, he crept through the house and out the front door, pausing on the doorstep for any sound of the specials before slipping out into the night to see what was happening.

Drawn by noise, Moss stood on the street opposite the Royal Tiger Hotel which stood proudly on the corner of Taranaki and Abel Tasman Streets. As Moss hesitated there several man were thrown out onto the road, one of them screaming his head off. "You bastard! You're giving free drinks to the specials!"

"Piss   of   home,   Si!

"You shouldn't serve the bastards at all!"

The man called Si shoved his protagonist and received a punch in return.

Before long a full scale fight was in place as men carrying their batons emerged from the pub and started in on Si and his friends. Moss turned away. He'd already seen enough blood exploding under the batons of the specials. Anyway, he had to tell Samuel.

Sprawled out over his mattress, Samuel slept the sleep of the dead. In his dreams he and Mick were attacking Massey on horseback as a man with a familiar face stepped from the shadows with his baton raised high. Jerked awake by the dream, Samuel felt a hand on his chest and gave a strangled gasp, swore loudly, waking Cass.

"Woss going on?"

"It's Moss." Clutching his heart Samuel sat up. "Jesus, lad, what is it?"

Urgently, Moss signalled they had to follow. Grabbing their boots and grumbling the two men shoved their jackets and caps on as they trailed after the boy. In minutes they were watching the melee outside The Royal Tiger.

Someone shouted the warning.

"Coppers!" And men staggered off bleeding, throwing final punches as police whistles sounded.

Samuel grabbed hold of Si who clutched at his face as blood streamed through his fingers.

"Si! What the hell's going on?"

"The bloody Tiger's giving free drinks to the bloody Cossacks!"

Si's hand slipped down the blood on his wounded face revealing a thick chunk of flesh hanging from his cheekbone. With a gasp Samuel grabbed his clean handkerchief and placed it on Si's cheek to hold the torn flesh in place. "Go and see about that face, Si. We'll send the Tiger a message it won't forget in a hurry."

Moss was standing beside Cass who swore using words the boy hadn't heard before but mentally stored away for future use.
***

All through the night and into the next day the sounds of protest were audible through the stone walls inside the barracks. What began as a couple of hundred people grew steadily over the hours until over two thousand people gathered at the intersection of Taranaki and Buckle Streets decrying the use of special constables.

Every now and again a stone would land on the roof causing the horses to shift nervously in the courtyard while the specials saddled them. Jimmy was passed his baton and pistol, felt ashamed at his heartfelt reluctance.

"Remember what Police Commissioner Cullen told us, 'If they won't go, ride over them.'"

A voice from behind Jimmy called out tentatively, "But, there are women and children in those crowds."

"They've been told to keep the streets clear. If they're protesting, they're trouble and we're here to keep trouble at bay."

Jimmy hadn't dare mention his misgivings to Dray anymore, going about his duties with a set face and trying not to head out on too many patrols, keeping himself busy within the barracks. But the call came through that all troops were to be ready for action forcing him to saddle up with everyone else.

Beside him a short, finely built middle aged man was staring at the pistol he'd been handed. "There's oldies out in those crowds, too," he said wretchedly. "Are we really meant to shoot?" He raised troubled eyes to Jimmy who couldn't reply.

***

"No, Alex! Absolutely not."

If Samuel expected her to back down after he had resolutely expressed this opinion, he was to be sorely mistaken.

She met his angry glare with a cool expression, belied by the glint in the silver grey eyes he loved. "Everyone I know is there."

"It's dangerous."

"It's been dangerous since Massey brought the first lot of scabs riding into the city." Her lips set in a determined line. "I'm heading up to the barracks, Sam."

How could he be angry at Alex's independent resolve when it was just that attitude which had brought her into his life in the first place? Exasperated admiration seemed to be Samuel's lot when he was bested in confrontations like these between them.

"I can't be there this afternoon, Alex. I've got to see the lads down the wharf."

"Then I'll go with Cass." She saw the genuine concern in Samuel's eyes and slipped her arms around his waist. "I'll be fine, love."

He weakened as they both knew he would. He drew her close, kissed her deeply.

"I love you."

"I know." And she waited just long enough before adding, "I love you, too. Now let me go raise a bit of hell."

Samuel watched her stride confidently towards Cass, slip her arm through his. They gave him a final wave, Cass blowing Samuel a kiss. A small shape emerged from the hallway, hoping to sidle by unseen. Moss's hopes of an unobserved exit were thwarted when Sam grabbed him about the collar, bringing the boy to a hasty stop. "And where do you think you're going?"

He gave Samuel an eloquent glare.

"I don't suppose I could tell you to stay home?" Samuel sighed as he received an adamant shake of Moss's head. "Then be bloody careful."

Moss slipped passed Samuel and began to jog up the street. Samuel saw the boy reach down to fill his pockets with stones before carrying on. He wanted to cry out, tell Moss to put the damn things back but didn't.

The sound of little wheels on the wooden floor caught his attention.

"Up, Smam. Up."

With a smile, Samuel lifted Peg into his arms and she snuggled happily into his chest, cooing, "Smam." He loved the way she said his name – didn't love it so much when Cass called him Smam, though.

"At least you'll be safe and sound, Peg." He kissed her soft hair. "I'm just not so sure about the rest of us."

Jimmy tried not to lash out to the people crowding around his horse. He kept his pistol in his pocket, knew others didn't. He'd already heard shots ring out as they charged the crowds, heard screams and cries but couldn't see who was hurt as people surged back and forwards.

"Over the bastards!" Dray shouted, tugging his horse viciously round as a hail of stones came their way.

Batons were swung up and bashed down across unprotected heads and shoulders, faces and torsos. Jimmy refused to hit out until one man grabbed his reins while another tried to pull him out of the saddle. In the mad desperation of self-defence, Jimmy flailed about with his baton, catching one man across the forehead and the other under the chin, sent him reeling backwards into the crowd. A roar of anger swelled from those who had seen this and now Jimmy was forced to fight as if his life depended on it. Because he wasn't at all sure that it didn't.

The Socialist Hall was once again full of wounded, the seriously injured quickly despatched to the Public Hospital on Riddiford Street in Newtown yet even with the worst cases off their hands, the women of the Distress Committee found themselves besieged as more injured people were brought to them. Alex worked with Jane Donaldson, trying to organise a rough triage to deal with each case as it turned up.

"What kind of man drives his horse into women and children?" Jane demanded of no one, her face flushed with anger and effort.

"What kind of man gives the orders to?" Alex replied bitterly. "Between Massey, Cullen and their kind, we'll be lucky to come out of this without everyone bearing scars."

A screaming child was brought up the stairs in the arms of a man Jane recognised.

"Jim! One of yours?" she asked, taking the sobbing child.

Jim shook his head tiredly. "Don't know whose. He got trampled under one of the scab's horses. I tried to find his parents but…." He gave a gesture expressing the uselessness of his attempt then sank onto the nearest chair, gratefully taking gulps from a cup Alex handed to him. "It's a war out there." He shook his head in disbelief. "There's talk of a demonstration outside the Royal Tiger. I only worry Massey will bring up the machine guns from the wharf."

Jane's eyes widened in horror. "He wouldn't Jim!" but doubt, reinforced by the last few weeks forced her to add, "would he?"

Jim finished the drink, passed the cup back and stood again, preparing to leave. "I would never have thought him capable of setting them up in the first place, never mind setting our country into this chaos." He laid a hand on the head to the crying child. "Take care of him."

"Of course. You take care of yourself."

For several moments after Jim had gone, Jane stood in the middle of the upheaval in the room, aware of the much bigger madness in the city itself and unable to move.   It took Alex's arm about her shoulder to bring her back to the job on hand.

Samuel struggled to find Cass among the throng gathering around The Royal Tiger. Shoving through the throng he finally ran him to ground round the back where he was arguing with an indomitable Vi.

"It's only gonna get worse, Vi. Get yourself home."

"And lose my job?" Violet shoved Cass away. "Yer know what the boss is like. I can't just go home."

"Can't the bastard hear the riot?"

Vi gave a scoffing laugh. "Yer think he cares? He's letting the specials drink here, isn't he? Giving them free drinks, helping them out. He don't care, Cass and I need my job." She pushed him further away. "So get yer arse out of it. He don't want no truck with the likes of you strikers and it'll be the worse for me if he sees me with yer."

"Vi...."

"Go!"

Scowling, Cass left and Samuel fell into step beside him. "The bastard specials are shooting off pistols now and I've seen one or two with bloody rifles."

"Bloody farmer boys out for a day's hunting." Samuel said bitterly.

A shout went up round the front of the hotel and they shot off to where large crowds were forming. It seemed like every striker was there and the slums of Te Aro had emptied supporters onto the streets as well.

As he took in the faces all around, the well-fed ones on horseback compared to the rest Samuel realised strongly for the first time, that this was a class war. Semple had called it so weeks ago but Samuel hadn't seen it until now. Just one of those fine horses was worth more than a working man earned in a year.

"Go back to your homes!" An arrogant looking man sitting on a handsome chestnut shouted over their heads, his baton hanging from his wrist, a pistol on display.

Mutters became cat calls as he tried again. "We don't want to have to charge you..."

"Then bloody don't!"

"But we will have order in the streets!"

"Head back to your farm, scab and maybe we'll go home!" A woman called out.

The word scab was picked up and shouted repeatedly until the man on the horse sneered at them all and rode back to his compatriots. More people surged forward and the first stones were thrown into the hotel windows where frightened patrons peered out. As the windows shattered, a fusillade of stones followed, the smashing of glass echoing out into the night. Men grabbed palings from fences and began to heave them through the lower windows. A shout went up from the specials and fire hoses were turned onto the rioters, knocking them back.

From that moment fury took hold of the crowds. Pavers were overturned and used to throw through the hotel windows or launched at the oncoming cavalry. Bottles were gathered, anything that came to hand and in spite of repeated charges into them and through them, enough made it through to the barracks themselves. Suddenly the hunters were the hunted.

Samuel and Cass held a paling in each hand as the rumble of horses hooves alerted to another charge.

"Stand firm." Cass shouted but Samuel needed no such bidding. He stood, heart thumping wildly as the horses charged towards them.

Jimmy heard Dray's voice calling for a regroup. "We go through the bastards or over them!"

Adrenalin surging through him, Jimmy no longer hesitated. He swung his horse's head and obeyed Dray, settling just in front of him as the charge began. There was a large group, maybe a hundred people, more than Jimmy could count and it looked formidable. His horse snorted in fear. As they picked up their pace, Jimmy swung his baton up over his head and behind him, Dray cocked his pistol.

Cass shouted a warning to Samuel that one of the specials was armed with a gun but Samuel heard nothing more than the chaos. He lifted his paling and prepared for the worst as the horse bore down on him, the special with his arm raised.

Eye to eye they were special and striker and recognition stunned them both.

"Jimmy?"

Samuel knew his brother couldn't hear him but Jimmy wrenched his horse's head up, only his skill keeping the animal on its feet and himself in the saddle as the pistol fired and Samuel went down, his face registering shock and astonishment.

Jimmy swung round in his saddle, saw Peter Dray, his arm still out, a smile of immense satisfaction on his face as Jimmy gave a roar brought his baton down on Dray's arm with bone shattering strength. "That was my brother, you bastard!"

Dray screamed, the pistol lost from his useless fingers, scooped up by one of the strikers never to be seen again. Still mounted, Jimmy scanned the spaces around him for his fallen brother but there was no sign.

As quickly as he'd seen him, Jimmy had lost him.

***

"Don't try to speak."

Samuel was panting in pain from the bullet in his side. "Cass….. it was Jimmy." He groaned, sagged as all strength went from his legs and lost consciousness.

Cass hauled Samuel more completely over his shoulder, half-carried, half-dragged his friend through the press of bodies and the pandemonium on the streets wondering desperately where to go. He lowered him to the ground, shocked at the amount of blood on his clothes. Cass opened Samuel's jacket, saw where the bullet had gone in and quickly, he tore a chunk off his own shirt, pressed it to the wound, thankful beyond measure when after what felt like hours of heart-stopping panic, the pressure worked and the bleeding eased. Deftly, Cass worked a firm binding before taking stock of where they were. They were closest to Maudie's. Decision made.

Cass lifted Samuel as carefully as he could as someone stepped up and offered help and together they carried the unconscious man home.

Maudie's front door crashed open. Expecting trouble, she reached down for a hefty fire iron, surprised when Cass and a stranger almost fell through the door into the kitchen, Samuel hoisted between them.

"He's been shot, Maudie." Cass panted. "I think I've stopped the bleeding, but the bullet went in his side."

With a sweep of one arm Maudie cleared everything off her table and they laid Samuel gently down. More carefully than anyone would have given her credit for, Maudie opened Cass's rough dressing as the blood began to pour. She rolled her sleeves up, glanced at Cass. "Gotta strong stomach?"

Cass swallowed, nodded knowing only too well that he lied.

"Good, 'cause we gotta get that bloody thing out of him."

As she bustled around her stovetop emptying boiling water from the kettle into an enamel bowl, Cass turned to thank his helper only to find he'd already gone. He faced Maudie once more as she grunted, "At least he's dead to it."

His face pale, Cass managed to say, "Don't say 'dead'."

"He'll be fine, Cass. It's only a bloody bullet. I've seen worse."

"Where?"

"Never yer damn well mind where." Maudie threw a knife and some other implements Cass didn't recognise into the boiling water. "Right. Get them sleeves up and wash yer hands." She gave Cass a controlled, steady look. "Are yer ready?"

He shook his head, "Yes."

***

Jimmy left Wellington to implode without him. Leaving his horse stabled at the barracks, he set off into the city alone. No longer mounted or carrying a baton he was as vulnerable as anyone else and he had to dodge cavalry charges and projectiles coming at him from every direction.

The Royal Tiger hotel was a wreck, all her windows smashed, bitter fighting still raging down Abel Tasman and Taranaki Streets.

Not knowing where he was headed, Jimmy found himself in Martin Square, a squalid collection of wooden and tin buildings, not a place for a stranger to be late at night. He retraced his steps back out onto Taranaki Street, headed down the hill finding himself on Courtenay Place. It was quieter down here away from the main hostilities but still men burst out from side streets trying to escape their hunters or disappeared just as quickly towards trouble.

Unsure of what to do next, he found a silent alleyway, leaned into the shadows as a detachment of specials cantered by.

Where would Sam be? Knowing he was here, in this city right now gave Jimmy a strange feeling of loss and connection. All he knew was that he had to find Sam even if it was only to tell him it wasn't his brother who shot him.

But coming to that conclusion was all very well. How could he find one man among thousands in a city he didn't know? Jimmy began to walk again, needing to be doing something, anything.

He headed along Courtenay Place, found himself on Cuba Street, feeling insignificant among the tall brick and wooden buildings and longing more than ever for home. Keeping a track of where he'd come from, Jimmy was confident he'd be able to find his way back to the barracks eventually and turned once more to head up Manners Street. There was more noise and bustle here, one building in particular the focus of much activity. Jimmy crossed the road to read the sign – 'Socialist Hall, Everyone Welcome'.

It occurred to him that these people would be active in the strike and if Sam was among the crowds fighting the special constables then perhaps he was known here? Feeling as if he was walking into the lion's den, Jimmy walked up the stairs and into wall-to-wall commotion.

People were clutching head wounds, one man moaning as a doctor bent over the ruin of his face. Hot guilt rushed through Jimmy but he swallowed it, tried to get someone's attention. A woman in a stained apron came over to him, concern in her eyes. "Are you hurt?"

"No. I'm….. I'm just looking for someone."

Jane wiped her hot forehead and gave a tired smile. "Well, I might be able to help. It's madness in the city tonight. Who are you looking for?"

"Sam Brodie." As Jimmy spoke the words a young woman with her arms full of clean linen for bandages came to a halt beside them.

"Samuel Brodie?"

"Yes. He's my brother."

Alex stood unmoving for a few seconds before passing the linen to Jane. "Jane, do you mind?"

"Not at all."

Aware of undercurrents she couldn't define, Jane bustled away while Alex regarded Jimmy searchingly, seeking some family connection in his features. "Sam never speaks of you."

He gave a shy smile shot through with regret. "We …we…. lost touch." He met Alex's eyes beseechingly. "I thought he was gone forever. I thought maybe he was dead. But today, I saw him in the crowd but by the time I turned my horse, he was gone." The words were out of Jimmy's mouth before he realised what he had revealed.

Alex gasped, grabbed the young man by the arm and drew him into a corner. "You're one of Massey's Cossacks?"

"Yes."

She took a step back from him. "You shouldn't be here. Look what you lot have done!" Her gesture encompassed the room, the whole city.

Jimmy laid a hand on her arm but again she moved back, revolted.

"I've got to find Sam. Please."

"He wouldn't want to see you. He's fighting men like you."

"I know. But he was shot and I have to know he's all right."

To Jimmy's alarm the woman looked as if he'd slapped her. The shock on her face brought Jane back to them. "Alex? Are you all right?" Her eyes darting from Jimmy's pale face to Alex's.

"Sam's been shot." Alex uttered in despair.

"When?"

Jimmy gave a helpless gesture. "Hours ago. I'm sorry…. I saw him fall and…." He was dismissed as Jane reached for Alex's coat and hat, dressed her friend quickly.

"He might be at the public hospital."

"If Cass was with him, he'd have sent word to Maudie's. I'll try there first."

Jane gave Alex a warm hug. "Let me know. Whatever happens."

"I'll come with you." Jimmy's voice accepted no refusal, not that she gave him any thought. She nodded absently and led the way out of the hall, barely aware of his presence.

They turned into Tory Street when two patrols came down the street. Alex flattened against a dark doorway. As Jimmy followed suit she gave him a bitter glance. "You've nothing to fear from them. You're one of them."

Not giving him any chance to explain, she checked the road was clear, moved swiftly on and in minutes was standing outside Maudie's boarding house. "You're putting yourself in danger if you come in." she warned Jimmy. "You're the enemy here."

"I've not had my brother in my life in too long." He told her thickly. "I'm not leaving without seeing him again."

Unwilling to waste any more time, Alex shoved the door open, nearly fell over Moss and Peg, huddled together on the floor in the hallway, their tear stained faces and numb expressions telling their own story.

"Where?" Alex asked Moss breathlessly and the boy pointed into the kitchen, suspicious eyes on the stranger who followed her closely.

Maudie and Cass had set a mattress on the floor of the kitchen in front of the woodstove. There, covered in a blanket lay Samuel, his sweaty hair plastered against his skull, his breathing ragged and uneven.

At the sight of Alex, Maudie moved swiftly to her side. "We got the bullet out. Think he'll be all right."

"Think?"

"There's always the risk of infection but I don't wanna to move him to the hospital or anywhere yet. I can keep a close eye on the bugger here."

Alex knelt beside Samuel, ran a gentle hand over his face. He murmured wordlessly. "Maudie, how did you know how to….?"

"She won't say so don't bother asking." Cass spoke from his place leaning against the wall. He gave Alex an awed grin. "But she was amazing, Alex. Saved his life."

"Not yet I bloody haven't. Let's get the bugger back up on his feet first."

Maudie squeezed warm water out of a cloth, began to wipe Samuel's face as Alex's hand stopped her, took the cloth and the job, not seeing the warm smile Maudie gave her, the raised eyebrow she sent Cass's way.

It was then they noticed the stranger hovering awkwardly in the doorway, his eyes locked on Samuel's unconscious body.

"Who's this?"

Alex lifted her face and Jimmy sent her a wordless plea. "He's Sam's brother, apparently." She spoke the words carefully.

Cass shoved himself away from the hall. "Jimmy?"

The young man turned to him. "Yes." A strange look came over his face. "Sam… he spoke of me?"

Cass gave a harsh bark of laughter. "Don't be too happy. He said you'd told him to bugger off."

Jimmy faced Cass in anguish. "I was nine years old for Christ's sake! We'd been through….. terrible things….. " He raised helpless hands. "I was nine. I didn't know that he'd go." Jimmy looked down on Samuel as his eyes welled. "I've missed him."

Maudie eased herself down on a chair, eyed Jimmy. "How'd yer manage to track him here?"

Silence.

Jimmy shot Alex a look but she wasn't going to make this easier for him, she let him flounder, interested in what he'd say. He surprised her by telling the truth.

"I came from Murchison with others to be a special. I saw Sam in the crowd this evening…. I….I… recognised him moments before he was shot and by the time I looked for him, he'd gone."

No one knew what to say, staring at Jimmy in disbelief.

Cass found his voice first. "You're a bloody scab?" He growled the words, flexing his fingers.

"Not anymore."

But Cass was swept by anger and didn't hear the reply. He grabbed Jimmy, dragged him so close, his words spat on the younger man's face. "You rode us down like animals! Did you smash your baton down? Did you ride over anyone? Did you?"

Jimmy didn't even try to defend himself. He just stood there as Cass's anger broke over him. Cass seized Jimmy in one strong hand, drew his arm back.

"Don't… hit him, Cass….. Not yet." Samuel clenched his muscles to sit, collapsing when the agony hit him. As Alex and Maudie bent over him he hastened to reassure them. "I'm… fine."

"Yeah. Yer look brand new." Maudie drawled sarcastically. Seeing the already pale Samuel whiten further, she tipped a couple of drops of laudanum into a small measure of brandy. "Drink this and keep still or yer'll bust yer stitches."

Jimmy stood forgotten until Samuel spoke up again. "You… bloody …shot me, Jimmy."

"It was you?" Cass stared at Samuel. "I thought you were delirious or something." He reached for Jimmy again but the words poured from the younger man in a flood.

"No. I didn't, Sam! It's one of the reasons I wanted to find you. It was Dray. He was riding just behind me…. I saw you fall…. I broke his arm with my baton and by the time I turned to look for you, you'd gone again." Jimmy stumbled over the rush of words as his brother kept bloodshot eyes on him.

"It wasn't me, Sam."

Samuel knew Jimmy was a man grown, because here he was standing in front of him yet all he could see was the frightened seven year old, the conflicted nine year old and everything they had once shared filled the spaces between them so completely it was as if they'd never been apart. Samuel's eyes filled with tears and with a strangled noise, Jimmy shoved his way to his brother's side. Samuel put his arm around Jimmy's neck as his own tears fell.

Maudie signalled to the others and one by one they left the brothers alone.

Alex hovered uncertainly outside in the hallway, staring at the door. Moss lay huddled against it, refusing to move.

"I'm going back out." Cass said.

"Do you think you should?"

"Of course I should! Sam's as good as he can be but there are still bloody specials on the streets." Cass reined his anger in. "I can't just do nothing, Alex."

She nodded her understanding, watched as he slammed the door on his exit. With a final backward glance to the room where Samuel lay, Alex left the house as well, hurrying to return to the Socialist Hall.

Maudie leaned on the window of her parlour, puffing at her old pipe as Alex marched away. She didn't need to see the younger woman's face to know she was crying. Aware of little Peg's eyes on her, Maudie gave a sharp bark of laughter.

"Love ain't no good a lot of the time, Peg darlin', no matter what them poets might say. " As Alex turned a corner, Maudie added under her breath, "Can't see it ending well."

***

Cass found turmoil on the streets though the worst of the violence seemed to have passed. Shattered glass lay underfoot, blood dotted about on the stones, some clotting in pools. Specials led limping, wounded horses while injured people sat in doorways or were supported through the streets.

Knowing any regroup by Semple, Savage and the rest would be at the Albemarle, Cass made his way there. Sure enough, the place was filled with men wearing bloodied bandages or nursing unseen wounds, while standing among them was Joe Savage, desperately trying to calm their anger and fear.

"Fighting like this isn't the way. You can't send the strikers back out into that."

Bob Semple growled bitterly. "So what do you think we should bloody do, Savage? Roll over and let the bastards stamp us into the ground? Jesus!"

"There are machine guns on the wharf, Bob. Here and in Auckland. Do you want to send unarmed men up against those? After all that he's done so far, do you think Massey wouldn't use them if we gave him cause?"

Every man grew silent. Joe met Peter Fraser's understanding eye.

"Violence escalates," Joe continued urgently. "And we don't have an army waiting in the wings for the call to martial law. If we answer violence with more violence, we will lose." He dropped his voice, spoke to Semple. "And you know that, Bob because you've said it yourself– this isn't a fight we can win."

Angry at hearing his own words used against him, Bob Semple turned a battered, bruised face to Savage, his voice raw, his anger carrying a presence of its own in the tense room. "So what do we bloody do?" he demanded again.

Peter Fraser shifted against the table he was leaning on, reluctant to say the words but knowing there was no other choice. "We have to back down."

The room erupted around him but even when the angriest pressed closer to him, Fraser held his ground. He looked sadly at Savage who nodded. Let them have their anger, the gesture said. It was all they had. But there could only be one outcome for the strikers and both men knew it. They would have to return to work.

Cass watched and listened but felt strangely empty of all emotion. After a few minutes he left the building to stand outside in the fresh air. He knew someone had followed him out but wasn't aware it was Joe Savage until his voice spoke from the shadows.

"Are you as angry as they are, Cass?"

Cass didn't answer straight away. "I think I feel more…." he struggled for the word. "lost."

He heard Joe sigh. "In some ways that's worse. It implies you feel defeated."

"Aren't we?" Cass tried to light a cigarette but his hand shook too much and he gave up in exasperation. "Bloody hell, Joe, this isn't victory, is it?" He didn't think he was going to get a reply and opened his mouth to demand an answer when Joe's voice reached him.

"Peter and I have always believed that the only way to effect real change is through parliament. We have to fight, of course we do! But the government is always going to be stronger. Massey and the rest, they're fighting to protect their own self-interest and profits and that makes them implacable." Savage took a step towards Cass who saw something still burning in the exhausted face and red-ringed eyes. "But we will win, Cass. We will because we must. But we won't win, we can't win on the streets."

Some of Bob Semple's anger echoed in Cass's frustration. "Then, how the hell….?"

"By playing it by their rules." Savage smiled grimly, "Until we can rewrite the rules."

***

36

"For god's sake, Cass! Don't bloody fuss."

"Are you sure you're ready?"

"Of course I'm ready."

Alex chimed in. "Really, Sam?"

"If I stay inside this house a moment longer I'll go bloody mad."

Cass stood back from his friend. "I think you're bloody mad already."

"Well, I'm going out."

Hoping for support, Cass turned pleadingly to Maudie, sitting in her usual place beside the fire. "Maudie, tell the mad bastard."

But to his chagrin, Maudie was unmoved by the plea.

"He's the one to know if he's ready."

Samuel grinned triumphantly.

"See?" he told Cass and Alex. But at the real concern in their eyes he relented. "Look, Jimmy and I are only going for a wander. If I get too sore or anything, we'll head straight back. Promise."

Cass's gaze fell on Moss, waiting near Samuel as he had been from the moment the man had been brought back home bleeding and unconscious. "Then take Moss. If you need help or anything he can run back and you'll still have Jimmy with you."

"Oh, for god's sake!" Samuel huffed in exasperation until looking down into Moss's eager face. "Fine. If it makes everyone happy, fine."

Moss gambolled about, getting under everyone's feet while Alex popped a bottle of cold tea into one of Jimmy's pockets and Maude slipped a packet of something into another. She also pressed a small, corked bottle into her son's hand, giving him a knowing look which Moss acknowledged gravely.

Ignoring Samuel's moans, Maudie checked his dressing one last time before releasing them. They had barely made it to the front door when the sound of wheels on the wooden floor brought him to a halt.

"Smam?"

Stiffly crouching down and making a supreme effort not to show how much it hurt, Samuel hugged Peg to him.

"I'll take you out next time, my little love."

"Yes?" she lisped, her lips grazing his ear

"Yes. And we'll have morning tea somewhere posh. Just you and me." He was reluctant to end the hug for Peg felt so fragile that some unnamed fear tugged at Samuel's heart.

Happy at the promised outing though, Peg slipped from the embrace and raced her little cart down the hallway crowing. With a wince Samuel stood, hastily becoming nonchalant as Alex opened her mouth. He kissed her deeply to stop her telling him off. "We won't be too long."

Aro Valley seemed a lot further away to the aching Samuel but the brothers were in no hurry. With Moss running ahead or disappearing briefly down alleys, the three of them walked up the valley until Samuel came to a glad halt, resting heavily on his brother's shoulder.

Jimmy pointed to the view. " 'Show me the sights of Wellington', I said and you bring me to a bloody burned out, old wreck of a…….." But the words died away in his mouth as realisation hit.

….. *Jimmy heard the crackle and spit of flames, the colour of red and orange against a dark sky….. Mick's voice, angry, urgent….. "Your brother has seen bad things and had bad things done to him. He's allowed to do this." ….. Samuel bent over their mother's grave, struggling not to cry…..*

Without speaking, Samuel led them to the back of the old ruin. There was no smoky smell of ash and embers anymore just the tangy, vivid scent of green growth. The surrounding bush had begun to reclaim the place, tangled vines strangling the roof and reaching inside to choke the blackened timbers.

Side by side the brothers stared into the shadowy skeleton.

"It was here, Jimmy. Right here that I realised you can't forget some things or even overcome them. You can only carry them." He faced his brother. "I'm sorry, Jimmy. So sorry for all the lost years."

Giving a hiss of pain, Samuel moved stiffly to sit on a pile of collapsed roof beams. Jimmy studied his brother's pale, gaunt face. Knowing any show of concern would be rebuffed he hid his worry, sat beside Samuel while carefully keeping his gaze on the burnt interior of the cottage.

The silence between them echoed with the whispers of ghosts.

"I shouldn't have told you to go." Jimmy said softly.

There was another pause.

"I shouldn't have listened."

As Samuel's words faded they made eye contact, studying each other intently. Clearing his throat Jimmy fidgeted, kept his eyes on his brother as he replied, "Well, you bloody didn't usually."

As grin met grin they both began to laugh, Samuel clutching at his dressing as he did. "Brothers' code. The little brother is always wrong. Until he's right."

Eyes clouded with memories, Jimmy spoke hesitatingly, using that fragile bridge of humour to strengthen the connection between them. "Father wanted us both back, you know. He came looking for us when you left my adoption papers on his doorstep. I think it broke his heart to find you were gone." Jimmy swallowed painfully. "And I wouldn't go back with him."

Samuel drew in a sharp breath, ignoring the stab of pain. "Why didn't you? I thought you wouldn't have hesitated." But his brother averted his face. "I don't understand, Jimmy. Why didn't you go with father?"

"Because….. all those bloody years, Sam! I know Aherne hid the letters but when father didn't hear from us, why didn't he come looking? If we were important to him he should've come looking. And after everything, well, I'd changed. And then John and Emily took me on, ragged and broken as I was."

Closing his eyes, Jimmy fought the ghosts back into their shadows, wanting Samuel to understand but not wanting to be swamped by the emotions he'd struggled to repress. "I got sick when you left. Father came when I was sick but I wasn't the son he left behind all those years ago." Jimmy picked up some stones, threw them one by one at a piece of fallen roofing iron. "Father had a new family. And I was all John and Emily had. "

Through all his own struggles, Samuel never considered that his brother might have had troubles, too. And right at that moment a pair of bright, blue eyes danced on the edges of Samuel's memory, mocking him, reminding him.

"I paid Molly back," he said suddenly. "For her kindness to you and the money she gave me."

"I know. I wrote to see if she'd heard from you and she told me." Jimmy smiled. "She's married, now."

"Is she?" Samuel grinned. "Good old Molly. He's a lucky bugger whoever he is." He eyed his brother carefully. "And John and Emily. They are good people?"

"The best." Jimmy noticed the devoted Moss keeping a wary eye on Samuel, thought about Alex, Cass and Maudie. "We were both lucky buggers, too, you know. In the end."

Samuel moved painfully as he got back on his feet. "I suppose. Bit hard to believe it at the moment, though."

Moss rushed up as Samuel gripped his side and sank back to the ground, gasping. "I'm all right. Just a bit sore."

Jimmy stood over him. "Maybe we should have something to eat and then wander back?"

"Yep." Easing himself down onto the grass Samuel lay back, breathing as shallowly as he could, waiting for the pain to pass when Moss shoved a small bottle into his hand. "What's this?"

The boy mimed drinking it.

"From your Ma?"

Moss nodded vigorously and Samuel hesitated no longer, gulped it down.

While the patient waited impatiently for the pain to subside, Jimmy and Moss sat beside him, cross-legged. After a few minutes, Jimmy reached into his pockets and brought out the picnic lunch and he and Moss munched away appreciatively.

"Don't you mind me dying here." Samuel grumbled but they ignored him. "And don't eat all the sandwiches, you greedy bastards."

Moss carefully placed one in Samuel's hand, patting the man's face gently to reassure him. Samuel ruffled the boy's hair, then relaxed, letting Maudie's drugs and the warmth of the day do their work.

***

37

"You could come back with me, you know. John will find you work."

"Nah. Think I'll stick it out here. We lost the battle but the war's not over."

Jimmy looked at his brother with affection. "Well, at least you know you've got family down south. John and Emily will welcome you anytime."

"I've got a brother again, Jimmy. That's all that matters." Samuel grinned. "Anyway, I'm not sure how your farmer would take to a socialist in his house."

"There's always room in the barn." Jimmy's told him helpfully.

Before Samuel could reply a voice hailed from on board the ship.

"Looks like we're off."

"Yeah, well, I'll be glad to see the back of you."

They locked smiles and hugged. Jimmy swung his bag over his shoulder as he walked up the gangplank. "Give Cass my best."

"Nah. It'll be more fun to tell him you called him a bastard."

"And give my love to Alex."

"Ah, that I'll do."

Jimmy smiled down on Samuel. "I've always wanted a sister."

"Let's not rush things, eh?"

Once on board, Jimmy leaned on the metal railing, his bag at his feet, his eyes on his brother. As the boat slowly pulled away from the wharf he raised a hand and laughed as Samuel returned with it with a much more obscene gesture.

Samuel stood on the wharf and watched until his brother's ship turned to sail alongside the Pencarrow Heads out of

Wellington, watched until it was lost from view.

Whistling gently he turned, felt the Wellington wind pushing on his spine, compelling his steps back towards the city.

***

Author's Note: This book is not a non-fiction history of the Stoke Orphanage. It is an historical fiction, based on some of the terrible things that happened in that place, in that community and in others like it around New Zealand. I played with the dates of the fire to enable the story of Samuel and Jimmy.

But, facts there are. Abuse happened to those boys, terrible abuse, ignored until a report brought an end to the reign of the Marist Brothers. Life after that wasn't a lot better, the boys still starved and were not cared for as well as they could and should have been but at least the worst excesses were stopped. A boy named John Rogers ran away, his dead body discovered on the hills and buried in the graveyard and a boy named William Wilson was burned to death in the fire. I gave these boys a bit of history as the only pitiful bit of knowledge known about them is that they died there.

And of course, the Waihi strike happened and Fred Evans was killed. The Great Strike occurred and Massey did indeed set machine guns on Wellington and Auckland wharves. Less than a year later, the men Massey turned his machine guns towards, faced them again in a world war and the young men he branded as traitors and cowards, died for his country, their country, in foreign fields.

'Lest We Forget' was coined from the battlefields. It referred to conflict where men waged terrible war against men which is why I give those final words here after a story which ends on an urban battlefield where rich, privileged men chose to arm one section of New Zealand against another to defend their profits.

'Lest We Forget'

Read the next book about Sam, Alex and Jimmy.
'Between Two Worlds' follows them into the years of WW1.